how we are

POPPY MINNIX

Dedication

You are exactly who you should be.
Be proud. Be happy.

Contents

Author's Note   IX

1. Jolene is Out   1

2. Darius Gardens   8

3. Jolene Touches Down   16

4. Arlo Struggles   28

5. Darius Plans   36

6. Jolene Connects   41

7. Arlo Retreats   47

8. Darius Tours   53

9. Jolene Thinks   61

10. Arlo Advises   68

11. Darius Soothes   73

12. Jolene Cuddles   80

13. Arlo's Distraction   90

14. Jolene Schemes   97

15. Darius Instigates   104

16. Arlo Sucks   109

17. Jolene Worries   116

18. Darius Needs   121

19. Arlo Commands   126

20. Jolene Desires   132

21. Arlo Checks In   140

22. Jolene Explores   144

23. Darius Watches   153

24. Jolene Gets Ready   159

25. Darius Greets   164

26. Arlo Escapes   171

27. Jolene Says Goodbye   177

28. Arlo Lays It Out   185

29. Darius Feels The Tension   189

30. Jolene Fails   195

31. Darius Comes First   203

32. Arlo Goes Slow   210

33. Jolene Screams   217

34. Arlo Gets Marked   225

35. Darius Heals   230

36. Jolene Walks Funny   235

37. Arlo Questions   240

38. Jolene's Aching Everything   247

39. Darius Lets It Happen   252

40. Arlo Needs More   257

41. Jolene Wonders   261

42. Darius Is Concerned   265

43. Jolene Hurts   269

44. Arlo Shares   273

45. Arlo Screws Up   279

46. Jolene Gets Real... Uncomfortable   284

47. Arlo Takes It Back   290

48. Jolene Can't Catch A Break   295

49. Darius Is Done   301

50. Arlo Finds Out   306

51. Jolene Gets Her Answers   313

52. Arlo Does Something New   318

53. Darius Gets Some Clarity   325

54. Jolene Makes A Decision   330

55. Arlo Finds The Right Fit   335

56. Jolene Types It Out   340

57. Darius Is Pissed   346

58. Jolene Is   354

59. Arlo Owns   359

60. Jolene Spills   364

61. Arlo Notices   368

62. Darius Has To Go   371

63. Jolene Is So Sorry   379

64. Arlo Reflects   384

65. Jolene Wakes Up   389

66. Darius Gets Impatient — 394

67. Jolene's Luck — 398

68. Arlo's Dilemma — 406

69. Jolene Makes A Choice — 410

70. Arlo Breathes Easier — 415

71. Darius Is Complete — 422

72. Jolene Makes A Mistake — 425

73. Arlo Loves — 430

74. Jolene Accepts — 435

75. Epilogue: Hayley Arrives — 439

76. Next up... — 447

Holiday Hotel - A Tropical Christmas RomCom (3/5 spice level) — 449

Also by Poppy Minnix — 465

Acknowledgements — 467

Author's Note

Welcome! I'm thrilled you're here! However, let's make sure you're in the right spot...

The number one thing to understand about this book—it's wildly filthy in an emotionally intense way.

If you've read any of my other books and are expecting the fun, sexy antics that take place on Simona Island or the emotionally sensual heat waves and lovemaking in Duet of the Gods, stop that right now. Even Faetales's horny faeries don't hold a candle to what you're about to dive into.

There's so much love and antics, laughter and angst. But there's a ton of experimental, consensually kinky (sometimes BDSM-themed) sex, which at times is overwhelming with emotion.

This was not a book I expected to write. I struggled, trying to keep this book between Darius and Jolene, but they weren't having it, and Arlo, being Arlo, wouldn't shush about telling me what an awesome main character he is.

I'm so glad for that.

I'm really proud of this book. It made me feel so much while I wrote it, first on Kindle Vella under the pen name Georgie Monroe, and then I realized how much it was needed when readers found and responded to it. Comments like, "How can this be so dirty and so sweet at the same time?," and, "Oh, Jolene. My girl. My heart.," really made me understand that what I wrote resonated with many people who may feel trapped or know someone who lives under lifetimes of guilt for simply being who they are. And that's why this book is here!

So... if seriously kinky menage sex, blunt dirty talk, lots of cursing, and heart-clenching emotion are not your thing, this book isn't either. But if all that sounds like a great time, I hope you enjoy it as much as I do.

Love, Poppy

Chapter One

Jolene is Out

JOLENE

Mom sits on the end of my bed, tears flowing down both cheeks as she dabs at her sniffling nose with the tissue in one hand and strokes my frilly quilt with the other. She looks sadder than she did at Pawpaw's funeral.

Every inch of me is tight, making my stomach threaten to up-heave breakfast, but I don't have time for that today, so I swallow, and check my carry-on for laptop cords, lip balm, and then toss in an extra shirt just in case. "Mom, it's not that bad."

Her inhale is four stuttering breaths in one. "It is too. You don't have children. You don't understand what it's like when they abandon you." Our accent is thick, but she's playing the sweet-Kentucky-momma role a little heavy this morning.

"I'm not abandoning you." But I really am. I'm leaving her for my boyfriend in another state... finally.

My long-distance relationship with Darius has held strong for five years, and, despite the absolute need to be with him for longer than a couple days here and there, I stuck around here for two entire months after graduation to spend time with her. But is Mom thinking about that now? Nope.

I had hoped that doing everything she loves in one last hurrah before I start my life would comfort her, and maybe she'd even grow a little tired of me. However, our full schedule of garden tours, spa days, and country club luncheons only seems to have made her need me more. I even volunteered with her at the annual church picnic, and didn't walk out when she pulled my Miss Kentucky crown out of a box and placed it on my head, pinning it in place. Nor did I flick off the news cameras when they showed up, even though I really, and I mean really, wanted to. Pageant girls don't flick off the news. They wear their best scoring smile and graciously answer every question asked of them... again and again and fucking again.

I love my mom. I really do. She would give her only umbrella to a stranger in a downpour, and she tries so hard to make her family and friends happy, even if she forgets sometimes what we want.

But, although it's hard to tell us apart if you hold up two photos of us at the same age, I'm not her. I might have her thick dark hair, rare, amber-colored eyes, and dimples that upped my scorecards by at least a half-point in any category, but I can't keep living her pageant queen dream for her. Her parents didn't have the money to make her Miss Universe, and to her immense disappointment, her daughter didn't have the will to go all the way. I just needed the scholarship, because I knew if I didn't have control over college money, I'd either live with more debt than I could handle to be in the field I'm passionate about, or I'd end up with a full-parental ride to nursing school, because that's the judges' favorite career for who I was supposed to be. Everyone loves an obvious helper. And while I truly appreciate people in the medical field, when I think about the smells and fluids that go with that job, I'd need more help than I could assist with.

There are only so many hoops I can leap through to make Mom happy before I crack, and I'm there, one fake smile away from breaking out of my skin.

I need a job I love. I need to hug my boyfriend and have him tell me that every piece of me is perfect, even when it's not. I need to start my life already.

Her sigh is a wet snuffle. "I can't believe you're leaving me. And for Chicago. It's too big for someone like you, sweetheart." Says the woman who's been out of Kentucky twice in her life. "No one will see you for what you are in a city like that. You're going to waste your beauty and kindness there."

These are the times I wish I had a bunch of siblings to share the vast amount of guilt my mother can dish out. But if I keep trying to comfort her like I've been doing for months, I'll miss my flight, and we both know she won't be happy unless I stay in this room, town, and life forever.

Inhale, exhale, and fake smile. "You know I love you, Momma, but I have to get to the airport." I stand and turn toward my open suitcase.

She stands too. "But you haven't come close to finishing packing." She tugs at the quilt like she's going to fold it and fit it... who knows where, because I'm only bringing one suitcase and a carry-on, and both are full.

I touch her shoulder. "Mom, stop. I can't fit that anywhere. We've already sent everything I'm taking to Chicago. Except clothes. Obviously." I grin and snap the straps together before pulling the cord to tighten everything in.

"But what are you going to do for your bed?"

Tucking my lips between my teeth, I pivot and grab two more shirts from my drawer just to avoid conversation for a moment. Darius's best friend Arlo lives with him, which gives me complex feelings I'm trying to avoid feeling, but Darius has given me a virtual tour of their new apartment. While it's a massive upgrade from their tiny, creepy first Chicago apartment, it's still a city home. There are only two rooms and two beds, and the guys don't share. Mom is bound to know I'm going to be sinning with Darius under his cream-colored duvet.

It's hard not to laugh at her clueless behavior. Does she really believe all the uncomfortable scenarios will disappear if she pretends they don't exist?

I fight my grin as I turn back to her. "I'll think of something. Hey, I bet someone from the church would love this quilt." Like an eight-year-old who actually wants to be a pageant queen. When I was around that age, Mom had my hair and skin tone tested for my best complementary colors. Then every fabric in my room and closet, plus the walls, became nude, Jolene pink. I didn't mind the color before. Fifteen years later, I'd rather walk into a home of pylon orange. They can take everything in this room for all I care.

Her face scrunches. And she's crying again. *Shit.*

"Momma."

Fortunately, my phone buzzes from my gold and pearl Victorian dresser that I've considered lighting on fire about a dozen times.

"Do you have any lip balm I may have?" That will keep her busy for a while and out of my room.

She bobbles her head, dabs her eyes again, and heads to her room.

I snatch my cell and speed-walk down the hallway as I answer. "Baby, I might not leave this house without something pink."

Darius's chuckle dissipates a lot of stress right out of my body as I envision his wide grin, straight teeth popping bright against his deep brown skin. He's so damn handsome, and I cannot wait to kiss his face. "I'm sorry, Joles. Unfortunately, there is a no-pink clause in the apartment contract."

I blow out a breath. "Thank God—goodness." I glance behind me, making sure Mom isn't within earshot.

"Flight in two hours?"

"Yes. I'm scheduled to land at three sharp."

"You're so formal when you're at home. I feel like dirty talking you up a little."

"Please don't." My cheeks heat, as well as between my legs, because I haven't had sex with my boyfriend since he came home for Christmas, and I am a needy bitch.

Darius puts on his panty-dropping tone. "Are you sure, baby? I really miss those long legs around my hips, and I'd be glad to walk you through that entire experience in detail."

I turn into the living room to see Dad reading the newspaper.

"Oops." I halt. "And we will have to talk about that later."

"Did you get busted with wet panties, babes?"

I bite back a laugh. "Mm-hmm. I'll call you from the airport."

"Oh, public sex. I'm in."

"You are not," I say in a whisper. "Love you."

"Love you more."

And I'm back to getting myself out the door.

I'm shocked Dad's out of his office or not at the hospital. He doesn't take days off, even three years past retirement age, though with the gauntlet of activities Mom ran me through in two months, he'd probably be busier here than at work.

He lowers the corner of the paper and raises a dark eyebrow at me. Unlike Mom, he's aged naturally—dark hair now mostly gray and eyes bagged and tired from full calendars of surgeries. "Ready to go?"

"I just have to grab my bag."

He folds the paper and stands, signaling me to come over. Taking out his wallet, he pulls a wad of bills and hands it over. "Do not tell your mother." He nods toward the hall. "Get your things."

"Thank you." My eyes sting a little, but when he wordlessly turns toward the kitchen, I walk back down the hall.

My father is not affectionate and wasn't present for pageants, school events and all that, but money is still his love language, even if Mom is determined not to support my move.

I'm not bitter about it or anything. I earned my way through college, padding my savings through pageants and retail jobs, and it's not like I expect to be handed everything past graduation.

But ever since I mentioned I'd be following Darius to Chicago as soon as I graduated, there's been a heavy tone of disapproval in the house and a lot of reminders that as long as I lived at home, they'd take care of me like the princess they raised me to be. I don't want to lean on that, because being a princess means locked towers, royal rules, and a lot of expectations that don't fit what I'm looking for in life.

As much as it disappoints Mom, I love what I love, and it's not always what she loves. My dream job is one of my many disappointments in her eyes, preceded only by Darius and leaving the pageant circuit, but I can't let her expectations get in my way.

The top priority when I get to Chicago, besides getting my long legs around Darius's hips, is following up with the resumes I've sent to financial firms. While I'll be living with him, which will help financially, I'm going to need to contribute. I just want to do it by finding my dream job, and so far, no luck. Though it's been difficult to find time to research and write cover letters with Mom stalking my every move and making comments like, "Are you sure that's what you want to do?" It will be different when I'm there, though. Hopefully.

Mom is no longer in my room, but there's another bag on top of my suitcase—one with a hanger. When I unzip, all the tension that Darius and my dad helped get rid of just spirals right back into my chest. What the hell am I supposed to do with two pageant dresses in Chicago? And what a shock, they're both my perfectly matched to me pink. It's a beautiful color; I just wish there were less of it forced on me.

Shaking my head, I put them back in the closet and zip up my suitcase.

My room isn't as vacant as some of my friends' rooms were when they left home. Only one box of awards and pageant memorabilia made it onto the moving truck, courtesy of my mother. I'm not even sure all my stuff fits in Darius's closet, much less will find a place on the walls or shelves.

I grab my bags, flip the light, and make my way to the living room, where Mom blots her red, wet eyes, and Dad stands by the door with his hand on the knob, blatantly ignoring her pain.

Excitement flows freely through me, overshadowing the guilt of not being willing to make everything okay for my mom, the anxiety of traveling, and the nervousness I have about seeing Arlo again in person. Like Darius tells me, it's all going to work out, and this moment counts. It's going to be big, and change so much for me, for better or worse. Today, I'm starting my grown-up life with the person I love.

I grin widely. "All set to go."

Chapter Two

Darius Gardens

I stumble through the door, juggling six bags and two potted plants.

Arlo shoves himself off the new couch—the only purchase we've made together that wasn't thrifted or given to us—and jogs over.

While my shoulders might pop out of their joints, I take a long moment to eye the beauty of washable microfiber in all its soft, over-stuffed glory. "I love that couch."

"I know, right? Worth every one of your crisp promotion dollars." Tattoos and abs are on full display since Arlo's only in joggers. He took off work today too, so we both planned to sleep in. He's clearly getting his day going at a relaxed pace, but I've been too excited to actually sleep or pretend to relax. I'm glad he's here, helping to clean up and get our apartment ready for Jolene, as well as keeping me calm and somewhat collected.

He takes the plants from me, turning the big grassy one this way and that as he looks it over. "Last night, you said you needed a bottle of wine. What's all this?"

I grunt as I wobble from the entry to the kitchen, and lift what feels like a hundred pounds of food and things for the house, setting the bags on the brown-speckled granite-top kitchen island, struggling to keep them from falling off. "I went for that, but then I saw this blanket Jolene would like. And then this pencil holder and a couple of books. Cheese. Crunchy peanut butter."

"A garden." He snorts as he sets the pots beside the refrigerator. "Have you ever even had a houseplant?"

"No. But her parent's house has a bunch, and I need her to feel at home. I can't believe she's going to be here today. Not that I doubted it."

Arlo lifts his gaze from the instructions on the leafy plant's identification stake and raises a dark eyebrow at me. He knows me too well.

I sort through, picking up a box of pasta I apparently bought on autopilot as I was rushing through the grocery store. "Okay, there may have been the slightest doubt. I wasn't sure Donna would actually let her leave. Jolene is strong, but she's never going to be someone who shuts out her overbearing mother, no matter how much that woman sometimes deserves it."

Arlo leans over the piles of stuff, and grabs my wrist to check the time. "And we've got three hours until her plane lands?"

Renewed by that, I jump into sorting all the kitchen items I picked up. "Two and a half. Shockingly, her mother didn't lock her in their basement, so she texted me from the airport." And I sexy-texted her until she sent my full name in caps and told me to behave myself. She's so adorable. Apparently, her parents were staying with her until she boarded. I'm not sorry.

"Is it really that bad?" His tone is the one he uses when he's concerned, and I wince. I shouldn't joke about parental abuse to him, even if he's put the past behind him. He takes things like that seriously, though.

"Nah. Donna isn't a monster." The pantry is almost full for the first time since we moved in three months ago.

"She's not against Jolene moving here because you're Black, right?"

Yeah, he's still in defense mode for me, and I appreciate that. "Not at all. Actually, she was ready for us to get married and have children because of these lashes." I signal to the long, naturally curled lashes Donna has commented on more times than I can count. "That, and apparently mixed-race winners are trending in pageants."

"The fuck. She seriously said that?"

"She did." I sigh long. "While there's a lot about Donna that could use a few decades of therapy, she's not malicious. She's just... Donna. Granddad calls her 'whirlybird.' because there is no helicopter mother like Mrs. Shah. It fits." Kudos to him for not straight-up telling Jolene's mother she's an overprotective whacko, but still.

Arlo snorts a laugh. "To her face?"

"Not yet. Donna might not get that reference though, but I'm sure the rest of us losing our shit laughing might give away that it's not a compliment. He's just at that age where he does not care what he says."

Arlo grins wide. "There's an age for that?"

"Not for you, but with most people, yeah." I clip the tags off of the new towels and the blanket. "Speaking of. Go easy on Jolene when she gets here, please."

His amused gaze narrows. "We've gone over this. I'm not pretending I'm a *good boy*."

My jaw tightens. "I'm not asking for that—okay, I am a little, it's just, Jolene is amazing, but she's only been out of college for a couple of months, and her home life is not like this place and what we've been getting into. Nor am I going to be joining you with her here." Sharing sexual partners wasn't something I thought I'd be into before Arlo, but

Jolene and I have—had—an open relationship, and Arlo has shown me I enjoy taking direction and watching. With Jolene here, I don't need that, and I don't know how she'll take that information when we get around to talking about it.

He folds fabric bags and throws them into the one empty kitchen cabinet. "You've mentioned that, and in the same breath, said she's really open-minded."

"She is. But she's going to need a minute, and I'm going to need a minute with her to recalibrate this new—" I point around the room and grin. "Situation." I can't believe we're finally here. Moving in. It felt like forever apart and still doesn't seem quite real.

Arlo grumbles. "Help her get through that with a quickness. I'm losing my fuck-sidekick in this deal, and I won't become a monk so your girl doesn't pass out from blushing too hard. I love sex—loud, dirty fucking—I'm going to continue wanting that, whether or not she's here."

"Understood." I chuckle, folding the new towels.

Arlo is genuine to a fault, so I know his words aren't just for show. It is likely at some point Jolene will walk in on him, raucously fucking someone in the kitchen or living room, just like I did. She'll hear the sounds of skin slapping, begging, and screaming orgasms through the walls, even though our apartment is way more soundproof than the last one. What will she do?

There's as much thrill in the unknown as there is unease. She and I know nearly everything about each other. We're open and honest because that's the only way our relationship has continued to work through the years apart. Arlo is going to bring a new level of honesty to household communication, for better or for worse.

I put the towels in the bag with the incredibly soft blanket. "She's going to be fine. It's just going to take her time to adjust to the area and find the right job."

He scrunches his nose. "Still no luck?"

I shake my head. "It's been silent." That's been a sore point. I had my internship as a CAD engineer lined up months before graduation because the stars aligned for me, and it's only gone up from there with a promotion into my exact specialty.

The financial analysis industry is nuanced and lacks the openings my career path did. A lot of analysts start in something smaller, like banking, admin, or sometimes sales. I've encouraged her to aim for the gold and hold out. "She's so damn smart, she just needs to be discovered. I can get by supporting her for a bit, and she's got some savings—not a third of rent savings, but some."

"You know I'm fine with all that. I get it."

I nod. "Thank you for that. I just hope she finds something quickly. She's risking a lot to move to a new area without a job first, and her mother keeps reminding her of that. It's just one more lock on her Jolene cage."

"Fucking Donna." The way he says it is so offhanded and exasperated, especially since he hasn't even met her, that it reminds me why we're best friends. He's always on my side—no hesitation or question—and now he's on Jolene's as well, just because she's mine and I'm hers. She needs that.

I nod and match his tone. "Fucking Donna."

My watch beeps with a text.

Babes:

Taking off! Whoosh!

I type back to Jolene:

> **Enjoy the clouds. I can't wait to see you.**

Babes:

> Same. Okay, airplane mode on. Love you always.

I write back that I love her forever, but she doesn't respond. Such a rule follower.

"Okay…" The apartment is in decent shape, but is it in Jolene-shape? Probably not. "I've got to clean the bathroom. But there are dishes, and she'll see that first. When did we vacuum last?"

Arlo huffs and pokes a bird tea light holder I picked up. "I know you've waited a long damn time for this, and I'm happy for you, but you need to fucking simmer."

"She's really clean."

"As are we. We're not slobs. We treat our space like grown-ass adults, and we haven't been here long enough to fill it with shit like this." He displays a hand at the hodgepodge trinkets I picked up.

"I know but—" The deep breath eases my panic. "I thought it might make it homier in here."

Arlo grumbles, shuffling items back into bags. "Enough. Take all this and put it in your closet. We'll vacuum one more time, and I'll finish the dishes while you straighten up. Then we're watching a show." He holds up a finger before I protest. "Your girl loves you, and from how you've been acting, all you two will be doing for a couple of weeks is fucking. Then she can figure out what she wants to put all over the apartment."

I blow out a long breath and nod. "Yeah, okay." He's right. I just want to do this right. This will be much different from our open, long-distance relationship, and while that worked surprisingly well, this is a fresh path we're starting together. We will get to know each other more than we ever have. I've grown, she has too, and while we talk about a lot, we don't talk about everything. What's been missing on my end of the conversation might shock her. Has she changed more than I know in that department? What if her exploration bravery wears off and her mother tempts her back to Kentucky, or what if Jolene realizes that's what she's always wanted, but didn't know it? What the hell would I do with two soulmates in two different states? My jaw feels like it might crack, and when did I eat last? "I am so damn nervous."

Arlo comes around the island, grips my neck and drags me into a tight hug. "This is good. Stop worrying so much, and just let it happen."

I nod against his shoulder, hugging him back. "You're right. But you're going to need to put a shirt on, because you're hot, and I'd like her thinking of me, not your biceps, when I drag her to our room."

"I don't mind her thinking of me while you're banging."

"Dick," I say, but I'm grinning.

He knows I'm kidding by how he squeezes me tight, hands over the bag of junk I bought, then pushes me away toward the hallway. "Get your stuff done."

I smile at him over my shoulder, and do as he says, breathing easier.

It's crossed my mind—the things Arlo and I have done together with women—what if Jolene would be into that? She's more willing to explore than I am, and she's pushed us into a few places I tried, but ultimately didn't know how to handle. Arlo would.

After he met her for the first time a year and a half ago, something changed. He seeks me out when I'm on a video call with her and checks in, starts a conversation with her, though keeps things light. They're stiff with each other—cautious and too courteous, as if trying to find boundaries and get to know each other without pressing too hard. It's not an Arlo move to keep to small talk. It's annoying to him, so as well as I know him, as open as he is, I'm not sure what his thoughts are about my girlfriend.

He's been my best friend since our military families moved next to each other in Kentucky. His family moved to another base two years later, as military families do, but my dad settled, leaving my mom to chase the bacon, and me gaining stability in a home with grandparents, while staying at the same middle and high school—a luxury for a military brat.

Arlo and I stayed in contact through the blessing of video calls and gamer playdates, and forgot about the distance between us every time we got to see each other in person. I attribute my success with a Jolene-long-distance relationship to being in a long-distance relationship with Arlo first. It's different, but I know when to check in.

Living with him has been easy, but I can't let that mindset move to Jolene. There's bound to be hiccups. Adjustments. Especially with her need to please and not be judged, and his need for both space and control. How are the dynamics of this situation going to work?

Whatever, it will work. I hope. I love them and get along perfectly with them both, so they should at least like each other, right?

Chapter Three

Jolene Touches Down

JOLENE

I grab my luggage from the overhead and make my way down the aisle, still talking baseball with my seat neighbors until we get separated by an older couple who sneak their way between us with apologies. I wave goodbye, and they tell me I better get myself to a game since I'm now a Chicagoan.

Apparently, Cubs fans are dedicated, even if they moved thousands of miles away from the Windy City over two decades ago. That is prime city information right there. So far what I know about my new home is there's a shiny bean-shaped statue I haven't yet met, people are far friendlier than expected, the love of my life and his roommate love it here, and their signature liquor is utterly atrocious.

I learned that last fact from Arlo. I've only been to Chicago once, even though Darius has lived here for almost two years with Arlo, and that trip was... altering. I should thank him for the way he spoke to me when we were alone for a moment, even if at the time it really pissed me off. He was direct to the point of being rude, and basically told me that Chicago was the path if I loved Darius. In that part, he wasn't correct. There were many paths that would have taken our relationship into account, but thinking about all of them led me to one conclusion.

Chicago was indeed my path.

Even if I've only had one date with it. Even if it hasn't welcomed me with a job. I still think we're going to get along just fine.

It's Arlo I'm not so sure about. He's gorgeous. Darius is also gorgeous, but they're vastly different. Darius is down-home-comfortable hot, which is only enhanced by his personality. It's disarming. I can stare at him all day and get warm fuzzies of appreciation for just how handsome he is.

Arlo is *fucking* hot. Tattooed runway god hot. He's set-your-panties-on-fire, street-swooning fine. It's uncomfortable to look at him for too long, and I'm not sure yet if that's because I know I shouldn't look at him or because the intensity that rolled off him the night we met was breath-stealing. Lord, don't let him still be that level of gorgeous. I'm going to be living with him.

It's been a year since I've seen him in person, but he's said hello when I've been on calls with Darius, and seemed almost... nice? After our blunt conversation, or the quiz he gave me to figure out my feelings about the future and my boyfriend, it's almost like each interaction has been an unspoken apology, or maybe an olive branch to make sure I don't hate him. Which I don't, but I'm still uneasy about living with him.

My phone buzzes in the thigh pocket of my leggings. I sink my shoulders.

Mom:

Call me when you get in so you can tell me all about your flight.

How do I say I'll be too busy suctioned onto my boyfriend like a barnacle for at least the next two days without making her upset?

> It was uneventful. I'll be settling in, but promise to call later tonight.

Dammit. Now I have to remember to call. I shove my phone back in my pocket, but it buzzes again. With a sigh, I pull it back out again, but grin.

Hayley:

> City girl to city girl, virtual pizza night is Wednesday. Figure out the best slice before then so we can discuss. There will be an extensive quiz.

Hayley. Her pageant career was brief—she could only do free ones with borrowed dresses, and nearly everyone got taller than her fast—but she instantly became one of my favorite people. And with her recent move to New York City, we're now both officially city girls. I type out a quick response as I walk up the breezeway.

> It's a date.

As I step into the airport, Darius is there, tight black waves shorter than the last time I saw him. His get-into-my-arms-now smile makes my breath hitch. I love his sexy mouth, his tall frame, broad shoulders, and even his too-big feet. The nervous ball in my stomach shatters into a bright array of butterflies, and I can't stop myself from slipping around the meandering couple in front of me and running the distance between us.

He moves forward too, opening his arms as we get closer.

I squeal, drop my bags, and launch myself against him, inhaling clean laundry and spicy soap. "I missed you so much."

He lifts me against him, hugging me tight against his warm, lean body. "You have no idea how happy I am that you're here." He kisses my jaw, nudging me until he can reach my lips. He tastes of coffee, and I want to crawl inside him and live there forever.

I cup his cheeks, humming into his familiar, perfect kiss, completely forgetting that we're in public until an announcement blares through the dull murmurs of the airport's crowd.

He sets me on my feet when I release my legs from around his hips, then gives me one more hug. "Good flight?"

It seems I do have a lot to say, because I chatter about it all the way to the luggage carousel.

As if it's a usual meetup for us, we catch up on the day, family news, and friend gossip while going through the motions of gathering my bags, navigating to short-term parking, and driving into the city in the ancient BMW Darius's uncle helped him fix up with mainly Duct tape and prayer.

We fall silent as we drive into the apartment's neighborhood, because I'm leaning forward taking in everything. The concrete sidewalks are clean, and the only businesses between the huge brick buildings are an odd laundromat-deli combo, a gas station, and a law office stationed in a farmhouse that looks like someone built a bustling city around it. We pass a basketball court full of high school kids fresh out of school just before we turn onto a street leading to one huge apartment complex.

"How many people live here?" I ask, hand on the dashboard as I look up and up and up. He'd told me it was twenty-seven stories, but I didn't quite understand the meaning of that until now.

"No idea. There's probably about five-hundred apartments?" His brows furrow as he thinks, which is just the cutest thing. "About twenty apartments per story, with at least four levels of larger suites or management offices and community spaces. Average two people per apartment, so a thousand tenants."

"Oh, baby." I lean, tugging at my seat belt to loosen it, run my nails over the back of his neck, then suck on his earlobe. "I love it when you *flex* those CAD muscles."

He groans. "Do you want me to tell you my favorite layer property overrides or recite some non-uniform rational basis spline formulas?"

I gasp against his ear. "Both. Baby, do both."

"You're going to make me wreck," he says, breaking our game to laugh. "And look"—he points to a little building where there's a guard—"Larry's watching."

Grinning, I slide back into my seat.

The man waves, and we drive into an underground parking garage.

Darius grabs my suitcase and carry-on while I look at all the cars, and breathe in the stale, concrete air. It's not stinky, just cool and earthy.

"Does Arlo have a car?" I ask. What would he drive? Probably one of the four motorcycles parked in compact spaces. He would stop traffic on one of those.

"No. We decided to share." He nods toward a shiny metal elevator door.

Did not know that. My jaw tightens as we approach, and my insides jolt when the bell dings and the doors to my doom slide open.

"Let's get you a pass at the front desk, then head upstairs." The doors close, and he pushes the L-button.

"High securi—" I yip as we launch into fucking space. Just as quickly, the elevator slams to a stop.

Darius crinkles his nose. "You okay, babes?"

"Ask my stomach, which is on the previous plane of existence we just exited."

He bites his lips together and snorts as the doors open.

I leap out of the death box before it pulls a Dr. Who and I end up on another planet a thousand years ago. *Jesus.*

The lobby of the apartments is not elegant or even that clean, with the black streaks and dents all along the beige linoleum. There's an alcove beside the elevator with a "Mailroom" plaque on the wall, and a podium desk where a pretty red-haired woman in a security uniform sits on a bar-height stool.

"Good afternoon, Mr. Gates." She raises her, also red, eyebrows at Darius before giving me a long look over, letting her smile fall away.

I wave and hold out a hand. "Jolene Shah. I'm moving in today."

She shakes my hand like it's the last thing on earth she'd like to do—her weak, dead fish fingers a huge contrast to the pageant circuit's trained palm-to-palm power pressure.

"This is Sheena." Darius's voice isn't warm as he faces the security guard. "We're going to need another permanent resident ID badge."

I raise my eyebrows at him and the mask of coldness he's wearing. Is this a city thing? Does he act like this to all other city or business people, and I'm the one who still gets the boyish grins, and gentle words?

After another look over me that is blatantly disapproving, Sheena reaches under the wooden reception-desk overhang, shuffling papers before handing one to Darius. "She'll need to fill this out and provide proof of residence."

Ah, one of those people who like to pretend I don't exist. Fun.

A muscle in Darius's jaw twitches, and his lips part. I know my man and he's about to go to war for me like in the past when people made rude comments about my body or assumed I was dumb, once when someone who accused me of cheating, and another... a woman who thought she'd be a much better fit for him than I was.

Have they fucked? My stomach is going through quite the obstacle course today.

I loop my arm in his and grin until my cheeks hurt as I tug the paper from his fingertips. "Thanks so much. I'll get right on that."

She keeps her eyes on my boyfriend. "Tell Mr. Keller to come down and see me soon. He can give me some tips on security again."

Is Arlo in the security business? I thought it was computers. "We sure will. Thank you."

Darius remembers his manners, mutters a "thanks" and leads me to another elevator on the other side of the lobby.

I squeeze his hand as we wait. "You okay?"

He seems to shake himself and entwines our fingers, leaning to kiss my head. "Yeah. Just wish we could have gotten that for you faster. I should have prepared better."

"It's fine, baby. I'm just glad to be here." My lips twist as I watch the numbers drop. Fifteen, fourteen, thirteen... "Have you had sex with her?" I crinkle my nose. Not today. Not this soon. "Sorry. You don't have to—"

He whips his gaze to me. "No. No, babes. Arlo has a thing going on with her, but I'm not a fan." He huffs a laugh as the bell dings. "Not sure he is either."

So Arlo does indeed date, but it's not going well. I hold my breath as we step into another metal death box.

"Want to push the button?" Darius teases, snagging my waist and pulling me against him so he can nuzzle my neck.

I roll my eyes and arch back to point at the number fifteen button. When he nods, I poke it, then lean against him and the wall, holding onto the rail for dear life. I blow out a long breath, happy this one doesn't seem to want to race to the skies.

Darius squeezes my hip. "Want me to jump and make it pause?"

"You do, and if the falling elevator doesn't kill you, I will."

He's chuckling as the elevator slows and stops. The doors open onto a carpeted hallway and beige walls lined with mahogany doors marked with gold numbers. It's plain but pretty and smells faintly like peppermint.

We halt at the fifth door on the left. Darius pauses with his hand on the doorknob. "I feel like I should carry you in or something."

I shove his shoulder. "We're not married, and I drank a ginger ale *and* my bottle of water on the plane. Go."

"Alright." He pecks my lips with his and opens the door for me. "Welcome home, babes."

The apartment is huge compared to his first one. To the left are a television on a stand, a big couch, an older armchair, and behind that, a glass sliding door leading to a balcony. A hallway is directly in front of us, and to the right, a small rectangular table with four chairs and the kitchen made of warm wood cabinets and a full-sized stove. It's separated from the rest of the space by a nice island.

I get all teary when I notice Grams's console table and the pottery bowl my aunt made for me right beside the entrance. It has keys, a few bills, and a wallet in it, already being used exactly how it should be. "I love it. It's amazing, baby. I'm so proud of you." He's worked so hard to get here. This is a really nice city apartment.

His chest rises and falls, and he lets go of my suitcase handle to pull me close and kiss me. He sets his forehead to mine. "I'm so glad you like it. We're going to have so much fun here, Joles. I can't wait to show you the city. We can meet for lunch when you figure out the L-train. Pizza! We have to order a pizza."

There's no holding back my grin. "Yeah, let's do all that. But I have to pee first, so…"

He turns me and gives me a gentle push. "We're at the end of the hall. I'm going to make us a snack."

I leave my bags where they are and scurry down the hallway of beige walls. There are a couple of photos hanging halfway down, almost across from the only other open door and I turn my head to look at a picture of Arlo and Darius as kids, arms slung over each other's shoulders in what looks like Darius's family's backyard.

"Aw." I collide with a warm wall of a man. "Shit." I step back. "Sorry."

Arlo eyes me with a furrowed brow, and dammit if he isn't even hotter than when I saw him last time. He has a trim-fitted tee on, leaving muscular, tattooed arms on display and not much left to the imagination with his firm, mounded pectorals under that shirt. The dark lines of his ink creep up his neck now. He's gotten more since I saw him last, and it does nothing to deter the sexiness of his jawline, but it's his eyes that are the real treat. Blue like the deep ocean, gaze like fire. His dark hair is now short enough to be professional and long enough to be tousled and tugged. Fuck me, this man is too sexy for his own—or my—good. Because I'm going to be living here in this bubble of awkward... with my boyfriend.

"Hi." He raises an eyebrow, and his sexy pout kicks up on one side. "In a hurry?" Ugh, I already want to punch him in the face, and I don't know why. Okay, I do. Unfortunately, the fluttering in my belly reminds me.

I force a smile and point to the open bedroom door behind him. "Hi. Yes. Nice to see you. Be right back." Then I scoot myself around his unmoving body and run away, right into a nice, small bedroom that I barely glance at before rushing into the bathroom and hiding behind the door. My breath is runaway wild. This situation might not work, and yet it has to work. I just need to get laid—by Darius. Like right now. Stretch out this pent-up sex-drive. Orgasms will clear my mind. Are these walls thin?

The bathroom is quiet and seems sturdy. Nice big countertop and a small closet, along with a bathtub and shower combination.

My phone buzzes in my pocket.

Mom:

> Did you get to the apartment? Do you need anything?

Thanks for the verbal cold shower, Mom. I take care of business while I let her know I'm at the apartment and it's great, but we might be out all night, so I'll call her tomorrow. The responding sad face feels like a bad score at my best event.

I step back into the bedroom and inhale sweet orange, noting the lit candle on the older oak dresser. Darius's bedroom is perfectly minimalist. No pink. No ruffles or trophies, though there are pictures of us in a couple of frames and more propped in the lip of the dresser's mirror. He tossed a fluffy blanket haphazardly over the foot of the bed. I fold and straighten the cushy, soft material, then step into the hallway.

Arlo's door is shut, but as soon as I turn to the kitchen, he says, "Good trip?" He's chewing while sitting on the kitchen island, bare feet dangling.

"Yes. Thanks."

Darius cuts fruit on a wooden cutting board next to the stove, and I try to project into his mind to save me from awkward conversations with his roommate. I'm just not ready for Arlo.

Thankfully, Darius smiles, tossing strawberries into a bowl. "Drink, food, or…" He tilts his head back to the hallway and eyes my lips. My cheeks heat.

Not with Arlo right here, though I'm going to have to get used to being with Darius with another person in the apartment, unless I somehow can get Arlo out of here.

"Oh!" I snap my fingers and look at Arlo, or the cabinets behind him because his blue eyes are too intense. "The desk attendant said to come downstairs soon. Something about helping with security? That's what you do, right?"

Darius snorts and sighs, focusing back on the fruit. He really does not like that woman.

Arlo pops another strawberry into his mouth. "Yeah. But she doesn't want that."

I frown. "No?"

Arlo drops off the corner of the island and heads to the front door.

That gives me an opening. I make my way to Darius, who feeds me a strawberry, slipping his hand under my shirt and stroking my lower back, which he shouldn't do because he knows that turns me on and Arlo is, like, right there.

Arlo presses a button on the intercom next to the door. That makes a brief buzz and a red light blink.

"How can we help you?" the desk attendant's saccharine voice asks from the speaker.

"Take me off speaker," Arlo says, or demands. His voice makes my shoulders rise, even with Darius stroking lower, below the waistband of my leggings.

I nip his clean-shaven jaw. "Stop it," I say, though with amusement.

He chuckles and nips at my ear. "I fucking missed you." His rumbly tone makes me clench in need.

And yeah, maybe I do want to sneak off to the bedroom with him. I can say it's to unpack.

The line clicks, and Arlo grumbles, "When's your break?"

"About twenty." Her voice isn't as sweet now.

"Don't keep me waiting."

"Arlo," Darius says in a softly reprimanding tone.

The woman, Sheena, says, "Yes, sir."

Wait, what? For what? I peek up at Darius, who's watching me, but he doesn't give me any information or even a hint with his expression, besides looking slightly annoyed.

Arlo presses a button, making the light shut off, then stalks to the fridge, so close to us. He points to the four-person table tucked in the corner. "Sit down, Jolene. Beer or wine?"

I remain standing and raise my chin. I'm not at his beck and call like some people apparently are. *Sir.* I huff. "Bourbon. I brought my own."

Chapter Four

Arlo Struggles

ARLO

Defiant, innocent, sweet little Jolene. I want my cock in her throat more than my next breath.

Ever since I met her, it's been an irritating, prevalent thought I can't seem to tame down. Darius hasn't been helping the situation, and now that she's here, I can already tell it will get far worse for me.

Jolene Shah is a damn siren made of perfect curves, and upturned eyes the color of sex because I can't name the warm orangish brown color. And then there's that Southern accent tinting her deep, throaty voice every time she opens those lips. They always look fuck-puffed. She could start a riot with them if she knew what she was packing, which she doesn't. Woman doesn't have a damn clue what she does to others, which isn't a compliment. It's annoying. Especially as she bends at the waist, ass in the air as she roots through her luggage.

I glance at Darius with my jaw locked tight.

He fights laughing but also gives me a warning look that tells me to behave, even though he knows that's impossible, and not who I am. She's going to have to understand that about me and deal with it.

What she doesn't need to be aware of is that my lizard brain wants to grab her hips and tease my dick against the mysterious pussy that has Darius ready to say, "I do." Or that I'd like to punish her for merely existing in my space without being aware of my every dirty thought about her. It's not right for her not to know. What I'd like to do to her certainly isn't right considering our circumstances and how she is, but, fuck me, it would be good.

Jolene stands, cocking her hip and holding up a bottle of bourbon like she's a magazine ad promising one hell of a good night I can't partake in. She's not mine. I don't want someone for more than a night or two, and she's now living with me and Darius, her dedicated boyfriend and my best friend.

The man who told me a month ago, drunkenly offhanded, that he's been fantasizing about me fucking her. And that's all it took to wake my dick up to her presence.

I need to re-friend-zone her and fast because I'm struggling.

I pull three rocks glasses from the cabinet and open the freezer. "Of course you brought your own bourbon, Kentucky."

There are several choice tokens of knowledge I have about what Jolene loves and hates. And right now, I want to use everyone one of them to piss her off because—again—punish. She's a bourbon snob who's hosted tastings for charity. Sweet and hot. Good thing I don't like sweet.

I grab a handful of ice and turn toward the glasses.

"Straight up." Her voice is desperate and firm. "Please. Ice does not go into bourbon unless it's an Old Fashioned." Her jaw tightens like she wants to reprimand me more, and if things were different—if she were different, this night could relieve a lot of stress with a quick rip of silk. At least until the morning.

But for now, I've put her off guard, and she said "please," which will have to be enough. I raise an eyebrow. "You sure? It's good cold."

I'd like to feel that scoff tickle my palm when I'm gripping her delicate neck. But that can't happen because I would break her sweet brain and that siren body.

She and Darius make love. Innocent, calm, probably missionary sex with the lights off.

I do not. Ever. Which is why Sheena will be here soon. May as well get one thing straight from the get go—there's no place for discomfort involving fucking, bodies, and dirty talk in this apartment, and I'm not moving out of here. Darius insists he won't either, because we don't want to be apart ever, but as usual, he doesn't have a game plan if this all falls apart. It will just "work out" because "it always does." Let's test that.

Setting the glasses in a line, I rest my elbows on the kitchen island counter and beckon her with a finger. "Come on over, Kentucky. Don't be shy."

Her pretty eyes narrow. "I'm not shy."

Darius steps by me and picks up her bag, then grabs the handle to her suitcase. He kisses her pouting lips. "I'll put your bag in the room. Get comfortable."

Her eyes go all panicky. Such an interesting woman. Around me, she either looks like she's going to bite me or run from me. Nothing in between.

I smile and lift a glass—her glass, actually. The stained glass, high-end rocks glasses get her attention, and her panic slips away as she saunters over. "He really did unpack my things."

"We. We unpacked your things. Nice lingerie, by the way. Classy." I annunciate that last word like it's a curse.

And she's back in bite mode.

I grin and reach for the bottle, but she tucks it between her tits.

My mind goes to lapping a stream of bourbon from that exact location and how appalled she'd be by that notion. I'm tempted to go for the bottle anyway, skim my fingers over those gorgeous mountains when I do. Instead, I signal to the glasses. "Would you like to pour?"

"You unpacked my lingerie?"

I flick my eyebrows at her. "Yeah. We left only a few things boxed up. We didn't know where to put your pictures, pretty princess sash, and shit like that. You'll have to figure that out." What will she do?

Blush. She will blush. Her jaw twitches, nostrils flaring. She slides her navy-painted thumbnail across the label and jerks the cork from the bottle. Her hand shakes as she quickly pours. Maybe I should lay off for now. She's been here for ten minutes, and I'm acting like I'm going to pounce.

I'd like to pounce. I spin the glass she pushed in front of me. "Tell me how your trip was."

She looks put out, as if a simple conversation with me is so difficult. Though it probably is considering who she usually talks with.

"I don't like flying," she says. "But everyone's been helpful and pleasant. I met some baseball fans who told me a lot about Chicago and said I should go to a game." Smiling, she glances at me, then quickly down to her glass.

That raises my hackles, because I want her eyes on me. We're going to get to know each other, dammit, so maybe I can stop seeing her as the fucktoy she's not. I lean closer. "Ever been to one?"

"Yes."

I dip my head to grab her eyes again. "Would you like to elaborate?"

She lifts her chin. "I threw out a pitch for an All-Stars league. My boyfriend at the time was a catcher."

"Boyfriend?"

She's been with Darius for six years, and she's fresh out of college. That doesn't leave much time for others.

"Right before Darius." She sucks in her cheeks just a little, pouting those fucking lips. Then she looks over me, shoulders to chest, forearms, and back up again. What new game is this? "He looked a little like you. Less ink, because he was sixteen. Little bigger though." Her lips tip up.

Is she taunting me? Didn't think she had that in her. Maybe she's trying to tell me she's not intimidated by me, which she clearly is.

I tilt my head this way and that to keep her flighty eye contact. "And these baseball people on the plane. What were they like?"

Her tight features soften. "Really nice. They'd moved to—"

"Don't care. They hot? Give you their numbers and tell you they could get you into a game?"

Eyebrows raised, she holds up a finger. "You know, they did give me a card." She shifts around in her back pocket and pulls out a rectangular piece of paper.

"Lemme see." I hold a hand out, and, like a good, trusting girl, she puts it in my palm. Without checking the name, I rip it up and drop the shreds on the counter.

She blinks at me, wide-eyed. "You don't think I should have called them?"

"Don't take cards from strangers in Chicago, Kentucky girl. They're only trying to fuck you."

She gives a little gasp, but I can't tell if she's joking or not. "Well, I never."

I narrow my eyes. Her accent is even thicker, and who says that phrase in this century?

She smirks as she shifts through the destroyed card with a pointed finger. "Now I'll never get my free sandwich. Not that I was planning on being in Lexington enough to fill it up."

I glance at the pile of paper pieces and, sure enough, it looks like one of those punch cards for a buy five, get one free deal. Alright, maybe I went a bit overboard. "Well, the sandwich guy was probably trying to fuck you, too."

She leans closer, tits on the island, and picks up her glass, swirling the liquid that matches her eyes. That's it—she has bourbon-colored eyes. "Oh, she was, but the couple on the plane were just excited about baseball. Arlo, honey, I know when someone is trying to fuck me."

The hell she does.

"Fair enough." I force a chuckle and lift my glass, shooting the alcohol in one swig. The smooth, smoky burn is exquisite. "Damn, that is good."

"Especially when you savor it." She sips hers, humming a moan that makes my dick twitch.

"All set." Darius strides in from the hallway, steps behind Jolene, and kisses her shoulder.

She goes all melty as she looks back at him. Cute. And an even better reminder that she, what they have, is not for me. But I'm glad he's happy. He's been waiting for this day for too long.

At least they've had an open relationship since he went to college, which surprised me about Jolene. I thought the pageant girl would be too uptight to even consider sleeping with another man and then would be catty about others sleeping with her boyfriend. I asked him while we were tag-teaming a bar take-home if what we were doing would hurt his woman's feelings. He said he'd stop if it did.

I snag the bottle while they're staring at each other and pour another, then splash a little more in Jolene's glass.

Her brows furrow. Is it confusion or distaste? I really hate not understanding her expressions. Most women are easy to figure out when they look at me. It's *fuck me* or *I'm afraid of you*. She's both swirled together, plus a random glare.

I push the third glass towards Darius and clink mine against Jolene's. "Drink up so you'll relax." *Unpucker that pretty ass.* I barely refrain from saying that out loud, which would break Darius's request about behaving, so it's better for his sake if I ease her in.

She narrows her eyes.

Darius picks up the glass, sniffs and hums approval. He clinks his glass against hers and then mine. "Welcome to Chicago, Joles."

"Welcome," I echo, trying to catch her bourbon eyes.

She keeps her gaze on the glass. "Thank you." She takes a sip, and Darius and I do the same.

The doorbell chimes. I take down the rest of my glass, liking the burn in my stomach and the looseness of my joints. Instead of opening the door, I head to my room and grab a condom.

Sheena can wait. Like a lot of the women I bring home, she gets off on the anticipation, but her real orgasm trigger is being treated like shit. Used, degraded, discarded. She fucking eats it up, which works for me. I'm here to please, get off, and maintain distance.

"Should we answer?" Jolene asks from the kitchen.

"Don't you dare." I call back, walking back down the hall.

Darius has Jolene on the island.

Her face is flushed, eyes lusty. Woman needs to be fucked, but she slides off the granite like she's in trouble.

I glare at her and open the door.

"Come on, babes," Darius says.

"Hey." Sheena left her hair down, maybe knowing I'd just fuck it up if she put it in a ponytail again.

I grab the front of her shirt and drag her inside, slam the door, and push her against it, crowding her. "Having a good day?"

Her eyes quickly cut to Darius and Jolene, and she grins, lifting her sharp chin. "Not thrilled about having to deal with *some* people, but I'm better now." This is what I expected from Jolene. Not that I've seen either of them around other women. *Catty fucking showoff.*

I shove my thumb between Sheena's teeth and pump it against her tongue a few times to get her attention. "Where are your eyes supposed to be?"

She glances my way, dropping the peacock-preening she's trying to get away with. Why in the hell did I ever start anything with her? She circles my thumb with her hot tongue.

Oh yeah, that... "On your knees."

Chapter Five

Darius Plans

DARIUS

*D*ammit, Arlo*. Not that I should expect anything different, but he's just showing off here, setting expectations for how life will be with him using the most convenient woman available, even when she is radioactive-level toxic and he knows it.

I didn't realize he'd be insecure about Jolene moving in. I didn't really think about that at all. It was all just supposed to work.

Jolene stares, probably wondering what the fuck she just walked into. *Me too, babes. Me too.*

Of course, Sheena obeys him, kneeling on the blue front door rug.

I cup Jolene's glorious ass and lift her against me. No need to hide PDAs when Sheena's going to be choking on cock in a few seconds.

Jolene wraps her legs around my hips, but she's stiff, eyes glued to Arlo's back.

I hold her tight, tucking my face against her neck, kissing her lavender-scented skin while toting her toward the hallway. There wasn't a choice in having her here—I need her too—but I don't have a clue how this is going to work out between the three of us if Arlo is going to test her this way.

The idea of having my two soulmates under one roof has occupied my mind ever since Jolene said she wanted to make things work here. I've mulled over what movie nights will be like with them both and pictured social bar visits after work where we catch up and meet each other's work friends. Arlo would cook and shock Jolene with how good it was. She'd gush until Arlo rolled his eyes, but he'd be smiling for days. She could help him realize that every woman isn't out to control him, and he can rely on her just like she could rely on him. Then how he could help her realize more about herself...

I can't believe where my mind has gone with just how much she might enjoy the things he could show her. But, no. This isn't how we bond, and maybe I overshot my roommate-daydreams. Should have planned better, and not assumed that just because I get along with both of them, they would get along as easily.

There's always been a thick tension between them. I could say it's because he's too harsh and she's too sweet, but that's not it. They're both deeper than their initial reactions to each other, and with time, I'm hoping they will learn to at least respect each other, if not more, because I won't give either of them up. That's not an option.

"Don't act like you don't know what to do," Arlo says, harsh and low.

Jolene's legs tighten around me, bringing the heat of her core against my hips and making me hard. Her grip tightens on my shoulders, and she gives a little grind against me, something I'm not even sure she knows she's doing.

It stops me in my tracks.

I kiss her jaw, then the corner of her lips, which she licks, still staring past me. We talk about everything but sex. That hasn't been on the list in a long ass-time unless it was about us together. Discussing others almost broke us up at one point, and we realized the subject was too hard to be rational about while apart.

But we're not apart anymore.

"Do you want to watch?" I ask. We've watched porn together and mimicked what we saw, but a live show is far different, especially when Arlo is involved. And as much as I wish he'd have given her a damn moment before proving that his viewpoints on sex are not what she's used to, he is who he is. Who is she at this point in her life?

Maybe we *all* need a moment to get to know each other, as long as the process doesn't explode us apart. She might crack under his intensity or push him until he lashes out. I have to be ready for that. Keep the peace so I don't lose either of them.

Her eyebrows furrow, and she glances my way for a split second before she turns her gaze back to the front door. She clearly wants to watch. But how much? How close?

Turning, I press her against the wall, so I can see what she sees.

Arlo holds himself upright with one hand on the door, fingers splayed. I assume he's gripping Sheena somewhere with his other. His tense body is blocking the view of her, but I think not seeing her is far hotter. His pants ride low on his backside, and his shirt is tight over mounded shoulder muscle. He's directing in a harsh grumble, too low to hear, but I wish I could.

Maybe Jolene *is* interested. He certainly has my attention.

I press my hips between her thighs until she moans, though she tries to hold back.

"Do you, Joles?" I ask in a whisper as I trail my lips along her neck. "He wouldn't mind." Fuck, he'd love it. Especially if it made her a little uncomfortable. That might be another reason he jumped at the chance for a visit from Sheena, because he keeps that one at a distance.

He's upfront about what he wants, which isn't a relationship, but she'd like to be here more often.

Several women would like to be here more often, or they think they do. He gives them what they want—a temporary, domineering sex fantasy—and he blows off steam, continuing to stay detached to prevent the complications that come with relationships. He doesn't get it yet—how great it is to have night after night of stability, and the relief of being vulnerable without judgment. Having full trust in a life partnership.

I'm here for him, and he trusts me soul-deep and forever, but I'm not everything he needs. It's not the same.

Jolene trembles and squeezes her eyes shut before looking at me with blown-out pupils. Her lips are puffed and flushed. "Ah, I, um, I—"

Got it. I shift her onto my hips and walk into the bedroom. She's curious, but not ready.

Maybe I shouldn't feel so guilty about the part of my roommate fantasies that involved sweat and orgasms. It might turn her on. A lot of things she hasn't done would turn her on, but that's for another day, or month. Whenever we come up for air and have a discussion about what we've grown into sexually. But I need her first, thoroughly. I've missed her more than I ever thought possible. I just need to touch her, lose myself in her to make sure she's real and my hopeful mind hasn't dreamt her into my best life—her here with me in Chicago, maybe forever, definitely for now.

I shut the door with my foot, drop her gingerly on the bed, and run a finger down her sharp nose. "You okay, babes?"

She blinks, inhales, and blurts, "They're just going to..." she swishes her hand in the air. "Out there?"

I don't need to answer because Sheena's sharp cry comes muffled through the door, and it's not pure pleasure. She must be pouting about something. Arlo doesn't tolerate pouting.

Jolene's jaw drops.

"Yeah." I kiss her puffed bottom lip, then slant my lips over hers.

She refocuses on me, giving a soft hum of pleasure, sliding her nails across my neck before she tugs at my shirt.

I drag it over my head, then pull at hers too, need surging through me.

We work together to get her bra and pants off.

Her gasp against my lips when I brush her nipple with my thumb makes me harden fully. There's never been another that can make me hard the second I touch her, breathe her in, or simply say her name.

"Jolene. What you do to me is..." I sigh as her sexy little bud tightens under my thumb. "Just the best." Truly. All of it. The scent of the candle still burning on the dresser mixed with her is perfection. The way she dips my mattress and creases my duvet—sublime.

I'll play with her body excessively all night and tomorrow. For a month. We have time now. All the time from now on.

"I missed you," I whisper, sliding down, hugging her bare torso and soaking in the heat of her skin against mine. "And these." I rub my face all over her heavy breasts.

She laughs. "They missed you too, baby. And I need your dick because I missed that too, a whole heck of a lot."

I raise an eyebrow at her. "Yes, ma'am."

But she looks at the door again, brows furrowed.

Her cheek is warm under my fingertips, and those lips. Damn, I missed everything about this woman. I kiss a dimple. "I need you."

Chapter Six

Jolene Connects

JOLENE

I'm so distracted by what's going on at the front of the apartment that I nearly miss Darius's sexy tone. He needs me. It's been a lot of months. Of course he does. I ache for him too, but focusing is still hard because... was the desk security personnel seriously going down on Arlo in the living room? Isn't that against company policy, or something? I crinkle my nose. That was judgy and I know better. I hate being judged.

Good for them, or something.

I could have watched for longer?

Arlo had just started to rock his hips as Darius carried me down the hall, and I'm not thrilled about how perfectly biteable Arlo's ass is—all round, tight muscle that's highly grabbable. Is that why I want to sprint for the door and crawl down the hall for a secret front-row seat? A really great ass? No, it's only curiosity. It's nothing. Just banging in a pseudo-public manner.

"Hey, babes?" Darius's hot mouth encircles my nipple, shocking a gasp out of me when he pops off. "Want to stop and talk about it?"

Yes, and no. But not right now.

My man's gorgeous dark eyes are on mine, questioning, but patient, and they don't even slip to my exposed hard nipples, though part of me wishes they would so I didn't feel so busted.

"No." I shake off my thoughts, and grin up at him, shifting my legs to signal that I want him closer, up here with me.

He scootches back up to kiss my neck, then lips. His sides are firm and tense.

I run my fingers down until I reach the bulge hidden underneath his slacks. "I want you."

"Good." He gets back to kissing me, sweet and slow, twirling tongues and sipping at lips. "Because I've been dying for you."

I tug at his waistband, releasing the button, and slip my hand in to wrap my fingers around his hard dick, squeezing.

Is Arlo fucking that girl against the door by now, or is she going down on him? Is she touching him like this?

My stomach flutters as my breathing increases. I'm too horny, and now my mind is grasping onto things—people—it should not.

Darius's eyes flutter closed, and he hisses a breath through his teeth.

He slides down my body, taking my panties with him. He kisses up my legs, starting with my sensitive ankles, but when he gets to my thighs and doesn't veer, I giggle and squirm out of reach.

After being apart for so long, I won't have my unshowered vajay be his first impression of me. "I've been traveling all day, baby. I just want you inside me."

"You sure? I enjoy going down on you." He pouts his lip.

I crinkle my nose. "I like it too, but later."

"Soon." His growl is hot, and he nips my hip, making me squeal and giggle. Instead of his mouth, he presses his fingers exactly where I need him, grazing my clit, then slipping a long middle finger between my folds, teasing me with shallow thrusts.

I arch, moaning. "Okay, yeah. Let's do this forever."

"I'd like that." He presses two fingers in, deep. "All night. And tomorrow. I took off work, and then we have the weekend. It's just bed and takeout. Then forever. Deal?"

"It's unfair asking me to make deals when you're doing that." Even though that's the best idea ever. Exactly what I want. But how am I supposed to think with his fingers so deep inside me?

"You needed this, babes." He licks his bottom lip.

I can't even find an ounce of embarrassment for how wet I must be. "Y-yes." I cry out as he speeds up his thrusting fingers.

When it comes to this, to us, he's a maestro and I'm his instrument. He knows my tells, my signs, even if I try to hide them to prolong a game.

He sucks my nipple. "Are you going to come for me?"

I widen my legs, digging my heels into the mattress to roll my hips against his hand. I'm already close. "You know I will. Just come up here."

He kicks off his pants and settles between my hips, pumping his fingers a few more times while I grip his length and line him up at my entrance. He sucks his wet fingers. "You taste good."

My core clenches, surprising me with both his boldness and my reaction to it. I drape a leg over his hips when he slowly presses inside me, and tap his fantastic backside with my heel. "Please."

He slides in until hips meet mine, and I sigh at the fullness. He strokes my cheeks, smiling down at me. "You're here." His eyes glass up a little.

"I am." I pull his lips to mine, as he slowly makes love to me, hands moving over my skin, getting me where I need to be in a slow building flame I never want to extinguish until everything from my belly-button down tightens, and I have to chase the brink of orgasm to keep from losing my mind.

Darius keeps his slow rhythm even if I'm rolling my hips to get there faster.

I whine, wrapping my legs around his hips. "Faster."

He kisses me, smiling. "So impatient." But after teasing me another moment, he relents and quickens his thrusts. Deepens them too, which I love. He pants, breath tickling my neck between kisses.

My body goes chaotic, writhing and gasping as it panics to reach bliss. So close. "Right there. Darius. Oh, God."

"Joles." Darius kisses my neck as I cry out and pulse in pleasure, heartbeat in my ears. The last three grinds of his hips make me spasm again before he gives a pained gasp, pushes in deep, and comes.

I slide my fingers up and down his sweat-slicked back, catching my breath and grinning at his weight settled on me.

He stays inside my body, gently running his lips over my temple as his cock makes slow-pulsing aftershocks.

"So much better than sexting," I say, wrapping my arms around him and squeezing.

He chuckles, pushing up onto his elbows.

We kiss like we need to catch up, then squirrel away each touch for when we part again. Except we're not parting again. This is it. Home.

Two sharp knocks on the door jerk me out of my warm afterglow. "I ordered pizza since I figured you'd rather fuck than cook."

My jaw tightens, and my face heats.

Arlo isn't wrong. He clearly knows what we're doing in here, and while he may take his antics public, I do not.

"Go away," I yell.

Darius props his chin in his hand and raises his eyebrow at me.

I give him a *What?* Face.

"Because I'm *behaving*..." Arlo sounds like behaving is gross. "I won't walk in to have this conversation."

"That's behaving?" I whisper to Darius, tugging at the duvet to cover us. He would walk in? Who would do that? Just because he shows his ass doesn't mean I do. And Darius is still inside me.

Darius snickers.

I bite his shoulder until he whines, "Ow," and laughs harder.

"But another day... another day I'll just bring the pizza in and join you."

"Join us?" That comes out louder than intended, and I stretch to grab a pillow and throw it at the door.

He would not. He's joking—probably trying to lighten the mood after doing what he did a few minutes ago.

How long will it take to get the memory of that out of my head? Between my legs clenches. That might not happen soon. My entire face heats as if I'm too close to a campfire. "Go away, Arlo. We'll come join you *in the kitchen* later for dinner."

"Oh, Kentucky." An amused huff carries through the door. "Pizza in half an hour."

I glare at the door and the small creak in the hallway as Arlo walks away. "That was intrusive."

Darius runs a thumb across my furrowed eyebrows. "Want me to talk to him?"

I shake my head. "No. But is he always like this?"

"He's... bold." Darius's brows furrow. He opens his mouth like he's going to say something more before he presses his lips closed again. "You rarely have to wonder what he's thinking. It's a nice trait once you get used to him. Don't walk on eggshells around him, okay?" He gently kisses my lips and moves his hips back, parting us. "You don't need to. Not here." He seems to want to tell me more but pulls me up with him. "Shower? We should hurry, or he really will join us."

Why doesn't that seem to bother him at all? Like that's the norm. Is Arlo going to walk in while Darius has me bent over the bed and decide to... what? Talk about electrical bills or something? I've been here for an hour and have no idea where the boundary lines are.

"Intrusive," I murmur as Darius leads me to the bathroom by my hips.

Chapter Seven

Arlo Retreats

ARLO

When Darius and Jolene arrive in the kitchen, hair wet and both smelling like Darius's soap and shampoo, I've already downed two slices and a beer, though I thought about keeping on with that fucking good bourbon.

I'm leaning against the counter next to the pizza box, but Jolene slips around the island, keeping it between us. She acted this way around me when I met her last year—as if the thought of touching me after that initial handshake was an unthinkable act. At first, though, I thought she wanted to fuck me. That could have just been the alcohol in her glass, or me being hopeful because, as off-limits as she was, she was walking sin. Still is. It feels good to catch her watching me when I look at her.

But the tension is too much, and Jolene looks like she may grab her bourbon bottle and retreat.

"Good sex?" I ask. That will either give her the excuse to bolt, or calm her tight ass down.

She surprises me by lifting her chin in defiance. "Always. You?"

Oh, Kentucky. You want to have an actual conversation? "It was a decent game." I shrug like I'm not itching for her to ask me more.

Darius grabs plates and nudges me with his shoulder, though he's smirking. He knows what I'm talking about.

And I have Jolene's attention. She bites that puffed bottom lip and stares at Darius like she's waiting for him to take action. Does she even know him? That's not a fair thought—she does, just not when he's with me. She doesn't know what we discovered we like together, or the conversations we've had about her. How she wears a pageant girl persona until she's comfortable with someone. Apparently, then I'll really get to witness how amazing she is.

I find that to be bullshit. Why waste energy getting to know someone's fake side? I'd like to break that right out of her. I'm doubtful she'd be all that interesting with how prim she is, but I'd love to get to know her tits, and what sounds she'd make if she got spanked. If her throaty, sharp gasps from the bedroom were a sign, she's a screamer. I could have her right on the edge until there'd be no hiding who she really is from me. I huff a laugh at the thought of her reaction—tears? Cursing? Begging? It doesn't matter because it's not happening.

Her lips part, but then she bites them closed and looks toward the front door. Is she curious about what went down in that exact spot? *Ask, Kentucky. Ask me and I will tell you things that will make you blush to your thighs.*

She grabs a plate from Darius and keeps her eyes on her food. "Thank you for the pizza."

Yeah, I'd like to see her open and raw, no stupid-fucking princess etiquette.

A muscle in my jaw twitches, and I head to the fridge for another beer. "Water, beer, more bourbon?"

"I can get it." She pulls an olive from her slice and licks it off her fingers.

"Sit." The command comes out more harshly than it should, but she's frustrating.

Darius is watching the two of us like we're a boring tennis match, then grins when she makes her way to the small dining table.

I narrow my eyes at him. "What do you want?"

"Beer."

Jolene stands at the table. "Water, please."

I stay put, keeping my eyes on her until she lowers her fine ass into the seat.

"Good girl," I say, but so low, I doubt she heard me. I gather what we need, set their drinks on the table, grab my plate, and sit next to Darius, since I'm afraid Jolene will scatter or I will pounce on her because her presence is doing things to my body and mind it shouldn't.

She's living here now—talking to my best friend in a low, serious tone like we're at a fine dining restaurant and she doesn't want to offend the old oil tycoon two seats over with a less-than-proper public volume.

I want to make her scream so damn bad, my palm itches. Would that make things normal, or would she be on the first plane back to Kentucky? She'd run. For now, I need to lay off and make things right for my best friend. He's what matters here. So we'll do what he wants and get to know each other. Maybe that will help me stop thinking with my aching dick. "Tell me about the job search, Jolene. You're looking for a finance career?"

She swipes her lips with her thumb and swallows a bite. "That's the hope. I have two interviews coming up, and I'm really hoping for news on a third soon. That one's exciting."

"Mm, accounting. The thrill." What is it about this woman that makes me want to push every button she has?

She surprises me by raising an eyebrow and smiling. "While crunching numbers *is* fun, I'm hoping for a position in portfolio management." She does a little jolt, like something shocked her. "Oh, baby? In all the excitement, I forgot to tell you. You're going to want to grab more Burgundy shares, at least twenty. They pulled in a really young director, and the price tanked, but she's brilliant. Her restructuring plans are the future. They're going to blow up as soon as the old guys who bailed figure that out. Grab 'em quick. I don't think they're going to get any lower this week." She takes a dainty bite of pizza.

Darius's fingers fly over his phone. "Damn, that is low. Alright, I bought fifty."

Jolene gives me a smug smile. "If you have any money to invest, you should think about it. Also, Reed Holoform and Spigno, but the returns won't be as great as Burgundy."

"She's rarely wrong." Darius side-eyes me, probably because of my accountant dig. He knows I know what she went to school for and is obsessed with. I've even invested a few times when Darius mentioned it.

She's got a knack for finding penny stocks that avalanche into hundreds. She'll make a corporate investment business very happy as long as they stay ethical, because along with finance, her minor was law and only because she wants to stay in the right. Come to think of it, I don't think Darius is correct when he said she hasn't found herself yet and she's got a rebellious streak. There's no bad girl in this sweet treat. *Unfortunately.*

I pull out my phone and snag thirty shares from each company, just to see what she can do.

"And you do information technology?" she asks with a timid inflection.

I lean back and cross my arms. "I hack into security systems."

Her brows furrow.

I nod. "You heard that right. As a consultant. Companies hire me in a package deal to test data security. They build it, I break it."

She takes a gulp of water. "Sounds fun if not borderline criminal."

"Not illegal if they hire you for it."

"How did you get into that? Wasn't your whole family in the military?" She squints like she's trying to figure me out, and were she a different person, I'd distract her from this line of questioning with orgasms, or better yet, denying them.

But she's not a different person. I can't just bend her over the table. I set the crust of my fourth slice down. "Yeah. Four generations, all siblings, and cousins too." And they will never let me forget it anytime I see them.

She gives a short whistle. "Did you live on the base? I imagine they would monitor the internet."

I flick my eyebrows. "Unless you hack it." I grin at her shocked expression, and stand to take my plate to the sink. "Or you go to a regular school, and find you excel at programming. I'm sure you were good at math in school." She needs to be diverted. I don't like where she's taking this conversation, and I can't tell her to fuck off with the personal questions like other women who try to pry into my life.

She blows out a breath through her pouty lips and puts her hand on her chest like she's actually relieved I'm not a criminal. "I was. You didn't go into the military though? Did you ever try?"

"No." For a plethora of reasons I'm not interested in recapping.

Jolene hums. "Interesting. Sounds like that legacy runs deep. Were both your mom and dad's families in—"

Darius reaches to take her fingers, and she falls quiet as they exchange a look I'm positive means *shut the fuck up*. Looks like Darius didn't tell her too much about me. Good man.

"It's the family's legacy, not mine." I grab my beer and head to my room.

I don't need her zeroing in on my past. Not the first day she's here. Not ever.

Chapter Eight

Darius Tours

While Arlo's at work on Friday, Jolene talks to her mom, unpacks and explores the apartment, getting familiar with kitchen cabinets, and changing things around in the bathroom. She nearly cries when she finds her keyring in her pottery bowl. I added the apartment key to it and upgraded her dingy pompom with a new tassel and horseshoe charm.

The night was quiet, with Arlo holed up in his room and Jolene and me in ours. I should have let her know Arlo is sensitive about his family, but I didn't expect that to come up so soon.

For someone who craves pushing boundaries, he really hates it when anyone steps close to his. He had to know she would bring it up eventually. Her question was a gentle segue from work, and I don't think she meant to hit such a sore subject so quickly. I don't *think*.

She's sly with her intelligence, playing the fool more often than the goddess she actually is because it helps her navigate social situations. I wouldn't put it past her to have honed in on Arlo's discomfort and prodded at it as retribution for his earlier act with Sheena, though Jolene wouldn't have poked if she'd understood what he's gone through.

Was she truly offended or just frustrated because she was curious? It's not a simple conversation to have so early in living together, but if she can't accept Arlo for who he is, I need to tell him and work something out. We can at least set up a schedule so we can all get what we need without crossing paths. I don't like the thought of that, though.

When he gets home, they quietly gravitate like two polar-opposite planets, though they talk and no one seems offended. Arlo tolerates small-talk while Jolene avoids asking about his family and the past while we eat dinner. They're being peaceful, and yet there's tension—a shift in the energy of our apartment.

It will settle. It needs to.

Jolene wakes earlier than usual on Saturday, and grins widely. "Can we explore a little? I've been told I need to visit a big 'ol bean."

I put my book down. "Of course we can. What do you think about starting our day with waffles?"

She gasps.

Obviously, she wants them. When she visited last year and I introduced her to one of my favorite Chicago foods, she stole my leftovers for the plane ride home. I even brought her a bag of them at Christmas, and then she gave me the best blowjob I've ever received in my whole damn life. Waffles are magic.

"Yes, please. But I told Mom I'd call her." Her smile falls away, and she sighs, looking at her phone.

I drag her warm body closer under the duvet, and kiss her T-shirt-covered shoulder. "You could call her later." She was on the phone with her for almost an hour yesterday, talking about the apartment, plane ride, food, and being caught up on country club and pageant news as if she'd been gone for a month instead of a day.

Jolene crinkles her nose. "I'm going to say something really mean, and I need you to tell me it's fine, even though it's not, okay?"

Some of the warm glow of this dreamy morning skitters away. "Alright. What is it?" I hope it's not about Arlo. She might want to talk about him to her mother.

She drags her thumb back and forth over the screen, waking it up, and showing there's already a phone call and text messages from Donna. "If I don't do it now, I'm going to dread it all day. And since we haven't had breakfast, that will give me an excuse to make it short. See? So mean."

"Aw, babes. It's okay." It's not, but not because of how Jolene feels. Donna is a lot. It's overwhelming for me, and I'm not the one she's trying to leash from four-hundred miles away.

"I shouldn't want to avoid her. She's my mom."

I toss my phone to the side and roll over on top of her.

She covers her mouth with her palm.

"Stop." I uncover her for a kiss. "I don't care about morning breath. This is important. You're a good person, Joles. A good daughter. And you're an adult. You have a great big world to explore, and she can't be with you—"

"Because she won't leave Kentucky?" Jolene raises an eyebrow.

"Because she doesn't want to, and you do. You're an explorer. There's no shame in that."

Jolene twists her lips to the side, but nods.

I move her legs apart with my knee. "And there's also no shame in fucking first thing in the morning because you want to."

"Do I?"

"Mm-hmm." I nip her neck until she's laughing, and get to it.

Arlo is always up early, but he surprises me by joining us for waffles and a walk around the neighborhood. He glares at me when she sinfully moans around her mouthful, and then I have to lie to her about why I'm laughing. I'd told him that her throaty moans had made me come early before, and now he knows why.

Every new city sight makes her eyes sparkle, from the old architecture to a squirrel carrying around a full-sized croissant. She cringes at some of the city smells like garbage and Chicago sulfur, then her jaw drops a second later when we get close to a bakery or one of the many small gardens lining the street. She was made for new experiences, and the thrill of showing her a tiny taste of this city makes me appreciate she came here for me. I'm so damn lucky.

I'm glad I left Kentucky. Not just because of the job I love, but because I've had time to get close to Arlo again and live in a city with new people, food, and shops. My family is happy I'm here, too. They say that while they miss me, I've grown into myself. I can't wait for Jolene to find what she needs here. I'll show her everything I can.

Arlo dressed for a run, but stays with us, mainly keeping quiet while I jabber on about the city. As I walk between them, he answers and adds to the conversation if Jolene has a question I don't know. He chuckles as we come across a group of pigeons and Jolene tests how close she can get to them. Very close, actually.

"You're not adopting any of those," he says, leaning against a building.

"You're no fun." She rounds them up in a cooing circle, grinning and giggling like she does when she's fully entertained.

It makes my chest expand and a grin feel permanent on my lips. I lean against the wall beside him. "That is definitely something she would try to do."

"That one's purple." She follows one around. "She's so cute."

Arlo and I exchange a glance that says we agree. No pigeons in the house.

A group of boys walks by with a basketball, eyeing Jolene and whispering.

The tallest kid catcalls.

Arlo pushes off the wall, and I surreptitiously take his fingers in mine and squeeze. He glares daggers at me, which isn't like him at all.

I expected Jolene to have a lot of adjusting to do, but maybe I need to consider Arlo's needs as well. He's protective to a point that could get him in trouble. I need to be a step ahead to deal with that, and he's going to have to get used to situations like this with Jolene.

"She's got it." I drag him back next to me.

"What are you, ten?" Jolene puts her hands on her hips as she faces the kids. "Go home and tell your momma you just did that and see what she says."

The kids duck their heads and speed up.

She abandons the birds and makes her way to back us. "Looks like no matter where, boys are dumb."

I give her a dropped-jaw huff. "I was never dumb."

"Of course not, baby." She cuts her eyes to Arlo and gives him a conspiratorial nod that makes him huff a laugh and thrust his hands in his pockets. Turning back to me, she kisses my cheek. "Where are we going next?"

Arlo pushes off the building. "Catch you at home. Be safe out here. Call if you need me."

"Want to come with us?" I ask. "We're taking the L-train to Millennium Park."

Jolene grabs my hand.

"I've got some work to catch up on." He steps into a jog, leaving us alone.

I think Jolene likes the train about the same as the elevator, but we make it to Cloud Gate—or, as I like to call it, the massive metallic bean—and take pictures of us in the city's reflection along with dozens of others doing the same thing. Some people stare at us, mainly at Jolene. I don't blame them. Even her selfie poses come naturally. She's captivating to those watching.

At sixteen, she looked older, wiser than her friends. It's what drew me to her. That and her boisterous laugh when she really gets going. You can't hear her and not join in, even if you don't have a clue what she finds funny. That's exactly what sucked me in when we met at a senior party she shouldn't have been at. And that was it for us. We fell hard—all in. She gave her innocence to me weeks later. We were inseparable then, and even when the clock ticked towards my exit to college, we couldn't stop being anything but devoted to each other.

That doesn't mean there weren't others. What kind of sex has she had beyond what we do? We know *almost* everything about each other, and it feels weird to leave that part out.

When we sit at a cafe for an afternoon coffee, I lean over the table and brush my thumb over her knuckles. "Can I ask you something? It may be uncomfortable."

She stirs her latte, tilting her head. "You know you can. What is it?"

I keep my eyes on her hand, my dark thumb moving over her tan smooth skin. "When we were apart, did you date?"

Her eyebrows raise, and she leans back, chewing her lip. "Yes, and no. What do you mean by 'date'?"

"This is awkward."

"Hell yes, it is." She grins. "But I get it. I'm curious too. About you, I mean."

My breath is long and settles me. I wasn't alone in wondering.

"Dating, there's only been you." She shrugs, then sighs. "But I went on dates. I was *with* others."

"Do you mind telling me how many?"

"Three."

I give her a smile so she knows it's okay, even if there's a hefty twinge of jealousy. We've done what worked for our relationship, but that doesn't mean it's been easy to think about someone else touching her without me there, or doing something with her I didn't—something she liked. "How was it?"

She leans back toward me, taking my hand. "The first was really awkward"—she rolls her eyes and huffs a laugh—"probably because of me. It was so weird. One was absolutely terrible, and the other was… good. Not what we have, but good. Sorry, is that too much?"

"No, I wanted to know." I purse my lips as I consider. "Do anything we don't?"

"Not really. I mean, it was different, but you know me, my body, and they…" She looks to the sky for words, which means she's trying to be kind instead of honest. "They needed direction, or weren't there, uh, physically. It's like once we got to that point, they didn't know what to do with me." She crinkles her nose. "Is that weird to say?"

"No, babes. I get it." She's gorgeous. The kind that stops traffic, makes you lose your breath and stare. It makes her difficult to approach and talk to. It makes some people hate her, others avoid her, and the worst want to use her. I could see how that would translate to sex.

"What about you?" Her words are slow and cautious, but we've never been dishonest with each other. It's why we're still together.

"Ten. But…" I glance around to make sure there's no one too close. "Many of those were with Arlo, too."

I'm staring at her face so hard, I can see the shift in her pupils as her eyes widen.

"You dated the same women?" she whispers.

I shake my head and hope this conversation isn't too much for her. We're in Chicago, day three, and she's already seen a woman suck off Arlo, fought with him, been hit on by boys, and now we're talking about kinks we didn't know about each other. What are we doing? I stroke her hand in mine. "We were with someone at the same time. Just sex. I haven't really dated anyone either."

"Oh?" She sits back again, brows furrowed, until they shoot up. "*Oh.*" She stares out at the street, not really looking. Thinking. Coming back for a sip of her coffee, she exhales a lengthy breath. "Are you with him, too?"

It's a valid question. "We tried at one point, but we like women. So we share sometimes."

"Share." The word nearly gets lost in the wind.

"Shared," I blurt. "Used to. I don't need that. Um—"

"Got it." She nods, but takes a long swig of coffee like it's a beer. She stares out at the city, blows out a long breath, and... what the fuck have I done?

Chapter Nine

Jolene Thinks

JOLENE

Sunday is all about grocery shopping and other prep for the week ahead because I have an interview and the guys have to work.

I send resumes, follow up on resumes, and stare at my resume wondering if my Miss Kentucky bullet point is helping or hurting me. And when I'm not focused on that, my mind continues to whirl around Darius's words from yesterday.

They share. Like at the same time.

Watch each other go at it, naked, with a woman between them, I guess? Do they go for her mouth and vajay, or vajay and ass?

I've never done butt stuff. Hayley says it's sometimes better than vaginal sex, especially if a guy isn't familiar with a clit. Is she right, and what if Darius thinks that too? I should have asked, but it caught me off guard and made me wonder about all the things he's probably done that I haven't.

I can't imagine there's anything Arlo hasn't done because he's walking desire, and clearly has no boundaries. Whips, chains, public. It wouldn't shock me if he had a sex club membership. They have memberships, right? I think I read that somewhere. That brings up more spiraling because, unfortunately, every time I envision a woman with him, doing things I've never done, that woman turns out to be me. And wow, wouldn't that be awkward? We're all living together. Talk about complicated.

At least it's just in my mind; for me only. And maybe Hayley, because I'm dying to talk this out with someone and, while that someone is usually Darius, I don't want details on what he's done with others. He's been here, having wild sex in Chicago, while I was living the subpar college experience. There's a lot I haven't done. Like threesomes and public sex. Anal and spanking.

What would it feel like to be spanked?

Darius bit me once because I dragged him to my neck and asked him to, but he was worried about hurting me. I liked it though. I didn't know how to express that in the moment, and we moved on. It hasn't come back up.

I love sex with Darius. It's earth-shattering, emotional, and sweet, but I can't deny that imagining Arlo's tattooed fingers digging into me makes tension coil between my thighs. I need a new fantasy man. Too close.

When I first met him, I thought he was stunning. He could have been a tattooed, too-muscled male model. But then he had to introduce himself as my boyfriend's best friend and roommate. And then he had to stare at me like he could see my thoughts through my skull. He still does that, and I panic and want to get snippy with him. I don't need anyone rooting around in my mind.

Except for Darius. He's the most open, honest, and least judgmental person I've ever met. Even on my worst days, he loves me.

"You okay?" Darius asks in our dark room as I'm staring at the ceiling, wondering if the Chicago library has books on threesome positions. I'm too afraid to do a web search.

"Yeah." I crinkle my nose in the dark. What do I even say? *Did you like it more than what we do? What about it turns you on? Please don't tell me it was with Sheena.* "I have an interview tomorrow." *Nailed it, Jolene.* I roll my eyes.

"Babes, you studied all day today. You're ready. They're going to love you."

"I hope you're right."

He finds my hand under the duvet, and that's how we fall asleep.

***

Twenty minutes before I need to catch the train to get to my first Chicago interview, I'm pouring a half cup of coffee even though I'm already jittery. When I turn, Arlo is stepping around the kitchen island.

I'd jump, but my goodness...

He's in a black suit. *A suit.* And as if that's not distracting enough, the button of his crisp white shirt is open enough to catch tendrils of the ink rising from his chest. I have a strange need to reach out and trace the lines downward.

"Morning." His voice is morning-gruff as he steps close and squeezes my hip with so much confidence, I almost lean into him like I'm used to this kind of touch from him. "Good luck today." His growled words against my ear send a jolt through me, and the moment he turns and storms out the door, I prop myself against the kitchen island for stability.

"Thank you," I whisper to the heavy presence he left behind.

Darius finds me dazed in the kitchen and kisses my head. "You really are nervous."

I blink up at him and remember why I should be nervous instead of turned on. Interview. Oh, yes. I nod. "I made the mistake of talking to my mother while you were in the shower."

He groans and takes the mug from my hand, walking to the fridge to add creamer to it. "Did she go through the pageant personality checklist with you?"

That makes me laugh. "She did. Wear red lipstick, try not to be too cute, but flirt, be strong with the woman, and pay the most attention to the men. And now I want to vomit."

"Ignore that garbage and be yourself. You're going to do great."

But I don't do great.

I'm ten minutes late for the interview because building security needs to search my bag, print a visitor pass, and send me on a quest to find the correct office on the tenth floor where there are a thousand damn offices.

Then the interviewer is a snippy, arrogant man who glares at me the entire time while he scoffs about my research methods and tells me I have a lot to learn. He elbows the men beside him. One laughs. The other looks uncomfortable. The others in the stuffy room stay silent and unreadable. When the interview really starts tanking, instead of being myself, I get snippy too. I go in the opposite direction of what my mother told me to do. Sinking to that man's grumpy level is just as fake as being on stage, except the mean version.

Some days, I hate people. Some days, I hate myself. Today is both, wrapped up in one craptastic experience.

I spring for a cab so I don't have to be looked at by all the people on the train.

All I want to do is take a bath and sulk for the rest of the day, but when I walk in, Arlo is lounging on the couch, still in suit pants, but no jacket, fully open shirt, showing a white tank underneath. All the tightness in my chest withers, because he is one impressive distraction.

His laptop is open on his thighs, and he has on rectangle, clear-framed glasses. Glasses! For fuck's sake, how adorably hot is that?

"See something you like, Kentucky?"

His cocky words interrupt the mini fantasy of me pushing aside his laptop and straddling his hips. Stupid man. Even if it's for the better. I shrug. "Your glasses are cute."

He doesn't seem like the type who would appreciate being called cute, but he smirks. "On me?" He pushes them up his nose with one finger, then studies me slowly from my straightened hair to my nude pumps. That shouldn't make my body coil with pleasure.

I stalk toward the bedroom. "Just the glasses. Sorry to interrupt." I need to get out of this pencil skirt because I can't breathe.

Darius tells me he's in meetings until five when I text him, wondering how long I'm going to be here alone with Arlo. So, for a while.

I'm tempted to put on a robe, seeking soft comfort after the shit-show of this morning, but I'm not walking around in that, and I need wine, food, and bubbles. I kick my heels into the closet and jerk my shirt from my skirt. Good enough.

Keeping my gaze as far from Arlo as possible, I putz around the kitchen. We went grocery shopping yesterday, but I don't think we picked up anything easy to grab and eat except a box of cheesy crackers. Why couldn't that be a box of chocolates instead? Or some fries that are miraculously hot.

Arlo doesn't catch on that I want to be left alone. "What are you looking for?"

"Food." I sigh. "And wine."

"How'd the interview go?"

"It sucked." I open the wrong cabinet for bowls again because I think the guys put kitchen stuff on whatever shelf was closest when they were unpacking instead of thinking about where things should logically go, like over the dishwasher. Then again, their mothers didn't send them to home organization classes, not that I minded those.

"Tell me about it," he says.

I crinkle my nose. "Well, after telling me my analysis skills were elementary and would never work for *this business*, the CFO mansplained why inexperienced agents weren't capable of getting the numbers the company needs. Then he walked out when I asked why they were interviewing applicants fresh out of college, if that was the case." I really hope that man doesn't know others in the industry because I just torched a bridge.

"Bold," Arlo says, right behind me.

I jolt and spin, facing the wall of suit and muscle. He smells sweet and smoky—cologne or deodorant? I will not stick my nose in his armpit, even if it would only take a simple lean to do so.

From his grin, the deviant likes that he startled me. He steps beside me and opens the upper cabinet, pulling down a stemless glass. "Red or white?"

"I've got it." I grab the glass.

He holds tight, so I'm just holding onto him. "And you just left?"

I swear he must have weight training days for his fingers. "Left what?"

He raises an eyebrow and relaxes his grip, letting the glass slide into my hand. "The interview, stubborn." He crosses his arms, brows furrowed as I retrieve the bottle of gewurztraminer from the fridge.

"It was so embarrassingly done." I pull the cork. "Want some?"

"I'm working. And you don't think they'll give you the job just so they can stare at your ass in that skirt?"

The chilly bottle tinks against the glass as the shock hits me from his words.

It's like I'm backstage, getting ready for the next round. Mom is shifting my clothing, telling me to present well to the fourth judge because he can't take his eyes off my backside. That's what matters most—not my quick, solid answers, or my personality.

And now, fucking today, it doesn't matter that I've been obsessing over stocks for the last three years, learning everything possible I can without the guidance of an industry professional. Nor will I be great at my career because I work with passion, care, and dedication. No, I will only go far in life because I look a certain way. Nothing else matters.

I put the bottle in the fridge and slam the door as much as a refrigerator door will slam before turning toward him. "Kiss my ass." I hate that my tight voice betrays my attempt at being stoic.

And I hate that no matter how many times someone says something like this to me, it still hurts.

And I really hate that Arlo was the one to deliver that blow.

Chapter Ten

Arlo Advises

ARLO

"**W**hoa, Kentucky." I catch up to Jolene at the bedroom door, and grab her elbow to stop her escape. "That one stung, huh?"

She may be grinding her teeth as she glares at the wall with how tight her jaw is. Kudos to her for keeping her chin up, but I'm going to need her words for this, because yeah, that hurt her. Her eyes are all watery.

I didn't expect this reaction to what I thought was clearly a joke. An eye-roll or a middle finger; that was the response I expected, so either the interview went worse than she's letting on, or I hit something really raw.

"Why?" I slide my fingers from her elbow to her wrist and run my thumb over her soft skin.

Her jaw loosens, and she takes a long breath. Good. That spot isn't ticklish, or if it is, she enjoys it. "Like you care." She flinches as if she regrets her words.

That is not what I want. I need honesty, and crave her base reactions so I can get to know her.

I snag her wine glass, leaning into their room to set it on the dresser, but keep stroking her wrist to keep her with me. "We're roommates now, and Darius loves you. I care. And I want to get to know you. So tell me why you took that joke seriously."

She stays quiet, pressing hard on my patience.

I step closer, trying to catch her gaze, but she's not having it. There are a lot of things I want to do to her right now, and leaving her alone isn't one of them.

She glances at me, then back at the wall. "I thought you were working."

"This is more important." And interesting. That's saying a lot since I'm ninety percent through a project with millions of dollars on the line.

I see the moment she decides to give a little. Her shoulders sink, and she sends me a cutting glare. "That was an asshole thing to say."

I can't help the lifting of my lips. "Because I'm an asshole, but it should have pissed you off instead of hurting you. I want to know why. Your delicious ass brings you pain?"

Her nose crinkles into a brief snarl. "You wouldn't get it."

I will prod every angle until she tells me how someone this gorgeous, this impenetrable yet aloof, gets hurt by a snide, outdated comment meant to prod her into giving me more about this interview and the mansplainer. They were mean to her, weren't they? That makes me want to head over there right now, which is why she needs to fucking tell me why she's upset. I lower my voice. "Try me."

She lifts her chin. "And you called me stubborn."

That catches me off guard, and I chuckle, but squeeze her arm to tell her she's not off the hook just because she's trying to divert me. "Was there more to the story than you're telling me?"

"Not really."

"Then fucking explain your reaction so I understand you."

She rolls her eyes. "Fine. I hate interviews. Being judged. I'm too young, have an accent, and I've been told that fuckability is my top trait by people who've known me for less than five minutes. I'm supposed to act a certain way, and when I don't, I have guilt." She puts her hand over her eyes, which I remove because she won't be ashamed of sharing truths with me. "Just ignore me. I can't believe I just said all that."

The words "good girl" are on the tip of my tongue, but we're not there yet. "I'm glad you did." I tighten my grip on her wrist when she turns toward her room. "You are very fuckable."

"Arlo!" She swings back, aiming to smack me.

I snatch her other wrist and lean closer to get her full attention, a slight mistake because my mouth waters to taste her puffed, smirking lips. "See? That one didn't sting."

"Because it was just an assholy joke."

Assholey, yes. A joke. Not so much. She's beyond fuckable. She's a borderline obsession.

Not wise to share that, though. I nod. "Why the guilt when not acting like you think you should?"

Her lips firm. "No."

Is she serious right now?

"Just no?" I nearly laugh, but she's keeping a serious face and shakes her head. I want to push—crowd her and nip words out of those lips, but I'm going to let that go for now. She will tell me, though. I let go of her wrist and drift my fingers up her arm to grasp and give a slight tug to her dark hair. "Okay then, Kentucky. Let's talk about the interview. Did they say all that? Did they comment on your accent?"

She shakes her head, and it gets hard to steer clear because little puffs of breath come from the slight parting of her lips and she's flushed. Is this what she looks like when she needs more touching? My body certainly thinks it is, but this conversation is important; demands trust, and me throwing her on the bed and burying my face between her legs wouldn't add to that important link between us. We have no bonding to stand on, not that fucking wouldn't be a bonding point, but it may make things worse since we're roommates and both love Darius. We need to get to know each other.

I release her and lean against the bedroom's door frame. "Did you walk into the interview wearing this battle-ready attitude?"

Her sexy flush goes red, and she looks away. Embarrassment. Truth often hurts.

"Look at me." I demand.

Her eyes focus so well on mine that my chest warms. She swallows and shrugs. "What?"

"Someone really told you that fuckability was your best trait?"

"Yes. Said it like it was a good thing. As if I were lucky to at least have that going for me."

I'd take bravery and honesty before fuckability any day, but many choose to see the shallow depths, the instant prize. That's too bad for them. Especially when they mark someone internally like they did to Jolene. "What a fucking asshole."

"You just said they should hire me to look at my ass."

I grin. "And now I see why that stung. Look at us getting to know each other."

She rolls her eyes, but she's smirking too.

"So you have some hangups about how people perceive you?" I ask.

The widening of her eyes says I'm right. Interesting. "No."

"Don't fucking lie to me." I tilt my head, looking her over. "If you walked into the interview expecting them to treat you like others have, then that's you being judgy, not them. When's your next interview?"

She makes a motion, like she's trying to tuck her hands in pockets, but she's wearing a skirt, so she unfurls her fingers and smooths the material instead. "Friday."

I cup her hip as I lean to pick up her glass from the dresser. I'd like to follow that curve up and down and everywhere in between. Handing her wine over, I cup her shoulders. "Walk into that interview thinking about your future, not your past, and you'll do better." I turn her body, then nudge her toward the bathroom.

She glances back at me. "Thank you?"

"Welcome. Oh, and next time you tell me to kiss your ass, I will."

Her furrowed brows are sexier than they should be.

I hold her gaze—her stare down. I want to bite her lips, then hike that skirt up and reward her for sharing so much. She looks so vulnerable and confused, and for a second, I'm worried she'll take me up on that offer right now and I'll have to refuse until I talk to Darius. She's not mine to play with.

She tucks her bottom lip under her teeth and shuts the door.

I blow out a long breath and make my way back down the hall with a smile on my face. That went well. Hopefully, she'll take my advice to heart. She seems like she takes way too much on from others, and won't talk about it except, probably, with Darius. If she's letting others decide who she is, she's fucking doomed.

Chapter Eleven

Darius Soothes

DARIUS

As soon as I walk in, I can tell something's wrong. Arlo sits on the couch, alert, with narrowed eyes. Did Jolene press for family information again or something else?

"What's wrong?" I set my keys in the bowl and my bag on the floor.

"Her interview didn't go well." He points his thumb toward the hall. "She's in the bath."

I scrunch my nose. "Shit. Glad my meeting ended early. It was supposed to go until five. Is she okay?"

He rubs a finger under his lip and keeps his voice low. "She's got some baggage, huh?"

I raise my eyebrows and peer down the hall at the closed door. "She talked to you about her mom?" That would be a wild breakthrough for Jolene.

His expression relaxes. "Ah. She said she felt guilt for not acting a certain way, but wouldn't tell me more."

She feels guilt when she doesn't do what her mom wants, then more if she admits her mom makes her feel guilty, and it gets even worse if she tries to talk to Donna about it. I sigh. "She's basically a walking guilt sandwich. One that avoids the topic as much as possible." I sit next to him and grip the back of his neck, massaging tight muscles. "I'm surprised she told you that much. Did you spank that info out of her?"

"Fuck, I wish." He drops his head forward to give my fingers more room and huffs a laugh. "That would probably insult her more than anything, and though I'm into pushing lines, I'm not out to break your girl. Need to get to know her." He hums as I rub my palm hard across his shoulder. "Have you two done that?"

"Spanking?" I ask. When he nods, I shake my head. "No. I'm too afraid of hurting her, and she hasn't asked, but I have a suspicion she may like it." There are some things we should explore now that she's here and we're together. "She hasn't tried a lot, so she doesn't know what she's into." His muscles only seem to tighten. "You okay?"

He closes his eyes and blows out a long breath. "Well, she enjoys fucking you. Her sounds are driving me mad."

I groan. "Her sounds." Her voice when she comes gives me chills. "You should hear her little whimpering gasps when she's headed toward orgasm. Holding back just isn't an option when she's there."

"Are you offering?" He shifts in his seat. "Because this chat is making me hard."

Fuck, am I? I release his neck and lean back. "I don't know. It's not something Joles and I have talked about, though I told her I'd been with other women along with you."

He turns his head to look at me. "Did you?"

I nod.

"And?" Dammit, he's so clearly interested, and I'm not sure if that's good or not.

"And now she's in thinking mode. I don't know how she feels about it yet. She'll tell me when she processes." I take his hand and squeeze his fingers. "I want you two to have a strong relationship, however that works for all of us. Because I love you both."

"Love you too." Arlo leans to kiss my temple. "So that means I shouldn't drag her from the bath right now and lick her pussy, right?"

I huff a laugh, but also my dick wakes right up. What would she do? *Scream.* Smack him *and* me. "No," I say, resigned. Unless she didn't smack either of us and instead let him taste her.

He sighs dramatically. "Fine. Just fingering then?" He laughs before I do, but the visual comes to me with clarity. Jolene sprawled out, wet everywhere. Or Arlo crowding her against the counter, telling her to spread wider for him—

Okay, I should not be thinking about that, especially when she just found out we shared women before. I don't want her thinking what we've done in the past would be anything like what could happen between us in the future. Plus, she may have had a rough day. It was just her first interview though, and we talked about how it likely wouldn't be her last if she was going for her dream job. That's going to take a little time and interview practice.

We settle back, and I peek at his screen. "Almost done with the Grist project? Did you crack it completely?"

He taps his screen over a line of numbers. "Found three holes, but they had backups in place. They did a damn good job. Should finish in the next hour."

"I'll leave you to it." I lean forward to push off the couch, but pause. "Are you two okay for now? She upset you the other day."

"We're figuring each other out." He looks at me intensely. "Tell me if I push her too far, too fast. She's hard to read."

"That would be her pageant training. So we're not going to talk about her bringing up your family?"

His expression screams *off limits.*

"Then, I'll keep you posted." I squeeze his knee, making him jump with ticklishness as I pop up from the couch and dodge the swipe of one of Jolene's throw pillows as he aims for retribution. I grab the other he throws and set it gingerly back on the couch. "Hint. Do not let her know you're ticklish. She will wage a damned war and win." I head to the kitchen. "Did she grab a wine glass?"

"Yeah."

I take the Gewurztraminer from the fridge.

"How did you know she wanted white?"

I point down the hall. "Bad day necessities. Hot bath and cold wine."

His brows furrow as he eyes the bottle. He would handle a bad day far differently.

Stepping into the bedroom, I grin at the low music and Jolene's quiet, slightly off-key singing behind the bathroom door. She hasn't fully taken over the speaker-system with pop-country music yet, but it's bound to happen.

I remove my clothes and put everything away, then step into the bathroom.

From her sea of bubbles, Jolene startles, then blows out a long breath. "Scared me."

I raise an eyebrow. "Did you think I was Arlo?"

"I wouldn't put it past him." She smiles at the bottle in my hand and holds out her empty glass.

"You have no idea," I say under my breath. I pour, grinning as she looks over my body, eyes heating. Yeah, I'm still hard. "Rough interview?"

That makes her wince. "Yes."

She tells me how it went, and that she's nervous they may contact other companies she's interviewing with.

I slip in behind her in the lukewarm water, barely fitting us both. "You may have felt you were super rude, but I don't think you were, and he sounds like he was worse. You're safe. They won't pursue retribution, and the next will go better."

"I hope you're right." She grabs the soapy washcloth on the edge of the tub and runs it over my exposed knees and arms.

I wonder if she talked to her mom yet, but don't bring it up. She'll tell me when she needs to, and Donna will interrupt soon enough if she hasn't yet.

I take the washcloth from her, pushing her forward so I can scrub her back, then the rest of myself before I pull her back against me so she can keep me warm. I trail my hands over her heated thighs and hips, over her stomach and up to cup her breasts as I kiss her neck. "Ready to get out of this chilly water?"

She sighs like that's the worst idea. "Are you going to make it worth my while?"

I'm pushing her up and out before she gets the full sentence out.

Wrapping her in a towel, I kiss her as we stumble-dance our way into the bedroom and onto the bed.

I nudge her knees open, and grin at her, all pink from the bath, and spread for me. My heart races, cock full and tight.

She gasps at the first lick, and grips my hair when I settle in, playing with her clit and trailing her puffed folds with my tongue. She tastes like water and smells like fake lavender bubbles—nice, but not her.

She's nice, though. Loose. Spreading out as if the only care in her world is enjoying pleasure. I love when I can do this for her. Her eyes scrunch shut, and her lips part, sounds going haywire, making me groan against her pussy.

I bet Arlo can hear from the living room. It wouldn't surprise me if he stepped in. Part of me wishes he would. It may scare Jolene for a second, but he wouldn't allow her to cover up or back away. If she said yes to him, he'd pinch her nipples until she cried out. Ravish her mouth with his until she was lifting her hips against my face. That view would be… a lot.

Jolene arches back, nipples hard and perked.

Arlo would nip them. See how much she could take.

She'd either come hard or hit him. Not sure yet. We'd figure it out, though.

I slip fingers into her soaked entrance, focusing on her clit as I feel her tighten.

"Darius." Her hips roll against my face. "Fuck!"

She'd say that with a much different tone if Arlo told her she couldn't come. She'd squirm and whimper, or maybe growl. Would she beg?

I grind my aching dick against the bed.

The things he would growl to her while I fucked her—Christ, that would make me lose it.

Her legs tremble as she keens, lifting her hips so I can sink my fingers deeper inside her and feel her fluttering pussy.

I pull them from her and grip her thighs, dragging her to the end of the bed. Lining myself up, I ram my cock inside her.

She yips, but arches, widening her legs to let me in deeper.

I come in three thrusts, yelling out at the electricity raging in my spine, forehead between her breasts, panting like I ran a mile.

"Holy shit," she gasps out, weaving her fingers into my hair.

"Yeah." I kiss her sternum. "You okay?" That was out of hand. Arlo would be proud.

She giggles. "Are you seriously asking me that? That was intense."

I glance up, still inside her. "You liked that, then?"

"So much."

So did I.

Chapter Twelve

Jolene Cuddles

When I need a break from reviewing stocks and interview questions, I reorganize my clothing and ignore my last box in the closet instead of unpacking it.

I sit on the floor wondering if I should open it just to look, even though I know what's in there. I watched Mom lovingly wrap and put in every item while my guts twisted and my shoulders felt heavier and heavier. The black-marker words written on the side say, *Jolene's Accomplishments* in the beautiful script Mom spent years perfecting.

What do I do with my framed high school diploma, pageant sashes, crowns that were small enough to fit in the box, modeling photos, and trophies? There's a specialty case at my parent's house—that's where all of this should have stayed. The Miss Kentucky replica crown probably looks so lonely in there. Maybe it needs its friends back. I crinkle my nose.

The thought of shipping it back to Mom doesn't sit right. She'd blame Darius for convincing me there's no room in the apartment for these things, but really, even having them in the closet seems to weigh down the person I'm aiming to be. These accomplishments were young Jolene setting her future in the only way she was allowed.

She was trying to make it to graduation day, because she knew things would change. The real world would be different.

But is it?

There are still catty bitches trying to establish their dominance the second they meet me. There are still old men cutting my points when I don't say what they expect me to. I still have to step onto a stage. Perform. Pretend I'm something I'm not because what I am isn't good enough for them.

I blow out a long breath, lay back on the floor and grab my phone.

"Womannnn," Hayley yells in lieu of hello. "You caught me in line at the coffee truck, and my crush isn't even here today to distract me. How's the city?"

I laugh. "I didn't know Micah Milford was in New York." The soccer star is handsome, but maybe Hayley's obsession is because she actually knows him, since he's friends with her brother.

"He's not a crush, silly woman. He's a god I will worship until the day I'm dragged down to hell."

"You shut your mouth," I say, though with laughter. "So who's the new crush?"

"You first. City. How's it going? Are all the companies throwing money at you to come work for them yet?"

I groan. "Not even close." I end up blabbing about the shitty interview, and Sheena, who hates me. Then I tell her about Arlo's foyer blowjob, and promptly apologize for taking too much time when she's at work.

"Oh, fuck that. We already missed our first Wednesday pizza night because of my job. I'll be late back from lunch, and I don't care. They owe me, and I'm caught up on scheduling company newsletters for a month."

"Oh, how's that?"

"Don't divert. Did Arlo's voice get all growly? Are you living with a dom? Is he alpha-ing all over you? What's Darius think about all this?"

And that's how I end up telling almost every detail of my week to Hayley, including sniffling because there's a box in the closet I don't want and I might be attracted to Arlo—am attracted to Arlo. Really, the rest of our conversation is just a hyperventilated mess of jumbled events that Hayley can somehow sort through because she's Hayley. She's two years younger than I am but has the experience of a sixty-year-old. She's fallen down in life so many times without a safety net like I've always had the privilege of having, that it's a shock she seems whole at all. I'd be a scarred pancake.

"So..." I can practically hear her mind sorting through my chaos. "Was Arlo right?"

"About what?" I can't even remember what I said.

"Are your demons coming with you to your interview?"

"Oh. Um, are they demons, or just me?"

"Oof, Jolene. I want to hug you so hard right now."

My eyes water again. "I want to hug you too."

"Okay, so distance hug, and I think you need a power pose or something. Wonder Woman stance and feral scream those demons out. You're exceptional, and you fucking know it. You've got spreadsheets, which are better than crowns in your business, and yes, it's your business. Your career. You take that bitch and own it."

I feel like I can breathe again and nod. "Okay."

"Arlo's right, you're fuckable, but it's okay. That doesn't make you less intelligent, 'kay? If it did, I wouldn't be in the running to head the newsletter at my company."

I gasp. "Hayley! Why didn't you tell me?"

"I'm telling you now. Awesome, right? And you know how fuckable I am. You've seen my ass." She is the prettiest pear, and she owns it, even if her body didn't fit the pageant circuit. It fits her.

I laugh right out of my soul, and it feels like it opens something in me. "I really needed to talk to you."

"I'm so glad you called. But also, if I'm going to lead this team, I should probably get my fine ass back to work. But we clearly need to talk again soon."

"We do." I didn't get to ask her about her threesome experience—I'm sure she's had at least one. A lot of the rumors circulating about her in school weren't true, but some of them were.

We hang up, and I shut the closet without acknowledging the box.

I head into the bathroom and stare at my reflection. I put light makeup on this morning out of habit, though I cried off my mascara and much of my foundation. Do I enjoy putting it on every day? I think so. Does it feel necessary? Absolutely.

I grew up with the motto, "Put your best face forward." Mom has a cross-stitch in her bathroom with the phrase. It doesn't mean your actual face. And now, the thought of taking it off—baring myself—gives the stomach dropping sensation of being on stage again, looking at paper numbers that sting, my frowning mother, and an audience only there to see who was best because of their makeup, body, and hair, or if they had an extraordinary talent, though that was only the icing on the pretty cake. In a classroom, we learned scripted, pretty, sellable words, and it was never from the heart, because that wasn't good enough.

We were always striving to be the perfect person someone else wanted us to be.

I blow out a long breath, and shake my head at myself. Who would I be if I hadn't spent so many years posing as someone else?

I'm going to need to confront this before tomorrow's interview.

So, it's interaction time, starting with a difficult subject. I went to the store yesterday, and Arlo's hookup gave me the same snobby stare down the interviewer did. I need to find a way not to be pageant-perfect about it or opposite—rude and bitter. I need to find myself somewhere in the middle.

I wipe off the lip stain and go with the simple chapstick I use at night in the dark, put my hair in a comfortable bun, and refuse to change out of Darius's sweatpants. They're so comfortable. I can be comfortable. Before I grab my keys, I partially take Hayley's advice.

Hands on hips, feet shoulder-width apart, chin high and chest out. *I am Wonder Woman.* It feels great. Powerful even. I bet Hayley's right and a feral scream would be cathartic, but then someone would probably call the cops, and nothing diverts confidence like having to explain why you're screaming to law enforcement. I take big breaths and quiet-roar them out.

I'm not even scared of the elevator as it dings. Then the doors open, and my confidence wheezes right out of me.

Arlo stands there in a gray suit with a dark green button-down under it. Man can dress. He's laid low since our conversation in the hall, and I'm a little hurt about that, oddly. I guess I thought that opened up something between us, not closed all conversation.

"Hi." I wait for him to step out, but he doesn't.

"Taking a study break?" His eyes rove over my outfit—sweatpants, tank top, and my sweater wrap that hangs off one shoulder—then he gets to my face, and there is something unreadable there, but it tightens my stomach.

I tug my sweater back in place, and smile. "Just going to get the mail."

His eyes narrow. "Why? Darius gets it."

I bite my lip, tasting peppermint wax, and shrug. "Just... because."

"Let's go." He holds the door open.

I study him for a second, but his serious stare is in place, so I step in. The doors shut, and this was a dangerous plan. One, his smoky sweet scent encompasses me, and my mouth waters in this small, private space. Two, his presence will not help my test with Sheena. And three, I grip the bar along the wall because I was wrong in my confidence about the elevator. I don't like it, and Arlo doesn't need to know that.

I hold my breath as it begins its descent.

"Not a fan of elevators?"

Dammit. "Not really, and this one is long." I close my eyes.

Warm fingers touch my chin. Arlo's blue irises are rimmed in gray, and his pupils are the deepest black. Wow. He drags his thumb along my jaw, making the side of my face tingle. "Closing your eyes will only give you motion sickness."

"Okay," I whisper.

He moves his heated touch down my neck, and it feels entirely too good to question, even when his fingers enclose and give the slightest pressure against my throat.

My breath hitches, and I sink into the hold like a scruffed cat. I swear I feel my racing pulse slow down against his fingers.

The bell dings and the corner of his lips raises. "Not bad." He drops his hand as the doors open.

My neck stays warm and almost gooey. Oh, and we're at the lobby. Right. I blink, swallow, and walk by him, feeling the tightness between my legs with each step. What was that? I refrain from fanning my face, but it feels like it's boiling.

As soon as I turn the corner, Sheena looks over, a fake smile in place, but that drops away. Until she sees Arlo behind me. He gets a real, eye-lit-up grin. Of course he does. So it really is me she doesn't like. Wonderful. Making friends all over the place already.

"Hello, sir." She looks at him from under her eyelashes.

"You remember Ms. Shah." His voice reflects boredom; no commanding presence or warmth at all. It sounds like a hollow echo.

"Oh, it's just Jolene." I grin and wave, slowing to a stop. "Hi, Sheena. Having a good day?"

I swear she eye-rolls as her gaze makes its way to me. "Could be better."

Arlo grips the back of my neck hard and pulls me along with him. Sheena gives me a death glare.

As soon as we pass into the mailroom, I elbow him. "Let up."

He gives my neck a squeeze that feels like the start of a killer massage, then releases me, swiping the keys from my hand and going to our copper mailbox door among the hundreds lining the three walls.

I cross my arms. "Want to tell me what that was all about, because I'm trying to get to know people, not have them hate me."

He glances back with a raised eyebrow. "Why would you try to get to know her?"

"Because she works here and I live here now, and you two are—" I swish the air. "Women don't like it if it seems like someone is stepping in on their man."

His laugh is a single, boisterous huff that crinkles his nose. "I'm not her man, nor ever will be." He pulls four envelopes and a small package from the box.

"Well, whatever you are or are not, leave me out of it. I'm just trying to get to know people. Make friends."

He tucks the package under his arm, holds the envelopes, and grasps my hand, dragging me out of the mailroom.

"Arlo," I growl under my breath.

"Yes, angel?" He leans as if he's going to kiss me before he brings us to a stop, looking away from me to Sheena. "Any packages?" His voice is warm now, amused. Did he just call me an angel? My body is fritzing out—hot like embarrassment, tingling like lust. My ears are stuffed with pulsing rage.

"No," Sheena says quietly.

I can't stop myself from smiling as I try to detach from his strong fingers. I blurt out, "Thanks. Have a great day."

"Right back at ya," she says with venom.

As soon as we're in the elevator, I jerk my hand, and he lets me go. "Is that part of your game with her?"

"Not this time." He raises an eyebrow. "Are you curious about my games, Kentucky?"

My mouth gapes before I snap it closed. "No." *I really, really am.* "Do you treat all women you do stuff with like that?"

He grins. "So curious." When I cross my arms and lean back, he steps closer. "You mean, do I parade a gorgeous woman in front of one I've fucked? No, my games are far better and much less petty. That was entirely for you."

What the fuck? "For me?"

"Yeah. She's not going to be your friend. You don't need her to like you."

"I wasn't—" My brows furrow. "I was trying to see if I was imagining her being rude to me or if I was just being judgy like you said."

His expression softens. "She was being rude to you. You weren't being judgmental."

"How did you know I was going down to see her?"

He eyes my face, my lips, and under my eyes. "Intuition." He stands close, seeming to wait for me to do... something.

I glance at the rising elevator numbers. "Did you call me angel?"

"I did. That was for show, but maybe you'll grow into it."

The elevator dings before I can ask what that means.

Arlo tugs my fallen sweater up over my shoulder, sliding his thumb over my skin. His touch makes the spot light up, and everything is so confusing. He slaps the envelopes against my hip. "Come on. It's movie night."

We're silent as we go inside and stay that way until Darius arrives. Then we all have dinner and talk about normal stuff—meetings, traffic, family updates only from Darius, and food we love.

I clean up the kitchen while the guys change into comfortable clothes.

Darius seemed surprised that Arlo proclaimed it movie night, so that must not be a regular Thursday night thing.

I need more interview practice, even though I've been going over questions, and researching fund statistics all day. Or at least when I wasn't shredding my soul to bits with Hayley, staring at the problem in the closet, or replaying the feel of Arlo's fingers on my neck. Why did he do that? Why did I let him and also kinda like it?

Focus. What if the interviewer asks me about the valuation of a company I've never heard of but should have? What if they hate my asset allocation method because it's wrong? It's not wrong, though. It's fine. Maybe.

Darius microwaves popcorn while I sit on the counter looking through the latest stats.

We lie on the couch, stretched out in a half-spoon, and Arlo strides in, grabs a handful of popcorn, shoving it into his mouth like a beast. I giggle and go back to stats when he snags my phone and tosses it onto the armchair.

"Hey." I glare at him, but he lifts both Darius's legs and mine and sits, one foot behind me, the other stretched out under Darius and my knees. I'm basically in the middle of a snuggle pile.

"Can I have my phone back?" I move to get up.

"No." He presses me down with his forearm as he reaches for more popcorn. "Movie night." He pins me with a heavy arm over my legs.

Darius puts on a new action release we haven't caught yet, and I side-eye Arlo.

"Relax." He squeezes my thigh. "No more studying tonight. You're ready."

I could protest. Stand. Leave them here to watch their movie while I keep prepping for tomorrow. But I'm tired, and this couch is really comfortable. Maybe just for a bit.

Chapter Thirteen

Arlo's Distraction

ARLO

R ivulets of sweat tickle my chest, and I'm glad for another test. I will not swipe it away. I will feel it and ignore it. So what if it's making my skin itch and tighten? With a hard right hook, the hundred and fifty pound base of the punching bag lifts and thunks back onto the hardwood. I want to do far, far more, and wish I had the strength to rip this bag to shreds and kick around its foamy guts.

I'm an idiot.

This is why I don't have a woman in my life, especially one I'm not fucking.

I made a mistake. At my fucking job. A big-ass, glaring, black hole of a mistake because I was *worried* about Jolene and the interview that made her all frowny, then followed her down the hall to impart advice instead of orgasms. Then, as my good-behavior reward, I got to listen to her throaty moans while Darius fucked her behind a closed door. Instead of paying attention to my million-dollar project, I was fucking my fist, daydreaming I was with them.

Goddammit.

I nail a left hook so hard, my teeth clack together and the bag groans. I set my forehead against it and let it hold me up as I give punches to its sides. My muscles scream for mercy. *Fuck you, muscles. We stop when I say so.* Five more hits. Then three. A knee strike. My jaw loosens, and the rage ebbs away. I grab the towel from the floor to wipe the sweat stinging my eyes as I gulp the sweat-scented air.

"Hey, are you okay?" Jolene's voice is quiet against the fast-pulsing blood in my ears.

My body tenses right back up, tugging at my spine from her damned rasp. My cock still works, so I clearly didn't wear myself out enough. I chuckle, dark and humorlessly, grabbing a swig of water from the bottle on my dresser. "Fuck. No."

"Can I help?"

Yeah. She can crawl her way to me and do a vast array of depravity, but that would be for my temper and not for either of our fun. I'm so worked up though, even the wrongness of it sounds right. "No."

Her presence remains thick on my back. "You sure, because—"

"Go away, Jolene."

"Fine, cranky pants, geez. Just trying to check on you because you're not looking—" She pauses and damn if I don't turn around to see her eyes wandering me from tattooed calves to mesh shorts and bare back. She swallows. "Uh...good." She bites her lips together, and I'm three seconds from breaking. Two. And one.

"No?" I turn to her and take another swig of water. It soothes the burning in my throat. "Because you can't seem to keep your eyes off me."

Her pretty lips frown. "I wanted to make sure you were okay. You were loud." She sticks her gaze to the wall and I don't like it off me.

I huff a laugh. "Says the porn-star screamer."

That makes her face go rosy, but she puts her eyes back on mine. "What?"

"You." I throw my water bottle on the bed and unwrap my hands. "You're fucking loud when you come. It's distracting." And hot. So damn hot, it's making me mad not to see her face, too. Does she bite that lip while her eyes roll back? I bet right before she blows, her low straight brows furrow like she's in pain. The best kind of pain.

I move toward her.

She steps back. "Asshole."

"You certainly enjoy calling me that." I slide between her and their bedroom.

"Would *bag of dicks* work better for you?"

"Maybe." I glance at my tented shorts and smirk when she does, too.

"You know, I came to check on you, but since you're acting all—" she flits a hand towards me, then stops. Her brows furrow. "Wait. Did something happen? You okay?"

I lean back and scratch my itchy, slick chest, then wince because every muscle aches at the motion. "Go, Kentucky. Wait for your man to get home and then you can bring down the damn walls with your carrying on."

"First, that's rude. I'd think you'd be immune to the sounds of sex since you happily do your thing in the living room."

"And kitchen, couch, balcony—"

She waves her hand at me to stop. "Two, you're not acting like yourself."

"You don't know me yet."

"Ditto. So I'll tell you I'm perceptive."

I laugh at that. "Like hell you are." If that were true, she'd realize that I'm fighting to keep myself from pushing her against the wall and choking her with my tongue and hand. Then my cock. I want to hear how she whimpers around me while she comes apart. I want to see her disheveled—kind of like this, but in broken-down bliss, not irritation.

"Are you mad at me? I thought after last night, um—"

Last night when I should have checked my email and found the meeting request instead of curling up with the happy couple on the couch. I shouldn't have let myself feel the softness of her thighs, or let my chest expand and warm when her calves relaxed under my palms. I started massaging them because I couldn't stop myself from exploring her, just a little. Like friends, but not at all. I shouldn't have gotten caught up watching Darius kiss behind her ear whenever she gasped at a suspenseful moment. Or have been mesmerized at the way she'd look at him or me at a funny part just to see if we got it, too.

"Just go. Seriously. Let me work this shit out." I step back into my room.

"Tell me." She tilts her head. "What did I do?"

"You came here." I growl when her stance tightens up like I kicked her proverbial puppy, then grip her arm when she tries to escape. I should let her go to her room and leave me to sulk over this unstoppable irritation. But I don't. Instead, I make another mistake and jerk her against me, cupping her neck, thumb against her jaw, forcing her face up so her attention is fully on me.

To her credit, she doesn't slap me or try to escape. Her tee-covered tits press against my chest, and a thousand ways I can fuck her run through my mind, starting with those.

I grin with malice and dip my head until I can feel the puffs of her sweet breath against my lips. "Your voice while he fucks you is making me lose my mind. You wouldn't be able to say a damn thing if my cock was in your mouth, but I bet even your hums would tie me into even more of these knots. I had a bad fucking day. Now leave me the fuck alone before I make you kneel and—"

"Go to hell, Arlo." She shoves at me. When I let her go, she sneers at me like a cat hissing after getting dunked in a bucket of ice water. "Bag of flaccid dicks."

She stamps down the hall and slams their bedroom door.

I don't feel any better. I actually feel flaccid. Another round of rage sears through me, and I slam my bare fist into the bag as I make my way to the bathroom to shower.

I can't even rub one out. Every time I picture Jolene, I get a gut check of guilt from her worried eyes. That wasn't trust I demolished. It was devotion to Darius, or curiosity, or plain confusion. I'm not getting trust from her anytime soon, if ever, and maybe that's for the better. She'll leave me alone, and I'll get my head on straight.

I finish up, wrap a towel around my waist, and fall into bed.

A shoulder poke wakes me. "You okay?"

I blink at Darius through a fuzzy sleep-haze. "No. Why?"

He's in sweats, not workwear. "Because you slept through dinner, and I know how much you like pasta night." He holds out a bowl.

I push myself up, hissing through my teeth at my sore arms. "What time is it?"

"Eight. Want to talk about it?"

Taking the bowl from him, I nod. Here is where he tells me in his serious Darius-tone that I can't say things like that to Jolene or they're going to move out. But he doesn't look mad.

"Jolene said you had a bad day and were working the bag."

I take a bite, and my body remembers that it burned five-thousand calories. I shovel a spoonful of chicken Alfredo rotini. There's broccoli and carrot slices in there, too. Those must be Jolene's add-ins. It's good. Salty and creamy, with different textures from the vegetables. A little more garlic than usual, but I like it.

I swallow and sigh. "I made a mistake." Several mistakes both starting and ending with his woman.

"Your project?"

"Yeah. I missed a hole. A big one. I've been distracted and didn't catch what I needed to."

"Are you in trouble?"

"The intern pointed it out." I cram another bite into my mouth. Fuck, that's so good.

He gives a one-eyed squint. "Oh, damn."

I nod as I swallow. "Yep. The project is okay because it was caught. But I should have caught it, and everyone knows it. I got a half-hour inquisition from Sam that I almost missed because I didn't get the meeting request until this morning."

"Joy." Darius reaches out to grip my shoulder, which makes me wince. Gentling his touch, he sighs. "You went hard on the bag, huh?"

"And your girl." I should apologize, but I'm not ready yet. While it's not her fault she distracted me, I still need to settle down the frayed nerves enough to think clearly, and not act like a—I huff a laugh remembering her words—bag of flaccid dicks. Funny.

Darius raises an eyebrow. "What kind of hard? Did she let you do anything?"

I furrow my brow. He's acting like he wishes we would have. "She didn't mention what I told her?"

He shakes his head. "What did you say?"

"Bunch of shit I shouldn't have because I was running my mouth off. She's not mad?"

"Worried and a little frustrated because she hates being worried. And her interview went, 'meh.'"

"Fuck, I completely forgot that was today." I could not have picked a worse day to be shitty to her. "How did it go?"

"She impressed them, but they're looking for an unpaid intern"—his eyes widen—"for at least a year."

I'm pissed for her. "What fuckery is that?"

"A company that wants free workers in desperate times. Someone will do it, but not her." He takes my empty bowl. "More pasta? We made extra." When I nod, he leaves.

She didn't tell him what happened? Why? And why do I feel uneasy, like I don't know what to expect from her now?

Chapter Fourteen

Jolene Schemes

JOLENE

Arlo thinks I'm a distraction? I've been a ball of chaos since I walked in the door; wavering between wanting to bite him and wanting him to bite me. There's an energy that rolls off him that's as frightening as it is alluring, and that's a confusing mix. And his words? Did he say those things just to make fun of me? Or was it to push me away? Were they true? There was something off—a pain I wanted to know more about if he weren't being such a prick.

I spear another carrot when Darius comes back from Arlo's room and scoops an even bigger bowl of pasta. "Is he okay?"

"Sweetness." Darius comes over to kiss me. "Eh. He made a mistake at work and doesn't handle that well. He'll be cranky and working his ass off for a few days even though it's the weekend, then he'll turn back into his *easy-going* self." I get a deeper kiss with a smile before Darius heads down the hall, bowl in hand.

So that's why Arlo was punching the bag until I thought he'd fall over. And he blamed me? Had the audacity to bring up the sounds I make with Darius? I bet Arlo can't even hear much, if anything, and he's just trying to make me uncomfortable because he was mad about screwing up at work. Is that a thing he always does, and will continue to do? We're going to need to handle that better.

I blow out a breath, leaning back in my chair, shoulders relaxing. What would he act like if I really were a distraction? Since I'm so fuckable and all.

That is one dangerous and tempting puzzle.

Arlo is intense and dominant. Even with Darius, who seems to enjoy the occasional times Arlo grills him about a decision he has to make, or even when Arlo tells him to sit and eat. It's so normal for them. Though last night was nice—being abducted from my studying to watch a movie. Not so much being paraded in front of Sheena, even if logically, I understand what he was trying to prove.

Darius returns, sitting beside me, putting a hand on my knee. "What do you want to do tonight?"

Press my luck. Get a little drunk. I think I've whined all I can this week to Arlo, Darius, and Hayley, so that's out of the way. "Let's go out for drinks. Will Arlo be okay without us for a bit?" I don't want to discuss him here.

"Of course. I've been wanting to show you a place you'll love." Darius takes my empty bowl and rinses it out, then we walk down the hall towards the bedroom.

Arlo's door is shut, which is probably good because I think he can read my expressions, and I don't need him to catch onto my annoyance, worry, and especially not my curiosity. He'd been right on the nose when he said I couldn't keep my eyes off him. Of course, I couldn't. He's a solid wall of muscle with geometric ink that runs down his firm side, and into his shorts. What would he do if I asked to see all of it? Not that I would.

Darius and I cozy up at the bar of a venue that looks straight out of the roaring twenties, complete with flapper servers. I twirl my straw, take a sip of a damn good Old Fashioned, swoon, then put my *Jolene needs answers* face on. "So what happened at Arlo's job? Is he in trouble?"

Darius puts his martini down and runs a hand over my back, making me smile because it's still new to be able to touch while having a conversation. "He missed a security risk. An intern found it instead, and Arlo got lectured by a new manager. You okay? You seem... out of sorts?" His thumb trails down the nape of my neck, raising chills. "Arlo said he was rude to you."

He did? "A bit. His tantrum could have rivaled a pageant girl looking for her stolen boob tape."

Darius snorts and covers his mouth as he coughs on his martini. "God, I hope not. Just know that he lashes out when he's upset at himself. Pushes people away while he beats himself up for a while."

"Yeah, that bag was having a rough day, too." I smile at Darius's amusement. "Does he do that because of his family? That seemed to be a sensitive point."

I get an eyebrow raise for that, but take a sip of my drink and blink with innocent curiosity. Darius tucks my hair behind my ear. "It is. And that's possible. His childhood was pretty fucked."

"Can you tell me about it?"

Darius nods. "Both his parents controlled every move in his life until he snapped when he was a teen. His father beat the shit out of him, and his mother left his dad because of it."

I grimace.

Darius spins his glass on the wooden bar. "Arlo said he learned more about both of them that single day, then he did in his entire life. And now, he's hard on himself, but maybe because he's the only one controlling things."

Every bit of that information hurts my heart. I swallow down the tightness in my throat. I can't even imagine that happening, much less Arlo going through it. He's made of steel. Maybe that's the reason for that, though. I think about the picture of him and Darius when they were kids, all smiles and innocent, mischievous little faces. No one would see that photo and worry about him. "I should have been nicer. I knew something was wrong."

Darius kisses my shoulder. "Stop. You couldn't have known, and none of his behavior is your fault. And if you act like it is, he'll be even more pissed at himself. Just let him go through his motions."

I shift on the barstool. My butt's going numb. "Thanks for telling me."

"Of course. And whatever he said to you, know he didn't mean it to be cruel. He's just really blunt, and sometimes he says things to see how someone will react, though not when he's really pissed. There's not much he does without purpose."

I look around the bar's shiny bobbles, not quite focusing. If Arlo is testing me, he's expecting me to act a certain way. And I went and called him a bag of flaccid dicks. I probably didn't score very high with my insult, but I don't want to let him off the hook for what he said, either. Actually, I want to push for more, or find out if what he said was the truth and not him being a defensive beast. So far, his reactions prove he will either make fun of me or jump me. I'm not ready to face either of those scenarios.

"What are you thinking?" Darius shifts toward me.

I take a long swig of the Old Fashioned. It's a little smoky, reminding me of Arlo's scent. Goodness, I can't stop thinking about him. "I'm trying to figure out how to handle Arlo."

"I'd recommend handcuffs"—Darius smirks as he tugs an olive from his toothpick with his teeth—"on you," he adds quietly.

Another thing I haven't tried.

I take his hand. "Being with Arlo too—is that something you need?" I lean closer, and my cheeks heat. "Like in the bedroom."

His eyes widen the slightest bit, and his lips twitch before he takes a big breath. "Are you interested in that?"

"Is that a 'yes'?"

"No." Darius's reply is quick and serious. "I love what we have and don't need anything else." He shrugs and kisses my hand. "But if you were interested, and comfortable? I think I'd enjoy myself."

I purse my lips and nod. This situation was not what I expected to face when I moved here. There are too many things that could go awry, including me. There's no possibility of denying that whenever Arlo puts his hands on me, there's a wild spark between us, demanding more. But this is not what I do or even consider. I belong with Darius. I don't know how that would work, or what we'd be left with if we went through with it.

Mom would faint if she found out what I was considering. She would tell me she didn't raise me that way and that I'm not that kind of person. She would give me a one-point-one out of ten.

My breathing comes fast as I think about her disappointment-face. Is a sexual experiment worth a moral downfall I might replay over and over again with regret?

Darius squeezes my tight fingers. "Joles, listen. There are no expectations here. Not ever. I love you and love making love to you." He palms my cheek as he stares at me with worry. "You are exactly what I need. Just you. Okay?"

I smile and peck his lips so he knows I'm not upset. I'm just processing. "Okay. Thank you."

He takes a swig of his drink when I do. "Arlo is a lot, and I never want you afraid or uncomfortable around him, so anything that would happen between you and him or the three of us would only happen if you fully wanted it to happen."

"Arlo and me? Like alone?" I don't want to continue an open relationship, so where would that put us?

"There are no rules here, only the ones we make. I love you and trust that you love me."

My attention snaps back to Darius and his concerned stare. I squeeze his fingers. "I do. You're everything to me."

He gives me his full grin. "Same. What we've already done—the long distance, the openness—we've handled that gracefully, and it's worked for us. I trust us to handle anything as long as we keep talking."

"I agree." I take a deep breath and release it. "So, I should tell you I'm attracted to him."

Darius smiles. "He's gorgeous. You can say it."

I roll my eyes and take a bigger swig, smiling around the lip of my glass.

Darius leans over and whispers in my ear. "You should see him fuck."

My eyes pop wide and my jaw drops as I stare at Darius, who smugly smiles back.

"I can't believe you." I tuck a strand of hair behind my ear. "He's intense."

Darius chuckles. "Mm-hmm."

"But..." I scrunch my nose.

His expression goes from amusement to concern. "You can tell me anything, babes."

God, this man is everything to me. I nod. "I want to push him, tease him—which seems like the exact thing I shouldn't do with someone like him—but then..." I stretch my neck. Just when I think Darius and

I can't have a bigger conversation than what we've already had, here we are. "I like the way he looks at me like he wants to bite me."

He nods. "I can tell. I think you would probably like things rougher than what we do."

I shrug. "It makes me curious. But it's not something I need."

"Hey, there's nothing wrong with wanting to experiment. And Arlo is demanding, but would never hurt you."

"Because of you."

That makes his brow crinkle. "No. I've seen him do a lot of things with women that made me worried, but none of them disliked what he did with them. I don't know how he sees where a line is and takes someone to it, but never beyond. Never enough to break someone."

"What do you mean?" I lean closer as the bar is filling out, and this isn't a conversation for others. "Like with sex?" I can't imagine just sex would break someone unless he was really pounding them, or he broke their heart, maybe.

Darius purses his lips. "More like control with his hands and words. And, uh, spanking, toys, and choking."

I nearly fall out of my chair. Yeah, I'm not ready for that. I don't think.

Spanking? Why does that make heat flood to more than just my cheeks? Toys I handle on my own, alone in the dark. And choking? I wouldn't like that. A quick recall of Arlo's fingers encircling my neck in the elevator has my heart rate quickening. Fuck, would I like that?

Darius kisses my temple and downs the rest of his martini. "Want to catch a movie or go bowling?"

That sounds like the best subject change. "There's a bowling alley in Chicago?"

He waves over the bartender to close out our tab. "Several. America's pastime, remember?"

Chapter Fifteen

Darius Instigates

DARIUS

After our weekend of deep conversations, bowling, and another trip out exploring the city, Jolene has fallen into a quiet contemplation bubble. I love her for that.

Though the long conversation she's having with her mother is only going to muddle her thought process. Jolene is toying with the idea of experimenting with something far beyond how she was raised. And as much as the thought excites me, I'm not sure she'll ever be ready to go that far, and that's okay. I just hope she never has regrets about us—which could happen whether or not she explores some things.

I listen in while hanging a picture of the Kentucky hills in the hallway.

Jolene's voice goes from apologetic to firm annoyance when it's clear Donna is telling her to come home to the many available jobs that Jolene doesn't want. I can't tell if Donna is blind to Jolene's wants or just can't deal with her daughter not loving everything she does. Jolene is doing amazing things for herself, but Donna is still trying to push her into an escaped dream. She needs to stop that bullshit.

Jolene and I celebrated the scholarship pageant win that set her free by burning her winning pageant dress in a bonfire and toasting the flames with god-awful moonshine. The joy my woman exuded that night from being freed from a lifelong shackle was one of the greatest things I've ever witnessed.

But Donna cried for weeks when Jolene told her she was done, even though Jolene had been telling her she didn't want to continue for years. Donna told Jolene to leave early for college since that's all that mattered to her, though she rescinded that threat the moment Jolene packed a bag.

Donna still follows the ranks and gossip, pretending her daughter didn't do the unthinkable—the unacceptable.

I roll my eyes when I overhear Jolene trying to explain that she doesn't need to come back to Lexington to find a good man. *Every damn time.*

Donna sends Jolene photos of the brothers of local pageant winners, no doubt trying to get her set up with someone who will help Jolene pop out pageant grandchildren. That stings a bit—Donna did like me at one point. I lost her favor when I left Lexington, because I think she knew Jolene would follow, even if we weren't technically "going steady."

And now that Jolene is living with me and looking for a job, it's probably finally sinking in that Jolene isn't returning to Donna's beloved pageant life. By moving in with a man, Jolene has made a public statement that she's not interested in the facade of virginity so many contestants pretend they have. Rumors have started, and there's no coming back from that, not that Jolene would.

Arlo walks up behind me, looking at the photo. "I'd hike that. Is she talking to her mother?"

"Yep." I pop the P.

My jaw tightens as Jolene says, "No, thank you. I don't want to meet up with anyone except the man I love. Please stop asking."

"Fucking seriously?" Arlo says.

"Completely." I tilt my head as I balance the frame. "Is this crooked?"

Arlo stands beside me, tilting his head, too.

"I'm not being rude, Mom, and I don't think I owe anyone a chance to date me when I'm happy with Darius and living in another state." Her voice is tight with stress, and I'm done.

Arlo is as well, apparently, because he tips the picture slightly left, then balls his fists. He steps into his room. "End that before I do something I shouldn't."

Something I'm positive would embarrass Jolene, and not because he'd be mean to her. He would create some interesting questions from Donna, though.

"Are you ready to go?" I yell, leaning against the wall. "We're going to be late." We're all in sweats and have zero plans this evening. I take one last look at the picture that is almost straight and join Jolene in the bedroom.

She looks so downtrodden as she clears her throat. "I have to go now, Mom. Love you." She pulls the phone slowly from her ear as she says goodbye four more times before hanging up and flopping face-first on the bed with a groan.

"Aw, baby." I crawl onto the bed, slipping my fingers into her silky hair to massage her head.

She groans again and rolls over. "Why do I feel like an asshole when she's the one being terrible?"

She must not have realized Arlo heard some of that shitshow too. I lean over her for a kiss. "Because you're sweet, care deeply for others, and because she raised you to respond to her guilt trips."

"She's only doing this because I stupidly accepted one date she set up. *One.* And he was such a turd." She blinks up at me and gives me a mischievous grin. "Kiss it and make it better?"

"Gladly." Thank God her mother didn't take her mood down too much. I grin, crawling over her and lowering to the cradle of her legs to give her a sweet, brief peck. "Are you happy here, Joles?"

Her amber eyes are tired but brighten. "Every day gets better with you."

That helps me breathe more easily. I never want her mother's manipulation to get so deep that Jolene can't dig her way out from under it. "I'm glad. Let me know if I can do anything to make it even better." I kiss her for real—taste her tongue and play with her soft lips.

She groans. Loudly. When I lick her neck, she arches and gives an open-mouthed purr of pleasure.

The door is open.

I push up on my elbows and raise an eyebrow.

"What?" She loops her long legs around my hips. She's the perfect mix of innocence and sin.

"What are you up to?" I ask, twirling a lock of her silky hair around my finger.

Her pursed lips say she's feeling mischievous.

I tickle her side until she squeals.

She lowers her voice to a whisper. "I'm just testing something."

"What are you testing, babes?" I nip her bottom lip. It's hard not to be distracted by her mouth. Actually, we should take a shower so she can wrap those gorgeous lips around my cock.

"If Arlo can hear me when we have sex."

Chuckling, I glance towards the open door, just in case he's watching, but the hallway is empty. "He can." I kiss her parted lips again and slip my fingers between us, seeking her heat. When I press against her clit, even with the fabric between us, she gasps, but it's real and makes me hard in a second.

The floor creaks from his room, and I swear I hear a growl of frustration.

Grinning, I keep kissing Jolene, circling my fingers against her center, waiting for her to tell me to stop or for him to show up and then... who knows.

She only moans into my mouth and rolls her hips.

"If you want my fingers in you, babes, these pants are going to have to go." Moaning with the door open is one thing. Naked with my fingers deep in her pussy is entirely another.

Water pipes whoosh in the walls. Arlo's shower. Yeah, he heard her. Jolene relaxes under me, panting.

I crawl off the bed, pulling her up with me. "Let's get clean, then dirty, unless you want to join him?"

She looks toward the hallway, biting her puffy bottom lip.

Tension pulls tight in my groin, and I hold my breath as her mind works behind her sparkling eyes. I envision Arlo's reaction if she were to step into his bathroom and drop her clothes.

He'd probably spank her for teasing him so much, then soap up her red ass. He'd want to play with that more, but wouldn't at first. He'd touch her all over, though. Make me hold her tight while he teased her to the edge of orgasm. And then—

Jolene pulls me toward our shower.

But she wanted to go to his.

Chapter Sixteen

Arlo Sucks

ARLO

Jolene's trying to kill me. She has to know that, right?

The micro shorts she wears may as well be lace panties because they're tiny and tight and hotter than the hell she's keeping me in. Every day, I swear her fuck-me moans are louder, and her clothes are smaller, giving my fantasies more realism as I get to witness firsthand the shape of her thighs I want to grip, and the scar on her knee I'd like to explore with my tongue.

I'm finding more excuses to work from the couch than I ever have before, because apparently this kind of hell is exactly where I long to be.

In the kitchen, she lifts on tiptoes for the damned wine glasses again, which she can't reach, shifting in her tank top. No bra. Fuck me sideways.

I practically throw my computer and stalk over to her.

She has one second to blink at me over her shoulder before I press my hard dick against her ass and get what she needs, setting the wine glass on the counter with too much force. She gasps and, I swear to fuck, arches enough to give the most teasing friction against my cock.

Killing. Me.

"Just fucking ask," I growl against her ear, inhaling the naturally sweet scent of her. My mouth waters to nip her lobe, then her neck. How would she react to my tongue tracing down her spine?

"What?" Her word is a breathy pant.

I squeeze her hip hard, just like I'd do if I fucked her against this counter or the door or my bed.

"When you can't reach a glass. Ask for help." My fingers twitch to tug down this cotton and sink into her wetness. I bet she's soaked. Not that it's any of my business what her pussy is doing. Unless she's trying to make it my business. She's not, though. This has to be a punishment for being an asshole to her—something I haven't yet apologized for.

She sidesteps me, cheeks pink, and I forget my damn name. Those bourbon eyes are blazing. "Why, thank you. I'll do that." There's a shakiness to her voice that dissolves the confidence she's aiming for, and my pants loosen the slightest bit.

She's not ready for what she's teasing, and that makes me wonder if she has a clue what she's doing to a man like me. It's not only the way she's been dressing or her sounds. It's the need in her eyes, and the way she's been glancing at me like she wants me to react to her. That's not right, though. I'm imagining it because I want her. Badly. So, I'll keep my dick in my pants where it belongs around my best friend's girlfriend.

I keep the loudly yelled "fuck" in my mind.

She bites her lip, then turns to flee.

"Hey." I snag her waist to hold her still. "I'm sorry for how I acted the other day. I shouldn't have taken my anger out on you."

Her deer-in-the-headlights demeanor drops immediately to confusion, then she relaxes. "It's fine."

"It wasn't. I'm sorry." My hand fits her torso as if it was made to grip her like this. I roll my thumb in the fabric of her tank, lifting the material until I land on soft warm skin and can feel the intake of her breath. "So you can stop teasing me."

"Teasing you?" She looks honestly confused.

Against my better judgment, I glance down at her tits. I could trace the ring of her areola with my tongue, wetting the fabric of her shirt so it was clear I'd been there. Nip the bud so I could hear that whimper right next to my ear while I touch every inch of her exposed skin. Not something I should bring up, though. "Those shorts are vicious, Kentucky. You know what you're doing."

She raises an eyebrow and runs her tongue over the tips of her teeth. "Do I?"

I roll my eyes. "You love Darius's sweatpants."

"I really do." Her grin is mischief and I'm not sure how to take it, but thinking about anything other than her ass as she struts away from me is impossible. She didn't even take wine with her.

The next day, she's doing yoga in the living room, ass-up, as I'm walking out the door to work. Her sports bra is overflowing. At least she's not in shorts. Instead of jerking those tight fucking pants off of her and demanding she stretch her legs over my shoulders while I eat her pussy, I tell her to have a great day.

She moans at dinner, and every hair on my body stands on end.

Darius smiles and shakes his head. Does he know what she's doing? He said he wasn't pushing her, but he also didn't say not to touch her. Is she asking me to touch her? Because it's getting harder not to.

I glare at him, and he shrugs and tips his head toward his girlfriend like he's saying *Have at it* or *Fight back*. Don't mind if I do.

Later, when she's making tea, I walk into the kitchen in my boxer briefs, still sporting a semi. I don't think she breathes once while I refill my water bottle, take a swig while I eye her hard nipples through Darius's tee, and say goodnight.

I have to jerk off three times before I can sleep.

We are at war, and the very air between us is prepping for battle.

The next afternoon, I come into the house to find her blasting country music while she vacuums the hallway, completely oblivious to my early arrival home. She dances back and forth, shaking her ass in sweatpants that swallow her up and a cropped shirt that gives an amazing view of her lower back. She'd be about the cutest thing I've ever seen if not for the distracting music and the fact that I now know she's been trying to get my attention. The only thing she's let me see her in this week is skimpy, tight, and tempting.

I stand behind her and wait as she bops her way back and forth, forward and—she bumps into me, screeching even louder than the twangy noise coming from the apartment's speaker system.

She slams herself against the wall, even though she looks like she wants to punch me. "You scared me."

"Obviously. Thanks for cleaning." I tilt my head as I blatantly look her over so she knows I'm noting her outfit. Still sexy as fuck—I swear, this woman...

She clears her throat. "Sure. I'm not busy, since no one wants me to work for them."

I snap my eyes back up to hers. "You didn't put that you were a country music lover on your resume, did you? That won't get you anywhere."

Her mouth drops open in insult, and she pulls the vacuum to the side of the hall and signals me to go. "Shoo. I need to finish this."

Shoo? I grunt and pass her. Pulling off my work clothes, I put on a pair of loose mesh shorts and nothing else, wrap my wrists, and work the bag.

"Bad day?" she asks from my doorway.

I give a sharp right hook, then pummel the bag with a left before looking at her. "No. But your music enrages me. Leave the vacuum out so I can do my floors."

"Okay." Her straight eyebrows crumple. "What do you like to listen to?"

"Nothing you'd like, Kentucky."

"Try me."

Oh, how I'd love to. I pick up my phone from the bed, connect to the system, and flip the shit to something worthwhile.

She scrunches her face.

I turn up the volume and smile before taking a few more swings at the bag.

"Can you turn it back to what I had on, please?" she yells.

"No can do. I'm allergic."

I hit the bag a few more times, then turn to ask her if she wants to learn how to punch, but she's gone.

The music cuts out, and something with a goddamn banjo comes on.

Oh, hell no. I turn it to the song with the most "fucks."

Two punches to the bag, and the music changes to a man singing about tears in beers. How is this music actually getting worse?

I put on a screamo song, but lower the volume so she can hear me yell, "I can do this all night, Kentucky."

Country starts again. "Kiss my ass, Arlo."

Everything within me pauses, and I smile with malice. I warned her.

Leaving her music on, I unwrap my hands, flinging the cloth to the floor before striding down the hall.

She's already facing me, leaning back and gripping the counter with both hands. Her eyes are wide, bourbon color eaten up by her pupils. "Um—" She yips when I snag her around the waist and haul her to the couch, where I drop her over the cushy arm so her gorgeous ass is up in the air.

"Arlo!"

I pin her with a hand on her back, and grip the waistband of the sweats. "Remember what I said?"

She goes still, peeking back at me and biting her lip.

"Answer me, Kentucky." I should probably lay off a little, but something tells me that this is exactly what she was looking for. "I told you I'd kiss your ass if you said it again. Did you remember that when you said it today?"

Her face goes flame red, and she crinkles her nose but nods.

Fucking hell. I raise an eyebrow. "Need me to leave you alone?"

She visibly swallows and gives the slightest shake of her head.

Fucking yes. I jerk her pants down. That is one seriously perfect ass with the tiniest freckle on her left cheek.

She attempts to push herself up.

"Hold still." I smack my hand hard against that freckle.

She sucks in a breath and stops struggling.

"Good girl." Holding her wide-eyed gaze, I kiss the red splotch, loving the way she sucks in a breath. Her ass is hot from the strike, and my lips probably feel like a brand on the sensitive spot. Moving to the other cheek, I suck her soft skin into my mouth.

She gasps, then drops further over the arm of the couch, but lifts her hips.

My mouth pops when I leave her skin. I run my thumb over the bright hickey I left behind. "I'll do this every time you tell me to kiss your ass. Private, public, I don't give a shit. Got it?"

She blinks, lips parted.

I slap the warm red splotch again. "Answer me."

She squeaks. "Got it."

I want a "yes, sir" from her lips so badly. And I want to plunge my fingers into her pussy. I didn't pull her pants down far enough to see if I made her wet.

Next time.

Putting her sweats to rights, I scoop her up under my arm like she's a football, and leave her leaning back against the counter in the kitchen with her terrible music.

When she's ready for more, she'll come to me.

Chapter Seventeen

Jolene Worries

JOLENE

I'm too hot. Probably because my ass cheek is on fire. It stings a lot, and I'm dizzy. The hallway seems like a black hole of... I don't know what. Danger? Yes. Desire? Too much. Temptation? I'm going to lose this battle.

Scrubbing the counter like it's insulted me by being present for that show, my face heats further, but from exertion. There's a tightness between my legs that's far hotter. I lean to peek down the hall, then slip my hand down the back of my pants, and flinch. The skin is hot, and there's a place that's really tender and tingly. Did he seriously give me a hickey? On my butt cheek?

I can't contain my grin.

But what now? An odd sadness rolls over me, and I ache to go down the hall and ask that exact question. I don't know how to do this. I've never met anyone like Arlo before or had anyone spank me and give me a hickey on purpose. If I pass him to go look at my butt in the bathroom mirror, will I insult him if I don't say anything? What would I even say?

I shouldn't go in there anyway because I'm turned on when I should be mad. Right?

I clean the fridge, feeling my butt twinge with every movement. When my playlist ends, it's silent except for the thuds of Arlo's fists against his punching bag. I stay frozen, waiting to see if he changes the music.

He doesn't.

I creep down the hall.

The rhythmic punching pauses, and so do I, like a rabbit hearing a crunch of leaves nearby and waiting to see if they need to escape from getting eaten. My heart hammers in my chest.

But the punching starts up again. It's not like the other day—not desperate and punishing. These are lighter and more like a metronome. Tap, tap, tap.

I peek around the corner and nearly sigh at the view of his muscled, tattooed back. Here's where I could lean against the doorframe and ask him what this means or tell him to do it again. Would he kiss me with those frowny lips? Do I really want that? If I know anything about Arlo, it's that he's intense and does everything to the limit. It would change everything.

My butt tingles, and I realize I'm fingering the spot again. Things already feel changed.

Holding my breath, I walk down the hall and slip into the bedroom.

The punches continue as I carefully shut the door and skitter to the bathroom.

I drop my sweatpants. One butt cheek is still pink. The other has a red, swollen oval from his mouth. His lips. I can hear my mother's outraged voice echoing in my brain. "Well, I never. How dare he. Who would do such a thing? That man needs Jesus."

Except... I liked it. The thought is mind-blowing. My reflection in the mirror is flushed, lips puffed, hair tousled. *I. Liked. It.*

I want more.

The heat of the shower stings, and I carefully scrub down the area, then the rest of me, not so carefully. Sensations feel needed, like the rest of my skin craves equally fierce treatment. My breasts tingle, and I'm swollen between my legs. As soon as I let my hands wander down to wrestle with the ache, there's a knock on the bathroom door.

Darius steps in. "Hey, babes. Good day?"

Throwing on a smile, I pull my hand away and hold my palms under the water, focusing on the massaging streams. "Hi. I cleaned." And got my butt kissed.

"I noticed. Thank you."

There's something else he's bound to notice. I turn off the water and open the shower door, trembling at the chill or maybe the adrenaline flowing freely through me.

Darius looks over me with heat in his eyes but hands me a towel.

"Did you talk to Arlo on the way in?" I pat my face and hold the soft fabric to my chest.

"No. Why?"

Taking a deep breath, I turn around to show him.

"What happened?" He steps closer and runs a finger over the mark, making me flinch from the sensation. "Is this a bite?" He says in a deep whisper.

I close one eye, squinting over my shoulder at him. "I told Arlo to kiss my ass."

His eyes pop wide a second before he barks a laugh and covers his mouth with his fist to stay under control. But that fails, and he laughs harder.

That makes a giggle break from me too, and the ball of scary unknowns dissipates.

Darius pulls me to him, even though I soak his work clothes. He kisses my forehead. "Are you okay?"

That makes my giggles subside, but I nod. "I'm confused about it all."

"What exactly happened?"

I tell him from start to finish in a way that sticks to facts and not feelings because, by the heat in my face, and the way I want to cringe, even though it didn't feel cringy, I'm fragile about this. Am I wrong to have instigated Arlo like that? To have basically laid myself out for him to do whatever he wanted?

Darius's heated gaze and smile tell me he doesn't think that's the case.

Being in his arms helps soothe my jittery body and pulls my scattered mind back together. "I think I liked it."

"There's nothing wrong with that, Jolene." He eyes me with seriousness because he knows me. "I'll tell you as many times as you need to hear it. Anything you want to explore is okay. I'm glad you said yes."

I bite my lip and nod, then rest my wet head against his chest. "I love you. So much." No matter what happens, he will keep me together because we do that for each other.

"I love you back so much." He kisses me and gives a light pat to my sore backside, making me hiss, which makes him laugh again. "I can't believe he gave you a hickey on your ass. You should show it to him. He'd be so proud."

That raises my eyebrows. "Proud?"

"Absolutely. He'd like to know how well he marked you. It's a thing for him."

What on earth am I stepping into, and why do I want to run there?

***

Arlo and I haven't talked since he kissed my ass. The tension has lowered in the house though, and his boss took him out to dinner last night to discuss a newly awarded project, or so I'm told from Darius.

He was out late though, and I'm left wondering if more than dinner was involved. Darius wouldn't lie to me, but maybe Arlo had other plans too. Plans with other people. It's not like I expected him to always be around like he has since I moved in.

The mark is still there, light pink. I touch it as I wait for the coffeepot to finish and wonder if it will always feel a little sensitive or if I will remember the heat of his mouth for the rest of my life.

Arlo comes around the corner in chinos and a cream button-down, sleeves rolled. He tilts his head, and I realize I'm frozen with my hand down the back of my pants.

Darius's words come back to me, and I have the need to extend a sexy olive branch to see if Arlo will accept or whip me with it.

I slam my eyes shut and turn. My heart hammers as I drag down my sleep shorts to reveal the mark. My lungs burn with my held breath.

Arlo's warm hand slides over my backside, making me jump. He brushes his thumb back and forth over the mark, sending my skin into tingles. "I'm going to be hard all day thinking about this." The growl in his voice makes me wonder if he's mad about that, but then his lips brush my ear. "Good girl."

Then he's gone. The door shuts, and I slump against the counter. I'm wrecked because I am definitely a very bad girl.

Chapter Eighteen

Darius Needs

DARIUS

All I can think about as I'm finishing the second phase of the CAD layout for our latest engineering partner is getting home to Jolene and Arlo.

I'm burnt out.

I need Jolene to hug me and tell me I'm doing a good job, and I need Arlo to hand me a beer, grunt in understanding, make me sit and eat, and not think about work for an hour.

I shut off my computer and stretch my sore neck. When I stand, my back pops. It's far too late, and I wince, pulling out my phone to text Jolene that I'll be home soon.

Gathering my things, I shut my office door and stride through the nearly empty office. I say goodnight to the few who are working late, and a voice calls my name. The elevator was so close.

The vice president flags me down from her office.

I turn in her direction, pasting on a smile.

Martina has gray streaks in her short, brown hair and a warm grin, despite her ability to chop heads in the boardroom. "Come on in. This won't take long." She heads back into her office of dark wood and bright pops of color from the couch pillows, art, and her lime green vinyl chair. When I'm settled in the chair across from her, she nods. "You've made quite an impression on the TechMote team. They really enjoy working with you."

That makes my day brighter, despite being tired of working on their project. "Thank you for telling me that."

She swishes her hand. "They appreciate you so much that they've requested you for a meeting at their headquarters to discuss a new project now that the one you're working on is finishing up."

That surprises me. They don't meet with underlings. "Isn't that in Canada?"

"Toronto. Just a little plane ride away. You in?"

"Of course. Who else is going with me?" A team can make or break a project. If I get stuck trying to muzzle our accountant while he gasps and challenges every number, I'm going to have to see what I can do to leave him back at the hotel.

She smiles. "No one unless you'd prefer it. I think you'll do a fine job representing us as a senior CAD designer."

My heart feels like it stumbles in my chest. I grin. "Really?"

"Yes. Paperwork is incoming, along with a sixteen percent promotion increase that will retroact to the first of the month. Also, there are additional bonus stock options, which I'm sure you'll want to run by your other half. When are we meeting Miss Darius, anyway?"

My chest feels like it's made of warm cotton candy. "I'll bring her on Monday for lunch. I should be done with the project by then."

Martina's nod is sharp. "You better. Now, your trip is in a month. Reach out to purchasing so they can handle your details." She stands, holding out a hand to shake. "Congratulations."

I'm in the clouds as I travel home on the train. Jolene is going to hit the roof. How are she and Arlo going to do by themselves for five days? They'll be fine by then. I hope.

When I step into the apartment, Jolene is sitting on the counter eating a chicken finger. I grin at her busted expression. "Where's Arlo?"

She shrugs a shoulder, eyes going to the hallway. Is she even dicier about him today? She shoves the last bite in her mouth and slides off the counter. Holding up a finger, she chugs down half a glass of water, then turns to me with a smile. She's wearing one of my tees and a pair of shorts. "How was your day, baby?"

"It sucked until I got promoted to senior designer with a raise, stock bonuses, and a business trip to Toronto to meet with TechMote about a new project."

She gasps, hands flying up to cover her mouth. "Oh, my God!" She runs over to me and leaps into my arms. "Congratulations! You're so amazing."

This is exactly what I needed today. I'm more appreciative than ever to have her here with me instead of on the phone.

She cups my face and kisses me. Her excitement and sweetness are so easy to bask in. It just warms me up from the inside out. Then something shifts when her fingers slide down to grip my shirt like she's going to pop open my buttons. *Need.* She's been revved up lately, and I'm all for helping her out with that. She taps her tongue to mine.

I drop my bags and push her against the kitchen island, cupping her ass and grinding against her heat.

She moans into my mouth.

"Good day?" Arlo says from the hallway. He's in sweats and a tee, so he's been home for a while.

Jolene squeaks and slips behind me to hide. "Sorry. We were just—"

"About to fuck on the kitchen island?" Arlo asks, stepping into the kitchen and around the island in question, so we're across from each other.

I chuckle.

"No. Um…" Jolene grips my shirt, still hiding behind me like what we were doing wasn't obvious.

Arlo's eyes narrow, and his shoulders lift. I know that look, and a different excitement veers my lust. "Don't be fucking shy about it, Kentucky. You should." He licks his lips, glancing at me with a raised eyebrow—a question.

I smirk at him and nod.

"Right now," he says.

I tug Jolene out from behind me, sweeping her lips with mine. "We could."

She blinks up at me, cheeks and lips flushed. "Now?" she whispers.

"If you want to."

"Hands on the counter." Arlo crosses his arms and stares her down. "Now, Kentucky."

She looks back at him as she holds onto me. I don't know what she'll do here. She may run, but that would give Arlo an excuse to chase, and I'm not sure she's ready for that. I don't really know what she's ready for.

He leans, staring hard at her wide eyes. "Would you like me to put your hands on the counter, or will you do it?"

She glances up at me, but I keep my eyes on Arlo for his next direction.

Slowly, she turns, placing her spread fingers on the marble. The energy in the room shifts, leaving us cushioned against the world so the only sounds are Jolene's quick breaths, the thrum of Arlo's fingers against his forearm, and the squeak of my dress shoe as I shift to make room in my pants for my growing erection. A thousand things I want to do with them run through my mind on speed drive.

Arlo puts his elbows on the counter as well, putting him eye-to-eye with Jolene. He tilts his head. "Look at this good fucking girl." He keeps his voice gentle before he leans closer and hardens his tone. "Take her pants off, Darius."

The command makes my cock go even harder.

Jolene twitches when I slide my hands down her sides and loop my fingers in the waistband, tugging until the fabric hits the floor. Pink lace covers her ass.

I run my fingers over the scalloped edge, and glance up at Arlo to find pleasured heat in his gaze. He's proud of her. My chest warms. I wrap my arms around her and kiss her neck. "So good, babes."

Arlo holds his palm out, arms still half crossed, looking like he's a little bored. Like this isn't a huge fucking deal. "Give her panties to me."

Chapter Nineteen

Arlo Commands

ARLO

J olene stares at me and my extended palm with the prettiest confusion I've ever seen. Yet her hands stay on the marble island. Her
lips are parted and pink, cheeks are flushed but just on the crest of
her cheekbones, not all over like she was when I caught her grinding
against Darius's thigh. I could have kept my mouth shut, but when I
watch them fuck, I want her to know I'm there.

I am very much here.

But I need to make this right for her. No more denying what she
wants because she's teetering on the edge of shame. That is a fucked-up
place to exist, and I can't allow it in this house. If I do—if I let her
hide her wants—we'll go through years of walking on eggshells, pissed
about missing out, until we have a fallout fight over something stupid
because the tension from our unsatisfied lust was too much.

That will be the end.

She and Darius will move to the burbs to start a family. They'll have
good enough sex and be happy. And they'll go to their grave wondering what could have been if they had just said what they wanted one
time and opened that door.

But they won't. It's not in Darius's nature, and if my guess is correct, Jolene doesn't know how because she overthinks. I don't know her completely, but she wants me. She's been teasing me to make a move. That paired with the overheard phone call from her mother… she needs, and most likely wants, a push, whether or not she realizes it.

I'm so willing to be the one that gets her there. Slowly.

She's not someone I would pick up. She's Jolene—a sweet, burdened princess who needs to embrace that she likes to fuck because fucking is the best.

Darius tugs her panties off, lifting her stiff legs one at a time with gentle hands. He looks like he might burst with excitement when he passes them over to me.

I take the warm, damp lace and bring it to my nose to inhale. Lavender and woman. Fuck, I want to taste her. Soon.

Jolene cringes as she watches me, and I narrow my eyes. No more shame. When I put them against her nose, she turns her head.

I snag her chin, forcing her to look at me. "Smell or taste? Your choice."

Her eyes pop wide, then glare, making me want to inflict a string of delicious punishments. But then she smells the lace and visibly relaxes.

"If you taste as good as you smell, when I go down on you, I won't be able to stop until you're begging me for mercy, tear-streaked and jerking through your orgasms."

The innocence rolling off her is delicious, and I can't stop my smile. How fucking cute is she, all squirmy with discomfort? It seems like her thoughts say, "This might be wrong," but her body says, "Give me everything."

I've got you, angel.

"Touch her, Darius. Anywhere but her pussy." I stalk to the refrigerator and lay her panties over a box of lasagna in the freezer before walking back to the island, across from her, so I can watch every expression we earn from her.

Darius slides his hands over Jolene's curved hips and down her thighs. His thumbs graze the backs of her knees, and her breathing goes rapid. He brushes kisses over that perfect backside, and her skin peppers with chill bumps I'd love to feel as well.

I settle my elbows on the counter. "Do you like being touched while I watch?"

Her parted lips need to be bitten.

"Answer me, Kentucky. I need your words."

She licks her lips and swallows. "Yes."

"Good." What else does she like? I can't wait to find out.

Darius steps against her, running his hands up her thighs. "I love every inch of these legs."

She bites down on that lush lip when he traces up, lifting her shirt.

"May I take this off?" he asks.

"Yes," I answer.

Jolene's lips part, and she blinks. She thought she needed to respond? Nope. That would have taken too long and let her get more nervous than she is now.

"Arms up," I growl. "Now."

She obeys slowly, but she does it. Darius kisses her neck and tugs the shirt up to reveal the most suckable nipples—dark pink and hard. I could clamp them as is.

"Fuck," I let slip.

She must like that reaction because she raises her chin, pushing her body into a confident stance.

I nearly come around the island to see how well her plump breasts fit in my hands, but inhale long to calm myself. That would be too much for both of us because once I touch, I'm going to take her, and she's new to this. "Hands back on the counter."

She does, demeanor calmer; as if she's ready for anything. She's not, but my chest fills with pride.

"How do those incredible tits feel, Darius?"

Darius's hands cup and massage. "The best in the universe." He leans to nip her ear, and she arches.

I lean in. "Do you enjoy having your nipples played with?"

She nods.

"Outloud."

She doesn't flinch at the command in my voice, which is good. "Y-yes."

"How?"

Her brows crinkle at the question, and she squirms. "Um."

Darius dances his fingers over her nipples, giving her teasing circles. He's so careful with her. Worshipping even. Like every slow touch requires memorization.

I brush my knuckles over my scruff, needing some kind of contact. "Stop."

His hands fall away, and Jolene looks like she wants to bite him, which is a glorious reaction.

I lift her chin with one finger. "How do you play with your tits when you're all alone?"

"I..." She licks her lips.

The struggle is apparent on her face, and I really hope she can get past this. We'll know soon enough. "Answer now, or this stops. Do you want to stop?"

"I thumb my nipples. Tug them." Her face goes red with embarrassment, and she sinks into her shoulders. "But maybe—"

I place my thumb over her lips. "Always go with your first reaction. That one's the truth. Keep going, Darius." *Get her mind off what she thinks others want and back on what she wants.*

He strums both nipples, then pinches them, and tugs.

Jolene whimpers like she's dying.

It makes the hair stand up on the back of my neck in the best way.

When her lips part, I tug at the bottom one, feeling the heat and puff of it, sweeping it down to see her straight teeth and gather some moisture. Sinking my cock into her mouth would be a gift.

Darius eyes me for instruction.

"Harder."

He presses what I'm sure is his rock-hard cock against her ass, and extends her nipples with his tugs.

Jolene jerks and her eyes roll back as her hips shift in rhythm, making him groan.

I pull my thumb away from her lip and lick it.

She watches me, eyes my mouth like she wants me to fuck her with my tongue, but I'm not rewarding her for hesitance and silence. She's going to have to accept her needs, and she's not there yet. "You could come from this with enough incentive, couldn't you? Is this making your pussy clench?"

She nods, then adds hurriedly, "Yes."

Damn. "Good girl." I glance at Darius. "Is her pussy wet?"

His hands trail down, and his eyes flutter closed as he kisses her shoulder with smiling lips. "Soaked."

Of course she is.

I give her a wicked grin, my pulse kicking up at her need. "What would you do for his fingers to fill your cunt right now?" We're going to do a lot more, but I need reactions first.

"Ah—" She whimpers, rocking her hips, and clawing at the marble. "What do you want me to do?"

Darius watches me with raised eyebrows.

I narrow my eyes at her. "I should whip you for not answering. Do it again, and I will. What would you do for us, Jolene?" I run my fingers across her cheek before gripping her hair until she grimaces. *Come on, angel. Work with me. Push through so we can get to the best parts.*

Her lips part, but nothing comes out. She's thinking it through, and I need to give her time, though it's killing me to wait. She may call this whole thing off, and that would be a shame, but at least I'd know a boundary.

I keep my eyes on her, though Darius's gaze is hard on me, waiting for direction.

Jolene licks her lips, eyes meeting mine. "Anything."

My heart thrums wildly. This is turning out to be one hell of a day.

Chapter Twenty

Jolene Desires

JOLENE

I don't think my face could get hotter without bursting into flames. But the heat only starts there. My brain is fuzzy, my breasts feel heavy and ache in Darius's hands, and between my legs is a painful inferno. My body wants whatever Arlo will do—make Darius do.

I meant it when I said, "anything," because there are too many options that I know nothing about. I don't even know what I wouldn't do at this point because I just need... something. Something to shift or break between us.

Arlo has to feel it too. His muscles are tight and flexing, even with his elbows on the island, as he watches me like he's going to come around the island and touch me. I wish he would. "Anything?" He brings his ridiculously gorgeous face closer and bites his lip. "Are you sure about that?" His soft tone whittles away more of my nerves, making me feel like maybe this pose—bent over and naked—is the most powerful one I've ever been in.

"Yes."

"Fuck yes, you would." His glance at Darius is more like a flit before his attention is back on me. "You really are an angel."

Darius pumps his finger into me, making my eyes half close at the instant gratification of being filled. He slides his other hand over my hip and down my thigh, sending my skin into tingles. His thumbs graze the back of my knees, and I'm back to panting. Every touch tingles and seems to connect directly to my clit. I love it when he touches me, but it feels amplified with Arlo's eyes on mine.

"How do you like getting finger-fucked in the kitchen?" Arlo's lips almost catch mine, close enough to smell mint tea on his breath.

I moan and thrust my hips. "I like it."

He clucks his tongue in a tsk-tsk fashion. "Of course you do. You needed release and instead wanted to hide. That's not allowed here." He slides his fingers into my hair and slowly tightens until my scalp tingles. The way he jerks me where he wants is aggressive, and I completely swoon. "I should have spanked you for that, but you're getting off free because you're being such a good girl right now." He looks over me, strained neck to arched back to raised hips. "You're so fucking sexy, angel."

Possessed. That's what I feel like because I want to do anything he says if he will keep looking at me like he is. I crave it. I want to tell him, but my throat is dry—the words are stuck there.

"Look at this pretty blush." He runs his thumb under my bottom lip. "Darius is dying to fuck you, and this tells me you need it. Two fingers."

Darius slips another finger in and pumps faster. "I want you so bad, Jolene. You're killing me, baby." He strokes down my back and hip. Back up to cup my breast.

I groan, and my fingers curl against the marble.

"Spread your legs." Arlo practically pants against my lips. When I do, he smiles at me, and warmth hits my chest. His eyes, half-lidded, move to Darius. "Let me taste her."

Time seems to stop as Darius's fingers leave me and he offers them, glistening, to Arlo, who sucks them and groans. My core lights up, then Darius plunges his fingers back inside me and moves quickly, curving them deep.

"Oh, my go—"

Arlo kisses me, tongues me hard as his fingers tighten. He's tangy and hot and I'm so desperate for more I want to... I still don't know but I want him close. So close.

But disastrously, he pulls back.

"No," I whisper, following his lips, but then Darius's fingers slip away and I can't have that. But I want more. I want them both, but closer. I'm coming out of my skin, wanting to grab Arlo and bring him back to me, but my fingers lock to the counter. "Darius?"

The sound of a zipper makes me gasp, and I glance back to find him stroking his cock with slick fingers. Slick fingers that were just in Arlo's mouth. A new flood of wetness seeps from me. I can feel it when I shift.

"I'm right here, babes." Darius leans forward, looping his arm around me in a chest-to-back hug. His hard cock rests between my ass cheeks. "Right here. You good?"

Yes, and no. I bite my lip.

Arlo palms my face and swings my head back to him. "Are you done here? Say it."

"No." I blurt the word so fast, I'm afraid I might have said the wrong thing.

Arlo nods. "You sure?"

"Yes."

"Does Darius's cock feel hot against your ass?"

Holy shit. His words make my brain melt, but I'm nodding, nonetheless. "So hot."

His lips kick up. "There's our good girl." He drags a single finger down my jaw and neck. "Did you like tasting yourself on my lips?"

I tilt my head, leaning in, hoping he'll touch more of me. "Y-yes." I'm going to short out. Explode. My legs are shaking so badly, they may collapse. "More?"

His lips quirk. "Didn't hear you, angel. Say it again." The command in Arlo's voice is a warning I want to snuggle up against. I don't have a clue why it's doing it for me, but it is doing it well.

I lick my dry lips. "More, please."

Arlo hums. "You want him to fuck you?"

"Yes," I whisper. I blink. That seems like a lot. But my core tightens, seeking to be filled.

Arlo grips the island's opposite edges with white knuckles and stares with eyes that burst through my soul. And there we wait. Darius's fingers move tortuously slow over my body until he finds my center and slips one finger back inside me. In and out. It's only enough to make me need to come. Whimpering, I clench my teeth and try to grind, but he squeezes my hip, holding me still. I'm trembling and wondering if I said something wrong. Should I ask? Say please again or sir or something? Offer to do more? I'd love to reach over the counter and see how hard that massive bulge is. Maybe I should ask. Or maybe I'm doing this wrong and he doesn't like—

"Do it." Arlo's voice is demanding, but somehow soothing. Or maybe it's his intense gaze that makes me want to nuzzle against his neck. Even though he's breathing like a pissed-off dragon.

The relief that I did something right is instant, hot and flooding.

Darius moves back from me and rubs the smooth tip of his cock against my entrance.

I bite my lip to keep from screaming at him to fuck me hard, then look to Arlo. "Please," I whisper, hoping he can read my body or the desperation on my face and do something, anything, about it.

He leans in, sinking the fingers of both hands into my hair to grip and hold me still. "What is it?"

I give a jerky shake of my head as well as I can, with him gripping tight. I don't know. Whatever is trying to burst out is big and confusing. It's lurking in the shadows, unattainable but needed. There's so much tension running through me, I feel like all of me is going to burst open.

"You can't say what you want?" His voice is so soft and focused, and he glances up for the quickest second.

Darius's teasing cock drops away, but he covers my back with the heat of his body again and kisses my spine.

"I—I don't know what I want."

Arlo leans close and bites my lip, making my whole body shudder. He licks the sting. "Darius is going to fuck you. Hard and fast, and if he comes before you do, you're going to lie down on this cold marble and he's going to fuck you again with his fingers until you soak this island with your cum. Say no if you don't want that."

I shake my head in a quick twitch. "I want that. Please. Sir." I just want to come, and I think I need a cock to make that happen. I want to be stretched—

Arlo's lips part in an exhale, and he squeezes the strands on both sides of my head in his fists until I whimper from the twinges of pain and my eyes burn.

I can't stop a smile from curving up, and I blink open my eyes, breathing fast but not panicked.

Arlo's lips crash down on mine while Darius pushes all the way in and groans.

Arlo is a relentless, vicious kisser. His tongue invades and I open fully, melt for him, then squeal into his mouth as Darius grips my shoulders and gives a harder-than-usual thrust, filling every inch of me.

Just as fast as Arlo started this lip mauling, he pulls away. "You let him fuck you bare, angel?"

I eye his puffed, wet lips. "Yes."

He moves closer to whisper in my ear, keeping my head in his hands so I can't move back to his mouth while Darius pounds into me, hot huffs of breath searing my brain. "That trust is everything. You look so beautiful getting fucked right now." He lets me go to run a palm over the bulge in his pants. "I'm going to replay this in my shower while I fuck my fist and wish it were you."

I want to tell him it should be me—I'll join him and he won't have to replay a thing, but all that comes out when I open my mouth is gasping groans as Darius quickens his thrusts.

Arlo traces my lips again, then pushes his finger into my mouth. I suck his salt-tinged digit with my tongue.

Darius groans and touches between my legs, getting me so close to that ending pleasure.

Arlo's eyes blaze before he pushes too far.

I fight gagging, pulling back.

He removes his finger. "Let me hear those screams up close. You better fucking come for us." His last word is a gritted-teeth growl.

I want to please him. My body is tense. So tight, it should be pulsing. My world reduces to the rhythmic slap of skin, my racing heart, and ferocious blue eyes, but the orgasm Arlo is demanding is just out of reach.

Darius grunts and shouts my name.

That's when I shatter, soul exploding, body wrecked apart. The orgasm pulses hard and just keeps pulsing. I cry out, slap the counter, whimper, gasp for air like I'm dying because for a moment, it feels like I may.

Darius's hips slap against my backside for a few more fast strokes before he groans and twitches, fingers digging into my hips. "Fuck, Joles. Fuck."

Arlo sweeps a lock of sweaty hair from my forehead as I catch my breath. "Beautiful."

I give him a loopy smile.

Darius slowly slips out of my body and kisses my back. "You're incredible, babes. That was..." He sighs.

Arlo stands and turns.

I press my burning-hot face onto the marble, breathing hard.

He goes to the fridge and pulls out my panties, then approaches almost cautiously.

Darius steps away, and tension creeps back into my muscles and bones.

I'm naked, half sprawled across the kitchen island, dripping from Darius and my pleasure. Is Arlo going to fuck me too? Heat returns between my legs and I twist my hips like I can hide my slit from his eyes.

"Be still." Arlo's hand comes down hard on my backside.

I yip and relax as the sting melts into pleasure.

"Lift your left foot."

My eyebrows scrunch, but I do what he says. The chill of the fabric makes me twitch. "Cold."

"Yes." Arlo's lips trail my right thigh. "Now this one." He drags the freezing fabric slowly up. Chill bumps rise all over my body, and when he settles what feels like ice against my center, I jolt, then moan.

My skin feels like it's on fire compared to the icy crotch of my panties, and new sensations swirl within my blood. "Oh, my God."

Arlo stands, digging his fingers into my hips, and leans against my back to whisper in my ear. "Tomorrow we're going to talk about this. You are not to retreat, Jolene. Do you understand me?"

Why does he have to ruin this with words? Can't he just slide in too? He's right there. Against my naked body. He just watched us fuck. That was brand new.

Okay, I might need to talk this out. With Darius. Soon.

Arlo steps back, but keeps a hand on my ass, stroking the sensitive spot he gave me. "Answer me, Kentucky."

"Yes."

"Yes, what?"

"Yes, I understand."

But that doesn't mean we're going to do that.

Chapter Twenty-One

Arlo Checks In

ARLO

Darius steps out of our apartment and grins when he notices me. "Checking in?" He steps next to me and takes my hand, squeezing my fingers.

Damn right I am, and not just on his girl. He's told me—hell, shown me—she's the love of his life, and I will never impede that, even if playing with them tops my wants list. I pull his fingers up and brush my lips over them before tugging him toward the elevator. "She's hiding this morning. How did you two handle last night?" It's not like what we did was over the top, but it felt heavier.

"Lots of quiet cuddling. She's thinking. And she ignored a phone call from her mom, which could mean she's stressed about what happened, or is happy about it and doesn't want to think about what her mother would say, not that she'd ever tell her."

So she really is hiding. Not a fan of that, but I could tell from the yip she made when I spanked her and how hot her blush gets, I'm leading her into fresh territory. But did she like it?

I certainly did. I'm not sure I've ever come that hard on my own. There's no way she didn't hear my wrecked growl, even with the shower running.

We step into the elevator, and I nudge Darius's shoulder. "And how are you feeling?"

He rubs his fingers over the back of his neck, but the way he's trying to hide his smile says everything. "That was amazing. I didn't think she'd be so bold. Not like that."

"You want more?"

He nods. "As long as she does."

"Ready for me to see what she's all about?" She's shown herself now—at least given us a peek that Darius was right, and she might be more experimental than I believed. If that's true, last night was only the start.

He glances at me, eyes full of trust and excitement. I love him for that. But then he shrinks a little, and yeah, there's the rational side of my best friend. It pokes through his constant optimism once in a blue moon. "Not yet. Let her think it out."

How long does she have to think through something to know if she liked it or not? And he just lets her? His worried expression says he does, though the last thing I want to do is leave her be. I want to go back inside and push her until she tells me every thought and feeling about yesterday. Tasting her for real just topped my to-do list.

Darius squeezes my shoulder and chuckles because there are days he can read my mind.

Fine. I roll my eyes and push the elevator button.

"Tell me everything is going to be okay, Arlo," Darius says the second we step into the elevator. "If we move forward, is it going to make it weird?"

I nudge his shoulder. "Has it ever been weird with us?"

He purses his lips. "The first time was a shock."

Maybe, but it seemed right. He interrupted, so I invited him in. It worked for both of us. "You just weren't used to it yet. But you like it."

He nods as we step out of the elevator. "This is Jolene." He swallows, and maybe he's more stressed than he lets on.

I wave at Gregory, the morning security guy, and open the door for Darius. "I know. We can call it a day on this. You know that, right?"

"I do." He looks so damn conflicted.

I drag him into a hug, squeezing the tension out of his neck. "What is it you're always saying?"

He huffs a laugh. "It will all work out."

"So there you go. Stick with that." I grin, letting him go. "Get to work and earn that shiny new title."

There are two people in the world I want with me for the long haul. My stepfather, Ian, changed my entire trajectory and my way of looking at the world. He will always be a part of my life. And Darius taught me that family can come with different DNA.

If Jolene is part of the package now, then now I have three important people in my life, and I'll do everything in my power to keep my household happy. I have to approach this differently—form something with Jolene that won't crash to the ground if we fuck, and she inevitably decides that what I do to her, what I am, is a fun, but temporary game.

Women are like that. They get a taste, a night, a few trysts to satiate their curiosity. Only that or I'm being commanded around, told I'm not as good as my dick, and need to change. They like to place me inside a picture they have in their heads of what I should be for them. But for my first fourteen years, I tried that. I accepted that I'd never be good enough if I was myself, and that let others control me. Never fucking again.

Yet I have to form a relationship with Darius's woman, because we now all know that staying away from each other isn't a possibility. It would be easier and smarter to walk away, but I'll do it for him. And because I need more of her moans, and more of her fucking sweet lips.

These are my tortuous thoughts during my entire work day—Jolene's whimper, and how her tongue felt against my finger. The mark from my mouth on her ass. Yeah, if she accepts she enjoyed last night too, we'll play until she's done. Afterwards, I won't let her make it weird, though that has potential, too. I've fantasized about her since I met her, though I wasn't able to fully wrap my head around the reality of it because I didn't expect her to be interested.

That reality punches me in the guts the moment I walk in the door and find Jolene lounging on the couch in only a shirt. She stands without saying a damn word and makes her way to my room, bites her lip as she pauses in the doorway, and crosses those long legs like she's already primed and trying to prevent her pleasure from escaping.

How fast can Darius get home?

Chapter Twenty-Two

Jolene Explores

Oh my God, am I really doing this? I drag my shirt off, holding my breath as the air hits my heated skin. My nipples are tight behind the black lace bra, and my panties are already a goner.

In his doorway, Arlo drops his shoulder bag on the floor, pulls out his phone, sweeping his thumb over the screen while keeping his eyes on me. Then he tosses that to the floor as well and steps towards me, undoing the top button of his shirt.

Are we going to do it? I want to. Hell, I've been thinking about it all day.

I walk backward toward his bed.

He catches up in one stride and snags my waist, grinning when I gasp. He drags me against him, and the scrape of his work clothes against my skin lights up every nerve, and that's before his smoky-sweet scent hits my nose and makes my mouth water. Yeah, I want to do this. He runs his fingers down the indent of my spine and confidently cups my ass like it belongs to him now. "What's this all about?"

I shrug.

His eyes darken, and he crowds me, lips an inch from mine. "Tell me what you want to do, Jolene." He's got to realize what I want, right? And now I know, unlike me, he can think up a sexual game plan in seconds. He had me naked in the kitchen in less than ten minutes, and I'm not feeling bad about it in the slightest. It's why I'm here now. Whatever magic he possesses, possesses me, and I need more.

"Um…" This is wild. I've been on stage hundreds of times, and it didn't feel as important as whatever I'm starting, which I can't even define yet. Whatever I'm seeking, he's the key to figuring it out. I lick my lips. "What would you like to do?"

The twirling butterflies in my stomach take flight as his eyes drop to my mouth.

He swings us around, pinning me against the closest wall and holding me there with his hand on my midsection, bracing his forearm just over my head. "I don't want questions when I ask you a question."

"Okay."

"Yes, sir." He raises an eyebrow as if daring me.

I glare back. "Yes, sir." The word feels odd and generic.

"Why the kickback, angel? You said it last night."

I'm not sure I like how well he can read me, or that he chooses when to read me and when not to. If he were really paying attention, he'd be inside me right now on his bed. He'd realize the word had slipped from me in a moment of desperation. But now I'm thinking. I clench my thighs together to stave off the ache, but it gets worse. Fine, I'm still desperate. I roll my eyes. "That's what you get Sheena to call you. That's what I say to older men as a courtesy."

He pulls his hand from my waist, then brings it down hard on my bare thigh, which should be wrong and weird, but satiates the ache a second before my whole damn body gets hijacked by horniness.

"Exactly," he grumbles. "It's what I want you to call me while we play. Understood?"

I blink, then nod. "Yes, sir."

His demeanor goes from demanding to gentle in a heartbeat. "What a good fucking girl." He rubs the sore spot on my thigh as he places a gentle kiss on my lips.

Now I'm horny *and* gooey.

"Now," he says. "Tell me what you want."

I blurt out the first thing my swirling mind lands on. "You to touch me."

He hums. "Because you need release, or because I didn't touch you yesterday?"

"Both." I've been thinking about it non-stop, and my body has been in a near-panic state about needing more. That's new. I love when Darius fucks me. But with Arlo there, looking like he was coming apart while Darius listened to his every word and later on cuddled me like I'd given him the best damn present... it opened something in me. My body isn't satiated today. There's more to this, and I need to follow my curiosity. Just for a night.

The kiss Arlo gives me is a peck, and I melt against the wall. How can someone who has no problem making my skin red with his palm, make me feel like thin glass he'd never, ever break?

"There's something you need to know about me." His grip tightens on my hip, and he lifts my chin with his finger. "I'm not sweet."

"No." The word that slips through my lips is long and sarcastic. But seriously, who would first think of that word for Arlo? "I'm not that sweet either." Though I've been called it a thousand times. Those people only saw the pageant persona, not the cursing, eye-rolling woman who would get obsessed with finding her way into someone like Arlo's bed.

"Bullshit," he growls. "I've tasted you."

I don't have time to blush because his mouth lands on mine, nipping and sucking. I cup his cheeks, practically purring at the sharp tickle of his scruff against my palms.

He grips my hair hard enough to send a searing tug to my scalp, licks my tongue when I gasp, then bites the center of my bottom lip. The spike of pain is sharp, but it slides into pleasure so quickly, I groan. He trails his tongue over the sting.

I close my eyes and exhale.

"Fuck, you're delicious. Do you like my teeth on you, angel?"

"Yes, sir." Okay, fine, I kinda like calling him that. It takes him away from being my new roommate Arlo, and into a category I'm unfamiliar with but want to visit.

"This is where I should demand you to strip and kneel while I get a condom and fuck your mouth."

I pull back to look at him all wide-eyed and *whoa what now.*

He grins and slips his fingers around my neck, not squeezing, just holding, like in the elevator. Makes sense because I feel like I'm about to plunge. "If you were good, I'd pin you down and feast. After that, I'd fuck you against the door, then go shower. If that didn't satisfy me, I'd tie you to my bed for hours while I played, threatening to keep you and only let you up after you screamed yourself hoarse. I'm tempted."

My lips part, but nothing comes out because what would? *Yes, please, sir?*

"But you're Jolene. You moan for Darius while you make love. And you probably haven't even dreamed up a shadow of what I can be."

"You're right." My cheeks heat. "Because I haven't dreamed up a shadow of what *I* can be, Arlo. So how could I understand what you're like?"

His eyes soften. "See?" He releases his grip on my hair and thumbs my cheek. "Look how sweet you are. We need to be on the same page about a few things."

"Arlo…" I want him worked up like I am. This energy is riled up inside me, and there's nowhere for it to go. It needs to go. I slide a leg against his hip and press the ache against the hard length in his pants. "Please? I've been thinking about this all day."

He traces under my ear with one finger. "What exactly have you been thinking about?"

I lick my bottom lip. It still stings. All of me stings. "The way you kiss."

"How's that, angel?"

"Vicious."

He chuckles. "You have no idea."

"Show me." I lean in, arch, and spread. *Show me like I'm trying to show you.*

He lifts my chin with his thumb and sucks the base of my throat, dragging a whimper up and out. "What else have you been thinking about?" He trails his knuckles down my neck, gathering the moisture he left there, and drags the chill over my collarbone. Why does everything he does feel wildly inappropriate and perfect? It makes no sense.

I'm sucking in air like I've just been for a run. "Just. Everything."

He clucks his tongue. "Let's talk more when Darius gets home."

But I need this now. I want to know what Arlo is like when he's not with Darius, and I need to see what this feels like outside of my love for my boyfriend. "He said it's okay." I pop open the next button on his shirt.

And, thank fuck, intense Arlo is back, watching me like a sexy predator. "You two spoke about us? This?"

My face goes hot. "We did. I told him I was attracted to you, and he told me we could explore together or alone." I widen my eyes, hoping he understands what I mean. *Fuck me. Please. Sir.*

"In that case, maybe a hard orgasm will clear your head enough for conversation. Yes?"

Whatever. Sure. I bobble my head. "Yes."

He grips my throat and slips his hand into my panties, going right for my clit, slipping around it in tight circles.

"You were thinking hard about that *everything*, angel."

I grip his shoulders, holding on so I don't fly off the planet at this moment. "Mm-hmm."

"Did you already make yourself come today?" He growls the words right next to my ear.

Twice, but can we just focus on the one I'm spiraling toward now? Everything is tightening painfully.

He stops his hand.

No! I grit my teeth and crinkle my nose. "Yes. It didn't help." I roll my hips, trying to get friction.

He follows my motion, giving me nothing. "Did you think about me?"

So obviously.

"Outloud, angel."

"Yes, sir."

"Was I doing this to you?" He kisses me with that hard, unyielding nature like last night, while fingering my clit hard and fast.

I twitch and pant, then move my hand from his shoulder to his hip, then go inward.

"You touch my dick, angel, and I'm going to fuck you hard with it. I can't do that until I trust you can tell me to stop."

"I need..." my voice is deep and jagged even to me. "Please?"

"So fucking sweet." He pushes my hand up to the wall, then the other, gathering them tight together in his fingers. "You want to come? Today, I'm going to let you. Nod if that's what you want."

I nod frantically and widen my stance because I need to be filled.

Fortunately, he gets it, and sinks his fingers deep, pressing his palm hard against my clit.

"Oh, fuck." I struggle against the hold on my wrists, because I forget he has me pinned. I want him closer. In me. Surrounding me. I want the weight of him to press me down. "Arlo."

"Someone hasn't been tied up before."

I laugh before the pleasure winds tighter, bringing me so close I need to chase it so it doesn't get away. "Harder."

"Look at you fucking my hand. Say please."

"God, your words... please."

"Put those bourbon eyes on me, angel."

I blink, and take in the wild blue that feels like it pierces into my chest.

Arlo rams his fingers deep, curving them, fucking me with them as he grinds his palm against my clit.

And I'm done. I cry out, bucking my hips toward him in the rhythm of the pulses of pleasure.

He nips my parted lips again, and drops my pinned wrists, which flop helplessly to my sides as I slump against the wall. He grips my neck and moves me from the wall, keeping his fingers inside me while walking me backward to the bed in stumbling, awkward steps. "Did you enjoy your orgasm?" His work pants are tented hard. Does this mean...

"Um..." I did not prepare responses to questions like this. I need a study guide.

"Ready to quit?" he asks.

"No." The back of my legs hit the bed.

Arlo lowers me down to the brown comforter. "Stay still." He lets go of my neck and tugs my panties down, then groans as he pumps his fingers slowly in and out of me. "My fingers look hot as fuck inside you. Take your bra off for me."

"But?" Light is bright from his window, and I'm used to darkness for the first time at least. I go silent when his intense gaze moves from his hand to my eyes.

He pulls his fingers from me.

Okay, things are different with this man. I already knew that. I grab his wrist, sitting up to reach back for the clasp. The lace falls, and I lie back, hoping he doesn't stop.

"Touch your nipples for me."

No one has commanded me like this. Darius and I just let our bodies guide us. Then the words—slight adjustments and requests—came later, as we figured things out.

Arlo seems to want to figure everything out, then do, but I don't have his brand of experience. It's as scary as it is enticing. I've had to practice relentlessly for everything I've done, but this is just winging it and the reward is orgasms. Okay then.

I palm my breasts, then pinch like I did last night. It feels good, but I'm not sure I'm doing exactly what he wants as he looks down at me. Is this too much? Not enough?

"You don't like when I watch you?" Arlo sucks his wet fingers and moans.

My pussy clenches, clearly not ready to give up on what we're doing. "I'm not used to it." I shake my head when his brows furrow. The swimsuit competition leaves little to the imagination, and I'm positive more people have seen my boobs backstage than I'm aware of. "Not like this, Arlo. I'm—"

He grins widely. "Exposed."

"Yeah." Exactly that. I can't hide behind makeup and smiles and rehearsed words. Actually, I'm worried about what my mascara is doing right now.

"Well, angel, if you want to continue, know I'm going to be exploring every inch of you. Thoroughly." He drops to his knees on the bed, straddling my hips, then takes my hands and presses them above my head. "Are you done for today? Want to leave?"

I really, really do not. "No."

"Leave your hands there or I'll punish you. Understood?"

"Yes." Is this the handcuffs portion of the program? My lips kick up. "Sir."

"Good girl." He teases his lips over mine. "I'm going to touch you now. Learn you. And you're going to say stop when you want to stop. Right?"

"Yes, sir." What would I want to stop for?

"That's my good girl." He tugs a strand of my hair. "And while we play, you will not come. Tomorrow, without taking our clothes off, we're going to set rules, ask questions of each other. Then you may ask me to make you come."

Wait... what?

Chapter Twenty-Three

Darius Watches

With furrowed brows, I glance at Arlo's text message once more before stepping out of the elevator.

Arlo:

Come home

So weird. I'm just glad my meeting ended early. He would have called if it were an emergency, but I don't like that he won't answer back, nor will Jolene. I'm sure it's fine, but the silence isn't doing good things to my imagination.

I step inside the house and drop my keys in the bowl. "Hey, where is every—"

Jolene's gasping moans stop all functioning of my brain as my blood pulses to my cock like some Pavlovian response. Whimper equals orgasm; therefore, whimper equals instant hard-on even away from her.

I race toward the sounds. When I get to Arlo's room, my breath catches.

Jolene is on his bed, bare chest heaving as she lies on her back, fingers wrapped tight around her ankles, knees up and spread, soaked pussy grinding air.

"I said no moving." Arlo slaps her thigh, making her cry out, but her voice stumbles into a choppy moan. His collared shirt is unbuttoned, sleeves rolled up. The gleam in his eye is straight-up feral. She's either being very good or very bad.

"Y-yes, sir." Her golden hazel gaze finds me. "Hi, baby."

Oh, good God. *Very good*. I can't stop my grin and walk closer. This was an unexpected welcome home.

Arlo glances at me, lifting his chin in greeting before his gaze goes back to the wonder on his bed. "I came home to talk, but Jolene wasn't interested in having a conversation. She'd rather tease me with lace and fuck my fingers" He grins and runs his palm over the blotchy red spot where he spanked her.

My eyes widen as I take that in. I have so many questions about how this fucking sexy scene came to be, but deep down already know the gist of it. "She's good at getting her way." I lean to kiss her bruised lip. Her skin is flushed and gleaming, and her hair is in utter disarray from writhing. Disheveled like this, she looks glorious. "Your lace is missing, babes."

Jolene gives the slightest wince.

Arlo's hand comes down on her reddened thigh again, making her suck in a breath and exhale a groan. "No regrets, angel. We've gone over this." He kisses her knee. "She's being so good for me. And this is the most perfect pink pussy I've ever seen." He trails his fingers down her thighs, spreading her wide, dipping his head to kiss her clit.

She jerks and hums a little whimper. She looks tortured, ravished, and so close to orgasm, I'm surprised she hasn't come yet.

I move around to see him tugging at her swollen pussy with his lips. He's being very careful.

I take off my shirt and hang it on the doorknob. "May I taste her?"

Arlo gives me a mischievous smile and bites Jolene's inner thigh. "You may." He steps beside her, running a finger down her sternum, then firmly gripping her breast. "But she's not allowed to come until tomorrow."

My mouth gapes, and I look over Jolene with a fresh perspective. She's a whole new level of turned on. She likes this kind of torture then?

Arlo likes to keep lovers on the edge for a bit, but until tomorrow? He doesn't plan to see them again, so this is a new play area for him, because Jolene isn't going anywhere. Where will that go with his type of creativity? This isn't a one-time thing, right? My shoulders feel like a rod connects them and is winding upwards. Is this a one-shot weekend?

I kiss her clit, getting lost in her taste and how needy she is. No matter what happens, I get to do this from now on. She's not temporary to me.

She mewls, lifting her hips to me like an offering, and warmth relaxes me down to the mattress. She really must be desperate, and I'm here for that.

Arlo sucks the tip of an elongated nipple.

Jolene keens a string of mumbled curses, turning her head to muffle her sounds with her upper arm.

"Poor thing," I whisper, running my thumb over her soaked slit. "Does this ache?"

"Darius." Jolene's voice is firm, but I grin. I love it when she gets desperate enough to lead, but we're both passengers on this ride.

As if Arlo understands he needs to prove that, he lets her breast go and grips her hair. "You look at me while Darius tastes you, okay?"

Her tense body relaxes. "Yes, sir."

I dip my tongue into her channel until her hips are shifting in rhythm.

"Don't you dare, Kentucky." Arlo grumbles. "Slow," he says to me.

"Harder, please," Jolene whispers, arching back.

I want to so badly. I love to give her pleasure. It feels wrong not to do what she asks when she's being completely unguarded like this. I won't interrupt their dynamic, but that doesn't stop me from barely biting back the words and giving a look of pure begging to Arlo. *Let me give her what she wants.*

He raises an eyebrow, smirks, and places a kiss on her lips. I've never seen him be this gentle. "I'm proud of you for telling me that, but no." He gives me a look that tells me to stop touching her. He really is going to leave her in agony. All of us.

She jerks and growls. "Let me touch you, then."

He leans in, giving her another kiss. "You think you're ready for that?" His eyes meet mine.

I haven't told her about his piercing and am not sure how she's going to respond to it.

She starts to sit up before sighing, tightening her fingers on her ankles and settling down again. "Yes. Then maybe you will let me come?" She uses that soft, lulling tone of hers.

He trails his lips over her shoulder and to her collarbone, where he bites down until she squeals. "If you ask me again, I'll make it two days." After a kiss to his bite, he licks his finger and plays with her nipple until she's back to thrusting her hips against the air. "Do you only want to touch me because you think I'll let you orgasm?"

The shake of her head is determined. "No. I want to see you. All of you."

Arlo pries her fingers from her ankles, massaging them before he pulls her up and grips her hair, jerking her head back to give her a deep kiss.

I take in my fill of them, getting harder by the moment. Are she and I this hot when we're kissing? I'll have to do more of that in front of Arlo and find out.

He pulls her from the bed and turns her to me, giving her ass a light swat. "Welcome Darius home for real. You were occupied when he walked in and didn't give him the attention he deserves."

I step in and pull her naked body against me. "Hello, babes."

"Hi." She smiles with half-lidded eyes and kisses me. Then she rubs against my hard dick.

I groan in agony. "I can't make you come."

She blinks up at me, and bites her lip like she wants to talk. I bet she does, and so do I. We have a long conversation ahead because she's made a massive leap, and I'm not a hundred percent sure she's fine.

Behind her, Arlo undresses, then gives his cock a hard squeeze. He presses against her backside.

She jolts, eyes widening.

"Okay?" I whisper.

Her brows furrow. "Yeah."

Arlo runs his teeth over her shoulder. "Then touch me." He turns her around and puts a step of distance between them. His cock juts, the ball of his piercing glinting.

"Oh," Jolene says, breathless and low.

"You want to touch me? Come here."

Jolene moves forward.

I want to drop to the floor with her, unzip, then fuck her from behind while she gets to know Arlo's dick. The idea is so vivid, I grit my teeth to keep from saying it. That's not in the cards today, because when Arlo sets a game, he sticks to it.

Arlo grips her neck and pulls her closer. "Touch my cock."

She sets her palm on his chest and grips his dick with her other hand, but avoids the silver balls. "Did it hurt?"

"Yes." He grins. "Doesn't now, though." He wraps his hand around hers and closes his eyes, lips parting. He touches his lips to hers, just panting against each other's mouths, and my lower stomach is so tight with lust right now. "Good conversation today. Looking forward to the one tomorrow."

I could hug her from behind, tell her how Arlo looks like he's about to fuck her hard, but I don't want to disrupt what's happening between them.

"I like my cock in your hand, angel. Now stop. When you suffer punishment like this, so do we." He glances at me. "No orgasms until tomorrow." He takes her chin between his fingers. "If you come without permission, I'll know, and then we'll have to start all over again."

Chapter Twenty-Four

Jolene Gets Ready

I wake to the covers being dragged off me and fingers seeking between my legs. I moan, spreading for Darius.

"Good girl."

My eyes fly open to land on intense blue irises. This shouldn't embarrass me—Arlo had his fingers inside me a lot yesterday. And his tongue—but light is blazing through the window, and I probably look a mess and everyone has morning breath. I freeze up and glance to the other side of the bed.

Darius watches me, head on his pillow, expression calm and blank. Not judging, but assessing. Last night, he said he was interested in continuing to see where this goes, but wouldn't interrupt interactions between Arlo and me.

"You don't like when I touch you?" Arlo's fingers slowly retreat from my panties.

"No, no, no, no, no..." I slide my hips toward him and grip his neck to stop his retreat before realizing, in my sleepy, panicked state, that I skipped the getting to know you phase before the all-out touching phase of a relationship.

His brows furrow, and I think I'm scoring low here, but I don't know how to approach him with intimacy yet. He approaches me, touches me. Not that he didn't start it, but I haven't even said good morning.

I let go like he's on fire and ball my fingers. "Sorry. Shouldn't have—"

"Put your goddamn hand back on my neck." His voice is a rough grumble that hits me right between the legs. I do as I'm told, and he dips down to tug my tank strap over my shoulder with his teeth. His tongue drags pleasure over my collarbone and right into my nipples. "Always do what you want to me unless I tell you otherwise, understand?"

I swallow and nod. "Yes, sir."

His jaw clenches, and his eyes flutter closed as he pushes two fingers inside me and grinds his erection against my hip. "Ready to talk?"

My breath comes fast as I ride his hand, wishing he'd thumb my clit. That would send me right over, and my body is tingling with need. I don't want to talk. I want to touch his piercing. With my tongue. I wanted to last night as well, but he stopped me, and I wasn't ready to push. But now I want my hands all over him. I want to grip his muscular backside as he thrusts hard inside me and—I groan and arch as he presses his fingers deep.

"Stop thinking and answer me, Kentucky."

Kentucky. I don't mind it. No one has called me that before, probably because I was *in* Kentucky, but I prefer angel. The nickname feels like a reward whenever he uses it and makes me want to do right by him. It makes me want to obey, yet also tumble right over the edge he has me riding, just to see what he'd do. His expression warns me of an imminent spanking. I wouldn't mind, but I need his fingers more.

"Yes, but—" I lift my hips for more. With the ease of his movements, I'm flooding his fingers. I whimper and gasp. "I want this. Please."

His smile makes my stomach flutter and between my legs tighten. He nips my sore bottom lip. "Don't you dare come."

"I need it." This has gone from game to utter, devastating need. My breaths quicken. I need him inside me. And Darius. My fingers tighten on Arlo's neck. I want them both. Right now.

Arlo pulls his fingers from me and sucks them.

"No," I whine.

"Yes." He kisses me hard, slanting his head to mingle with my tongue. I taste him and me. It shatters every idea about what should and shouldn't happen between two people in a morning. He growls, grinds hard against my hip, and steps away from the bed, holding a finger up when I open my mouth to tell him to please let me play with his cock some more. "I'll make breakfast. Do not finish yourself off." Then he's out the bedroom door. "Watch her, Darius. She's not ready for the punishment that would entail."

I prop up on my elbows. "What punishment?"

Darius rolls on top of me and kisses me with such fervor, I'm back to whimpers and moans. He pushes himself up and pulls me along. "One day, babes."

"Tell me."

He grins and pushes me against the bathroom doorframe, dancing his fingers over my hips, then up over ribs, until he cups my breasts. His eyes are dark and intense. "I can imagine it would entail restraints."

I grip his shirt with both hands and press farther into him.

"You'd be sore and red for days." He raises an eyebrow. "You like that idea?"

My face heats. "Maybe. Has he done that with others and you? Punishment, I mean?"

"Some, but he hasn't cared enough to threaten like that ahead of time. Or hasn't found someone he thought might enjoy the anticipation of the threat and stuck around long enough to play it out."

That's a thing? "You think I like the anticipation?"

He gives me a sweet, knee-weakening kiss and strokes between my legs, over silk. "You are loving this. You and Arlo have been dancing around this since you arrived. How do you feel right now?"

I roll my hips. "So horny I could die."

He pulls his fingers away, grinning at my grumble. "And?"

"Excited."

"So excited." He kisses me again, sending warmth through my soul. "I'm so proud of you for exploring this for yourself."

"And us." I rest my forehead against his. "I love you, what we have, but I'm not the only one excited, am I?"

He shakes his head. "Let's go have that conversation, okay? We all need to be on the same page before this goes further."

I groan and give his hard dick a gentle squeeze. "Fine. Though we're really tempting that death-by-horniness thing."

Darius pulls on sweats, and I stay in my tank in case Arlo wants to have fun with his teeth some more. Can he take a shirt entirely off without using his hands? I bet he can.

We walk down the hall, smelling eggs.

Arlo is wearing a tee and jeans as he stands at the stove, looking positively delicious. His heated gaze roves over me before he lifts his chin toward the refrigerator. "Grab the juice."

There's a knock at the door. All three of us freeze and look in that direction.

My stomach drops. Is it Sheena or another woman coming to visit Arlo? He's not the type to be sneaky or quiet about sex, so I think he's been holding out for me. Which makes me feel special, along with a slew of other emotions. But I also don't know him or his games. Maybe he invited someone.

Darius leaves my side and flips up the peephole cover. His body goes rigid, and he presses a palm to the door, glancing back at me with a look that makes all the remaining warmth in my body freeze over. "Go get dressed, babes," he whispers. "Your mother's at the door."

It feels like my heart halts in my chest. Did she somehow know what I was getting up to? *Shitty, shit, shit.* Guess I should have answered her calls.

I glance at Arlo, who looks like he'd like to go a round with his punching bag. Maybe this is a sign. What am I bringing to the table here besides nerves, whimpers that apparently drive him crazy, and a mother who will see him as a demon? Maybe she won't, though. It's not like she needs to know what we're doing. What we were about to do. Oh my God, I was about to have sex with two men at the same time.

"Jolene?" Darius's voice is calm, and I want one of his *it's going to be fine* hugs.

My mother knocks again. "Anybody home?" she asks, muffled through the door.

I suck in a breath and sprint down the hall.

Chapter Twenty-Five

Darius Greets

DARIUS

This interruption is the very last thing I want. *The very last.* I can't say I'm shocked, because Donna's happiness depends completely on Jolene, and Jolene has been avoiding her. But really? This ambush violates every Southern etiquette rule Donna's ever muttered. And she mutters all the damn time.

She knocks again. "Y'all home?"

I shake my head and look at Arlo. "This is going to be weird."

He works his jaw as if he's grinding a wad of gum as he looks down the hall. "What do you need me to do?"

Smoothing my frayed curls, I take a deep inhale and whisper. "Donna is sweet, but will say things with a smile that will drive you out of your mind. Just... be patient. Let's figure out why she's here and how long she's staying."

He nods, returning to breakfast.

I plaster on a smile and open the door. "Donna?"

She's in a cream-colored pantsuit and added more highlights to her hair, most likely to mask the gray coming in. She's a gorgeous woman who is literally the last person I'd like to look at right now.

"Darius!" She steps into my hug, then leans back, holding my shoulders. "Surprise, handsome." Her accent is thick and reminds me of home—family potlucks and saying hello a hundred times in a day, mostly to strangers who mostly have that same Kentucky drawl. But I'm still really pissed. Granddad and I are going to have a very interesting conversation about this later.

"We weren't expecting you." I step aside to let her come in.

She pokes my chest with a Jolene-pink polished fingernail. "Well, when something's going on with your daughter, you know. Plus, I wanted to see this apartment she apparently loves so much." She rolls a beige carry-on inside. Thank goodness it's only one bag and not moving boxes. Her eyes land on Arlo and go wide. "And where's my Jolene?"

"Just waking up. This is our roommate, Arlo."

"Oh, goodness. Aren't you... handsome." She sounds like she was really reaching for that word, and my spine straightens.

Women literally swoon on the street when they see Arlo—like stumble-step and lean against something. Guess he's not firefighter-hot enough for her. Or maybe he is, and that's a concern with her daughter and how he might tempt her. If Donna only knew.

I snort a laugh.

Arlo raises an eyebrow and steps close enough to shake her hand. "Some would say." He gives her a smile. "Jolene's mother. Hmm."

Donna giggles and goes all smiley at that, apparently thinking Arlo meant something complimentary.

I take a step back. "I'll check on Jolene."

"I can do it, honey." Donna sets her purse on the table and takes a step toward the hallway. "I'm just so excited to see her."

"I've got it." I wave her off, walking backwards in case Donna attempts to race me down the hall.

Arlo steps in front of her. "Do you like eggs?" Fuck, I love him so much. And also shouldn't leave him alone with Donna for long, so he doesn't end up saying something that would make her stage a Jolene-kidnapping.

Donna goes into a rant about cholesterol as I jog down the hall.

When I open the door, Jolene is fluffing pillows so roughly, I'm afraid she might rip one in half.

"Babes?" I step in and close the door. The room was already neat, but she somehow made it look pristine in minutes. "Do you not want to see your mom?"

She slams the pillow down and shoves her hair out of her face. "I do. And I don't. I've been avoiding her, yeah, but she just *shows up*? What if she—and now—" She slaps her hands against her hips and blows out a long breath. "Okay."

I grimace and intercept her as she darts to the door, dragging her into a hug. "She's here because she loves you, but it's okay to be angry. She shouldn't have dropped in like this, but everything is going to work out today and in time." I say this to both of us.

Jolene clings to me and sighs. "Thank you for that."

We make our way down the hall, and Donna runs to Jolene as if she hasn't seen her for a year instead of two weeks. When she parts, she touches Jolene's face. "You look tired, sweetheart. Are you using enough moisturizer?"

Jolene rolls her eyes. "Yes."

Donna's brows knit, and she reaches to touch Jolene's lip. "Is this a bruise? What did—"

"Oh." Jolene jerks back and touches the mark Arlo left on her last night. "It's... uh, I got overzealous with a spoon. Um, how long are you staying?"

Arlo raises an eyebrow, and I bite back a laugh. He's going to have something to say about that later.

Donna smoothes her shoulder-length hair. "I have to get back to work on Monday, so I'm only here until tomorrow night, but, oh, how I wish it could be longer."

One night, two days. Could be worse.

"Sounds great," Jolene says, her pageant smile fully in place. How Donna doesn't see when her daughter is uncomfortable is beyond me. It's so clear.

Arlo clunks plates onto the kitchen island and runs his hand along the edge, eyeing Jolene, who seems to pretend he doesn't exist.

I was afraid this was going to be awkward, and I was correct. We need a game pause.

"Where are you staying?" I ask.

Donna's big grin doesn't waver. "Well, I thought here. Where's your guest room?"

"Mom, we don't have one." Jolene's shoulders hunch inward like she's personally responsible for apartment sizes. "City spaces don't sprawl like they do where we're at." Her eyes dart to me, then back to her mother. "You're at. Kentucky." She clears her throat.

The need to pull her into my arms is intense. I loop an arm around her waist and squeeze.

She pats my forearm.

"Oh. Well, that's fine, I'll just..." Donna glances around as if she may find a spare bed beside the television. "Think of something. I just needed to see you, since you won't return my calls." Her eyebrows raise in question.

"Sorry. I've just been settling in and distracted." Her eyes flit to Arlo, then to the floor. "Uh... busy with stuff, you know?"

"Breakfast." Arlo takes a plate to the table. "Sit."

When Jolene turns, I can see why there's a sharp warning tone from Arlo. I've been to Jolene's pageants. Right before she stepped on stage, there was a moment when she wanted to run and never, ever return. Panic, regret, indecisiveness. She has that look now.

I grab her hand and sit next to her at the table.

Donna remains oddly quiet as we tell her about sightseeing in Chicago. Jolene pulls up pictures for her mother, who gasps and coos as they scroll, but a furrow remains on Donna's forehead.

Jolene diverts when Donna asks about Arlo's family, but unfortunately that gets us on the conversation of his job, and my promotion. Those should be safe, proud topics, but they lead to the topic of Jolene's job hunt.

"I have another interview on Tuesday." Jolene sips juice. "And I need to call three other places to check up. So it's going really well." She takes a dainty bite of eggs.

Donna reaches over the table, covering Jolene's hand with hers. "Well, you know you can call me anytime."

"I know."

Donna's intentions seem good, but I know better. She means, *"You can call me, and I can get you a job in a second, but it will be in Kentucky and will be the job I feel is best for my reputation."* I swear if she somehow guilts Jolene into considering giving up on Chicago, I'll kick her out myself.

"I'm always here for you, sweetheart."

Arlo huffs a laugh, then wipes his hand over his mouth.

"What?" Donna asks. "Is that funny?"

"Not in the least. But Jolene is highly capable, and finding the right job takes time." Arlo stands, picking up his plate and Jolene's, and stands beside her until she looks at him and nods with the slightest smile on her lips. I appreciate his check-in as well. She needs more of that kind of support.

But Donna's eyes narrow.

I clear my throat. "That's true. Joles has some fantastic leads she couldn't pursue while she was spending the summer with you." *Hint, hint, Donna. You held her back.*

"You found your job before college was through." Donna tilts her head at me, softening her parry of words with a smile.

Dammit. "My situation was unusual. It was a well-timed internship."

"It took me five months to find my job," Arlo says, putting dishes into the dishwasher.

"But your job seems pretty unique."

"So is Jolene's. If she took something mediocre, she might miss the opportunity she's seeking."

Donna's grin fades. "Mediocre?"

Arlo's smile is tight. "Yeah. Mediocre in the context of what she's looking for in life. Why waste time on the wrong fit?"

Donna's huff basically says, *"How dare you?"*

Jolene's laugh is brittle, but distracts Donna. "It's good to see you, Mom. Do you want to see... a Chicago park or maybe a show? They're always having those here on the weekends. All over. There's always something fun to do."

"If the timing is right." Arlo wipes his hands on a dishtowel. "I'm going to head out. Be back tomorrow sometime."

He can't take it, and I get it. Jolene is not herself around her mother, and that is a trait that Arlo loathes.

I nod, and he heads down the hall to his room.

Out the balcony doors, the sun glints off the distant buildings' rows of windows. I turn back to the women at the table and rest my chin on my hand. "Maybe a trip to the ice cream museum?"

Jolene's jaw drops. "There's an ice cream museum? Why didn't you tell me?"

"I was saving it for a rainy day."

And it is pouring.

Chapter Twenty-Six

Arlo Escapes

ARLO

After applying to companies all over the world, it was a coincidence that I ended up in the same city as my mom and Ian. At least I like to think so. I sent more resumes and visited more companies here than I did anywhere else, and I breathed a little easier when the company I work at made an offer. It's not that I was trying to stay in Chicago or near family. But in times like these, it's nice to shoot Ian a text, because *we don't just drop in on someone*, and know that he'll be glad to see me, talk to me. Maybe we'll get a drink, make some dinner together, catch up.

I've now lived here for three years, not counting the two before college, the longest I've lived in one area ever. I still only need one suitcase and a backpack to move my belongings, but with each life event—my mother meeting Ian, them getting married and him taking early retirement so I'd have a home base, the job, and Darius moving here—things are feeling more settled.

Which must be why my skin feels tight as I drive toward my mother and Ian's house. This morning things felt like they might be locking into place again, and now? I'm extremely unsettled.

Did I imagine the smug glare Donna gave me as I walked out the door? Was getting me out of the house intentional? There's no way. But now I want to go back, and not because I want Jolene to moan some more for me, though I want more of her moans very, very badly. My hands tighten on the steering wheel, and I force myself to breathe out and relax back into the seat. I want to show her so many sexy things.

But that's not what I'm struggling with now. I have the utmost desire to walk back into *my* fucking house and have a passive-aggressive verbal throw down with Jolene's mother. What crazy shit would fly out of her mouth if I politely asked why she didn't believe in her daughter's ability to get a job? I bet I could get her to righteous indignation in under an hour.

But that isn't my place.

Jolene is just my roommate. And while I want to call right now and check up on her, maybe give her an escape too, I need to leave them be. Just like all women, she's going to want me to stay out of her business, not her bedroom. When I go back, we'll have a chat and then if she's on board, we'll have a good time fucking, and that's all we're going to need from each other. Just a good time experimenting with orgasms and loving life with Darius.

As soon as I park in the driveway, I unclick my seatbelt and stare at the forest green garage door. Should I go back? Friends do not leave friends to fend off their future mother-in-law without backup, even if Darius seemed relieved I was leaving. He was probably just throwing himself on the grenade like he always does.

But what if Donna really was happy to have me out because she knows it will be easier to drag her daughter back home if Darius and I aren't a force together? I scoff at my ridiculousness. Donna hasn't a clue who I am or how Jolene and I interact—I'm still figuring that out too—why would she think I'd want to keep her daughter with us? She didn't pick up on how I can't stop looking at or touching Jolene when she's in the room, right?

I grab my overnight bag and step out of the car. Part of me hopes my mother is on a business trip or golfing, but when I ring the doorbell and it opens seconds later—no such luck. I have her blue eyes, her sharp cheekbones and scowling lips, but my father's build and dark hair. My ears and nose are my own, so they like to say. There are days I look in the mirror and hate that I can see them in me.

My mother and my relationship has morphed over the years, becoming more civil, but I doubt there will ever be affection between us.

Especially as her Roman nose crinkles. "Did you get another tattoo?"

I smile like a shark. "Two."

Eyes to the entrance boxwoods, she nods and turns, leaving the door open for me. She's never outwardly condoned my pastime of getting ink, but this response—acknowledging the change, then ignoring it for the rest of eternity—is normal.

Their house is incredible, even if it's far too big for the two of them. They bought it as a home base for the whole family, so it's probably for the best that it's only a half hour from the apartment. Staying under the same roof with my sister, uncles, and cousins is never happening. It's hard enough walking the halls and through the living room where every wall holds military memories and dead relatives that glare at me and my dishonor for not joining their ranks like a good soldier.

I'm just glad that my grandfather's face isn't among them, and I'm not sure if it was Ian or my mother's idea to leave him and his medals in a closet instead of on display. While standing over my hospital bed, he told my mother I deserved the beating my father gave me and tried to convince her to drop the charges against him. I'm not sure if she's spoken much to either of them since that day. I doubt I ever will. We never talk about any of that.

"Office?" My voice echoes against the large spaces and hardwood floors.

"Yes," my mother calls from somewhere near the kitchen.

I head down another dead-relative hallway and step into Ian's space, which is blissfully free of photographed judgment and war ribbons. It's all dark woods, leather, and burgundy paint. There's one candid photograph of his Air Force reconnaissance squadron goofing off on an F-16.

"How's my favorite corporate hacker?" He stands from his leather wingback chair with effort, throwing his arms wide. He's a big, barrel-shaped man, but I haven't seen him in person for over a month, and he's thinner. His eyes carry dark bags, and there are red veins on the tip of his nose.

"You okay?" I ask, stepping into his hug. "Or does my mother have you on a diet?"

His raspy laugh is not entirely convincing. "Having a few health things. You get old, and this is your shit-ass reward."

Tension draws tight through my jaw. "Anything to worry about?"

He shrugs, pushing me down into the other chair before he sits. "Normal old man garbage. How are you?"

I open my mouth, then close it. I'm frustrated, worked up, edged, and disappointed.

He raises an eyebrow and pushes up the sleeves of his sweatshirt, exposing the tattoo of a shot glass with a cat silhouette on his freckled skin. He went with me when I got a SQL-coded version of "I do what I want" on my forearm and decided he liked whiskey and pussy so much, he needed it on his body too. My mother didn't talk to either of us for a week.

"Tell me what's on your mind, son."

"I have a new roommate."

He whistles. "That's right. Darius's girlfriend." His brows furrow. "And it's not going well? Don't tell me she's awful."

"She's not. At all." That makes me smirk. "You would like her immediately. But her mother, who just showed up at our damn door, is a real fucking peach."

He winks one eye as he grimaces. "Alright. Let's hear it."

I give him the story—how Jolene is this gorgeous, funny woman who lights up like a damn tourist even at the farmer's market, and how she just caved inward and stopped acting like herself the second her mother walked in the door, which is why I'm here. I'm not watching that ship sink. Or, I'm trying to preserve us all because if I were there, I might get in a war with her mother.

Ian gets that smirk. The one when he's about to lay out some truth I'm probably not going to like because he sees things from a different angle. I can admit it's typically a wise angle because he's had a big life.

"What's the damn verdict?" I ask, circling my finger at him. "Your wheels are going."

He shrugs. "You're protective of her."

"Of course I am. She's my roommate and the love of Darius's life."

He purses his lips and leans forward, linked fingers in front of him. "Think you're protective of her because of the way you handle your family?"

My brows furrow hard. "How's that?"

He leans back. "I love your mother, Arlo. I'd do anything for that woman, so we're not going to play the blame game here. But I know what your payment has been in order to do whatever the fuck you want." He holds up a finger. "For which I'm endlessly proud of you.

There is no one in this world who is you. So, don't expect others to act as you would in a situation."

That's a high compliment, but still feels a little like a reprimand. "I just don't get it. It's not that she doesn't have a backbone. She told me to kiss her ass the other day." Which I did. I still love that she pushed me—pushes me.

Ian snorts. "Yeah, I am going to like her, aren't I?"

"You want to meet her?"

He tilts his head and smirks. "Uh, yeah, son. I do."

I rub the wrinkle between my brows. "She just needs to grow the fuck up first."

"Her situation isn't yours. She has her own path to figure her shit out, and all you can do is support her without rolling in and smacking down any threat to her. Especially her mother. Not your place."

I really hate when he voices what I was thinking. "Yeah, it's not my place, but should I do nothing?"

"She's young. Give her time and be there for her as she figures her shit out, so she's not alone when *she's* ready for battle." He tilts his head. "Right?"

When I figured my shit out, I was isolated. There was only so much leaning I could do on Darius since we were halfway around the world from each other, but talking to him helped me through that rough, damn time. My throat goes tight. "Fucking fine."

Ian grins and pushes himself out of the chair. "Want to do some yard work, then drink?"

My bark of a laugh knocks the remaining tension loose. "What do you need done?"

Chapter Twenty-Seven

Jolene Says Goodbye

JOLENE

Flight announcements blare through the airport chatter, and people shuffle into a line at the gate.

I hug my mom as she cries. Her signature perfume mixed with recycled air from thousands of people makes my eyes water, though not for the same reason as hers. I squeeze her harder. "It was so good to see you." Guilt has been a knot in my stomach since yesterday, but it flares brighter because that's not entirely the truth. I love her hugs, her need to make sure I'm settling in, and that she cooked chicken casserole for us last night because it's my favorite dish, even if she complains about the calories and carbs.

But my skin feels like it's coated with lead. I'm utterly spent emotionally.

She releases me from the tight squeeze and pats at her eyes, mouth pulled into a tight line as she looks at me as if I'm a lost puppy. "Oh, I wish you were going with me."

This move to Chicago has scored me a two out of ten in her eyes. It's a half-point above quitting the pageant circuit. I just can't seem not to disappoint my mother.

She steps into the line and waves, blowing me a kiss before ducking into the jetway, smiling wide with a hopeful gleam in her wet eyes that her words will sink in and I'll come *home. "Anytime you want, Jolene."*

This weekend, she caught me red-handed in the failure department—I don't have a job, and I haven't unpacked my box of pageant trinkets, meaning I'm not fully settling in with the multiple men I'm living with. My apartment is small. There's canola oil instead of olive oil like I grew up with. Nothing is Jolene pink.

Pick anything in the apartment and city besides me, and it's all wrong to her. I don't belong here, and there's nothing within my control to make her think maybe I could belong here. No job and no ring yet. People don't stop and say hi because they don't know us, and the apartment doesn't look like I've settled in, because she only sees my style as the one she handed to me.

And if she knew what I did with Arlo, she'd ask me where *she* went wrong. The thought of making her feel responsible for my faults makes me nauseous as I walk through the outside doors to grab an Uber.

Darius dropped us off, and I sent him back to the apartment because I wasn't about to let him sit with my mother for another two hours. He's already the best boyfriend on the planet. I can't let him reach Saint level while I'm wondering what the hell he sees in me.

When I pull out my phone to check the app, there's a message waiting for me from Arlo.

Arlo:

Text me when you get this and I'll pick you up.

My heart speeds up. I've been thinking about him a lot. He just left for... where? Did he stay with a woman? I suppose my mother's arrival voided his no orgasms rule, and I don't blame him, though the thought makes my jaw clench harder.

I'm still behaving, and I'm sure Darius is as well. Last night, he slept in Arlo's room, because my mother wanted a "girl's night," but really, she disapproves of us sleeping together and didn't want to be under the same roof with sinners if she could halt our misdeeds. As if I could have had sex with her there.

I text Arlo back.

> I can get an Uber.

Arlo:

> See you in five. Terminal 3 departure lane.

Well, okay then. He must have looked up Mom's flight details. That was... sweet.

Will Darius be with him? My love has been quiet, leaving Mom and me to our sightseeing and conversation, biting his tongue half the time like he always does around her, poking at her the other half. She likes him, but he's not who she would have placed me with. For once, she didn't bring up other men, though. Maybe my curt end to our last conversation finally got through to her.

In the chaos of the airport drop-off lanes, I get another text.

Arlo:

> Four cars to your right.

Arlo stands next to the silver BMW, his tattooed arms on the roof, phone in his hands. "Let's go, Kentucky."

Butterflies swoon inside me, dispersing a bit of the tight tension. He's here. I didn't realize how much I needed to see him.

"Damn," the older woman next to me says under her breath.

"You can say that again." My feet move forward, while my eyes take in every detail of his expression.

He's not exactly happy, but is studying me as much as I am him.

I speed up as he slides into the driver's seat, step in, and drop my butt on the leather, then fasten my seatbelt. I fidget with my purse strap. "Thank you for picking me up. You didn't need—"

With a speed that makes me gasp, he snags my neck and jerks me to him, lips crashing onto mine.

I balk and look up, out the window as if my mother might peek out of the airplane that already took off and see my misdeeds. She couldn't, I know this, but still. I turn back to his narrowed eyes and grimace. "Sorry."

He pulls me closer, more gently, and my mind blanks as I lean in. Mint flavors our kiss, and his lips are sinfully distracting. Exactly what I needed.

He nips the still-sore place on my bottom lip, sending tingles through my entire body. "A spoon?" he growls.

I giggle at the ridiculous excuse I gave Mom for my lip bruise. "I panicked."

"I marked you and want to do it again." He licks the seam of my lips, diving in tongue first when I open for him.

I suck in his breath, and a spark of the lust we were working toward before my mother arrived, flames to life in my core. I want to fall into a vat of his scent. Live in the smoky goodness.

"Fuck, angel. I wanted to mark you harder right then, so everyone in the room knew what I did, what I do, to you."

My fuzzy brain imagines how that would have gone, and I freeze up, closing my parted lips.

Mom would have passed out, then disowned me when she woke.

Arlo tuts, fingers tightening on my neck as he nearly drags me across the console. "Quit, Kentucky." His eyes are the fiercest blue.

I feel the reprimand in my chest, and it's not helping with the stress that moved in over the weekend. "Quit what?"

His jaw works as if he's chewing his thoughts. He relaxes his hold on me, letting me drift back into the passenger seat. "Did Donna's flight leave okay?" His nose gives the slightest cringe, as if that pained him to say.

I clear my throat, fighting the urge to crawl into his lap and hug him so hard. Would that make this tension go away? From the way I'm doused with more guilt for even wanting that, the answer is no. My mother just left. This is too much, too soon, and I'm crumbling. I need a bath to wash this all away. "Yes. She was sad to go, but..." I shrug. What else is there to say? *Sorry she invaded? What now?* I'd like to ask that, actually.

His hum makes me feel like he understands whatever I can't seem to say. "What would you like for dinner?" he asks softly, pulling from the curb.

"Indian?"

"Not a chance." The corner of his lips tips up, and some of the lead from my skin lifts away, letting me breathe easier.

"Why not?" I can't help the whine in my voice.

"Because you'd just order tikka masala again. We need variety."

"But I like tikka masala. I just discovered it."

Arlo shakes his head. "Then you're going to get sick of it and never want it again."

"It doesn't work like that, Arlo."

He glances my way and raises an eyebrow. "No?" Why do I feel like we're talking about more than food? The leather on the steering wheel creaks under his hands. "Text Darius. Tell him to meet us at Sal's Italian Bistro. You'll like it."

My hands shake as I do what he asks. I'm not sure if it's from the adrenaline of being near Arlo or the worry and tension still spiraling from this weekend. I put my phone in my purse, staring at the city as we drive on the interstate.

He shifts, elbow resting on the console. "I'm fighting myself not to pull over and punish fuck you right now. Do you think that would help whatever is going on here?" He lifts a finger to signal between us.

"Punish?" I clench below, clearly not immune to the effect of his words. The interstate is full of cars. We'd be seen, probably reported, and arrested for indecent... everything.

He glances my way, then back to the road. "Yeah. Hard." He inhales and holds it. "So fucking rough."

I squirm in my seat.

"Do you always act like a kicked puppy around your mother, or is it with others too?"

"Rude." I glare at his profile, then look out the window.

"But not wrong. Why the fear when it comes to her?"

"It's not fear." Is it? I'm not afraid of my mother, but I can't say I'm not afraid of what she thinks. "I just don't want to disappoint her." Or Arlo. Especially Darius. He was so perfect this weekend, despite not getting what we all wanted. It was just supposed to be a night of experimenting. And we didn't get to talk about anything before Arlo was out the door.

"How in the fuck would you disappoint her? Have you seen you?" He glances my way, eyes trailing from my knees, up, and pausing at my boobs.

I slap his shoulder. "Eyes on the road, sir."

He hums, focusing on driving, but puts his hand on my thigh. "How though? I'm not talking about your fucking glorious tits either, angel. You've done so much for your age."

"I've accomplished what she wanted me to." I huff a painful laugh and glance at my chest. They're just boobs. All boobs are glorious. "She got a prescription for anxiety meds when I quit the pageant circuit, Arlo. She's probably popping those babies daily until I get a job, and get on the right track, which I'm not in the least."

"You've been here for two damn weeks." He bites his bottom lip, and his chest rises and falls like he'd like to lay it all out, maybe in punishing words instead of a punishing fuck. I have mixed feelings about that. The last thing I want to discuss in this car, with the man who's making me feel things I shouldn't, is my mother, but I kinda wish he'd just blurt it all out like he did when he was having a bad day. He wasn't kind, but he was raw, and purely honest. Maybe I want him as mad as his energy feels right now. Maybe I want him to make me mad, too.

My eyes sting, and I yawn to relieve the ache in my tight jaw. But she's my mom. Family. I'm supposed to honor that. Appreciate all the things she's done for me and try to make her happy.

He moves his hand up, and down my jeans, then puts it back on the wheel. It feels wrong, so I lean closer, and touch his thigh.

"You're not ready for me, Kentucky." His voice sounds dejected, and another wash of disappointment flows through me, this one sharper, and very close to gutting me wide open.

I furrow my brows and rest my head against the seat, staring at his beautiful profile. Is anyone ever ready for Arlo? I can't imagine. But the idea of not having him near me, not drowning in his intensity, seems as wrong as wanting him. "How do you know I'm not ready?"

He takes my hand and moves it so I can feel the hard length of his cock under the soft joggers.

I'd shoot from the seat if my seatbelt weren't there.

"See? You think too much. I'm not interested in being one of your many regrets." He takes the steering wheel with both hands.

"How could anyone regret you, Arlo?" The words just slip out, and I'm glad for that, because I'm tired of thinking, even when it's impossible not to.

His fingers clamp tighter on the wheel, and he leans back in the seat, arching toward my touch. He'd let me do anything to him. He's inviting me in, but can I take that chance? What I want and the emotions holding me back feel like they're at war. I'm cracking, stuck in the crossfire of the painful jabs.

Why can't I just stop thinking so damn much?

So I try to let go, letting my fingers wrap around him over his pants. My mouth waters as I remember how much I want to taste him, and didn't get to. There's no regret surrounding those feelings, so what's holding me back? "I—" I think ahead and weigh the consequences. Burning my pageant dress felt great, though I broke at how hard Mom cried about it. I give his tempting cock a squeeze and pull my hand away. "I only regret things when others get hurt."

"Will fucking me hurt others?"

"*No*" gets lodged in my throat. "What if it does?" How do I tell him I want to be in bed with him and Darius with zero consequences? That's a nonexistent situation. It's all just too complicated. "What if a night with you and Darius just crashes everything?"

His lips kick up. "Would you regret not fucking this cock, Jolene? Would you wonder for the rest of your days what it would have been like to be pounded by me while choking on Darius's cock? Be very, very honest."

Chapter Twenty-Eight

Arlo Lays It Out

ARLO

Jolene is willing—fuck—eager to explore what she wants, but her empathy is putting her in the backseat of her life. It's sweet... and I hate it. That needs to change, which is an asshole thought since I'm a mountain when it comes to change, but she's holding herself back. I should probably rein myself in more.

I consider the data. Talking about sex is a sore point, but her mother is a landmine. These are the reasons I've wanted to talk about boundaries first instead of bending her over the counter. If she can't tell me something hurts, physically or mentally, I could truly harm her. It's happened before, when I was young and exploring my needs with others who were also figuring their limits. It won't happen again. I'm too wise for that now.

I keep my eyes on the road, though they want to stray to her. "I'm not used to being patient for what I want, nor am I used to having someone like you around all the time."

The nervous tension in the car shifts, and I feel her eyes on my face. "What am I like?"

That hit something. Good. I can cast a wide net and tighten it until she channels in where I need her to be. The turn signal clicks as I exit the interstate. "An innocent temptation."

"I'm not innocent, Arlo."

I glance at her offended expression. "Innocent to what I want to do to you. Don't ask what that is if you don't want to know."

Her lips part, then close, and she makes a sweet little humming growl I'd like to feel against my cock. I keep quiet like I don't care one way or another, pulling into a parking garage, muting the lights and sounds of the city in gray concrete.

When I pull into a spot and shut the car off, Jolene turns towards me. "I want to know."

I lean, elbow on the console next to hers, eyes roving over her face. "You sure? Your mom was just here." Her little grimace and blush tell me that's a delicate, should-not-touch situation. So, obviously I want to break it open to see what's inside. "Wonder what naughtiness she's partaken in before?"

Jolene snorts. "She hasn't. She wouldn't risk her perfect reputation."

There she is. I fight a grin. "You'd be surprised."

Her eyes flit to mine and soften.

I like that look on her—the one where she looks to me like my words hold merit, and she really cares what I think, not just what I can do to her. I should change that. Get us on the right track.

"You think?" She crinkles her nose. "Nevermind."

I lean closer. "I bet she's done unspeakable things. You need to catch up."

She rolls her eyes at that. "You're changing the subject. I don't want to talk about my mother."

Actually, I'm testing the conditional statements. Yes or no, off limits or on. I thumb her bottom lip. "You truly want to know?" I wait until she nods. "I want to push every limit you have once you trust me. Then I'll take you to an edge of ecstasy you're positive you won't return from. I want to break you down into orgasms, but I'm not going there until you can handle that with pride."

I touch her chin and lean in, because I can't seem to get enough of her mouth. A kiss is a kiss is a kiss, but hers are so perfectly soft and giving that they imprint on me, making my lips tingle and my tongue impatient. I lean back. "But if you're looking for the minutiae, I want to choke you, fuck your ass, then watch Darius's face as he comes down your throat because the idea of us all together makes him lose it. I want to leave so many marks on you that you have to cover your body at the new job *you're going to get* so that no one knows what a fucking dirty whore you are for us. And when you feel shame or guilt for loving all the filthy things I do to you, I want you to crawl down the hall to me, begging for punishment."

Jolene's pupils dilate, and her lips part on a gasp. "Arlo." Her voice is a shaky whimper.

I cup her face, and she leans into my palm.

"But, angel?" I stroke her cheek. "I want to do all that without you getting attached to me." Ignoring the way the flames snuff out of her eyes, I grip her chin. This is important. "I won't be your boyfriend. That's Darius's job. I play with others and don't care if you do the same because that's who I am. You need to decide if you can handle that because I don't change for anyone. I will own your body sometimes, but I'm your roommate, the best friend of your boyfriend, and even if you intensely distract me, I'd be fine if we left it there."

As long as she didn't test me too hard, because if I have another music war with her and she tells me to kiss her ass, it's going to be difficult not to have my dick in her as well.

Her brows furrow.

I nod and let her chin go. Cards played. And I know her well enough to see she's going to need to process that for a few. "Ready for dinner?"

Chapter Twenty-Nine

Darius Feels The Tension

DARIUS

When Arlo and Jolene step into Sal's, my happy thoughts of a fun evening flit away.

Jolene's brows are furrowed, and Arlo glances around as if running security detail.

I wave from the booth of the Italian bistro. This place looks like a family moved directly from Italy and made this their big casual kitchen. The yellow stucco walls further warm the dark woods and make the red checkered tablecloths pop. Italian music sounds low, dimming the murmuring chatter of diners and the little tinks of silverware tapping against plates and bowls. A little candle in a jar flickers on each table, and there's no chance of not falling in love in this place.

Arlo spots me and snags Jolene's waist.

She steps away from him, but he tugs her closer, hand splayed over her hip, and leans to whisper in her ear. Her eyes meet mine, and she nods, but pulls from him to walk in my direction. What the hell did they talk about in the car? I was hoping when he asked to pick her up and have some alone time that they'd talk, and maybe he'd rile her back up. I've been half-hard sitting here sipping chianti while thinking about him fingering her in the car. She's not looking blissfully worked-up. She looked angrily worked-up.

Jolene kisses me with tight lips and sits next to me.

Arlo slides in across from us in the booth.

And they're quiet.

The air they brought into this bread-smelling paradise feels heavy. It's hard to tell where Jolene's mind is after her mother's visit, because her shoulders are still up to her ears. Is that because of Donna or Arlo?

I squeeze her tight shoulder. "You okay?"

She stretches her neck, giving me more room to massage. "Just fine." She snags a menu, but leans against me.

I wrap my arm around her and hold her close to my side. "We're going to need alcohol, aren't we?" I ask, trying to lighten the moment, and to keep from blurting out what I really want to know—which is what is making them both so prickly.

"So much alcohol," she says, studying the menu.

"Not too much." Arlo takes my wine glass and sips from it. "How about a bottle of this?"

"That would be good. What do you think, babes?"

"Maybe two bottles."

I raise an eyebrow. I'd need to carry her out of here, so I know she's joking.

Arlo glares at her, but she leans further into me.

I know how to diffuse both of them, but not together. Plus, I've said I'd let them figure things out between them.

"One." He leans forward, chin on his knuckles. "Because I have plans for you tonight, and don't want you sloppy drunk."

I inhale long and exhale longer. "So does that mean..." I trail off in case anyone else can overhear, though the booth is cozy enough to feel cut off from other patrons.

However, I'm not sure my words even register over the roaring inner conversation the two of them seem to be having.

"Did something happen with your mom at the airport?" I should tote her out of here and get her back to the apartment. Draw a bath and leave her alone with wine and candles. Her body is tight with stress, and I don't think Arlo is helping at all.

She gives a pitchy laugh. "Not at the airport." She leans forward. "Where did you stay, Arlo?"

My stomach tightens, and I crinkle my nose. Outside relationships have been easier to navigate and discuss because of the deep love and understanding between Jolene and I. But Arlo? He doesn't allow jealousy. Jolene and Arlo don't have the building blocks to withstand a wrecking-ball conversation about who Arlo fucks, which is whoever he wants. Not that he hooked up this weekend.

Arlo sets aside his menu. "You think you're going to be possessive now, Kentucky?"

She shakes her head. "I'm just trying to figure out if I can do what you're asking."

That raises my eyebrows. *Which is?*

"And what if I let someone, or even a couple of women, pick me up and take me home?"

She shrugs. "Did you?" She doesn't sound accusatory. Just curious.

I sip my wine and push the glass toward her.

Arlo tilts his head. "I went to see my stepfather and mother, stayed with them, pruned a holly bush, and went to brunch. Feel better?"

She takes a long sip from my glass, sets it down, and smiles. "I do."

"And if I had been with another? What fucking then?"

"Arlo..." I tip my head toward the table of suited people across from us, who are now staring.

Arlo turns his head fully their way until each one of them quickly puts their attention back on their plates. He looks back at Jolene and lowers his voice so it's just below the level of the music. "What then?"

"Then you would have broken your rules." She shrugs and leans into me. "I was just curious since I clearly don't know what I'm doing." Her laugh is self-deprecating, and I fucking hate it.

I hug her harder against my side. "Want to go?"

She shakes her head. "Hungry. I'm fine. Just thinking."

Arlo watches Jolene with a furrowed brow. At least he's not pleased he upset her, not that he would be.

I sigh and kiss her head. "Your mom might have interrupted Arlo's game, but his rules stand until he says they don't. Is that what you needed to know?"

"Yes, sort of."

Arlo's glare softens, and he reaches over the table to take her hand, stroking her with his thumb. "I didn't break my rules."

"And while I've been worked up..." I nudge her. "No rules broken here, either. Was that all you talked about?"

She pulls away from Arlo's hold before turning to me and lowering her voice. "If we, uh, do stuff, you're the boyfriend." She pats my chest like she's checking if I'm still there.

"Obviously?" I say with a question.

"I'm not allowed to get attached to him."

I throw Arlo a glance that says, *"You seriously went there?"* Her damn stressful mother just left, and Jolene is not a bar bunny he needs to stave off. If anything, he's the one obsessing.

Lips firm, he puts his menu on the edge of the table. "It's important for you to know how I am. It's a boundary. I'm not and will never be owned by another."

She snorts. "Wanna explain that history?"

He purses tight lips and shakes his head. "No." There is no give in his voice.

"Another boundary. Got it."

"I'm not trying to hurt you here. I'm just letting you know how things will be if you try this. Same page. I'd never hurt you."

I nod. "He wouldn't. Like I said, you can explore what you want, with or without me, but I'm there, babes. No one is doing anything to you that you don't want."

Jolene watches her fingers trace along the tablecloth. "So just sex."

"Exactly," Arlo says.

My jaw drops. "Not to me." I turn to her. "You know that, right? It has never been and will never be just sex with us." I don't want Arlo putting her in any category that would make her solely a plaything, and as much as it turns me on to think of them together, this stops here if that's how he feels about it.

She nods and cups my face. "Oh, I know, baby."

"Good." I press my forehead to hers, breathing her in because the thought of her not knowing what she means to me is terrifying.

The server picks that moment to approach the table.

I move back to see Arlo eyeing me with the intensity he's been aiming at Jolene.

I put my gaze on the menu.

We order, and Jolene takes another sip of my wine while Arlo tears into the crusty bread the man left behind.

When the bottle comes moments later, Arlo takes it and pours for Jolene. "What are you thinking?"

She swallows her bite of bread and sweeps her thumb under her lip before licking it. "How long it's going to take until you try to fuck me again."

Arlo and I both freeze, him with his wine glass halfway to his lips and me with my hand on the bread. That was literally the last thing I expected out of her mouth.

Arlo's lips spread into a grin. "Just say when."

Chapter Thirty

Jolene Fails

JOLENE

As Darius holds the car door open for me, I'm still not a hundred percent sure I won't smack some sense into Arlo any second. Figuratively. Probably.

While our conversation at dinner felt like a fight, it also felt like foreplay.

He won't stop checking me out. It was obvious, from the way he eyed my lips every time I sipped wine, to how he rested his foot against mine under the table like he needed to touch me. Maybe it's his way of saying sorry for being an unattached shit.

Even walking to the car, he stays quiet and close, energy rolling off him like a shield, tempting me to break it open.

All while Darius holds my hand and stays in line with me, always my warm, encompassing safe place. My *boyfriend* holds the passenger door open for me, then gets into the back seat when I'm settled.

Arlo slips into the driver's seat and turns to me.

I flashback to hours earlier and his desperate kiss, but he only brushes his knuckles against my chin, then leans back in his seat with a sigh. I'm still a little mad about being told not to get attached. How would I not get attached while trusting him with my body the way he wants me to? It would form a bond between us. And I already feel something like that. I lick the bruise on my lip.

He marked me. He wants to do it again. How is that not an attachment?

And even more so, how can we live together and not feel something for each other? That's not what he and Darius do. They've both told me they love each other. So where does that leave me?

Maybe Arlo is just trying to set the stakes if we get attached, because he knows who he is and how he reacts to women. Is he trying to protect me by pushing me away?

"You're thinking again, Kentucky." Arlo pulls out of the parking garage, pausing at a red light. The city is dark and busy with cars and people. "Do you want to stop that?"

I keep my eyes out the window. "Not really a thing, Arlo."

Darius huffs a quiet laugh behind me.

"It can be." Arlo's words are teasing, and I hate how I can't let it go.

I should let him keep his thoughts in his head and keep mine to myself as well. I purse my lips. Fine, I give. "And how's that?"

"Tell me you want to stop overthinking."

I roll my eyes. Now he wants to talk? "I'd just love to stop over-thinking."

"Good girl." His voice is deep, and the leather of the wheel creaks under his grip. "Darius, pin our girl's hands for me."

My eyes go wide, and I glance back at Darius.

He tilts his head. "Your choice, babes. We can go home and take a bath." He holds up the remainder of the wine bottle. "Finish this. Go to sleep."

We could. I know that. I'm certain Darius would do anything I asked of him. We could make it a normal night after an abnormal, stressful weekend. I'd think about everything my mom said while she was here. The crushing doubt and disappointment are still heavy in my chest. I'll go quiet and Darius will step around me, take care of me, while I process and regain my bearings.

Arlo keeps his eyes ahead. His profile is now lit by neon street lights against the dark of the evening, making him more structured and firm. More intense. More... distracting.

I swallow and settle back in the seat. "Where do I put my hands?"

The wheel creaks hard. "Grip the headrest."

I reach up and back, closing my eyes when Darius's warm fingers wrap around my wrists.

The car comes to a stop, another light, and Arlo turns to me, leaning close to my face. He unbuttons my pants and gives my lips a long, gentle kiss. "Good girl, Jolene."

He leans back in the driver's seat but slides his hand under my panties, seeking. His finger glides into my folds and lands right on my clit.

I gasp and arch back, feeling the pressure of Darius's grip as I tug.

"So responsive." His finger slowly glides back and forth over that spot with ease. "You want faster?"

"Yes, sir."

He hums. "I don't think you do, though." He keeps that slow pace as I try to rock against him, but the seatbelt and Darius have me constrained. "I think you want to be tortured for a while."

I huff a laugh. He might be right.

Darius's thumbs swipe over my sensitive inner wrists. Having both his hands occupied with mine, and then another giving attention to my clit, is wild. Tension pulls tight in my lower stomach, and I spread as wide as I can.

"I think she wants a cock inside her right now, Darius."

"Is that true, Joles?" There's a creak of leather and then warm lips surround my fingertips. "Do you wish you were on my lap right now?"

"Yes," I whine. How am I already this close?

We come to another stoplight—the one that's just before the apartment—and a little jolt of panic skips through me.

The car beside us has tinted windows, but—

Arlo circles my clit roughly.

I arch back. "Oh, fuck."

"There she is." Arlo chuckles, driving forward as soon as the light changes. "Let go of her hands so she can wave at the attendant."

Darius drops my wrists, but Arlo keeps his hand in my pants.

"Wave, angel. Show them how sweet you are while I fingerfuck you."

I bite back a whimper and raise my hand as we pass the guard on duty.

As soon as we're past, I gasp and try to roll my hips. "Close."

"I know." Arlo slides his finger over my clit with rough quickness.

I gasp, everything tightens and—

He pulls his hand away.

"Fuck! No."

He laughs. "I really love when you say that." He sucks his finger.

I drop my head back on the seat and moan. I'm tempted to finish the job, but the moment my hand drifts that way, Arlo tuts.

"You do it, and the cameras in here will record me making your ass very, very red."

I hiss through my teeth and squirm as we pull into the parking spot.

Darius un-clicks his seatbelt and leans in to wrap his arms around the seat and me. He kisses my neck. "Anything you want, babes. Seriously."

I'm panting, boiling hot, and everything deliciously aches. "I want to try this. Just for a night."

Arlo adjusts the bulge in his pants and steps out. "Get out of the car."

The love of my life kisses my neck, then cheek. "I love you, Joles."

My throat tightens, and I nod. He is exactly what I need.

Arlo's eyes narrow. Maybe I need him too. I crave his demands.

Darius opens the door for me, helps me out, then pushes me against the car and kisses the fuck out of me. We taste like minty vanilla from the puff mints the restaurant had as we were leaving. He always grabs about ten of the things. He pulls back. "You know you're mine, right? Whatever happens between us will never change that."

"I know." I place my hand on his chest and peck his lips.

He takes my hand, tugging me toward Arlo, who smirks and heads toward the elevator.

And of course, Sheena is the guard on duty. Why wouldn't she be when I'm feeling so damn vulnerable?

Darius stays close, holding my hand and being my comforting anchor. I can tell he didn't approve of what Arlo said at dinner. Asking for full trust, but also detachment, isn't possible. That's further confirmed when we approach the front desk and Sheena beams at Arlo as he steps out behind me. She wants him—what he does to her, how he makes her feel, how he demands intimate trust. He doesn't return any of that attachment? How?

"Mr. Keller, Mr. Gates, nice to see you."

Being completely disregarded shouldn't sting, but it does. It always does.

Arlo's shoulders rise, and tension weaves up my spine as I wait for him to reprimand her or grab me to show her how much he doesn't care for her rudeness by being rude, but he doesn't. He steps closer to the desk, putting his hands in his pockets.

Sheena preens under his gaze.

"Did you work yesterday morning?" he asks in a way that sends chills up my neck.

"You know my schedule." Her gaze finds me, and she smirks before looking back at Arlo.

"Actually, I don't." Arlo is calm, but with a simmering danger she doesn't appear to catch.

"Sure, you don't."

"Why did you send Ms. Shah's guest to our apartment with no warning?" His jaw tightens, and I want to wrap my arms around him and tug him away. He was right. This woman will never be my friend, so this doesn't matter.

Her smile widens. "It was a surprise."

My years of expression training are the only thing that keeps me from sneering at Sheena. Did she think she was being nice, or did she expect that my mother would interrupt exactly *what* she interrupted?

"Allowing someone to have free access to residents is a danger and against building rules."

"Oh. Would you like to punish me?"

My stomach sours, rolls, and twists so hard, I put my hand over it. Is this what he's asking of me? Is that why he's bringing it up? Maybe when he said he'd still be fucking others, he meant tonight. But then he said he had plans for me tonight. I hope he doesn't expect me to watch him fool around with Sheena, because I really will smack him. Maybe this is a jealousy test. I'm not sure if I'm failing or just uncomfortable with him being with someone who hates me.

Arlo doesn't flinch. Not even a muscle. He doesn't speak until her smile wavers. "I would like you to do your job. Do not force us to involve management over your pettiness."

She stands so fast the chair rolls backwards. "But—"

"No." Arlo turns and lifts his chin toward the elevators.

Darius squeezes my fingers and tugs me along in Arlo's riptide.

"Sir?" Sheena says behind us. "But... Arlo?"

He steps beside me, pressing a palm to the base of my spine as Darius smashes the elevator button. The doors open, and Arlo practically throws me in, crowding me. As soon as the doors silence the hum of the lobby, his lips crash against mine.

I shove him away. "Off."

"Why?" he rumbles, caging me against the wall.

Darius leans against the wall and raises an eyebrow at me. "Be honest, Joles."

The metal rail bites into my backside, and I grip it with both hands. They want honesty? *Fine.* "Is that what you're expecting me to do, Arlo? Be an asshole, then ask for punishment?"

His stare punctures my soul. It's so hard and deep. "No. What she did was a petulant call for attention by using others. When you do something you shouldn't, you'll either do it because you want to play with me or because you actually did something you know you shouldn't and I can make it better. I want you to give yourself to me so I can free you. You are not her, and wouldn't act like that." He grips my throat. "Would you?"

My whole body relaxes with the pressure from his fingers. That small move owns me, as do his words. *Give yourself to me.* Does he have any clue what that means? I drop my head back against the wall. "No, sir," I say on an exhale. "I'd never act like that."

"And that's why you're in this position. Here with us." Arlo gives me the softest kiss and wedges his muscular thigh between my legs, returning me to that worked-up state I was in days ago. "Darius? How many orgasms do you think we can give our girl tonight?"

Our girl. Chills rise on my arms and neck. My nipples peak painfully against lace.

Over Arlo's shoulder, Darius smiles at me. "Two." He knows me well, but it's rare to get to two. I shift my hips to get more pressure and moan. It may not be so difficult today.

The elevator dings, and Arlo steps back. "Let's double that."

Chapter Thirty-One

Darius Comes First

DARIUS

Sprinting down the hall might draw attention to the three of us, and would be difficult with my erection, but it's hard not to bolt when the elevator doors slide open. I'm sure Arlo is feeling the same way since he's refusing to budge from Jolene while she pants against his lips, a sign she's through with foreplay.

Her eyes flutter closed when he gives her neck a squeeze before letting her go and stepping out into the hallway.

I follow but drag Jolene against me, gripping her ass and kissing her as we stumble toward our apartment. I want her. I always do, but knowing Arlo will see her, feel her like I do? There's no better fantasy.

I pause in the hallway and cradle her gorgeous face in my hands. "Are you okay with this?"

She kisses me in that perfect way, pressing her tits against my chest, arms around my neck. When she pulls back, she smiles. "I'm so horny it hurts." She tilts her head. "But are you okay? We don't need to—"

"We don't but"—tightening my hold on her ass, I pull her closer so she can really feel how turned on I am right now—"I want to watch him fuck you so badly. I'm dying here."

She breathes out a whimper, nodding. Then she turns and sashays to Arlo.

He holds the door open for her, but as soon as we're inside, he jerks her toward him by the front of her jeans, then pins her against the door. He crashes onto her with biting kisses. His growl hums in my cock.

Jolene arches, helping him while he drags her pants and panties down. She jerks at his shirt, and he tugs it off for her. They are so hot together.

I rub a hand against my erection as he flips her, pushing her chest against the wood.

She arches her back, popping that perfect ass out. She enjoys being tossed around. I knew she would.

The crack against her backside from Arlo's palm is sharp, and she responds with a grunt. "You're going to be a good girl for me, aren't you?"

"Maybe."

I grin. There's her sass.

He flips her around, crowding her, gripping her chin and opening her mouth, pressing a thumb to her tongue. "Kneel, Kentucky."

She honest-to-God nips him away, then bares her teeth at him, holding his glare as she kicks herself the rest of the way out of shoes and pants. She pulls her panties back up. "I'm not kneeling in our damn foyer like a *guest*. I'll be in your bed." She ducks under his arm, striding past him toward the hallway.

I could cheer. Jolene is adjusting here, both to what she needs and to who she is. She's so strong, and I'm thrilled to see her remember that during this transition.

"Fuck me," Arlo whispers, balling his fists as I laugh and follow my gorgeous woman. Arlo and I shed shirts and socks. He pauses at the doorway, stopping me with a hand on my chest. He pulls me close, pressing his forehead to mine. "I'll take care of her."

"I never doubted that for a second." It's the truth, too.

For as callous as he portrays himself to be, he always cares. It's part of why he needs to control like he does. It's a way of communication, and I'm excited to see how he speaks to Jolene today, and later.

He kisses my cheek and steps into the bedroom.

Jolene lounges on his bed, propped on her elbows, one leg bent so we get an incredible view of her lace-covered pussy. She's the perfect temptation as she confidently waits.

"Shirt off." Arlo strides forward and climbs over her, pressing her to the mattress with his kiss. "Now." As soon as she tugs it off, he grabs her hair hard, jerking her head back, and crashes his lips back down on hers.

It makes butterflies shoot through my stomach. He likes her. He wouldn't be kissing her, giving her time to warm to this if he didn't.

By her flush and sweet hum, and the way she reaches up to caress his cheek with her fingertips, she likes him too.

He gives a quick bite to her lip, then licks it. "I want to watch you suck Darius's cock. We all need to get off right fucking now, but I own your first orgasm." He tugs her up and pushes her toward me.

I stay off the bed but lean to kiss her, then stand straight up and wait. I watch for any grimace or retreat as she leans forward, because she's not one for oral unless it's in a shower or right after. It's not that I'm dirty, but I've been running around all day. People smell like people. I like it, as does Arlo. But this may be a *no* for her.

As her hands go to the buckle of my pants, I whisper, "You don't have to."

"But she wants to." Still holding her hair in one hand, Arlo slides a finger down Jolene's spine. "I believe she wants me to call out just how much she wants your dick in her mouth."

Her cheeks blaze, and she bites her lip.

"Is that true?" I ask.

She nods, takes me out of my pants, and pumps my hard length in her hand. I curse under my breath and tilt my hips toward her.

"Outloud, Kentucky."

"I need you," she whispers, eyes on mine. "I want this." She squeezes hard, making my jaw drop as I groan.

Her cheeks go redder when her pink tongue swipes over my tip, sending even more blood into my aching cock.

Arlo quietly watches as she takes me in fully, forward and back, making my eyes close in pleasure. He loosens his hold on her hair so I can slip my fingers in, and gently massage.

Her hand goes to my thigh, and the other around the base of my cock as she sucks me down until I nearly touch the back of her throat, shifting as she works me, hips perched out, rolling the slightest bit.

"So hot, Jolene." Arlo kneels behind her, his thighs surrounding hers. He runs his hands up and down her hips and sides.

Her sucking stops when he cups her breasts, but she hums, sending reverberations through my entire lower half.

"Keep going, babes." I'm panting, heart racing. This won't take long. "This feels amazing."

She smiles around my cock, then runs the point of her tongue up my length.

"Focus." Arlo regathers her hair with one hand and unhooks her bra with the other. "Take him deeper."

She's panting as she lets me drop from her lips. "I'll gag."

"Good," he growls, pushing her toward me. "Take him down until you gag. It's pretty. I like it." He palms her breast under her dangling bra and thrusts against her ass. "Makes me hard. Feel that?"

"Y-yes." She takes me back in, breathing heavy. With furrowed eyes on mine, she pushes forward and back, then pauses and sinks me deep. Sure enough, her brows furrow and she gags, pulling back.

"It's okay." I stroke her cheek.

"That was gorgeous." Arlo kisses her neck, guiding her back to me by her hair. "Again."

Jolene closes her eyes and moans.

My cock hardens further.

She doesn't hesitate, which surprises me. I hiss at the pleasured shock of breaching her throat. This time she coughs as well, and her eyes water as she gasps for air.

I thrust into her hand. "I'm so close."

"He's being so kind to you." Arlo nips her ear. "Remember what I said?"

She pants and nods, leaning back against him as he toys with her nipple.

"I'd hold on until you were crying, gagging, foaming at the mouth. You're going to learn to open your throat to me. Would you like that?"

"I don't know."

"You'll find out." He pinches her nipples until she cries out. "He's going to come down your throat, and you're going to take it all."

I raise my eyebrows, remembering the only time she's done that. It was Christmas. She wanted to try it. My soul left my body, but she gagged then, too, and we ended up laughing, but haven't done it since. "You okay with that, babes?"

She grins up at me, likely remembering the same night. "I like when you're this far gone."

My eyebrows raise when she leans toward me again. She looks like she's already had an orgasm with her watery eyes and flushed skin. She trails her tongue up my length and gives my balls a teasing squeeze as I moan to the ceiling. Maybe there is something to pushing her out of her comfort zone, though I'm not the man to do that.

Arlo leans over to whisper in her ear. "I'm going to take over now, because I need to fuck you so badly, and with the way you're shifting against me, you need that, too. Okay?"

Jolene's brows furrow, but she nods.

Arlo moves her toward me, and she opens, taking me down.

My lips part in a gasp.

Arlo grins, strumming her nipples and grinding against her ass, no doubt getting her used to what this will be like when he's buried deep in her.

She breathes, and takes me down again with enthusiasm, rolling her tongue as he tugs her head back and forth. She places her hands on the mattress instead of me as she adjusts to Arlo's movements.

It's harder than usual, but wildly different with him directing her moves. I feel when she truly gives in, relaxing into his hold while being used by us.

Arlo must realize it too, because he leans to whisper in her ear, kiss her cheek, and slips his other hand into her panties.

She whimpers, then grins around my cock, tears flowing from her eyes from the occasional gag. I love her so much my chest feels like it's going to burst.

Each of my nerves tingles with frustrated delight. I can't take more. "Fuck, Joles, I'm coming." I shout, electricity ripping up my spine. My knees weaken, and I nearly buckle as she sucks my release from me.

It's not something she enjoys, but apparently she likes what we did because she bites her lips and proudly smiles up at me.

"Hells," I whisper, dropping to my shaky knees to worship those beautiful lips. "Incredible. You okay?"

"I am." Her cheeks turn pink, and she turns toward Arlo. "Did I do well?"

I grin. She knows she did, but I love that she's asking him. He'll love that.

"That was so sexy." Arlo moves over her, pinning her onto the bed. "You're next."

Chapter Thirty-Two

Arlo Goes Slow

ARLO

I'm going to wreck Jolene's world off-kilter. The neighbors will complain about the noise. I need her broken down with lust, so she gives me everything. For just one night. I snort. We'll see. That won't be enough time for me to do what I want with her.

Her pupils are dark voids, and she does a slow lick on the center of her top lip in the sexiest move I have ever seen—like she's remembering Darius's cum, or impatiently waiting for mine.

My muscles are tense balls of lust, and all my blood is in my cock, making my brain hazy and honed only to her and what she can give me. The wet spot of pre-cum in my pants is a constant, annoying reminder that I need her right fucking now.

She closes her eyes as I thumb her lip. She's so gorgeous when she's flushed, needy, and owning her depravity.

I grip the back of her neck and thrust my tongue into her mouth. She tastes of wine and basil, need and pleasure. "Need you."

Her groan is a siren's call, the way she opens her mouth and body to me—wisdom beyond her understanding. She hasn't a clue what she's doing, and I'm not sure if I like that she's this innocent, yet this fitting for me. Her panties break with a hard jerk, and she arches like busting her out of the fabric keeping us apart just gave her a mini orgasm.

I leave her mouth to slide the soaked lace from her, tasting her nipple, dipping my tongue into her belly button and running my teeth over her hip. I'm going to mark that later. My hip, my pussy, my fuck-puffed lips, my whimpers, my pleasure to divvy out for my fucking innocent country girl.

I shove the ruined lace under my pillow because that's mine too and nip her lips when she raises an eyebrow at me. "Arms up. You will keep them there until I say. Understand?" I'm not in control enough for her to touch me. Holding back from spreading her and sinking in right now is taking a remarkable amount of restraint.

"Okay." She drops her hands behind her head, pushing her gorgeous tits out.

I suck one nipple hard, then the other, groaning at the way her breath stutters out in pleasured whimpers.

Darius loses his pants and settles on the bed, wrapping his fist around his recovering dick.

Yeah, this is going to be quite the night for Jolene. She's going to feel us both for the next few days.

Her tits can take a lot of abuse, and I squeeze harder. Fist them, so they mushroom out over my fingers. I bite her nipple, smiling when she screams out. "Does our girl like a little pain?"

The little shock in her expression has me curious. Was it because she's also my girl tonight, or that I called her out for liking pain, which is already obvious? Those sweet lips curve into a smile around gritted teeth. "I think maybe so." Pain then. It's going to be a real kick when she realizes she's mine, too.

I prop myself on my elbows, pinning her under me, and dropping my weight down to feel the soft warmth of the woman under me. She smells like her, sweat, and sex. I can't help but kiss the hell out of her perfect mouth.

She whimpers and caves, gripping my hair and squeezing, and damn if I don't close my eyes and get pleasure chills on my neck.

Darius sucks in a breath through his teeth, though he's smiling. "Uh oh, babes. Bad girl."

He's right. I set a rule, and she broke it. I sigh and move off her.

Jolene struggles to follow me, wide eyes going between me and Darius. It's so cute. "No, I'm sorry. Don't go, Arlo. I don't want to stop."

Why do her words, or maybe her tone, make me want to change my damn rules? Just the game, though. I feel like tossing my plans out the window and just being with her, but that's ridiculous and not what any of us are here for. I hold her close. Soak in her sweetness. "You moved your hands, Kentucky."

Her eyes go wide, and she grimaces as she leans back, putting them behind her again, clutching the duvet.

I cluck my tongue. "Too late." Shoving myself up, I grip her hips and flip her, dragging her to the edge of the bed so her feet touch the floor. I pull her arms behind her back and make her hold her forearms. Even now, I find I've plastered myself to her warm back, and am grinding against her backside like non-stop touching is our normal state of being. I run my nose up her neck and inhale right behind her ear before growling. "Do not move from this position. Do you understand me?"

"Yes, Arlo."

"Perfect." I drag myself down her body.

Her ass is soft and round. Delightfully overflowing handfuls.

I bite her softness, making her squeak, then kiss the sting and trail my tongue along her spine, lifting chills on her skin. I brush my lips over her shoulder.

She smells good everywhere, but today, she's enhanced by jasmine and sweat.

Sucking a spot behind her ear makes her hips lift against my crotch, and she makes that moan that I've been dying for, but this time, I'm the cause of it. I can't wait to sink into her, but she needs to be physically and mentally ready for that. "I'm going to be rough with you. Tell me no or stop if you need to. No need for a safe word—"

"Pickles. My safe word is pickles." She eyes me as well as she can pinned on her stomach, then looks to Darius, who seems as surprised as I am.

I tug at her ear with my teeth. "You've thought about this. Did you pick that word because I hate pickles so much?" My hard dick is softening just thinking about that sour shit hiding in burgers and grilled cheese sandwiches.

"Yes."

There's no room to think about how that warms my chest because what's between us is physical. I grind against her ass to get that part of me back on track. "Use it if you need to." Parting her cheeks, I lick her from clit to ass. It's a fun trip because she relaxes, then tightens right back up when I get to the place where she's clearly not used to being touched. I do it again. Slower.

Her sweet little bud is peaked and swollen, as are her folds, but her muscles stay tense.

I bring my hand down hard on her ass and spear her with the tip of my tongue.

"Homagawd," she mumbles.

I can practically feel her blush from down here and chuckle. "Little innocent thing." I spit between her cheeks and rub her with my thumb, then slap her ass again as she squirms. "No moving."

She yips and tries to relax, but her hips are shifting as I circle her and put pressure against her unyielding ass. "Arlo?"

"Yes?" I raise an eyebrow at Darius, who's beaming.

"Can you..." She swallows, squirms, and bites her lip. Her fingers flex on her forearms.

I'm tempted to spank her perfect ass again. "Tell me exactly what you're thinking. Right now."

"More, please. Sir."

My dick jerks. *Yeah, me too.* "Feels good, doesn't it? Want me to play with your ass while I fuck you?"

"Oh, God." She nods against the mattress, and I can't bring myself to punish her for it or push harder for her words. She's being perfect right now.

I step back, ears tingling from the disgruntled groan she makes. I grab a condom from the nightstand, drop my pants, and roll it on. "You're going to come all over my cock twice, Jolene. Then Darius is going to fuck you until you come again. And I'm going to finish you off. Understand?"

She huffs. "I haven't come more than three times in a day ever."

I smile and slap her red ass. "And today you come four times." Rubbing the head of my cock through her folds is already a lot. She better come twice quickly.

I reach under her to rub her clit and barely enter her. Just the tip. It's clear she thought I was going to slam in because her brows are furrowed and she braces herself.

She remains stiff until the head of my dick disappears inside of her soaked center. "Can I…" She moans and presses her face into the comforter. "Can I please let go of my arms?"

She's a natural at taking direction. "You may."

She lets go, flexing her fingers before gripping the comforter in one, and my side with the other.

I keep moving slowly, centimeter by centimeter, into her heat. I can't imagine what being with her bare is like. Darius said she's so hot inside and takes all of him, which is impressive with his length. It would be kinder of me to let him take her ass first when we go there—he's long, I'm thick—but I'm not going to. That's mine.

I move her hair aside and nibble her neck. "You're squeezing my cock so well."

Her whimper is one of desperate need.

"Already, baby?" Darius says with amusement. "You like slow torture?"

"I-I didn't know." She gasps. "I can feel your piercing. I'm close."

I'm not even halfway in yet. "You didn't know edging would do this, did you? It's only been days. I could work you up for weeks."

Darius groans. "That would be hell."

"It makes heaven all the brighter." I grin. "Do you like my cock, angel?" Another little bit, then another, stretching her.

"I really do." She laughs. "Thought it would be rougher, though."

I chuckle. Oh, it will be. This is prep work. I tease her ass. "How close are you?" I bite my lips together and get a little deeper. Almost there. Fuck, I want to thrust in so hard. But I don't. Not yet. She's not ready for that. Her body is strung tight. No give. I'm going to need her pliable.

"More, please." She shifts, trying hard to take more, or get a better angle, but I press her hips down, thumb against her hole, breaching her tightness. A whimper escapes instead of words when she opens her mouth and her muscles tighten. She's trembling, probably right on the edge, and I can't stop my grin. She's so fun to torture. "More."

"More what?"

"More of you. Fill me, please. I'm dying."

"Good girl," I growl in her ear, setting my weight on her. "After you come, I'll fuck this perfect pussy so fucking hard, you'll cry for less instead of more." I go even slower, giving a couple of shallow thrusts. "Like this?"

"No, dammit." Her frustrated growl almost makes me pity her. Almost.

I stay slow, even though my balls ache and tighten. Not yet. I press in deeper, cock and thumb, sliding along the ridges of her clenching inner muscles. Fuck, she really is close, tightening by the second. I let go of her hip to wedge my hand under her chest and pinch her nipple as I take that last inch and push hard against her ass.

She bucks, cries out, and her muscles pulse and massage my dick so well, I almost let go. It's close, but that would mean I couldn't fuck her hard. And like hell I'm missing out on that.

I suck her earlobe as she pants and trembles, and keep my voice light and playful. "Did you come?"

Darius bites his smile and slowly strokes his dick. He's enjoying this game.

She nods, panting. "Uh-huh."

"Remember your safe word."

Chapter Thirty-Three

Jolene Screams

JOLENE

I've never come like that before. It shouldn't have happened.

I need deep, rhythmic, and fast, and what Arlo did wasn't any of that. It was torture from days past, an additional experience with my backside involved, and simply... delicious. My body hums.

Arlo runs his hands over my skin, leaving a wake of chills as my body slowly relaxes again after his warning to hold tight to my safe word. He's being sweet. Careful with me.

Darius strokes himself slowly, as if he's settling in for a long night of what we're doing, and a tiny part of me asks if they fuck other women just like this? It feels immature to wonder if someone else has been in this exact position, but I don't like that thought, not when—

Darius's happy expression slides to concern a second before Arlo pulls out of me and flips me to my back.

I gasp, staring up into a tsunami of blue. Did I tense up, or what?

Arlo slaps my thigh hard, making me yip. "Don't wander off." He glares with an intensity that makes me want to bite him. "I'm fucking you. The only thing that matters right now is you taking me like a good girl. Right?" He's so intense.

I bask in it, and something clicks into place within me. He wants the real me tonight. Not the makeup, fake smiles, and niceties. He wants the core of me. Just *me*. How could I not want this? Him. More. Darius is here, and he is always mine. Arlo's right. Nothing else matters but him and this experience.

I nod. "I'm sorry. Yes, Arlo."

"No more thinking. Let go with me." He shoves my legs apart with a knee and thrusts inside me.

Alright, then. I claw my nails down his chest and lift to take his lip between my teeth. I'll let go and show him a *good girl*.

He breaks his scowl with a grin and nips me back, looping my leg over his forearm. Then, he kisses me with deep, yearning tongue licks and hot, vicious lips as he slowly thrusts between my legs.

I clutch his hard body, digging in. He makes me want to fight—go down kicking, screaming, and cursing his name. But I don't ask for any of that, or get as rough with him as I'd like to. I don't know where the line is yet.

Darius leans against the headboard, calm and collected as always, a slight smile on his face as if Arlo fucking me is the most natural thing in the world.

A hot suck on my breast brings my attention back, and I scratch at Arlo's head, digging in my nails. He moans, then bites me.

I cry out, heat flooding between my legs. Why in the hell does that feel so good? It's like the pain only lifts the pleasure higher. My attention is everywhere. The sear of Arlo's mouth, the tension of his fingers against my hips, Darius's hooded gaze as he nibbles his lip. This turns him on so much. How could he not have told me he needed this?

Arlo grips my chin, bringing my gaze to his. "Look at me."

I drag myself closer to him by my legs, and rub myself against him as the tension builds in my core again.

His eyes close, and he licks his lips. "You are... quite the temptation." He refocuses. "I'm going to fuck you hard, and Darius is going to join in. It's different with two. Tell me you still want this."

He makes me melt. He's an ass. A pushy, horny ass. But there's so much more deep down, isn't there? Darius wouldn't love him if there weren't a big dose of good. Arlo's a protector, fierce and loyal. He cares so much, even if he claims he doesn't—connects, even when he's asking me not to. Does he even know that?

I cup his face. "Yes. Please. I need you both." That's as much as I can get out, because my voice tightens and breaks.

He encircles my neck with one hand, holding me pinned, and steadies himself with a palm on the bed, then pounds his way home.

I clutch at the duvet behind me and cry out. *Holy hell.*

He's hard and desperate; bold in everything he does. "Darius."

Darius leans over me and kisses me sweetly. "How does Arlo's cock feel, baby?"

"Good."

Arlo slaps my thigh on the searing spot, then he's back to pinning me down. "Do better, Kentucky."

"Thick," I squeak out. "Punishing."

Darius grips my breast. "And you like to be punished."

It feels right, like this kind of punishment is breaking down the ones I give myself daily. I'm too concerned with what others think and how they judge me. Arlo is my rebellion. They can't judge me when they don't know this feels like a dose of raw truth. Maybe this is me, and I'm allowed to figure it out. "Yes," I whisper. "I like it. Harder."

Arlo chuckles and spears me hard with his cock, sending flicks of heated pain through me.

It makes me moan and spread my legs in offering so he can get deeper. I am wanton, lost, and so needy for this. A flick of shame tries to weave its way back into me until Arlo groans like there's nothing better in this world than what we're doing.

He turns my face back to him and dives his tongue into my mouth as he grinds into me, forcing the tension back into my center like I didn't have an orgasm a few minutes ago.

It's not the sweet build Darius gives me.

Arlo changes things up and makes my mind flit. The moment I understand what he's doing and move with him, he maneuvers me, brings my leg over his shoulder, or spreads me wider to him, sinking so deep, he rams against my insides, sending a sharp pain that makes me jump at first, then simmer with the heat right after. He's not letting me participate—just take him. Accept this fucking while Darius's hands work me over my favorite places as well, a gentle calm against the raging storm.

Arlo grips my neck again and stares down at me. "Fuck, Jolene. You're good at this." He turns to look at Darius, who flicks his eyebrows and nods.

"She's a goddess," Darius says, voice husky. "And her pussy is pure heaven. Coming inside her is the pinnacle of existence." I widen my eyes at him, and he winks back at me.

"Lick your palm," Arlo says through heavy breaths.

"What?"

He slams in so hard, my teeth clack. "Do not question me."

I lick my palm. Twice.

He pushes my hand to Darius, who leans forward so I can wrap my fingers around his cock. Oh. *Ohhh*.

Darius tugs at my sore nipples.

I arch.

Slamming his hips against me harder, a blush of exertion paints Arlo's cheeks as he stares down at me like he's out to break me with his cock, except... he can't. I wonder if that's frustrating to him or fantastic?

"More," I whisper, on the edge, I think. The tension in my body is hard to follow because it's everywhere. They're everywhere. I pump Darius faster, so turned on by how firm his cock is and the whimpers he's making. "Fuck me harder, sir."

A tiny flicker of shock lights Arlo's eyes.

Darius stops my hand and chuckles. "You're going to make me come again, but I want to be inside you." He kisses my wrist and the inside of my elbow, sending sweet tingles up my arm.

"And right now"—Arlo loops his arm under me and slams in, angling me so his punishing thrusts hit my clit—"this pussy is mine."

I whimper. It's not a fall over the edge into bliss. It's a hard shove. Sounds break from my throat that make no sense coming from a human, but I'm not feeling mortal at the moment.

As I pulse hard, Arlo grips my hips in a vise and shouts, pressing in deep with jerky trembles, eyes angled with an expression that goes from the hard lines of pain to a relaxed, broken-down sweetness—not something I thought I'd see coming from him. A few more gentle thrusts, and he lowers fully onto me, kissing me with sweet tenderness and a promise beyond spanking and controlling words.

My eyes burn as the endorphins, adrenaline, dopamine, all crash and swirl in me. That was so much, and yet not enough. "Wow," I whisper, catching my breath.

Arlo pushes himself up and away from me, breathing heavy, looking beautifully disheveled. There's red streaks down his chest from my nails, even able to be seen through the dark parts of his tattoos. His lips are swollen and red. I did that to him.

I did that to *him*.

I want to do it again—want to make him lose control completely, come apart at the firmly muscled seams while letting me ride him. I want to pull off that filled condom and suck more cum from him with my greedy mouth while he shows me how he likes that piercing played with. The wonderment of even thinking those thoughts is overshadowed by one that feels more important. Would he let me do that?

He wants only sex, and I said just a night. Darius is mine forever, and even now, I feel like this might be part of who he is sexually. He's very comfortable in this role. Do I offer more? But what is more to all of us?

I'm already panting again—reeling with lust and questions—but Arlo turns and stalks towards the bathroom without a backward glance. The hormonal wonderland going on inside me shifts to a whirly ride I'm not sure I want to be on. What the fuck does all this mean?

"You okay, Joles?"

I turn and crawl onto Darius, who leans back fully when I push his shoulder and straddle his hips.

He urgently finds my center with his hard dick and surges up into me. His groan is exactly what I need to hear.

I press fully against him, desperate for more. So much more.

"You liked that," he says, caressing my cheek.

I nod, kissing his lips and cheeks with near-panic need. "What does this mean?"

"Shhh." He pulls me closer, holding me tight. "It means that I know you well. We'll take one day at a time, okay?"

"I need—" I press my hips tighter against him, roll them, taking over.

"Yes," he hisses. "Take me. Use me to get off. You know how much I love that." His brown eyes anchor me, slow the spinning confusion darting through me. His kiss is calming and familiar, and my heart rate slows a beat—doesn't feel like it's going to pound out of my chest.

However, all my nerves feel linked to my swollen clit. It's like Arlo fucked horniness into me instead of out. I should be satiated and tired. But I'm not. I'm sore, hyper, and I want more of something I can't even name or speak about. I'm on the verge of discovery but not worthy of the prize because I don't even know what the prize is. Is it only sex? That doesn't feel right.

I lean over Darius—focus on this man I know, this body I understand—palms to the bed, grinding against him while he smiles up at me, biting his full bottom lip. I love those lips. I love him. My throat tightens, and I choke on a groan.

"You're so beautiful." He strokes my cheek. "Strong. Sexy." Darius radiates love and compassion. He always has toward me, and I crave that now as much as the fire Arlo stoked in me.

"I love you," I whisper, throat tight.

He lifts to kiss me. "I love you, my perfect girl. There's none better in the universe." I didn't realize how much I needed to hear that until he swipes an escaped tear away. "Don't you think so, Arlo?"

I gasp and look over my shoulder.

Arlo's gaze is intense and all over me, lips parted like he forgot his jaw is typically rigid. And his cock... it's hard already.

I eye it hungrily, shifting my hips faster.

"You want more, angel?" His voice is business. Curt and demanding.

"Yes, sir."

He smiles, but it's tight and not in his eyes. "It will be too much."

"It won't be." I think I could take anything from him right now. Just anything.

"You have no idea, Jolene."

Then show me, I want to say. *Fuck me harder, again, because I need it and I don't think I'll ever not need it.* But only a whimper comes out when I open my mouth.

He smirks. "Keep fucking Darius that well and I'll have a treat for you after."

My tongue is useless, so I show him just how well I can fuck.

Chapter Thirty-Four

Arlo Gets Marked

ARLO

When Jolene's eyes go hazy at my mention of a treat, I expect her movements as she rides Darius to become quick to finish faster. But not Jolene. She takes over again, possessing my best friend with rolling hips that would put her on a stripper stage as an opener.

I bet it feels incredible to be inside her when she moves like that, working over a dick like it's hers.

Darius is hers, though. And she's his. Tonight she's also mine, but I didn't expect this amount of control with the submissive, needy way she acts with me. With Darius, her movements are confident, skilled, and sexy as hell. Did I stumble across a switchy sexpot and didn't realize it? Even after the orgasm that felt like it emptied my balls, I'm hard again.

I've watched Darius fuck women before, but this—what he and Jolene are doing on my bed—isn't that. I'm witnessing what making love is, and as much as I want to join, it feels intrusive to do so.

They talk to each other—not dirty talk, but kind conversation. Darius smiles up at Jolene, and his previous words about her being a goddess weren't false. He worships her. I can't imagine feeling that.

I rub at the tightness in my chest and get a jolt from the scratches Jolene left on me. They tingle and sear, as if she branded me for the night, and then—fortunately—need replaces the unsettling warmth inside me. I have to fuck her again. What else will she do when she's that far gone? I cross the room, eyes still honed on Jolene's hips and how her silky hair sways against them.

Darius grips her thighs as he gets closer, giving in to the movements. "Babes. So hot." He thrusts up into her, and my cock jerks.

Jolene's hooded gaze moves to me as I pull the vibrator box from my nightstand.

I ignore her pretty wide eyes and go back to the bathroom to wash the silver wand. When I return, Darius has Jolene on her back.

Her tan legs wrap around his hips as he rocks into her, kissing her, close and gentle. Good. She's going to need that before what I do to her.

When Darius glances back at me, he grins and rolls, bringing Jolene back on top of him, beckoning me with a flick of his fingers.

And just like that, I'm invited back into their moment.

I crawl behind her, straddle Darius's legs and press my cock against Jolene's lower back. I move her hair aside and lap at her damp skin, inhaling her addictive scent, then run the wand across her hip. She's so damn biteable when she jerks at new sensations. I nip her ear. "I got this for you yesterday when I was driving back home."

Her head drops back against my shoulder, and she moans as I roll it up her stomach and just under the swell of her breast. "Were you planning on seducing me, Arlo?"

"Quite the opposite," I whisper in her ear. "You've been seducing me—parading around in those tiny fucking pants and no bra under your tank. Putting your perfect ass in the air, asking for it to be reddened by my palm." I grip the crest of her hip and speed up her rhythm, matching it so we're grinding together. I run the toy over her nipple. "Did you want me to take you?" I know the truth, but want her to admit it.

She nods, lips parted, gasping at the ceiling.

"Yes, she did," Darius groans. "Close." He bares his teeth, working on staying in control, which he's not. I fucking love this moment.

I wrap my arm around her and flick on the vibrator.

Jolene sucks in a breath and arches. Her "fuck!" is so sweetly rasped.

I force her to keep rhythm, holding the vibrator against one nipple, then the other. Her left is more sensitive and makes her buck harder. Whimper louder.

"Babes, babes, fuck, Joles." Darius's urgency makes me smile. "Feel you."

Then they're both falling apart, crying out, cursing, and clutching at each other and me. My chest swells with pride. I don't let up on Jolene's nipple until she slumps forward, then I turn off the vibrator. I stroke Darius's cheek, and he kisses my palm, then Jolene's lips.

Besides the heavy breaths, it's quiet as I roll on another condom.

Darius turns Jolene onto her back, and both of them hiss when their bodies separate.

Jolene gives a quiet giggle, eyes closed and lips quirked up. She looks flushed and well fucked. After me, she'll look completely wrecked.

I push her compliant legs apart and stare down, breathless. Cum drips out of her, and fuck it all if I don't want that to be my mess inside her too. I want to mark her so deep, she's reminded of me tomorrow when a little more works its way out of her each hour. And when it's all gone, I'll put more right back into her.

I've never gone bare. Never. It's too risky and makes things too complicated—like now. There's no room for complications between us, and yet...

Out of frustration, I suck a dark hickey on her hip. *My fucking hip.* I suck another onto the top of her breast. "Sleepy, angel?" I grab the vibrator. Fuck four orgasms. How about eight? How about a hundred? I will give her so much pleasure, she'll never ever forget this night, me, or what I've opened in her world.

"Mm-hmm." She blinks her tired eyes at me, tempting me to snuggle against her, but that's not why she's here. She's too beautiful for words, but she's in my bed to be fucked. It's best to remember that.

I lean, nudging the head of my condomed-cock against her cum-soaked pussy. I place the vibrator against her clit. "Time to wake up." I turn it on and start fucking.

She splays out as if she's being electrocuted, back bowed, head digging into the mattress, a raspy scream tearing from her throat.

I hold her tight and unleash what I am: aggressive, intense, too much for anyone to handle.

Except Jolene wraps her legs around me. Her arms too. She doesn't try to escape. She pulls me closer. Tighter. The only word she echoes is "Arlo." My name is a chant, a sweet song that makes my balls tighten and my chest tingle. She rocks against the vibrator in time with my thrusts.

I glower down at this fucking dirty fallen angel coming undone underneath me—because of me. How dare she be exactly what I wasn't expecting? She wasn't supposed to be this level of good for me.

She whimpers, clawing at my hair with one hand, my back with the other. And—fuck it all—she bites my collarbone as she comes, screaming around my skin, shaking even more than the vibrator, her pussy trying to clamp me to her.

But I don't stop. I fuck her through one orgasm, then another.

Tears mar her gorgeous face. Her hair is a tangled mess from my hands and her reckless writhing.

After what I think is her fourth—or maybe the contractions of her pussy are just constant now—my dick can't take any more. Growling, I throw the vibrator, pull out of her, tug off the condom and orgasm so hard, my vision pulses in time to the spurts streaking her tits and stomach.

Darius is beside me, fisting his cock, painting her skin with his cum too. I never thought of myself as someone who enjoys marking in this way, but it's gorgeous. She's gorgeous. Our clean, sweet little Jolene, now a beautiful disaster.

Darius nuzzles my cheek. "You good?"

Fuck no, I'm not good. I'm wrecked. I nod.

He grabs a shirt to clean up Jolene.

As soon as he's taken the last swipe at her flushed skin, she bolts up and into *my* arms.

I hold her tight, my brows furrowed, confusion stealing my thoughts. Women don't come to me for comfort like this. They come to me to get fucked, demeaned, and pushed away.

Darius is the good guy. The hugger. The aftercare administrator, if that's needed.

So why do I pick her up, carry her to my bathroom, make sure the water is warm enough, and step inside, tugging Darius in too?

I don't know.

Chapter Thirty-Five

Darius Heals

DARIUS

My inner bliss wars with concern because both Jolene and Arlo are quiet. I expect it from Jolene, but Arlo...

There was a moment when he lost it. I'm not sure if it's because Jolene's need and actions were far more than he expected, or if it was because everything was so different from what we've ever done before. If it had been like a hookup in the past, what we just did together would have been colder, more transactional—an orgasm for each of us before he smacked her ass and told her to get the fuck out. He definitely wouldn't have picked any other woman up like she was glass and carried her to the shower.

But I get it. It was a lot for me to watch the two people I love most find pleasure in each other. I can't even pick a favorite point; how he watched and touched her, how she gave herself to both of us so freely even though she was nervous, her overwhelmed tears when she needed me and her clutching desperation when she needed him. My heart feels wide open. What if this can work?

But what if it can't? There was nothing simple about this evening. *Clearly.*

Arlo stands awkwardly in the shower, still holding her, his broad body blocking her from the water. Has he ever showered with someone before? Women get chilly in the misty remnants of the water streams.

I turn him around so the warmth hits her back.

She jerks like she might have been asleep, and Arlo glares at me. When she gives a sigh and snuggles in closer, resting her face against his neck, I raise my eyebrows at him.

His brow furrows further. *Interesting.* He really hasn't a clue what he's doing. And I thought I knew everything about him.

I grin, reaching over Arlo's shoulder to tuck Jolene's damp hair behind her ear. "Feet down, babes. Let's get you cleaned up."

She slowly unfurls from Arlo and slips around him to get closer to me. Arlo's shower is big, but not three-person-big. Especially when one is huge and confused.

Grabbing the soap, I sweep Jolene's hair aside and kiss her jaw. "Are you sore?"

That seems to snap her out of her stupor, and she leans into me for a kiss, though keeps a hand on Arlo's chest, like her palm has fused there. "A little."

Arlo watches me touch and caress Jolene with the soap and then joins in with meticulous determination, following my slow and calm method as we clean our girl from top to toes, being extra careful around the sore marks he left on her.

She takes turns resting against each of us, soaking in our attention.

We wash ourselves with Jolene helping. When she wraps soapy fingers around my cock, I hiss out a breath, and she grins. Good. She wouldn't tease if she were disappointed or feeling out of sorts.

She turns to run a gentle hand over Arlo.

His eyes close, and he leans against the tile, leaving her to do what she wants.

She's not the only one who relishes touch. When we're rinsed, she goes up on tiptoes to whisper to him. "I don't know what to say."

He wraps an arm around her, tugging her close. "Say you want to do that again."

I raise my eyebrows, as I'm back to wondering if this can work. She just wanted to experiment, but she's going to want to think things over.

She surprises me by nodding. "I want to do that again." She puts her attention on me, though stays in his arms. "Baby?"

"That was... yeah," I say. "I'd love to do more. Anything you want."

Arlo touches her chin, moving her face in his direction, and kisses her sweetly again. But when he turns the water off, it's like the calm magic of this peaceful afterglow slips down the drain. "Everyone, get out and go to bed."

I snag a towel and do a half-assed drying job, then wrap Jolene in it and steer her toward our room.

Arlo doesn't look up from drying off.

"Goodnight," Jolene says, pausing at the bedroom doorway.

"Night." He wraps the towel around his waist and steps closer, backing her out, and shutting the door.

The hallway is too quiet and gives off an eerie chill that I'm not fond of. Did he only ask to see what she'd say?

Her brows furrow as much as mine. In our room, I brush Jolene's wet hair and settle us under the duvet.

"You really want to do that again?" I ask, kissing her slack lips.

"Only if he does." She's asleep a minute later.

I'm not.

***

Jolene sleeps through my alarm. I wish I could. I begrudgingly drag my tired ass out of bed and get dressed for work.

I find Arlo in the kitchen, making coffee. He hands me a cup. "Update."

Taking a sip, I raise an eyebrow at him. "She's sleeping. As of last night, she wants a repeat *if* you do. Now your turn."

He purses his lips. "That was not typical."

I'm so glad he's been thinking too. After feeling booted from his room, I was worried he was going to pretend last night wasn't the enormous deal it was. I nod. "There's nothing about Jolene that's typical."

He breaks out in a grin and runs his hand over it like he can hide it. "I'm getting that. I'm at a bit of a loss on what to do here."

Please don't run from this, friend. "What do you want to do?"

"Skip work and go wake her up with my cock. But I was hard on her body last night and don't want to hurt her."

My insides do a dance, and I hide my smile with another sip of coffee. When I can contain myself, I clear my throat. "That's a new feeling."

"It is." Arlo doesn't seem to enjoy that thought.

I grip his shoulder and meet his eyes. "I know that was different, but in the best way."

He tilts his head. "You're seriously fine with this?"

I let his words sink in, and really think about it. I love both of these people and understand them implicitly. If there is one thing I trust about a future with both of them, it's that they would never try to hurt me. So yes, I'm more than fine. In my ideal world, I have them both forever. I smile and nod. "I'm still processing how right last night felt."

Arlo's shoulders sink with a sigh. "Okay. So now…?"

"Take it a day at a time, brother. We take care of her, she'll take care of us, and all will be well."

"Darius." He runs his hand over the back of his head. "What if it's not? What if she does that silent thinking thing she does and decides I'm too much, or that none of this is what she wants?" He scrunches his nose. "She's not… not what I expected."

And this is where it gets tricky and potentially painful because, as much as Arlo demands to be a solo being in this world, he craves pleasure and pleasing. It's why I love him, and why Jolene will love him. If he'll accept that what happened in his past isn't the situation he's in today. If he'll allow another into his life and get to know her. It takes so long for him to put his guard down that he might need to be challenged to put his guard down. But I'm getting ahead of myself again.

I hug him. Just plaster myself to his body, because it feels needed. "Be exactly who you are. You don't need to hold back with her. If it doesn't feel right, then we go back to being roommates, watch movies and eat dinner together. Celebrate each other's accomplishments." I step back from him. "But no attachments, right?"

The muscles of his jaw twitch. "Yeah."

We'll see.

Chapter Thirty-Six

Jolene Walks Funny

JOLENE

I hobble—literally hobble—down the hall.

Okay, I may have been a little overzealous with Arlo last night, but they wrapped me up in the moment. That moment was superb.

Now, it feels like my legs are going to fall off, and between those pained legs is an ache that is not sexy in the least. But my cheeks are still flushed, and my lips are puffy and magazine-shoot worthy. If I were still doing things like that, the makeup artist would have a happy fit all over me. At least I'll look decent when I meet Darius's coworkers and boss.

I warm up coffee and settle onto the couch, propping my legs up with pillows, my laptop on my stomach. It's not the most comfortable way to work, but it's not like I'm really working. I'm just researching stocks and cruising the internet for job listings in Chicago. My curiosity takes over, and I check Lexington jobs as well. There are accounting and tax jobs galore, lots of medical, but nothing that I want to do.

Ha. I'm not missing anything. Now if Mom calls, I have knowledge behind me. I'm prepared. At least in job discussions. I don't know what I'd say about Darius and Arlo, not that she'd ask.

By the time I'm leaving to meet Darius for lunch, I've shot off another two resumes for jobs that are not perfect, but could grow into decent opportunities. One company is new without a horse in the race yet. But I'm jobless, so literally anything on the same track as my career choice looks appealing.

I researched my dream company again. The building is shiny and modern, and the professionally done photographs of employees make everyone look happy and well-paid. It's so perfect.

What does Arlo's office look like? Modern tech with shiny chrome fixtures and neon lights? That's what I picture. I should ask him, because it's not like I'll ever see it. Talking about it might freak him out though, since we're not getting involved in each other's lives or any of that nonsense.

Each bump on the train jars my insides and reminds me of Arlo. The way his fingers dug into me to hold me close, then were so gentle as he held me close in an entirely different way. He's a perfect conundrum. Hard, soft, rough, gentle. So wild.

The slacks I'm wearing shift over the hickey he left on my hip, and my nipples tingle—not unpleasantly. Is he also replaying what we did over and over again?

By the time I'm off the platform and wandering the corporate block looking for Darius's office, the uncomfortable ache between my legs is uncomfortably wet. I push those thoughts away. The ones that hope Arlo pushes me for more tonight and maybe tomorrow morning and afternoon and then at night. Though he clearly doesn't do nights. He shooed me right out the door. That didn't feel great, but maybe he doesn't sleep well with others around. If I hadn't been so exhausted, I might have snuck back in just to see what he'd do.

Darius's office has typical older corporate office decor: short-pile patterned carpet and nicely framed stock photos on the walls.

The receptionist's eyes widen when I tell him I'm here to see Darius, and then he's on the phone singing, "She's here."

But it's not Darius who greets me. It's three of his coworkers who practically run up to tell me how funny, smart, and valued Darius is as they lead me to his office. Only one woman glares at me from a distance, and I'm sure it's because there's no shot at a date with him now that I'm here. She might be right. After last night, I'm not so sure about anything. I nearly stumble when it hits me that maybe she's had sex with Darius before. And who am I to judge? His best friend made me come like a hundred times last night. Do I really have any right to question anything sexually anymore?

"Hi," Darius says as he steps around his desk and pulls me into his arms. "You got the full welcoming committee."

Two coworkers lingering in the doorway coo about our sweetness while the other jests about getting a room. She has no idea what we do, and my face is so hot. Fortunately, Darius has a question about a project, and then they ask me about the job search, each of them giving me encouragement that the right one hasn't come along yet and it will.

Darius introduces me to his boss, Martina, who is terrifying to meet, but then, certain things she says remind me of Arlo.

As we're leaving for lunch, she stares at me from her doorway and scoldingly points. "You better wait for the right thing." I could see how her tone might rub someone the wrong way, but it feels like she has faith that I deserve what I want, and I'd disappoint her if I took something that wasn't the right fit.

I backtrack to hug her. "Thank you. I'll do the best I can."

With her wide smile, she seems to like that answer.

Darius squeezes my fingers in the hallway. "What do you think of Martina?"

I grin, antsy energy twinkling in my chest. "I love her."

He huffs a laugh and nudges me. "How did I know you would?"

"Cause you know me."

He hums at that.

At lunch, among the calming scent of curry and the not calming—but super fun—Bollywood music pumping from the sound system, Darius sets his elbows on the table. "You seem good. Are you after last night?"

I lean closer to him. "I can't stop thinking about it."

He grins. "Me either. I think you shocked Arlo." I wince, but he rubs the back of my hand. "In such a good way."

"You two discussed"—I look at the ceiling for words—"Um, everything?"

"No." His eyes twinkle in the bright lunchtime lights of the Indian restaurant. "He was just checking in. He does that. I told him you were sleeping in but were interested in more, at least as of last night. Are you still?"

"When I can move my legs correctly again." I can't stop my grin, but it appears Darius can't either.

"Is he? Um, interested in more of that?" It felt like it until it didn't.

Darius purses his lips. "He will have to answer that."

"Of course he will."

"It's a good thing. You two need to be talking to each other about these things, just like I talk to him and I talk to you. Do you know what I mean?" The corners of his eyes crease.

I take his hand. "I get it. Mostly."

It's easier to talk to Darius at the moment. There's just a lot going on, and maybe now isn't the best time to get this involved in something that's just an experiment. Still. I can't seem to help it.

I lean in and cup my hand next to my mouth. "I like being told what to do."

Darius raises an eyebrow. "Really?" His tone is sarcastic, but he holds a serious expression. "Then order what you already know you're going to order."

I crinkle my nose. "Maybe I'll branch out. I seem to enjoy doing that as well."

When the server arrives, I picture Arlo rolling his eyes at me as I order the tikka masala because it's fantastic. I won't tire of it like he says. I'm not someone who tires of the best things in life.

Darius laughs at me.

I just smirk. "Tikka masala for life, baby."

When I get back to our building, Sheena welcomes me with silence and a glare.

If she only knew the type of delicious punishment I got last night. If I were like some contestants I've come across at pageants, I'd tell her. Detail it out while watching her hatred bubble over. I'm better than that, and I know it. Arlo knows it. So I straighten my spine, lift my chin, and smile like I'm walking across the stage. In a way, I think I am. She doesn't get the real me because she doesn't care who I am.

Upstairs. I take a salt bath, touch every mark Arlo left on me, then wrap myself in everything fuzzy before I park it back on the couch for more stock and job research, but I'm distracted.

I'm already staring at the door when the lock turns and the door creaks open.

Arlo steps in and drops his bag, making my heartbeat kick up. Leaning his back against the door, he unbuttons the first button of his shirt, then the second, keeping those intense eyes fully on me. "I need you on your knees right now."

Chapter Thirty-Seven

Arlo Questions

ARLO

Work was a torturous day of meetings that could have been emails or should not have occurred at all. Especially when my thoughts were all on Jolene's mouth and moans and the way she trembled under me.

My body wants her so much, it trembles now.

I'm too worked up and should walk away—go hit the bag, masturbate in the shower, do anything except her, but I can't halt this pull to her. I just need a little more. A marathon to fuck her out of my system and clear my head.

She blinks at me from the couch, looking curled up, cozy, and frustratingly cute. But when she slides off the couch, she winces hard as she bends her legs.

The normal pride I feel when a night with me wrecks a woman's body doesn't land right. It's subdued by an odd guilt and the need to check her over. I could give her an out. My jaw tightens. I'm not the boyfriend, and I'm not sweet.

She shifts to her knees and nibbles her pretty, puffy lip.

"Good girl." I step close enough that my zipper nearly touches her nose. "Still think you can handle my dick?"

There's hesitation and a furrow between her brows as she nods. She leans back so subtly, I'm not even sure she realizes her movement.

"Then why don't you want to?"

I expect it's because she's sore or because I'm just walking in from work and she has that thing with bathing. A vicious inner voice tells me she didn't enjoy last night as much as I did, and she never wants me to touch her again.

What I don't expect is for her to twist her pretty lips back and forth, take a deep breath and say, "Are you sure *you* want to?"

More than she could know. "Yes. Why?"

"Because of last night."

I tug my pants at the knees and squat so I can look her in the eyes evenly. "What about last night?" It's a struggle not to lean in and taste her lips.

"I'm just—I wasn't sure how you felt after. You kinda…"

Was a second from a panic attack about wanting her in my bed? "Went cold?"

She nods. "Is that normal?"

"Yes." Because it is. What wasn't normal was pressing my forehead to the closed bedroom door and wishing I could sink through it and follow them.

There's no relief on Jolene's face though, and that makes the firmness of my cock a distant memory.

"Is that a problem?" Here we go. Of course, it was a problem.

She fidgets with her fingers. "Was that like it always is? I mean, was I different?" She rolls her eyes. "That sounds needy. I'm not, it's just, this is new and I don't have rules yet or know what to—"

I lean on my knees and cover her chatty, insecure lips with mine. I shouldn't be kissing her or gripping her neck to tug her closer or edging the tip of my tongue between her teeth until she opens with a groan, but I most definitely am. The relief from her floral scent in my nostrils and her taste is instantaneous. Was she different? Unfortunately, yes. When she relaxes in my grip, I move from her mouth and down her jaw. "Call me an asshole for kicking you out of my room."

Her lips quirk up. "It was kinda an asshole thing to do."

My chest tightens, and I let go of her neck so I don't hurt her with my fisting fingers. "Want me to change?" I prepare myself for her to tell me to be nicer, sweeter, more reasonable.

"Change clothes?"

"What? No. Me. The asshole. Should *I* change?"

She tilts, then shakes her head, leaning in to rub our noses together. "No. I like how you are, but am still getting to know you. I was worried that I had done something wrong."

At this point, I'm not sure she has it in her to do wrong. "You like how I am?"

She just hasn't had enough time.

Smiling, she pokes my chest. "I never know what you're going to do, but then, what you do is really fun." Her voice drops to a sex kitten tone, and my dick wakes back up. "And it's okay to need space after... stuff. It was intense."

"It was." I thumb her cheekbone, then slowly trace her jaw, following that to her chin, which I gently pinch, holding her in place as I drop a kiss on her lips. "You were so brave and fucking sexy while you took us. I wanted to wake you up with my cock this morning and have been hard all damn day thinking about last night."

Her lashes flutter, and she licks her bottom lip. "Do you want some help with that, um, problem?"

Fuck, she's in for it... but carefully because every movement she makes is stiff. I stand. "Take my cock out of my pants."

My demand to get back to getting us off seems to surprise her, but only for a second. Then she's eagerly undoing my pants and staring at my half-hard cock.

I cross my arms. "Play with the piercing. You want to, don't you?"

"It won't hurt you?"

I'm unable to stop my grin. "It feels good as long as you don't yank on it too hard. Other than that, use your tongue, fingers, teeth—but gently."

She stares at my cock, which hardens at her attention.

"Jolene, I want your mouth on my dick right now." I'm not babying her reluctance unless she really doesn't want to.

She tilts her head at me. "No condom?"

"Do you want me to use one?"

"No." Her answer comes quickly, and she blushes. "I just thought you didn't do that."

I thread my fingers through her hair. "I don't typically. But I went to the clinic to get tested last week just to be safe, and everything is negative. You're all clear as well, right?"

"Yes."

"Good." I give her a tug toward my now-aching dick. "Open that pretty mouth and taste my cock." The need to be inside her is overwhelming.

She touches the ball of my piercing with a hesitant finger, then looks up at me, sneaking her tongue out to see how that feels. Her eyes widen at the first swipe, then she traces circles around the top ball of the piercing, then trails to the bottom one and back up. She catches the ball with her teeth and sucks on it. The pressure boils my blood. This is the biggest tease I think I've ever experienced.

My lips part as my breathing quickens. "You're killing me."

Her fingers drift over my tip to catch a drop of pre-cum, which she slips over the head in the gentlest of strokes. "In a good way?" Her voice is a purr, and I'm wondering if she's meaning to be this sexy or if it's just her natural state.

"In a tortuous way."

That makes her smile. "Good."

"Bad girl." My breath catches as she wraps those perfect, hot lips over me. I could finish now. Just jet cum all over her face like a teenager with no control over himself.

She kisses me—an actual, soft kiss over the head of my cock. Then another. And another. I'm going to jump out of my skin.

Gritting my teeth, I tighten my grip on her hair. "You have one more minute to tease me before I fuck your mouth. If you need me to stop, pinch my hip. Understand?"

Heat billows from her gaze. "Yes, sir."

She takes her full minute to run the point of her tongue over my length and balls, lips tipping up as I grunt in frustrated pleasure.

I cup her face with both hands. "Open your fucking mouth." When she complies, I slowly press in, groaning long when she sucks me deeper, then gags. I let her breathe, and when she nods, we do it again. And again. She feels too good. "I'm going to open this throat, angel. Relax." After she gulps a breath, I press in, pushing through her gag.

She struggles and pinches my leg.

I drop to my knees and hold her face. "You okay?"

She nods. "Sorry. I thought I was going to throw up."

I brush my lips over hers. "No apologies. I'll slow down." She shakes her head, but I nod. "You will enjoy this too, and puking on my dick is not sexy."

Her shoulders sink with relief. "I want to try again."

"And you will." I slip my hand under her fuzzy shirt to play with her nipples until her eyes go half-lidded. "I plan to have my cock in your mouth a lot." We kiss until we're both shifting with need.

She moves down, kissing my neck and gripping my dick.

I stand again, and she takes me in, trying to force me down. While it feels good, I want her on board and doing it right. "Another day."

"But I want to now." She kisses my dick again as if it's my or Darius's lips. Does he get these teasing little dick kisses? "Teach me?"

That was one sweet beg, and I'll reward her for it. I thumb her cheek. "We go slowly. Do not force yourself. Trust me to take you there."

With gentle motions, I talk her through a deep fuck, gag, deeper fuck and hold, then let her breathe.

Her eyes tear and spit drips from her chin. She is everything right now.

We find a rhythm, and after a bit, she's playing with my balls and humming around my cock. The gagging has stopped.

I whisper praises through growls and clenched teeth. "My good girl likes to take my cock deep. This is the best fucking mouth. You're perfect. Do that again, just like that." Then, as I'm edging closer... "Where do you want my cum?"

That throws her off, and she gags hard and backs away to cough.

I grip her and pull her back to me. "Answer." The glare she gives me with her mouth full of my cock makes me chuckle, and I pull her off, leaning to kiss her perfect mouth. "Now."

"My chest—tits. Please."

Best girl.

I give her another hard kiss, then jack myself as she pulls her shirt off. She pushes my hand away and takes over. I gather her hair and thrust into her mouth. "Look at me."

Her gaze latches onto mine, and electricity jolts down my spine and into my balls.

I press in hard and whimper. Yes, this woman made me whimper. It's a sound of pained prayer because this is going to be out of control and there's no stopping it.

Jolene doesn't balk, though. She sucks me hard and moves her hand up and down my shaft like she's just as crazed as I am.

My dick swells, and I groan and pull from her mouth, then jet cum all over her gorgeous tits as I curse, grunt, and call her name in a pleasure-induced chant as my knees go weak.

Her covered chest rises and falls with her quick breaths. Fucking beautiful woman. I grab her under her arms and toss her back on the couch, jerking at her sleep pants and panties.

"Sore," she mumbles, though lifts her hips to help me.

"Do not move." I toss her garments behind me and head to the kitchen.

Chapter Thirty-Eight

Jolene's Aching Everything

JOLENE

Arlo doesn't return from the kitchen with paper towels. He comes back with a piece of ice between his fingertips. I never know what to expect from him, but ice wasn't on the list.

"Um, ice?"

He wears his mischievous grin. "Of course. Cold helps with soreness and—" His gaze lands between my legs.

I flinch when I close them.

He glares. "Swelling." He drops to his knees, but just studies the hickey on my hip, the mess on my chest, and my sore lips.

"But—"

He pushes my knees apart and teases the ice at the crease between my leg and vagina. My words disappear in a squeal.

His focus between my legs is sharp—like he's so into what he's doing to me, it's taking every ounce of his concentration. "Here, angel? Is this where you're sore?"

"No." I laugh and launch a pillow at him, which he blocks. The movement reminds me of the cooling cum on my chest. I go still. Do not make a mess on the couch.

He kisses my thigh when I expect a nip and then runs the ice over my labia. I arch and gasp. It doesn't exactly feel good or bad, but it feels a lot.

"Poor little pussy had quite the night." Arlo leans and kisses my clit, making me jerk, because his lips are so hot compared to the ice. "Did you like getting pounded hard?" He looks up into my eyes, as if everything rides on my answer.

"I... did."

"But?" He raises his eyebrows.

I shake my head. This is so hard to talk about. "No buts. I liked what we did. All of it." So much I'm not sure what is wrong with me, but something must be.

He hums and licks my clit this time. "So when this pretty pussy is feeling better, does it want to be pummeled again?" He pushes the ice inside me.

Gasping for air, I widen my legs, and whimper what I hope is a yes.

Arlo must have heard what he wanted, because he gets back to playing with my clit and pressing the ice cube so it slips in and out of me.

I grip the back of the couch and cry out. Does he like this done too? Maybe I should bring some ice in and—

He trails fingers up my stomach, through the mess he left on me and up to play with my nipple. It's slick and so sensitive. This—what we're doing—is so incredibly dirty. It makes me rethink everything I thought I knew about sex and what I like. I still like those other things, but why does him, stroking my nipples with his cum, make between my legs clench painfully? Maybe it's the ice. Or us, and what we can do together.

I'm close, rocking my hips at him, seeking his mouth. I feel every movement as my muscles tighten, and somehow that makes it even hotter. What is wrong with me? Jesus, the rumors this would start.

"Jolene, look at me."

I drag my eyes from watching his fingers and find intense blue.

He licks his wet bottom lip. "I can tell when you think about things that are not what I'm doing to you. Usually that would mean punishment for you, but I'm still reeling from that orgasm and I'd rather talk it out. What's making you tense up and edge away from me?"

"Sorry," I whisper.

"None of that." He inserts a finger and plays with the small bit of ice remaining. "What are you thinking about?"

My eyes burn, and I want to get up and run, but he's gripping my thigh and slowly swirling his finger inside me. I swallow hard. "That I shouldn't like this so much." I flinch in wait for the slap on my thigh or a scoff, but there's none.

"Why do you think you're not worthy of pleasure?"

"It's not that." I groan when he presses the ice in deeper, sinking two fingers into me. It's hard to concentrate. "It's—" I signal to my sticky chest. "I shouldn't like this, right? I'm sensitive to smells and cleanliness, yet this turns me on. A lot. That's not normal." I grimace at my words. "That was judgy of me. It's not that you're not normal or—"

He laughs. "I'm not normal. I'm okay with that."

"How?" The question just slips out, but I really want to know. How does he live so freely?

Arlo moves closer, thumbs my clit and plays with my nipple again. "It's just us here. Why should we give a fuck what others think about us making each other feel good? If you like my cum, if it gets you off, who does that hurt?"

I don't have an answer.

He lifts his slick finger from my nipple and raises his eyebrow in question.

I shift to take his finger between my lips, tasting the bitter salt that is unpleasant, but completely worth the fire it stokes in Arlo's eyes.

"So fucking hot, angel."

Licking his finger clean, I roll my hips to get him to work between my legs again. "Tell me it's okay to be dirty, Arlo."

He moves his hand to my neck and squeezes. "You want permission?"

I nod.

"How about a command instead?" He thumbs my clit in rapid circles, and I bite back a cry at the electricity he's weaving through me. "You are my filthy fucking girl. My whore. My slut—"

"Not slut." I shake my head. "I've been called that too much. Not sexy."

He nods, tightening his grip on my throat, making my blood pulse in my ears. It's not too hard or threatening, but it could be if he wanted it to be. "You will be so dirty with me, Jolene. If you want something from me, want to try something, you will ask me and I will give it to you. I'll never shame you unless you want to try that, too. Do you understand?"

"Yes." I struggle to get closer.

He rewards me by grinding his palm against my clit.

"Thank you, sir." When I come so hard, a universe of stars blocks my vision, I realize something very dangerous. I trust him *with me*.

This exploration I'm doing has backfired, because I can't imagine being denied *him*. All of him—the intensity, the teasing, the incredible, creative sex. Dammit, he's my tikka masala. I can't get enough, and I don't think there's a way to go back after this moment.

Chapter Thirty-Nine

Darius Lets It Happen

DARIUS

"Here goes." Jolene finishes kissing me hello, sighs, and picks up her buzzing phone. "Hi, Mom." She sounds far more chipper than she appears as she tucks the phone between her ear and shoulder and continues to put away the folded laundry she's probably worked on most of the afternoon.

I grin as Arlo peeks in after changing into sweats and a tank, like he can't get enough of seeing Jolene, and needs to wander the hall just to get a glimpse. I feel the same.

She gives him a coy smile and blushes as she talks to Donna about her week and visiting me at work. Then her grin lowers into a frown and her shoulder rise. She crawls on the bed, lying on her stomach. "No, I have enough." I take over putting the last of the laundry away and go to make dinner, but hesitate at the door when she says in a downtrodden voice, "I'll start chipping in as soon as I get a job."

I wince for her, and Arlo, who's making his way back to his room, sees it.

"Everything okay?" he asks, coming back to look past me into the room.

"Just Donna doing Donna things," I whisper. "She's not handling the move well and is just throwing bullshit around to get Joles back *home*." We thought the surprise visit would help things, but nope. If anything, Donna has doubled her efforts to make Jolene realize she doesn't belong in Chicago, from sending her crime and unemployment reports to making Jolene feel like she's drowning in debt, which she isn't. Not yet.

Arlo glares toward Jolene, probably wishing he could catch both sides of the conversation. He shouldn't. There's nothing good on the other side of that line.

"No, I still have savings." Jolene rests her forehead on her palm. "I know that, but I have to use some until I get a paycheck. That's kinda what savings are for." She sighs loud. I might as well draw a bath and head to the store for wine. Comforting Jolene every time her mother calls is getting out of hand. "I applied to three more this week. No, but—I know. Mom, I know."

Arlo steps into the room, and I'm not stopping him.

Jolene looks up when he clears his throat, and signals to hang up. Her brows furrow, and she shakes her head.

He straightens his shoulders. Here we go.

Maybe I should intervene. Or not.

Donna makes Jolene feel like shit every time they talk, and maybe him ending the call would help both of them get the point.

But Arlo doesn't snatch the phone and hang up. He crawls over Jolene, pressing her down when she tries to push herself up.

"Hey Mom?" She switches to her other ear when Arlo brushes her hair aside and kisses her neck. "Mom, um." She pushes at him—as well as she can pinned stomach down—and looks to me like I'm going to help.

I grin at her.

She glares, mouthing, "Stop it," to Arlo.

Arlo whispers to her and grinds against her backside.

Jolene growls, and the struggle begins. "No, it's fine. Everything is—" she gasps, then winces. She kicks him on the ass with a freed foot.

I cover my mouth with my palm to keep quiet.

"I have to go." She throws an elbow.

Arlo chuckles, easily blocking her, then re-pins her leg.

She stabs relentlessly at her phone, then checks it twice to make sure she hung up. "What the fuck, Arlo?" There's my girl. She tries to twist, but there's no moving him.

"Careful with that dirty mouth, angel, or I'll put it to good use."

"You're such an asshole." She gets a leg out from under him again, but Arlo takes advantage of that and lets her turn enough so that their bodies line up.

He gets his arm looped under her leg, stretching her wide, and pins her wrists over her head. "Your mother was being an asshole, not me."

I nod at that statement. "That's true. You're doing just fine. You know that, right?"

Her nose crinkles. "Intrusive eavesdropping is not okay."

"No?" He leans to nip at her lip.

She turns her head, defiantly escaping his kisses. "No."

"Why? She's making you feel like shit. That's not okay. Darius is right. You're doing just fine."

She stops struggling. "I'm not though. I'm dipping into savings even without paying rent and have no interviews set up."

My heart cracks for her. We'd both had so much hope that everything would snap together the second she arrived. Like all the waiting was worth an instant package deal reward—being together, getting a job, having Donna be fucking proud for once—boom, happy ever after. She just needed to get here. I'm so glad she is. But it doesn't feel permanent yet.

Arlo kisses her cheek. "They will come. Until then, you don't have to pay for rent or anything, for that matter."

I raise my eyebrows at that.

She doesn't, not yet, but we'd talked about all this before, and I'm the one supporting her until she gets on her feet. It's tight, but manageable, especially with the new promotion.

"That's true." I slide onto the bed beside them and stroke Jolene's hair.

She tips her head toward my touch. "Yes, I do, Arlo. I'm not going to just do nothing—be a kept woman—or whatever."

Arlo toys with her lips. It's not quite a kiss. "No?"

She deadpans. "Not even funny."

He grins at her. "Have you checked the stocks you told us about lately?"

"Which ones? I've been watching Burgundy. It's slowly rising."

"So distracted." He brushes his lips over hers. "Spigno. It's been on a steady increase, but started catapulting two days ago."

Her eyes widen. "Seriously? I have that one on a five-day check calendar because its stock moves slowly."

Arlo huffs. "There's nothing slow about it. I need you to watch it for me if I need to sell. At the moment, we've made a lot. More than rent. More than rent and utilities. You're doing fine. A job will come along and scoop you up because you know what you're doing."

My heart feels like it's going to burst from my chest. *We've made a lot.* Does he even realize what he just said?

And I'm not the only one.

"Um, *we've* made a lot?" Jolene asks, pursing her lips.

Arlo smirks. "The only reason I bought a thousand shares is because of you." His eyes go up as he thinks. "It was only thirty at first, but then I checked out the company, liked how ethical they were and how much their employees raved about them. Companies like that go far. So I bought more." He shrugs as if that's no big deal. "Too bad you weren't right about Burgundy blowing up."

Jolene huffs. "Give it a damn minute. That company is where it's at."

He hums. "So, should I buy more from them?"

"You should." Jolene nibbles at her smiling lips. She needed a win so bad.

I cup Arlo's face, hoping he picks up on just how thankful I am for him. "Told you she's always right."

"You did." He lets her wrists go. "All better?"

She purses her lips. "Nearly. Except for the interrupting phone call thing."

"Door was open," I say. "That's public domain."

She gives my curls a tug. "It's intrusive, even if well-intentioned."

Arlo runs his nose up her neck and gives an open suck to her pulse. "I don't like it when people make you feel like shit."

My lower stomach tightens.

Jolene's squirms differ from when she was trying to escape. "I wouldn't like that either if it were happening to you."

Their lips meet, and my heart takes off in a sprint. That's the closest thing to a confession of their feelings for each other I've seen yet.

Chapter Forty

Arlo Needs More

ARLO

When Ian and I have meals together, they're more of a confessional—sharing information that my mother says would be more fitting for a priest, so I can ask for penance.

But Ian knows what kind of man I am. I didn't go into details about the sex fest I had three days ago, or the oral fest two days ago, or the breast fest last night when Darius played with Jolene's tits while I fingered her. I fucked those perfect globes while she jacked off Darius until we both made a mess of her. No... no details for Ian beyond, "I got caught up with them and it was damn good."

We head toward the exit of the hole-in-the-wall sandwich shop that has grown into our spot. It's dark, and uncaring of fancy shit. The focus is on the best sandwiches and kettle chips the city offers, served on a cheap plate. I think they pick up the mismatched barware from thrift shops and estate sales. I love it.

He steps outside when I hold the door open for him. "I want to meet your girl next weekend."

I'm not sure how I feel about that. Or how she would feel about that. "She's not my girlfriend."

He puts his hands up, and even his palms look bony. The bag of leftovers drags his right arm lower than the left. I should have pressed him to eat more lunch, but at least he packed it up for later. "I said nothing of the sort, son. Have fun. Enjoy it before you get yourself locked down by some pretty little thing that knocks you sideways."

"Not happening, old man." I'm not like that, even if my mind immediately conjures images from last night—Jolene's open-mouth gasps and the way she lifted her hips as if she was created to seek pleasure from me.

"You'll know when you know, you little shit."

I laugh as he gets into his car and waves before pulling away from the curb, then I turn and head toward the parking garage. Unlike Ian, I never have luck getting a spot on the street.

A woman passes me. "Hey." She has short, jet-black hair, a nose ring, and huge floral tattoos on the shoulder exposed from a too-big sweater. She licks her top lip, and her tongue ring glints in the street-lamp. I'd wager she's pierced below as well.

I nod.

Would Jolene ever consider something like that? Her pussy is perfect as is, but it could strengthen her orgasms. I can't imagine the sounds she'd make if that were the case. She might crumble the walls.

Getting into the car, I grin as I think about what she'd do if I came home and pounced on her. Just ripped off whatever soft materials she's wrapped herself in tonight, pushed her against the closest wall, spanked her until she was soaked, then fucked her until she collapsed.

Is she still sore? Does she want to be sore?

As I pull into our parking space, I realize I've been thinking about Jolene's pussy and what I can do to it in great detail instead of getting the number or an orgasm from that woman. I should panic, but the need to go upstairs, inhale Jolene's neck and check about that soreness thing is too strong. I want to be back inside her.

Stepping from the car, I adjust my attentive dick, then make my way upstairs.

I open the door to Darius and Jolene sitting at the kitchen table, half-filled plates in front of them.

Jolene pops out of her chair, all grins. "Guess what?"

"What?" I drop my bag by the table.

She rushes over, practically tackling me.

I lift her. "Did you miss me, angel?"

Her legs clamp around me. "Yes." Her excitement electrifies the air. "But also, I have an interview next week with *the* company."

My eyes go wide. "Your first choice?" Her head bobs frantically, and I kiss her forehead. "Fuck, I knew they couldn't stay away for long. That's stellar news." When they see what she can do, there's no chance they won't hire her. When I set her down, we stare at each other, grins drifting away. This feels like it may be too much? Does she feel like that was too much?

I look at Darius, who's beaming at us.

"Welcome home," he says, lifting a beer. "How's Ian?"

I smooth the back of my hair. "He's good."

Darius tilts his head. "You sure?"

Jolene walks back to the table, sits, and takes a swig of wine.

I nod. "He's got some health things, but, as you know, he's a stubborn ass who won't talk about it if he doesn't want to. And he doesn't want to. But he's still full of shit and whiskey, so it can't be that bad. He wants to meet Jolene."

Jolene chokes and sets her glass down, coughing. "Huh?"

"He knows you're our roommate now, but doesn't know *you*."

"You've talked about me to him?" Her face is sharp but unreadable, and I don't like that. Is she happy? Embarrassed? She's not blushing. Maybe I should have asked her first.

"I have." The weird itch of energy trying to escape my chest is distracting. I step toward the hall and tug at my shirt. "Hurry and finish eating, then come to my room. I want to fuck." I walk down the hall. Barely. The urge to sit with Jolene on my lap while she finishes dinner is hard to fight. Did I kiss her on the forehead? *I did.* I've never done that to a woman.

I'm dizzy as I walk the hall, more aggravated by the moment because I'm impatient to have her. More of her skin and scent and adorable little vocalizations that she just can't hold back.

But then there are quick footsteps behind me.

I spin.

Jolene crashes against me, and our lips fuse, breathing calmness back into my raging mind with her wine-tasting tongue and perfect soft lips.

Curling around her, I nip her chin, and she drops her head back, exposing the long column of her jasmine-scented throat to me. I kiss a downward path and shove my hand in her pants to palm her ass and bring her close. "What do you need, angel?" Please let her need me.

She moans and arches, pressing her tits against my chest. "I need you to fuck me, Arlo."

I groan. "My filthy sweet whore needs my cock?"

"God yes," she whines, gripping my hard dick through my pants. "Please. I need it so bad."

I'm beyond dizzy with lust. I'm reeling, falling... *knocked sideways.* Fuck me.

Chapter Forty-One

Jolene Wonders

JOLENE

I'm not sure who's more frantic about getting the clothing off between us. I tug, then Arlo tugs.

He spins me out of my shirt.

I pivot right back into him and lick his tongue.

He groans.

I whimper.

He shoves me backward, and I squeal until I bounce on his mattress. Then he's over me, fingers gripping lace, jerking my panties down my legs as he pulls a condom from the nightstand and opens it with his teeth, flinging my lace across the room. He is an incredible multitasker.

"This one's going to be fast. I need you too much." Arlo pushes my legs apart and licks my clit as he rolls on the condom. "Perfect fucking girl. Already wet for me."

"Yes," I whisper. "Please, Arlo. Please." I clutch at his hair, pulling him closer.

He surges inside me.

My sore lower half cries for mercy, and I yelp.

Arlo stills, breathing heavy against my cheek. "Hurts?"

"A little." I dig my nails into his ass to hold him to me when he tries to back away. "Wait." I look into his eyes and my heart feels like it swells. He's so concerned, and my body unfurls for him, letting him in. I push myself up to bite his bottom lip. "I like it. Just give me a second."

"You sure?" His eyes rove my face, brows low and grumpy. He's so cute.

The pain turns into that ache I can't seem to get rid of when he's around. I spread wider for him. "Now, please."

He studies me for a moment longer, like he's looking for lies, and then he drags himself out, gritting his teeth, and thrusts back in with a grunt. "Goddamn, you feel so fucking good around my cock. Do that. Yes. There."

I lift and roll my hips.

He slams back in. "You're going to make me lose my cum, and then I'm going to have to make it up to you." He gives the hottest, longest "fuck" I've heard out of him yet.

Grinning, I roll my hips faster, grinding up into him, which hits my clit just right. "I'm not far behind you."

He chuckles, moving to kneel, and gripping my thighs. "Well, now I have to control myself." He blows out a long breath, then looks behind him to Darius, who's grinning, leaning against the wall. "Help us out."

"I was enjoying watching." He's serious, but steps forward anyway, crawling on the bed fully clothed. He places two fingers on my clit, rubbing exactly how I need him to, and his hot lips wrap around my nipple.

Arlo starts a pace and the sensations overload so fast it feels like seconds before I'm screaming, arching up, and Arlo's growling, biting at my leg that's looped over his shoulder. He presses in so deep as he jerks through his release. I love how he comes. It's almost violent, overflowing with passion, and that moment right after—the starry, sated, broken-down relaxation that crosses over his face makes pride swell inside me. I made him—the Arlo—forget himself and the world around him for just a split second.

He kisses where he bit, then sucks the spot until I laugh and try to pull away.

Darius kisses my cheek and moves as Arlo falls over me, pressing his weight on me, which feels so right. I run my nails through his hair as he kisses me, humming with pleasure. He doesn't stay long though, giving me a final, long kiss and pushing up. "Condom."

I beckon Darius. "I want you too."

"You're not sated, babes?" He tugs his shirt off.

"I always need you."

He steps out of his pants and sits on the bed, gathering me to him. "And that?" He tips his head toward the bathroom. "You really needed him."

I bite my lip, staring into the sweet warmth of his brown eyes; getting lost in just how much I love this man. "Yeah."

I remember when I first started having sex with Darius. It was so new and shiny, and we wanted each other so much it was hard to be apart. I feel that with Arlo, but is it just lust and experimenting? "I don't want it to stop," I whisper.

Darius nuzzles his nose against mine. "It doesn't have to." His hands make a soothing path from my shoulder to my thigh, reigniting the heat between my legs.

But what if it does? We can't just hide away and have sex all the time. Are we all in a relationship now or is Arlo just a sidepiece? I don't like how that sounds, even if it's in my mind. Do we all go out together? We can't do that.

Darius kisses me. "Babes?"

I kiss him back, letting him soothe my thoughts by pushing them aside for now. Arlo sits on the bed next to us and kisses my shoulder. It's a bit of a shock when he leans over and Darius turns from me, meeting his lips. It's not passionate. There's no tongue; but that doesn't make it less, because it's as familiar between them as kisses are between Darius and me. They love each other. It's clear. I love Darius, and—there's something there between Arlo and me. I just don't know what it is yet, and if we mess this up, where is that going to leave us all?

I'm still not sure as Darius covers me, his scent rolling over me as he gently slides into my body, which welcomes the familiarity. If I know anything, it's this man's body as he rocks against me.

Fingers on my cheek make me open my eyes.

Arlo looks down at me like he's the one making love to me. He thumbs away a tear, and entwines our fingers, but doesn't force my hand over my head. Instead, he presses our hands over my thrumming heart and leans to kiss me. It's sweet at first, but the build of lust ratchets up when Darius grips my thighs and I whimper.

Then Arlo tongues into my mouth and pinches my nipple.

Darius groans against my neck, and I'm falling too. Falling so damn hard.

After a shower and finishing my cold plate of food, I leave Darius and Arlo to their movie, making the excuse of needing to check my resume.

I dial Hayley, sighing in relief when she answers with, "Woman, are we ever going to do pizza night?"

I nod as if she can see me. "Maybe now? I have a confession."

Chapter Forty-Two

Darius Is Concerned

DARIUS

I wake to Jolene's whimpers. Not the good kind.

"Babes?" Turning, I pull her close and kiss her shoulder in the dark. "Joles, wake up. It's a nightmare."

She comes to with a jerk, puffing. "Shit, that was awful."

"You okay?" I wrap her up, looking past her to the clock on the nightstand. 2:40AM.

"Yeah." Her voice is calm, but she's still breathing like she ran a race, and her face is damp with sweat against my lips. "It's fine. Go back to sleep. Sorry."

"What was that about?"

Her huff of a laugh is slightly embarrassed mixed with slightly annoyed. "I was being chased by something I couldn't see. I hate those dreams. But I was in that pageant dress that was so tight around my thighs that I couldn't go up and down the stairs. Remember that? The red one?"

"Oh, I remember." I thought I was going to have to carry her onto the stage. It was the most awkward I've ever seen her, even if she looked like the temptress to hell—one that would be completely worth an eternity of torture.

"I hated that dress so much. Anyway, yeah, I couldn't run, and whatever was chasing me was right there." She turns to me, nuzzling my chest. "Ugh. Thank you for waking me."

"Anytime." I kiss her hair.

She stays fused tight to me until we both drift back to sleep.

***

The week is lost to days of prepping for the business trip, and nights with Jolene and Arlo.

He's holding back sexually—staying relatively tame while exploring her thoroughly—but he seems to be getting closer emotionally. Each morning, he tugs her close before he leaves for work, and drags her to him to kiss whenever she's within arm's length. He inhales her neck like he's sniffing rare brandy and watches her when she's not watching him.

But that's the thing—she's not watching him. Or she's fighting it. Unless he demands it while they're fucking, she's watching me like I'm a lifeboat in her choppy ocean.

Then on Friday, when Arlo kisses her before he leaves for work, she throws him a pageant smile that makes my heart sink.

When he's out the door, I text Martina to tell her I'm going to be late for work.

I warm up the coffee and sit her down at the table. "What's wrong?"

Her eyes widen. "What do you mean?"

"What do I mean?" I level a grim frown at her. "You're walking on eggshells around Arlo. You're opening up sexually, but shutting down at the same time. And you just fake-smiled at him. What happened?"

She studies her coffee cup.

Shit, shit, shit. "Do you want to stop with him?"

She glances up quickly. "No. I don't. I'm just"—she crinkles her nose—"I'm scared of how I feel with him."

"And how's that?" I've never truly needed to be inside Jolene's head like this before. I just want her to spill everything. Right now. Right. Now.

Jolene worries her lip, then sighs. "Obsessed."

My heartbeat quickens in happiness, but she looks on the verge of tears. "Why's that bad?"

"He said not to get attached. He told me there will be others."

"You don't want there to be others." I set my hand over her fingers.

She quickly lets go of her mug and grips me. "I still don't know. I'm not opposed to it entirely, I just…" She rubs her forehead.

"Gut reaction, Jolene. He leaves to go fuck another woman."

She winces. "I want that woman to be me." She pulls out of my grip to cover her face. "This is bad."

I come around the table, kneel, and pull her hands back. "It's not bad."

"He said—"

"Babes, he says a lot of things to put rules in place, but sometimes those rules change."

Her worried face shifts to the sweetest hope. "Did he say anything?"

"No." I hold up a finger. "And I won't ask him. I love you both so much. But you two need to figure out what's between you and if you want something more to be there."

"But what if we break it all?" Tears well up in her eyes. "You love him, Darius. You need each other."

"And I need you. I love you."

She nods. "You know I love you, but if I bring up *relationships* with him, I'm afraid of losing you both."

"You will always have me." I lean in and kiss her. Hard. She knows I'd do anything for her.

When I pull back and open my mouth, she puts a finger over my lip and growls, "If you tell me to take one day at a time, I'm going to bite you."

I laugh instead.

Chapter Forty-Three

Jolene Hurts

JOLENE

Periods suck. Periods that will interrupt newfound sexy times with Arlo and Darius suck so hard.

Halfway upright, I exit the bathroom and crawl back into bed, curling into a ball and groaning when Darius peeks under the sheet, letting light into my cocoon of agony.

"So..." He says, trailing off. "What's happening here?"

"My uterus is screaming mad, and I hate it so much right now."

"Period?" He's probably wincing, but I can't tell because I'm smashing my face into my pillow and I'm not moving.

I grumble, "Uh huh. Stupid uterus."

"Aw, babes. One day you'll appreciate it. Heating pad?"

"Yes, please. And the pink bottle from the cabinet where we keep the meds."

The sound of him rooting around seems extra loud with the headache. What a way to start the weekend. Darius gets me set up, threading the pad into my cocoon and telling me he'll make tea.

A few minutes later, the bed dips and a big body sneaks under the covers, snakes an arm under my head and presses a wall of warmth against my back.

"I've heard sex helps with cramps," Arlo whispers in my ear.

I laugh, then whine at the spike of pain through my skull. "I'm not having sex with you during my period. Messy." I wrinkle my nose.

He smiles against my neck, massaging my lower back with the hand not holding me tight to him. "Shower sex then."

"No," I groan at the kneading pressure that's distracting away from the tight pain. "This body is closed. You'll have to get your ya-yas elsewhere." I immediately regret my words and suck in a breath as if I can undo their escape.

Arlo's hand moves from my lower back to my ass, which he smacks, but it's more like a hard pat. "Shut up, angel."

So I do, right after I turn my head and kiss his firm biceps.

He didn't leave. He didn't even correct me or tell me he was going out tonight to do just that.

He called me angel.

There's a clink next to the bed and Darius whispers, "Tea. It's hot, so you'll have to wait a bit. I'm going to the store. Need anything?"

I recite the list in my head and tack on "chocolate."

Arlo adds bananas and soup ingredients, and I kiss his biceps again, then bite it because his closeness is making me feel better and apparently I now show love by biting.

Wait...

He nips my neck, making me squeak.

Darius laughs and kisses my head through the fabric. "Are we going for a run later, Arlo?"

"Absolutely."

Darius heads out, and I huff.

I like to cycle more than run, but I also don't like to miss out on exploring the outdoors. However, the ache in my center says there will be no movement today. I pull the heating pad tighter to me and shift until Arlo massages me more.

When I'm thoroughly melted, he says, "Ian wants to visit tomorrow after church service. Do you think you'll be up for it?"

The stepfather.

I turn to face Arlo, wincing at the movement. He's half under the sheet. Soft light filters in, making his eyes more gray than blue, and his lips so very kissable. How can someone so hard be so exceptionally beautiful? It's breathtaking.

His eyebrows raise. "What?"

I tap his nose. "You're gorgeous. It's distracting. I was going to ask you something and forgot what it was."

He grins at that, and he's even more gorgeous.

I push at his chest. "Quit."

"Quit what?"

"Distracting me by looking all hot. Stop," I whine.

He raises one eyebrow high and puffs out his lips, making a duck-like runway expression.

I can't stop the peals of laughter, even though it's putting pressure on my sore insides. "Ow. Cramps. Headache. Stop giving me super-model-face, you gorgeous ass."

He tugs me closer, unseating my heating pad but fitting me against his chest. It angles my head so our lips are a mere inch from meeting. "You're one to talk."

His eyes rove my face, which I'm positive is puffy. I have no makeup on, and I can't believe I didn't think of that until this exact moment.

He thumbs under my lip. "These lips haunt me." He trails up and taps my cheek. "And this freckle. It's almost as perfect as the one on your ass."

"I have a freckle on my ass?"

"Yes. I like to slap it like I did the day we had our music standoff."

I close my eyes and shake my head, but grin. "I can't believe you did that."

"I can't believe I didn't try for more. I wanted to touch you so badly that day. Wanted to see if you were wet for me."

I close my eyes and take a long breath. "I had been. That was... confusing."

"Are you still confused?"

Things are pretty clear on my end, but is that something we can talk about? I envision him angrily shoving himself out of the bed and calling Sheena up here again to prove a point. I can't exactly lie, though, can I? "I don't think so."

He makes a humming sound, and his thumb moves back to stroking under my lip. The look he gives me is of hunger and longing. It calls to my body, which it shouldn't do right now because—nope.

I recall what I'd been thinking of asking him before our conversation took this turn. "I'll be better tomorrow. The first day is the worst of it." I nibble my lip. "Will you tell me about Ian? I feel like I'm at a disadvantage since he knows about me."

I'd like to ask more about what he knows and who else Arlo has talked about me with, but that would pry, and family is a touchy subject for him. He keeps stroking under my lip, and when he speaks, what he tells me is completely unexpected.

Chapter Forty-Four

Arlo Shares

ARLO

It's easy enough to tell Jolene surface things about Ian. He loves whiskey, sandwiches, women, and wants a herd of cats, but won't do it because my mom is allergic to them.

Jolene sits up to take a pill, sipping tea in that dainty way she does, then settles back down, facing me and asking more questions.

I don't know how she does it, but she has me bringing up Ian's childhood—not that Ian would care, he's an open book—but sharing that Ian was physically abused as a kid has me slipping in tidbits of my own fucked up past. Maybe it's because our stories are so entwined that if she wants to know how my mom and he met, she has to know about my dad too.

"So yeah, we both had to deal with getting smacked around, but my mother pressed charges and left when it went too far. His mom hid the abuse on both their bodies until she died. It appeared self-inflicted. The day after her funeral, Ian packed a bag, forged a different date on his birth certificate, and took a bus to a military base to sign up for training."

Jolene swallows and nods. "He lied about his age?"

"He did. But when his father finally tracked him down, Ian was two years in, a team leader, and absorbing everything there was to know about planes. The first lieutenant had a discussion with them both separately. Ian confessed everything. His father told an obvious lie. And that's how Ian remained a year older, officially."

"They let him stay?"

"It was a different time. But really, only a monster would have let him go."

The pain-crinkles around Jolene's eyes have eased. "What happened to his dad?"

"He died of a gunshot wound in a back alley not long after. Cold case. They blamed it on drugs."

Jolene worries her lip.

I tug it from her teeth with my thumb. "No idea if that's what happened. Though I wouldn't blame Ian in the least if he did it." Fuck, that might scare her. "But he's a wonderful person and would never hurt anyone unless it was to protect another. He's the best man I've ever met besides Darius."

Jolene crawls closer, and I roll to my back as she curls against me, shoulder fitting snug in my armpit and my hand cupping her hip. She draws circles on my shirt, over my heart, hypnotizing me so well, I don't flinch when she says, "Your father abused you," as if she's trying to absorb the fact.

I can end a conversation even when answering using a tone, but I keep my "Yes" gentle. Maybe it was the way she said it—a fact, but not pushing me for more. That makes me want to give her more, even if it's not something I talk about.

Jolene stays quiet while I stumble through explaining the time-frame cage I lived in for the first part of my life. I tell her about my stringent schedule where, even as a toddler, every hour was planned out to lead to the path my father had chosen for me. My days were only interrupted if he needed me to perform for coworkers or visiting family. Then, I was to behave with perfect manners and follow the script he made sure I had memorized. *Nice to meet you, sir, ma'am. Please come into our home. Yes, I love school. Of course, I'm going into the military. Yes, I have big shoes to fill, but I'll strive to make everyone proud.*

My chest is so fucking tight.

The funny part is, I think I would have done well in the military and enjoyed it. It saved Ian's life and put him on a course for success. If I'd had him in my life from the start, everything would be entirely different. I wouldn't have rebelled so hard, or have been broken for so damn long. But as he's told me, I wouldn't be me, either.

I take Jolene's hand. It's easier to talk while focused on the elegant shape of her fingers and the sparkly blue polish she put on yesterday. She's so put together, but likes to be taken apart too. I love that about her. She's like a beautiful walking secret.

Maybe I am too.

I set her hand back against my chest. "Did Darius tell you what happened to me?"

"Some. He said your family was controlling, your dad hurt you, and your mom left him and met Ian." She tilts her head to blink up at me. "Sorry. I was being nosy about you."

I kiss her forehead, then get back to fidgeting with her fingers. "It's fine."

Something compels me to continue even though I shouldn't. It's not like she wants to hear my sordid past—or maybe she does, if only to fill in the gaps.

She squeezes my hand and looks up at me as if sharing like this is a normal thing.

It's not. And yet, I talk about the teachers that let me code during recess and lunch because I had a knack for it. I fight myself when that voice inside says she doesn't want to hear this part, then tell her about the day I told my father I wanted to go to college and study computer science instead of enlisting as soon as I graduated.

How he laughed until he realized I was serious.

How this path meant so much to me, I didn't back down.

Not when he hit me and not when he broke my ribs. Not when it took my mother tasing him to get him off me before the police got there to take him away from me for good. The week in the hospital solidified my decision and confirmed what I really needed to fight for.

No one decides what I do but me.

I survived a rotten existence of being forced to do someone else's will under the guise of discipline, and I won't tolerate anything similar again. I'm good enough for myself. That matters.

"Is he in jail?" Jolene whispers.

I clear my throat. "He served five years. Last I heard, he was working at a ranch somewhere in the Northwest. My sister keeps up with him."

"Why?" The distaste is clear in her tone.

"Because she doesn't have the history with him I do. He treated her differently because she's a woman, and she's five years older than me, so she was out of the house at that time." I smile, but it feels weird on my face. "She stayed on the path like a good little military brat. I'm sure he's very proud of her." I kiss her fingers because I can't kiss her lips. It would be too hard to stop if I went there.

"But he hurt you. If I had a sibling and…" She blows out a long breath. "Sorry. I don't have any siblings, so I can't really say what I'd feel."

Her anger drags past pain to the surface because it did hurt. But anytime I've confronted my sister, she's told me I was being ridiculous, and it was cruel of me to make her choose between her father and me. That's not what I had intended, and I felt like an ass for being so angry.

Thinking about it now though, if it had happened to my sister, I would have testified against him and done everything in my power to keep him away from my family forever. Maybe my opinion is skewed because it was me he attacked. Me he broke as he yelled, "You are nothing without me."

I loosen my too-tight grip on Jolene. "No, I think you're right. That was a real kick when I was down." I make a humph sound.

Jolene tugs her hand from me and turns my face toward hers so she can kiss me. "You have so much strength. It's incredible." She moves her kisses down my neck and slides to her knees, tugging at the waistband of my shorts.

"Stop." I lift her chin away from my cock that doesn't know better. "I don't want a pity blowjob."

She shakes her head and kisses my palm. "I just need to be close to you right now." Her expression is serious and determined. Something about the set of her lips dissipates any doubt of her intentions.

So, I watch her take my cock deep and let her control every move. Let her take me.

I hold her hair so I can see her and gently touch her hollowed cheek.

Her movements are passionate yet sweet. No teasing today.

I'm utterly entranced as she swallows down my release.

When she crawls back up, sprawling across my chest, breathing as heavy as I am, I feel empty. Not in a lonely way, but like she just opened a release valve and drained out every burden and stress I've ever had.

I wrap her up, hold her tight, never letting go.

Darius returns and watches us from the doorway. He must sense that something has changed between us, because he puts his sweats back on. "Maybe a movie marathon?"

"With chocolate," Jolene mumbles against my neck.

Chapter Forty-Five

Arlo Screws Up

Ten before noon, the intercom buzzes. I tell Ian and my mother to come on up and turn to find Jolene frantically wiping the already clean kitchen faucet before throwing supplies under the sink. She curses and grabs a newspaper, chucking it into the trash.

Darius quietly reads his book on the couch, bare feet propped up. He doesn't seem concerned at all that Jolene has turned into a disinfecting hummingbird.

I trap her against the counter and move in to kiss her, but she evades, murmuring, "Lipstick."

"Are you nervous?" I ask, tugging her silky tank aside so I can kiss her collarbone.

She nods. "It's your parents." Her nervous energy bounces around the apartment like quick-spinning lights from a disco ball.

"And you want to impress them?" I've already told her that Ian will think she's perfect and my mother will be polite enough, and not to take anything she says to heart.

In a quick move, she darts under my arm and dashes into the hall. "Yes. They're important to you."

I'm tempted to chase, but she really is freaking out, and I'll definitely make her disheveled and add to her stress if I get my hands on her.

When there's a knock on the door, she pops back out of the hallway with a long cardigan over her tank. Her earrings are big golden disks, and there's not a hair out of place. I pause, fingers wrapped around the handle. She's smiling, and her posture is both confident and relaxed. I wouldn't have guessed that she was nervous in the least. She raises an eyebrow. "Are you going to open that, or should I?"

"You're gorgeous." I don't know why I say it until her cheeks turn pink and the smile she's making slides into one that makes my stomach swoop because it lights up her soul. Beautiful thing. I shake my head and open the door.

Ian hugs me while my mother barges in. She gives Darius a side hug, and he takes the bags of food she's holding. Ian walks in after and blows out a long breath. "This beauty must be Jolene. Lord, honey, I can see why they gave you a stage."

"Don't embarrass her," my mother chastises, though she laughs. She holds a hand out to Jolene. "I'm Yolanda, and this piece of work is Ian."

I watch Jolene as she makes small talk with my family, taking the role of gracious host in our home seriously. *Our home.* It's the first time it's felt fully ours, and now we're sharing our new normal with others. After yesterday, it feels right.

Jolene, Darius and I had snuggled on the couch most of the day. Darius and I did some floor exercises while Jolene threw popcorn at us and said we needed a dog-shaped vacuum for food cleanup. That sounded like the best idea.

I made soup, and Jolene wandered in to press herself against me, arms wrapped around my waist while I chopped vegetables. She moved with me as I shuffled between cutting board and pot, as if she couldn't unglue herself from my back. I've spent a good portion of my dating years avoiding clinginess, and yet, when she finally let me go, I spun around and dragged her back into place, right where she belonged.

And it's clear she belongs at the table with my family, laughing at Ian's recount of his squadron days. She belongs with Darius and me, in this apartment with us. Warmth hits my chest at seeing her so comfortable, and that warmth buzzes strongly when her eyes meet mine every few minutes, when she seems to check for approval. *I approve.*

Ian pushes his plate away and leans back, crossing his arms. "Alright, Jolene. It's now time for the important shit. You ready to answer the big questions?"

I raise my eyebrows at him, and he winks.

Jolene's eyes go wide. She gives a shimmy to her shoulders and sits taller. "Probably not, but shoot."

"What was your pageant talent?"

Darius's laugh bursts out of him, and he claps as Jolene's eyes widen.

She shoves five fries into her mouth and makes a nervous humming sound.

How did I never think to ask that? Because I've been too busy wondering how she likes to be fucked, that's how.

"It's not singing," I mumble, taking another bite of burger. A French fry thwacks me in the forehead, and a chorus of laughter lights up the room. I give Jolene a look that hopefully conveys what would happen if my parents weren't here. It must, because she looks down at her plate, smirking. I wipe the spot with my napkin. "Answer, angel."

Her chewing abruptly halts, and her face goes red.

Darius clears his throat and gives me a questioning look, but I'm not sure why. Does he want me to drop it? Because I'm not going to.

She points to her full mouth and mumbles what I assume is, "Can't. My mouth is full."

Darius rubs her back. "You have to say it eventually."

"Yep." Ian sets his elbows on the table. "It's going to be one of the weird ones, isn't it?"

Mom taps his shoulder with the back of her hand. "Don't be beast-ly."

He chuckles, picking up her hand and kissing her knuckles. They exchange a look that's oddly intimate. Not something my ice-queen mother is known for.

Jolene swallows, takes a gulp of water, and rolls her eyes. "Fine." She squeezes her eyes shut. "Clogging."

"She is so good at it, too." Darius bolts forward, unable to contain himself any longer. He goes into a fast history of the folk dance and how Jolene found it—her granny—and then the part that's actually embarrassing to Jolene. Her outfits. Darius makes big arm movements. "A gold sparkle halter top with this red, white, and blue massive, billowy skirt and—"

"The worst hat," Jolene says, shaking her head.

Darius flops back in his seat. "Gold sequin cowboy hat with a blue star on the side. I shit you not."

"The worst." But she laughs with us too, then reaches for the empty plates. "I cried when Mom brought that thing home."

I stand and push her into her seat as she's getting up. "Sit. Talk. I've got this." I kiss her head and carry plates to the sink. But it's oddly quiet behind me.

Jolene's voice is tiny and tight as she says, "Excuse me." Then she's down the hall. And I mentally go through what just happened, quickly landing on the problem.

I kissed her head. And I called her angel. I just outed us to my family, even though they already know. As much as it pisses me off that she just darted away from that concept, I wince. We should have talked about it. "I just fucked up, didn't I?"

My mother scrunches her nose, and Darius nods, crossing his arms.

Ian stands up, gathering containers. "Depends. Have you talked to her about this relationship you're all in?"

"We're not in a relationship." Apparently, we're just roommates that give each other the best orgasms of our lives.

He covers a wheezy cough with his fist. "Yeah, son. You fucked up. In more ways than one."

She's not mine when my dick isn't in her, and I forgot that. It was too easy to do so. She's not ready for anything I could offer and probably never will be because even after the things we've done together, she won't accept that the only ones who should care what we do is us. *Fucking fantastic.*

I head to the door. "I'm going to walk."

As soon as I shut the door—too hard—it reopens.

My mom catches up with confident strides. "I'll join you."

"Okay?" When has she ever joined in on a rage walk of mine?

Chapter Forty-Six

Jolene Gets Real... Uncomfortable

JOLENE

I should have laughed, joked, played the part of the pageant queen who tripped on stage or kicked a clog into the crowd. But nope, I ran.

I snatch my phone and text Hayley.

> Arlo just told his parents we're fucking.

My phone buzzes.

Hayley's *WTF* makes me feel a little better, but then I get weirdly protective of the man who just ruined any chance for his parents to like me.

I roll my eyes.

> He didn't say it, but may as well have.

I was feeling really good about how things were going too, especially after talking to Hayley, who encouraged me to have the best kind of kinky fun with Arlo. She said it was good for me. That I needed this in my life.

This is good? This feeling like I'm going to burst out of my skin is what I need? I press my face into my hands.

How could Arlo kiss my head like I'm his girlfriend with his parents right there? Not after saying not to get attached because he never will. What the hell is he doing? If he was trying to prove something to them—if he needed them to think he had a girlfriend—he should have told me. Not that I would have played along. It's too hard. I want him too much to just pretend. But I can't exactly walk around with two boyfriends. *Right?* Right.

A knock on the door sounds through my near-hyperventilation.

I breathe deep, and expect Darius or even Arlo to walk in, but there's nothing but another quiet knock. I pace over and crack open the door.

Ian has his hands in his pockets. He's a man who's shaped like he used to be very strong, but now he's thin, and I see why Arlo thinks there's something wrong with his health. There's a pallor to his skin, and his eyes are bloodshot and tired. He tilts his head, assessing me. The gesture reminds me so much of Arlo.

"I'm sorry," I blurt.

His eyebrows lift. "For what?" Is he playing with me right now?

"For…" I can't even say it.

"Mind if I step in?" Ian smiles. "I'd like to chat with you."

My stomach roils, but I open the door. Here goes. He's going to tell me how lovely women like me shouldn't do things like I do. Ask what my family thinks. God, my mother would just die.

Ian leans against the doorframe. "You did nothing wrong, Jolene."

My eyebrows shoot into my hairline because he can't mean that.

He smiles. "And neither did Arlo. Well, mostly. It seems he should have talked to you about all the shit he's probably avoiding talking about because it's new to him."

My phone buzzes in my hand. Once, twice, then again.

I toss it behind me onto the bed. "But..." I crinkle my nose. "How much do you know?" God, this is weird and the very last thing I thought I'd be talking to Arlo's parents about.

"He told me you three are caught up and that it's fantastic." He shakes his head. "Don't look like you're going to pass out. I've had my share of nonconforming relationships and am not here to agree with your line of thinking."

Wait, what? "And what's my line of thinking?"

"That it's wrong to be with both of them."

"It's, I'm... but isn't it?"

"Does it feel wrong?"

I huff a laugh, even though my eyes burn. "Right now? Not feeling so great." I swallow hard. But I shake my head, which dislodges a tear. I swipe it away. "But usually? It doesn't feel bad at all. I enjoy being near them both." Nothing about being with Arlo and Darius together or separate feels wrong. It actually feels too easy when I give myself over to them completely. "But it's very new. And Arlo said not to get attached." Panic flows freely through me. I shouldn't have said that. It's really easy to talk to this man, but he's Arlo's stepfather. What if he tells Arlo about this?

Ian makes a grumbling groan. "Oh, that boy. I used to be the same damn way. Until I met his mom."

"You were like Arlo?" My shaking knees go weak, and I sit on the end of the bed. From our conversation yesterday, where Arlo broke my heart with his and Ian's past, yeah, they have a lot of similarities. But with relationships?

"If you mean, did I scoff and fight and look down on relationships outside of the bedroom? Yeah. Absolutely."

"How did you change?" I jolt, holding up a palm. "Not that he should change, I just meant—"

Ian waves me off. "I didn't. It's not about changing, Jolene. I just met the person who fit me, and I didn't want anything beyond her ever again. I settled into myself when I met Yolanda and her family."

I sniffle. Could Arlo find that? I don't know if I'm enough for him. "I love that for you. He's not you though, right?" I can't get my hopes up about something that happened to someone else.

"Look, I won't tell you how he feels because those are *his* feelings, plus he comes to his own conclusions on his timeframe. But I can count on half a hand how many women he's been with that I've met. He's never kissed one of them like it was his daily routine. Don't give up on him and do not let him tell you dumbass things like don't get attached. How is that even possible?"

I smile. "Right? I don't know how anyone couldn't get attached to him. I didn't want to at first, tried not to, but he's"—I bite at my smile—"There's a lot to him."

"I'm glad you see that." Ian's smile brings out a row of wrinkles that makes him even more approachable. "He is lucky to have you and Darius in his life."

He actually means that, doesn't he? This isn't how people really think, though, right? Could this thing between us really work out?

"I'm lucky they're in my life, too."

Ian grins and thumbs over his shoulder. "I need to head out and rest. It was such a pleasure meeting you, Jolene. I'll be back really soon to see you three. There's something I need to talk to Arlo about, and he's going to need you two, okay?"

My throat tightens for a different reason, but I nod and whisper, "Thank you," before he walks down the hall.

My phone buzzes again, and I check to see the string of curses aimed at Arlo from Hayley. I laugh and pat my cheeks with a tissue, then write her back.

> I don't know what's going to happen.

Will I ever know what's going to happen?

I check my makeup and breathe deeply a couple more times, then follow the sounds of dishes clanking.

Darius is at the sink. Everyone else is gone.

He peeks back and turns the water off. "You okay?" He knows I'm not.

"I didn't expect Ian to come talk to me. I thought you might." Because he's my person. Not Ian, my mother, or anyone else. Hayley is, but it's different. She's my vent session, and the tiny, feisty warrior that's always in my corner, even if I'm not being rational. Arlo is... I could roll my eyes. The guy I'm fucking who's not my boyfriend but sometimes acts like it.

Crossing his arms, Darius leans against the counter. "Ian wanted to talk to you."

"It was a good talk. I like him."

"I do too."

I stare at him staring at me. "Why are you avoiding talking to me about Arlo?"

His nose crinkles the tiniest bit, and he sighs. "Because I want you two to work things out without me."

"Why, when it—" I swish my hands around. "—whatever this is heavily involves you too?"

He rubs his forehead. "Babes, I'm worried. With Arlo getting more comfortable and you getting less comfortable, I feel like I pushed you into this, biased you, and you're not ready for any of it. And Arlo is..."

He blinks and looks to the ceiling for words in a way that tells me he's trying to figure out how to say something carefully. "This is new to him."

"And me."

"Yes. And me as well. I need to step back and let you figure things out, what you want, without pushing either of you or we're going to end up with a two on one situation during arguments and, babes, I just can't." The stress in his voice tightens mine. "I don't want to start out by choosing sides. It's not healthy."

As much as I don't like that, he's right. "That's fair."

He blows out a long breath. "Thank you."

"But I need to talk these things out with you. I was upset, and I just had a very real conversation with a stranger instead of the person I love most in the world. You weren't there for me, and I didn't like that."

He pushes off the counter and pulls me into a hug, muttering apologies. "What do you want to do?"

"I don't know."

Chapter Forty-Seven

Arlo Takes It Back

ARLO

After walking for fifteen minutes in silence, I crack. "Do you have something to say?"

My mother crinkles her nose and sighs. "You're different around her."

Even more tension floods my shoulders. I'm not different. I'm just me.

"Oh, stop it." My mother loops her arm into mine and tugs me to a stop. "It's not an insult, Arlo. What I mean is, you seem happy." She studies my eyes, and her brows furrow. "You really care for her."

"She's Darius's girlfriend and my roommate. Of course, I do."

I hate the way she purses her lips, like she's holding back words she should just fucking spit out.

I roll my eyes and turn to get back to the walk. "Just say you disapprove. That I handled that all wrong and shouldn't have gotten caught up with them like this, anyway. It was all a huge mistake."

"Oh, no, that's not at all what I want to say to you. It wouldn't be true, Arlo."

I spin on the street and cross my arms. "Then what was it?"

"Now's not really the time."

"It's never the fucking time with you."

She winces, and her throat bobs with a swallow. "I'm really proud of you."

That has me spinning my wheels. My mother doesn't show much emotion, and she's overflowing with it now.

She nods toward the path back to the apartment. "I've been trying to work some things out, from the past and now." Another swallow and there's something really wrong here.

"What's going on?" I step in line with her.

Shaking her head, she smiles. "Ian always suggested that I needed some therapy, but I'd been too scared because I was afraid that they would blame me as much as I do for everything." She puts up a hand when I open my mouth to tell her this isn't necessary. "But, Arlo"—she peeks my way—"You have claimed your life, built it the way you want it, and have people you love to share it with. I could not be prouder, and I know I'm difficult and don't know how to always say things the way I should, but I love seeing you care for someone."

I huff a laugh. I guess I am that obvious, except to Jolene. We haven't been able to keep our hands off each other. Did she think today would be different? "Ah, yeah, well, don't get too excited about that. She's *young*, as Ian puts it."

She grins. "She is. But she cares too. And Darius, he's just the best. How's his family?"

And I guess confessions are over for now, but the tension is also gone in my shoulders. We walk and talk about Darius's family, Jolene's mother, and my sister and her family, but Mom doesn't detail out all the accomplishments I usually hear from other family members. It reminds me she doesn't talk about the family with me. I get updates on my niece whom I've met twice, but that's usually it. It makes me realize maybe Mom was protecting me by what she wasn't saying, though I would have appreciated the kind of words she just said. How long will this new form of conversation last between us?

When we approach the visitors' parking lot at the apartment, Ian meets us at the car.

Mom squeezes my arm. "Go easy on her." Then she hugs me, shocking me even more than the conversation we just had. It's brief, but a lot.

Ian grins, then pulls me into his own familiar hug. "Figuring out what you want will help her. Be quick about that shit. Lunch soon."

Then he slides into the passenger seat, and I'm left alone, wondering how this day went sideways.

Does Jolene not know how much I want her? Was I not clear enough after holding her most of the day yesterday—after sharing my past—that this is different for me? However, I showed Jolene the part of me all women see first because I didn't expect her to be unlike any other woman I've been with. Now I'm acting differently. My feelings for her threw me off, so she's bound to be just as confused. But also, she ran, clearly embarrassed by my affection. She's not ready.

I stomp through a flock of pigeons and sit on the bench next to our building. The question is, am I too much for her outside our home?

Will she come around and let me touch her in public, be with her too, while Darius holds her hand, or am I relegated to bedroom antics only? I don't want that. The more I think about being a dirty little secret, the more my muscles bunch.

I flex my hands. Something like that never bothered me before, but it sure as fuck does now.

Dammit, what did she do to me? And the worst part of it is, I don't want to walk away. Yeah, I told her if it didn't work out, we could go back to being roommates. No harm, no foul. But the thought of doing that—seeing her reaching for a wine glass, vacuuming... or hell, when she's curled up in a ball with cramps—and not being able to palm her hip, kiss her neck, have her look at me with trust and need? Fuck no. I can't do it.

She'll just have to get over having us both, because that's exactly what she has.

But how to approach that with her? We could talk it out, but that would make it easy for her to put a stop to all this if she got too uncomfortable. She's already uncomfortable enough.

So we push through.

I walk back inside, nod to Gregory, who's on security detail instead of Sheena today, and head upstairs. When I step inside, Darius is hugging Jolene in the kitchen.

He gives me a tight smile. "They leave okay?"

"Yeah." I walk closer.

Jolene turns her head to blink at me. She's been crying, and that hits a dark place in me.

Hands in my pockets, I step behind her and kiss her shoulder. It's not an apology because I'm not apologizing for being so comfortable around her that I show it. That's her issue, not mine. But I want to know she's okay—to show her it will be okay. "You good, angel?"

She turns and wraps her arms around my middle. "I'm sorry."

"No need for that." There's a little need. That stung in a way I haven't felt before, and maybe I need some time to process that. I nudge her face up to mine and kiss her soft lips.

She hums a sweet sigh, then leans back against Darius. Her boyfriend.

He dips to kiss that smooth swoop between her neck and shoulder, then eyes me, lifting his brows like he wants me to do something.

I work my jaw, then cup Jolene's hip. "I should have told you they knew about us."

She nods. "That would have been helpful."

I want to pull her to me, take her back to their cozy bed, and get back into the space we were in yesterday morning. That was comfortable. Perfect.

We stare at each other.

Darius clears his throat. "I'm going to finish the dishes, so…" He thumbs behind him and backs away from Jolene and turns to the sink.

"So we're not public." I purse my lips.

Jolene sucks both lips between her teeth, then lets them pop back out. "What are *we*?"

I huff a laugh. "I could ask you the same thing." Because I don't know. "I just like being around you, Jolene." It's a lie, and I know it, but like hell if I'm putting it all out there for her to overthink, decide I'm not what she wants, and then have her feel guilty about it. "What are we to you?"

She studies me, then turns to the hallways. "I don't know Arlo."

It feels like she punched my soul. I grip her hand and pull her back. "Kiss me. So we don't know what we are. Who fucking cares? But don't shut me out."

"No, Arlo. I could never do that." She steps against me, cups my face, and fuses her lips to mine. Her tongue asks for entry and, fuck yes, I welcome her right in.

We'll just keep connecting like this until she figures out that I'm hers.

Chapter Forty-Eight

Jolene Can't Catch A Break

JOLENE

The floor of Diggory and Sons is gloss gray, and it's a little concerning to wear a skirt with the amount of reflection it's kicking off. Did the designer realize that before they installed it?

I keep sneaking peeks to see if these tiles could somehow reflect the ache between my legs like it is the flash of panties. This morning was... interesting. I was a mess trying to cram all the morning's numbers into my brain while chugging coffee and getting ready for this interview.

After a couple of days of being weird around each other, it seems like Arlo and I are back to some state of normal since he pinned me against Darius and kissed my lipstick off while Darius held me in place, both of them grinding against me.

I yelled at them both and went to fix the damage, grinning at myself in the mirror because what they do to me is unholy. And while I threatened to throttle them both, they helped get out of my head for a moment. Even now, my focus feels honed. I'm collected, not panicked.

The assistant to the executives I'll be speaking to points to a dark floor-to-ceiling door up ahead. "Good luck, Ms. Shah. They're nicer than they seem. Mostly." I'm concerned about her tight smile, but she leans in conspiratorially. "Little hint. Mr. Gant will rapid-fire questions at you. You're not expected to know everything, so don't pretend you do."

That is helpful. I thank her, and she walks me in to meet the three executives I'm interviewing with.

Lou Gant is intimidating despite his thin frame and trendy tortoiseshell glasses, but his energy is nothing compared to Arlo.

I stare him down, firmly squeezing when we shake hands.

Mrs. Sita Patel's gray hijab matches her pantsuit, and I'd love to know the name of the dark burgundy lipstick she's wearing. Another day, hopefully.

The third person looks younger than me. He introduces himself as Jeremy Jung and smiles a little too wide, stares at my chest, then asks if we've met before. My mother would tell me this is the perfect time to flirt. Another reason I didn't take her call this morning.

Fortunately, Mr. Gant cuts off the small talk with a speedy introduction to their roles, then quizzes me on my resume.

I quiz him back on the company, asking what markets they focus on, their ratio of maintaining portfolios to building them, and what working hours look like.

Mrs. Patel answers all the company structure questions, while Mr. Gant takes the lead on focal points. Then they both turn to Jeremy, who's reading my resume. He blinks, clears his throat, and asks what shares I would buy with twenty thousand dollars.

I smile, because I went over this last night with Arlo and Darius. I didn't expect Arlo to be the risk-taker with funds, but he was all about testing penny stocks and relentlessly quizzed me on projections per market-share while Darius wanted a slow-building portfolio he didn't need to check through the day. I want both. The thought makes me chuckle, and to recover, I ask if I can use the conference room whiteboard. Once Mr. Gant tosses me a marker, I quickly break down exactly how I would allocate funds for maximum profitability on a four-day exchange and re-allocation system.

When I'm done, Jeremy's phone has his full attention, Mrs. Patel is smiling, and Mr. Gant is resting his chin on his linked fingers, eyes flitting over my whiteboard of numbers.

He leans back, hands behind his head. "I don't like it."

My stomach sinks. "Why not?"

He comes around the table and points to my third fund. "Why would you dump funding into this?"

I tell him that a competitive company in their three-man market is declaring bankruptcy because of a pesky embezzlement issue, leaving the full market to the other two. The one I chose is not the strongest, but its business model is most like the bankrupt company, leaving those clients scrambling for some familiarity. I explain the pop that will create and when to sell, which he rejects until Mrs. Patel speaks up, reminding him of a similar situation in the past that worked to their benefit.

Mr. Gant still doesn't like that risk, and we go through ten minutes of erasing and rewriting my board while arguing over why I'd chosen some funds and not others. He tweaks my allocation system for round four, and I actually really like how he would bring in a secondary tier of low-risk funds.

Then he brings in another executive: a linebacker of a man named Michael Brown-Lewis, who hums and pokes at my board as well.

He wants to nix my entire third round until I show him how that would crumble step seven. He gives another hum and calls in Isadora Franklin, who gets so close to the board, she could lick it, then tells me to exchange my second fund, because a larger company is about to buy them out.

Seriously?

But she has another that could work if I wanted to do a little research.

Of course, I do.

By the time I leave the conference room of people, my feet are tired and I'm giddy from talking for so long with people in the industry. That went so great I could burst. I was there for over an hour, and to be honest, I would have liked to stay longer. The best part is that I feel more like myself than I have in a long time. I didn't act like a pageant girl or go the opposite and act mean. Even if they don't want me, it was a good interview. I'd give myself a solid nine out of ten.

"Jolene?"

I swing around on the sidewalk, and Jeremy nearly runs into me.

"Hi," he says. "Um, would you like to get a cup of coffee?" He scratches his neck. "Or, uh, early lunch maybe."

I tilt my head. "Does this have to do with the interview?"

"No. I mean, we could talk about it, but not really."

"I would except"—please don't let this hurt my chances at my dream job—"I'm involved with someone." *Two someones.* The thought bowls me over because both Darius and Arlo came to mind at the same time. I am *really* involved.

"Oh, well, okay. That's fine. Still, I'd like to talk to you for a bit. I have a couple of questions for you. Want to..." He points down the street.

Maybe he wants to talk about funds? It would be nice to talk informally with someone in the industry. "Sure. Just a coffee, though."

His face lights up. "Yeah. Of course."

So I go.

And then choke on my coffee when I learn Jeremy is the favorite nephew of the company owner and has a corner office and five stocks to watch.

I have a spreadsheet of fifty I monitor, and I'm not in the industry yet. My dread skyrockets when he holds his phone up and shows me a picture of me, in my crown on stage, with an armful of flowers.

For a few, I think it might be okay, because he mainly talks about himself, but then he touches my hand as he talks about how I should go to this new club with him or try a new high-end restaurant because they have a five course meal with wine flights.

"We can check it out together," he says, like it's a given that I'd want to do that.

I laugh and divert. "Don't think my boyfriend would appreciate that."

He laughs too, though I'm not sure why. I put my hands in my lap as I ask him about the stocks he's watching, and stay smiling, because that's what I should do, right? My chest tightens as I tune out his rant about Chicago's obsession with pizza while trying to think of a gracious way to get the fuck out of this coffeehouse.

Once more, I try to bring it back to business—the only reason I'm here—and he keeps bringing up places I'd like even when I don't ski or golf.

It's the worst first date I never agreed to go on.

The caramel latte tastes bitter in my mouth.

And when his dark eyes get that glimmer of lust that makes my stomach fall to the ground, I tell him, "I really have to go, but it was great meeting you." I regret those words the moment they're out of my stupid pageant-girl mouth. It wasn't great meeting him, but I've rehearsed that response so much it's become ingrained. A better response would have been telling him I wish I'd never met him. Too bad I can't say that.

Especially when, as I take his offered handshake, he jerks me close and kisses me.

Chapter Forty-Nine

Darius Is Done

DARIUS

J olene's tearful voicemail asking me to call her makes my heart rate take off in a sprint. I've been locked in meetings for hours, and now it's past lunchtime. *Jesus.*

I jog toward the elevator, texting Martina as I go.

> I have to leave for the rest of the day. Will catch you up later.

There's no phone service in the enforced capsule of the elevator, so I impatiently wait while I descend ten floors. I send a message to Arlo.

> Did Jolene call you?

I push send as soon as the doors open and the signal bars return. The interview had to have gone badly, right? If it were an emergency, I'd have gotten a call. Dammit, she really needed a win with that.

As I'm dialing Jolene, Arlo texts.

Arlo:

> No, why?

I return his message.

> Left me a voicemail. She was upset, but I was in meetings. Calling her now. I'll keep you posted.

I dial while I flag down a taxi, forgoing the train. She doesn't answer, but fortunately a cab veers to the curb and in seconds, the woman's tearing back into traffic on the way to our apartment.

Dialing again, I hold my breath until Jolene answers with a weak, "Hi."

"What's going on, babes?"

"Oh, um, hang on. Arlo's texting me." She sighs, the click of her nails sounding through the line, then says, "I'm fine," in that way that tells me she's not fine at all.

"What happened?"

She blows out a long breath through the line. "Well, the interview went great. Best ever."

My brows furrow. "That's good?"

Her sniffle makes me eye the traffic with disdain. "Oh, it was. But then the company owner's nephew asked me to get coffee with him. I didn't know that's who he was at first. He was just a guy in the interview with two others. He played the role of the aloof and nice one, and I wanted to say no, but didn't because my mother's voice was in my head telling me to be polite. 'Why not?' popped right out of my damn mouth. So dumb of me."

My spine stiffens, and I feel like mini spikes are shooting out of my entire body. "What did he do?"

"He kissed me." Her breath catches.

"What the fuck?" I hadn't experienced blood draining from my face until now.

"Yeah. That's what I said after I slapped him. Hard. It was just a reaction, but I had told him I had a boyfriend, and it was just supposed to be coffee to discuss stocks. I told him, I swear."

I wave her off as if she could see me. "I know you did, babes. What an asshole. What did he do after that?" I swear if he threatens or stalks her—I force my jaw to relax before I break teeth.

"I don't know. I rushed out of the place and walked. Got a blister."

"You're home now?" When she confirms, I breathe a little easier. "I'm so sorry. I was stuck in meetings and didn't get your message. You should have called Arlo."

"Yeah, I didn't want to bother him."

"It's not bothering him when you need us, Joles."

"I don't know where we stand."

I rub my forehead. They have got to figure out what's between them. The last few days have had us living in a haze of tension. They don't talk unless it's dirty, in-the-moment words. She's stressed, but she can rely on him, and should know that by now.

"I'm almost home." I rub my sweaty palm against my chinos. "I'm going to call Arlo and give him an update, unless you have already."

"I didn't."

"You should have. He's worried about you. You can always call him when you need him, and this was a time you needed him."

"Yeah, but..." I can visualize her nose scrunch. "I know."

We hang up with I love yous, and I call Arlo as the driver pulls onto our street.

Arlo's low, "Are you fucking kidding me?" as I explain is a good sign that both the asshole and Jolene are in for it when he gets home, but she's not the only one at fault for not reaching out when she needed to.

I pay and head inside. "Nope. Not kidding. She didn't think she could call you for help."

It sounds like he's moving fast, and the quiet background breaks into the familiar chatter of Chicago's downtown district. "Why the fuck not?"

"Because you two don't talk to each other outside of fucking, and she doesn't know where she stands with you."

"How can she not know?"

I shove into the lobby. "I don't even know, brother. You usually tell me how you're feeling with women, but not with Jolene."

Sheena stands up from the desk. Her blouse is unbuttoned enough that her bra peeks out. "How's Arlo doing?"

"It's none of your business." I keep walking to the elevator, switching the phone to my other ear. "See. That was Sheena, and I know where you stand with her."

"Why didn't you say something?"

"Because I love you both and don't want to play telephone when you should talk to each other about what's between you. I know you swore off relationships and anything beyond the bedroom, but it's more here. It's Jolene. Please don't hurt her and yourself because you're not used to speaking to women outside of the bedroom."

"Alright." He clears his throat. "Okay. Jolene means more to me than any other woman I've ever been with. I thought that was clear."

I check the bars as the elevator closes, but the signal stays. "More than Krisha?" She had us all fooled until Arlo got a tattoo of a snake on his shoulder. Then she told him no more if he wanted to be with her. When he questioned that, she told him he also needed to speak without cursing, would take a job her father had lined up for him when he graduated that would put them near her family, then they would get married at the beach—a small ceremony she'd already planned out.

She'd had a secret five-year plan lined up, and the dam didn't just break that day. It exploded with her bullshit.

In a way, I get why she held it all in. With the way she'd decided thier life would roll out, she had to have known it was over the minute he told her anything about his past. Maybe she thought she'd ease him into her plan and he wouldn't notice, but the tattoo got her too worked up to stay quiet. The funny thing is, he was thinking about a future with her. She was the last woman he thought about that with.

He sighs over the line. "Far more than Krisha."

That's something big, and also scary. If they can't work this out, where is that going to leave him?

"You and Jolene need to figure things out. Please. I'm headed up-stairs. I assume I'm seeing you in a few?"

"On my way."

Inside, I rush to the bedroom, stumbling when I step in.

Jolene's still in her interview outfit. Her eyes are puffy, and she's sitting on the bed next to an open suitcase half-full of haphazardly thrown-in clothes.

Chapter Fifty

Arlo Finds Out

ARLO

As soon as I walk through the building doors, Sheena pops out of her chair. "Hello, sir." She uses her sultry voice, but my dick doesn't even twitch. She's not getting that I'm so done.

Clearly, I need to work on speaking more. I'm eager to check on Jolene, but halt at the front desk, because this can't continue.

She preens under my gaze. "There's a place we could—"

"No." I wait for her grin to drift away before I say the rest. "I apologize if it wasn't clear that I'm not interested in continuing a sexual relationship with you, but I'm not. Stop trying."

"To tempt you? I don't think I can stop trying that, sir."

"You will."

She leans forward, pushing out her cleavage. "How about one more time, then?"

I step back and signal to my pants. "No part of me is interested. Go find someone who is."

As I'm walking away, she says, "Like your roommate. Since you're *not interested*, I can put some time into him. Find out when his bitch leaves—"

Fire burns along the back of my neck, but I don't have time for this, because I need to get to the most important woman in my world. How in the hell did that happen? No idea, but I don't regret falling for Jolene.

I stab the elevator's up button, and call over my shoulder to Sheena as I step in. "From now on, you only speak to us if you have something tenant-related." No more insults or bitch behavior directed at Jolene. No one is hurting her again if I can help it.

The doors close, and I exhale my rage. I'm filled with too many emotions right now and need to focus on Jolene and Darius.

When I get inside, the house is quiet. I head to their room and find them lying on the bed, facing each other, heads on pillows and both clothed. There's a goddamn suitcase with clothes thrown in.

"Fuck no." My words just pop out, but really—fuck no. She's not leaving us.

Her eyes are puffy, and when she looks at me, there's a pleading pain in her expression.

Walking to her side, I ball my fingers. "Can I touch you?"

Her eyes get watery again. "Of course you can."

I tilt her face towards me and wipe at her smudged mascara with my thumb. "You okay?"

She swallows. "Not really."

That's an appropriate answer. We can work with that.

I lower my voice to a deadly tone. "Why are you packing?"

She gives a sound that's between a laugh and a sob. "I was going to go ho—to Lexington. For a bit. Just to..." She scrunches her nose.

Heat floods my veins. "Was?"

She gives the slightest nod. "Not anymore. I calmed down after I thought everything through." She wipes at her mouth, and I notice the smeared lipstick on the back of her hand, like she'd been desperate to undo that kiss.

I've never had rage unfold inside me like this. It's wildfire in my blood. Someone put their lips on our girl when she didn't want it.

Darius looks just as enraged, his eyes murderous and jaw working as he sits up.

I tap Jolene's chin and swipe my thumb under her perfect bottom lip. "What's his name?" There is nothing but intense command in my voice, which should probably scare her.

Instead, she leans into my touch. "Are you going to hunt him down, Arlo?"

"Yes." Digitally, then physically. I don't like this worry inside. She can take care of herself. Logically, I know that. But that doesn't stop me from wanting to make that asshole regret every bad decision he's ever made, starting with touching Jolene. I will destroy his fucking world for messing with her.

She dips her head and kisses my thumb. "It's not right, but that actually makes me feel better."

"Good." I massage her hair, fingers shifting through her silky waves. "You should have called me. I would have been there for you in a second. And when I texted, you said everything was fine. You lied to me."

She huffs and rolls her eyes. "I can handle it."

I point to her open suitcase. "That's not fucking handling it."

She makes a huff of annoyance.

Well, I'm annoyed too.

Darius slips out of the bed and tugs his clothes off. For a moment, I think he needs to be with us, but then he pulls on jogging pants and a tee. "Going for a run."

"Baby?" Jolene asks.

He pauses at the door, back rigid and face sour. "I love you both, but I'm ready for you to stop avoiding what's between you. It's hurting us. Figure it out. Please." Then he's down the hall and the door slams.

Jolene sighs. "We're in trouble."

"We are." Especially if we can't work through this to avoid problems like this—not telling each other everything and running for it. No, I won't lose her. Refuse to. "I need you to tell me every detail about what happened."

"Arlo..." She swallows hard. "I don't want to."

I drag her to me, off the bed and into my arms, where she belongs. "Why not?"

"Because, um." She scrunches her nose and looks to the ceiling. "I just..."

"Tell me, angel. You've got to know I'd do anything for you."

Her eyes swing to mine and stick.

"I would." I nod. "Tell me what I can do to fix it. Do you need words? A bath, or whatever."

"Can you, um, punish me?"

I did not expect that request. "And what am I punishing you for?"

"For not listening to my intuition. I knew I shouldn't have gone."

"Not your fault." I cup her face. "He's the problem here, Jolene. Not you."

She shakes her head. "I know, but... this is hard to explain. I just need you to be *you* right now. Tell me I knew better."

Dammit, this woman. "You should have listened to yourself. You're always right."

She nods rapidly, and her breathing kicks up. "Okay. And I shouldn't have been so nice to him."

"He's a fucking asshole and a stranger. He didn't deserve a second of kindness from you."

Her throat bobs with a swallow. "Yeah. Okay. I need you to make me forget today." She grimaces.

It all snaps together, and my heart about leaps out of my body.

My girl needs me because I won't allow her to be anything but herself. She forgot that today and needs a reminder. Well, shit. She is so completely mine and is asking me to make her know it.

I take a long breath, step back from her, and sit on the bed. "Come here."

Her shoulders sink with her exhale, and she steps between my spread knees.

I capture her with a hand splayed over her ass and the other gripping her neck, and pull her closer. "Can I kiss you?" I whisper against her lips.

She grips my hair and tugs, making my eyes go half-closed. "You can always kiss me."

I shake my head, rubbing our noses together. "Not today, angel. I can be too much, especially after what happened to you. I would never make things worse for you if I can help it."

"Arlo, you're never too much for me." She runs her nails over the sides of my head, sending delicious chills down my neck. "You make things so much better for me all the time. Please do that now."

I tilt my head as I study her expression, seeking any kind of re-luctance. It's not that I don't trust her to know what she needs, but shit like what she went through can come back at really inopportune times, like when I'm getting rough, or if I make a movement that's too similar. I flinched for years when someone pulled their elbows back as they stretched. I couldn't join a gym because of that.

Dammit, if I could erase what happened to her, I would.

I palm her cheek. "Tell me it's okay to touch you like I do. I don't want to scare you."

She grips my ears and presses her forehead to mine. "I'm never scared of you, Arlo."

My lips quirk up. "You are in fleeting moments. I've seen you with Darius when you're fully comfortable, and it's not the same way you act with me."

"Because you're different."

"Good way?"

"So much." She bites her lip in the way she does when she's holding back.

I tug it from the cage of her teeth with my thumb. "There's something else."

She licks her lips and swallows. "Uh, I don't know how not to get attached to you."

My heart beats quickly for her. "Good. I want you attached. I *am* attached to you."

Her brows lift in a sweet, hopeful way that melts me. "Yeah?"

I give her my best, *how could you not see that,* expression. "I've been pining over you, needing you every second, sprinting to the damn train to get home to you sooner. Kissing you goodbye is a morning routine I never want to change."

Her grin is radiant. "I love that morning kiss." She pushes at my chest. "I've been a worried wreck, feeling like I was doing something wrong for..." Her expression goes a little shocked, and she goes back to biting that lip.

I raise my eyebrows. "Wanting me so much?" I know she does. Not as much as I want her, though, because that's not possible.

She runs a finger over my eyebrow, then my temple and cheekbone. "I need you to be you right now. Today did not go well."

I nod, taking a breath to pull myself together so I can be what she needs. "What's your safe word, Jolene?"

"Pickles."

"Good girl. Use that for anything. Do you understand me? Slow-down, stop, or if you need a second to process, you use it."

She blinks at me, all slow and sweet. "Thank you."

I stretch my neck and start unbuttoning my sleeves. "Don't thank me yet. I'm going to make your ass red until you fully understand that you are mine and I am yours. Then, you will unpack your bag because your home is here with me and Darius. Nowhere else."

Chapter Fifty-One

Jolene Gets Her Answers

JOLENE

My cheeks heat. So does between my legs, and I can tell he notices the shift because his eyes narrow, and his lips firm into the intensity I love so much.

He rolls up his sleeve cuffs. "Bare your ass and lie down over my lap." That's new.

I slowly drag my skirt up to expose my lacy thong.

He exhales a "fuck me" then signals me forward. "Leave that on."

That makes me smile. Throughout the day, I've thought of him peeling it off me, maybe in the kitchen or even the hallway.

I crawl onto his lap, settling down with my stomach against his hard thighs. "Like this?"

"Yes. Now, count." He grips my throat.

"Wha—" My words are cut off by my yelp when his hand comes down hard on my ass.

"That was one. Say it, Jolene."

"One." The sting makes chills rise on my skin.

His fingers give the slightest bit of pressure against my throat, holding me in place. "When you need me, you will call me. It doesn't matter what you need or at what time of day or how far apart we are. Do you understand me?"

I love the growl in his voice so much. "Yes, sir."

His hand comes down again, striking me harder than ever.

I hiss, scrunching my eyes shut and resting my forehead on the bed. The sensation is overwhelming, and I welcome it. Thrive in it. "Two."

"When you doubt how I feel about you, ask me and I will tell you. We're never going to let it get to a point where we don't know where we stand with each other. Right?"

Does he mean that? Because there are still a few things that I'd like clarified. "Yes, sir."

The next strike is so fast to my other buttock, it's shocking.

I yip. "Th-three."

"You are mine and Darius's. That's it. You do not go out with other men, even potential coworkers, without telling us. That way, we know where you are and who to bury if they don't behave around you. Are we clear?"

Is it wrong for that to turn me on? Maybe. But it makes me feel cared for. Important. I nod and stretch to kiss his forearm. "Yes, sir."

He slips his fingers under my thong and across my slit with ease, sending delicious sensations between my legs and over my stinging backside. His cock twitches and hardens against my side. I think it might be hotter with it caged underneath his work pants.

I whimper when his touch disappears, and groan when I hear him suck his fingers. My ass feels like it's radiating heat, and I realize why he wanted to talk this way. The pain makes his words feel like they're branding me, sinking in to stay forever.

His hand comes down again. "No one kisses you but us." He squeezes my backside in a crushing grip, making me squirm. "No one else touches this body, licks your sweet cunt, or turns this ass red unless we all agree. Do you understand?"

"Yes, sir."

"Good girl."

I turn as well as I can to look at him. "What about you? Do others get to touch your body?" I'm a little afraid to ask because he already told me they would, but the endorphin rush from his punishment makes me need to test out if he really meant I could ask him about these things.

He drags me closer by my neck, bending my back so he can kiss me. It's tender in the harshest way.

I smile at the irony that his severity makes me feel safe.

He kisses the crest of my cheekbone, then stares in a way that makes me study the deep soul under the blue of his eyes. "Only if you want to try something new. I'm completely devoted to you, Jolene. For as long as you want me, I am yours and no one else's. Do you understand?"

My pulse thrums wildly against his fingers. Devoted? That's not something he does. Ever, according to him and Darius. "You mean that?"

He shoves me back over his thighs, and his hand comes down again.

I screech a laugh. "Yes, sir. Got it. I understand."

Arlo's chest rises and falls in a deep sigh. He lets go of my neck and rubs my sore backside before giving it a light pat. "Everything okay? Did I hurt you?"

It's amazing how much I love the pain he gives me. I feel euphoric. Clean. My head is clear, and my heart is full. "Much better. You hurt me perfectly."

He hums. "I'm so glad. Now get this pretty red ass up and unpack your bag."

I don't want to leave his lap, because he's warm and solid. But I also want to please him, and maybe asking for him to punish me was for both of us. I need him in control as much as he needs to be in control. So I kiss his thigh and slide from his lap, but can't make myself move from him. I lean in close and press my nose against his neck. "I'm sorry. For so much." Most of my problem is that I should have just asked him how he felt, but my stupid manners are too ingrained. I didn't want him to judge me for needing him if that wasn't what he wanted.

He nods and massages the back of my neck. "The only thing to be sorry for is running away. Never do that again."

I pull back to look at him. "It wasn't from you two, though." That might not be entirely true. Feeling like Arlo would never return my love and what that would do to Darius hit a little harder when the hope for my career broke into rubble.

"It was. The moment you got in your head to go back home, you abandoned us. Never let it go that far again."

Swallowing the thickness in my throat, I nod and kiss Arlo's chin. "I shouldn't have panicked like I did. I should have called you."

He cups my cheek. "And I should have talked to you sooner. There's never a time that you can't rely on me. It's my fault you didn't know that." He kisses my forehead. "Unpack."

I step back and push down my shucked-up skirt, but Arlo stops me, taking my wrist. "No. Leave that up."

My face heats and I squirm, but smile at the way he eyes my thighs. I needed this. Not only clarification about us but also to be seen as a sexual deviant, not because of the way I look. There's such a difference with Arlo. It's like he knows who I am deep down and drags me to the surface just by appreciating this side of me. He doesn't sneer at it, or tell me I'm wrong.

I turn so he can see what feels like a second-degree burn on my butt, and he rewards me with a hissed breath.

"Bad girl," he whispers.

I refold clothes, then tuck the piles back into the drawers where they belong. All the while feeling Arlo's gaze all over me.

"Suitcase too," he says when I turn to him.

I zip it and put it in the closet, then return to stand in front of him.

He watches my eyes, staying silent.

I could ask him what's next, get impatient and poke at him, but I want to leave everything up to him right now. If he wants me to stand here all night because he thinks that's best... okay.

With a subtle nod, he hooks a finger into my thong, trailing a light touch along the lace. "Undress and come into my room. I'd fuck you here, but your headboard won't support restraints."

What good deeds did I do to deserve him and Darius?

Chapter Fifty-Two

Arlo Does Something New

ARLO

The way Jolene's eyes go wide with surprise and lust makes a trail of ideas sprout in my mind. I will give her everything her kinky side desires. And she has a strong, kinky side that we've only begun to unleash.

I stand and head toward the door. "You do not want to keep me waiting."

She walks in as I'm securing leather cuffs to the rungs. Like the best girl she is, she slides her gorgeously bare body onto my bed and kneels. I notice the tremble through her perfect body.

I turn and unbutton my shirt the rest of the way. "Are you cold or nervous?"

"Both."

I toss my shirt toward the hamper, then kick off my shoes and socks.

Jolene licks her lips as she looks over my chest and abs, then eyes my belt.

I signal to it. "Help me with this."

She's already reaching for me. Her fingers tremble as she undoes the latches, button, and the zipper. She palms my hard dick before tugging my pants down. "This feels different."

"My cock?" I push her onto the mattress before she can touch me more. I'm already riding the line of control, and I need to take care of her.

She rolls her eyes, but it's too soon to spank her again without making her too sore. "I'm talking about *it*, Arlo. This moment. I'm nervous because this feels different between us."

Trailing fingers up her soft arm, I watch her eyes flutter, then grip her wrist and fasten the cuff around it. "Because it is." I do the same to her other arm, then move back to pull the leg restraints from where I tucked them. Hiding a smile is impossible when she gasps and squirms as I pin her ankles.

Her spread body is a heavenly playground. I'll do this with ropes and a blindfold one day if she likes the restraints. A gag and a plug if she finds that enjoyable enough. But today, it's just us.

"We're together now, Darius and you and me. You look perfect, angel." I kiss the tops of her feet, then her ankles. Move my way up, taking my time touching every inch of my girl with careful fingers and lips. She squirms and lifts, desperate to get closer, faster, and I'm glad I decided on the restraints. If she had her hands on me, I'd already be inside her.

"More, please." She lifts her hips as I pass by, kissing each crest, then dipping my tongue into her belly button. "Arlo? Please."

"No," I grumble, playing my thumbs over her sides as I place an open-mouth kiss between her breasts.

Her harrumph makes me smile. My impatient woman. She likes it when we make her wait for her reward, though. She doesn't know that, but there's a difference in her moans and the arch of her spine as she gets truly desperate for more. It's so damn fun to get her worked up, just like this.

I trail my tongue so slowly over her collarbones. Her quick breaths against my hair raise chills on my neck.

"I didn't expect this." There's a smile in her words, and her body relaxes under me.

I rest my hard dick against her mound and kiss every inch of her neck while I send soft touches over one forearm, then the other. "You thought I'd be rough with you?"

She moans when I capture her earlobe in my teeth. "I'm being punished."

"This doesn't feel like punishment?"

The restraints creak as she tugs. "Maybe a little. But I like it."

"You like what I do to you." I settle fully against her, propped up on my elbows. I rub my thumb over her lips. "You scared me today." I kiss one dimple, then the other.

"I was scared today." Her eyes are so honest that heat expands in my chest.

"I know. That's what was most frightening to me. I'd burn down the city for you, and you were ready to run without a discussion first."

Her eyes tear up. "Thank you for telling me everything. I wasn't sure. I felt it in the way you look at me, but grew up surrounded by people hiding behind a mask of what someone else thinks they should be. It's confusing sometimes, and you mean a lot to me. I don't want to be confused about you."

I don't want that either. "I should have done things better with you from the start and trusted my instincts. Pushed you harder for more conversations like this one. Open honesty from now on, okay? Even if it's scary."

She tugs against the restraints. "I promise."

I seal Jolene and my promise of honesty from now on with a kiss—slow pecks at first, then harder, claiming her as I try to cover any mark the asshole made on my girl.

Jolene opens to me a little at a time until her trembles become rolling hips and frustrated jerks against the leather holding her back from getting what she wants, which is me. She wants *me*, all of me—the intensity, the possessiveness, the absolute loyalty I have to her and Darius. My life feels clearer than ever.

When I pull away from her, she growls in frustration and tries to follow. I suck a hickey on her hip.

"Yes," she moans. "Harder. I want it there for a week."

This woman is so mine. I finger her clit while I fulfill her request, making sure my mark is blood red, then I lap at her soaked pussy while she curses the restraints with a thicker accent.

"You want to ride my face, but you can't, can you?" I watch my fingers slide in and out of her swollen slit.

"Yes. Please, Arlo. I need you."

"And I need you so fucking much, Jolene." I bring my gaze up and find her staring back, raw lust and more in her eyes. I know mine reflects the same feelings. We're in so deep. I dip my head, holding her gaze, and suck her clit relentlessly while she cries out, spasming against my lips and fingers. When her hips try to escape my tongue, I give her two more licks, then un-tether her ankles.

Her legs are weak from her orgasm, but she clumsily tries to drag me closer with them.

I don't make her wait and rub the head of my cock against her wet heat, then slowly slide in.

Fuck, she is so hot inside.

I can feel every aftershock tightening around me. Each satiny inch inside her slick channel.

Her eyes flutter closed, and she arches with a moan.

And now I need her hands on me. Jerking at the buckles around her wrists, I free her and massage her fingers until she evades and wraps her arms around me, sliding her hands down to grip my ass.

"Arlo," she says on an exhale. "You're bare inside me."

"I am." I stroke her face, kiss her, and slide out, then back inside her at a torturously slow pace. "That okay?"

"Yes." She gives rapid nods and parts her lips in a silent moan as I give another slow thrust. Her legs wrap over my hips. "From the first time we fucked, I've wanted to feel you come inside my pussy."

"Fuck me, you're so fucking perfect." I have no hope of trying to stay calm after she says something like that. Our lips collide, and I thrust hard into my perfect girl.

She digs her heels into my bed, lifting like she needs me so deep inside, I'll never come out. I'm perfectly fine with that. Living inside her sweet heat seems like a good way to enjoy my days. Her little whimpers are impossibly sexy, and I get why Darius said he's come early because of her sounds.

I'm barely hanging on as my balls tighten and my spine feels electrified. "Are you going to come again?"

"Yes," she whimpers. She puts her hand on my cheek and rolls her hips. "There. Grind. Please."

I stay deep inside her and work the base of my cock against her clit.

Her eyes squeeze shut, and she gasps as the pulses begin.

I didn't know pleasure until now. There's no possibility of prolonging as I thrust, or more like sloppily jerk against her while grunting—my body giving a grand *fuck you* to me for attempting to be graceful and chill while my orgasm builds so tight I'm fearful the strength of it will hurt us both. But then everything aligns, snaps, and, fuck if it isn't everything and more than I ever thought it could be.

Stars—no—celestial bodies orbit in my eyes, shutting out anything except the heat of Jolene, her soft touches down my damp back, and the sweet floral smell of her lodging into an olfactory memory I'll keep until my dying day.

When I descend from heaven, I'm on my back with Jolene tucked tight against me. I tilt her face up to me. "Are you okay?"

"I am now." The way she says it melts everything inside me. She's okay because of me, because of us, and what we just did. It's only going to get better from here.

I turn, rolling over on top of her again and kiss her addictive mouth before crawling down and nudging her legs apart.

She slams her knees back together again.

I growl and glare up at her.

She's grinning, the little tart. "Did you want to see?"

"Yes."

"Say please."

I raise an eyebrow. "Please let me see the mess I made of your pussy before I spank your sore ass for not taking direction."

Her grin grows wider, and she slowly tips her legs apart. "Anything for you."

"Fuck, that's so hot, angel. You just gave me a new kink, and it might be my favorite." I push the escaping stream back into her pussy and tap her clit, just to hear more of her sounds.

She doesn't disappoint. She whimpers, squeezing her eyes shut. Her lips kick up. "How do you make me come so much, Arlo? I still want you."

"Good. You come so much because I make you come."

She laughs. She knows it's true.

"And you're going to do it again. Let's see what you feel like when you're slick with my cum." I'm already hard again and flip her, slipping back inside her with ease. This time isn't as sweet, but just as perfect.

She gets on her hands and knees, giving me the angle to grip her hips and fuck her hard.

I reach under her when I can't hold on much longer, sliding a finger over her clit, and then we're both crashing together again.

"Did you have time to talk?"

I lift my head from kissing Jolene's shoulder and turn to find Darius standing in the room, sweaty and unamused. His tented athletic pants lessen his full anger.

I wrap my arm around Jolene and hug her to me. "What do you think, angel? We clear on things?"

She gives me a heart-stopping smile over her shoulder. "We are."

Chapter Fifty-Three

Darius Gets Some Clarity

DARIUS

Has anything really changed between them? Looks the same from here. While I couldn't ever regret walking in on them fucking, they need to be solid beyond the bedroom.

Jolene was going to *leave*. For all I know, she still may. And then what? I don't want to be apart from her ever again, but I also don't want to live in Kentucky without Arlo.

And as soon as she sets foot in her mom's house again, Donna will do anything to keep her there—jobs, food, friends. She'll bury Jolene under a thousand pounds of guilt she'll never be able to crawl out of. Does Arlo not realize how bad this is? It's not *get Jolene bent over* time, it's *get Jolene on solid ground so she'll stay* time.

Any stress I ran off as I pounded down Chicago streets only took the slightest edge off the emotions rolling through me. Standing here with a hard-on, dripping sweat all over Arlo's floor isn't doing anything for my mood.

"Well"—I massage the tight muscles in my neck—"Wonderful, I guess." I'll believe it when I see it. I head into my bedroom, ignoring their quiet murmurs. After launching my clothes toward the bathroom hamper, I step into a chilly shower, pressing my hands to the tile and hanging my head forward while the water pounds on my back. I need to get my head on straight and then sort out how to help Jolene feel more secure here, so we all feel more secure.

The shower door opens with a click. "Goddamn that's cold." Arlo turns up the heat and steps in, holding a hand back for Jolene. Once the door clicks closed, Arlo turns me around and drags me into a naked, wet hug. "We're okay. I swear it." The clean scent of our shower can't overpower the smell of sweat and Jolene on his skin.

She presses against my back and hugs my waist. "I didn't mean to upset you, and I promise I'll talk to both of you more. It's just, it's been a lot to stomach all the rejection and then today..." she sighs.

"I know." I reach back to palm her hip. "But when I think about you leaving, I—"

"She's not leaving us. Not ever, right, angel?"

Us?

"I'm not. I just panicked. You know how I am."

I do, but I didn't expect her to pack like she was going to leave before the day was through.

"And now you know what to do when you're upset." Arlo shifts his arm to loop around her, pressing her against me hard.

"Yep." She laughs. "Stop squishing me and Darius."

"I think he likes it." Arlo shifts. "Yep. He's hard."

He's not wrong, but I'm still upset that someone hurt Jolene and her chances at a job she'd love. The ground isn't just shaky here; it's cracking open and threatening to take her away from me. I groan. "Shut up, you two."

"Start talking, shut up." Jolene rubs her hard nipples against my back and, yeah, there's no stopping the jump of my erection. "Darius has his bossy pants on today."

"Maybe it's time to boss him around. What do you think, angel?"

"I think that's the best idea."

That must have been one epic fuck to turn the mood around this much.

"Good." Arlo steps back and turns me around.

"What are you doing?" I ask.

He leans against the tile and pulls me back against him, tugging my wrists behind my back. "Do you need a safe word, too?"

I sigh, resigned to whatever they're planning on doing with me. "I'll borrow Jolene's."

She steps against me and gets close enough to my lips that I expect the kiss, but before I can connect, she ducks and runs her teeth gently across my nipple. My arms move to touch her, but Arlo holds tight. A thrill simmers through me. So this is what it's like to be tied up? Not bad at all.

He sets his chin on my shoulder, looking down at Jolene. "Trail that pretty mouth down."

She does, teasing my chest, stomach, licking my hip. "Should I touch this hard cock, or leave it be?"

That cock gets impossibly hard. "Hell, babes."

Arlo chuckles, probably at my shocked state. "One small taste."

We both watch on as she grips me and sets the head of my dick against her tongue.

She licks, then kisses.

It's a jolt to my balls, and I groan.

She's owning this space or role that she's fallen into. I've never seen her so comfortable playing with my cock, even if the water is cooler than she'd like and matting her hair down on one side. Even if she had the worst damn day that none of us were expecting. Even when everything could fall apart. Our life when she moved here was supposed to be perfect, because she is perfect.

However, maybe this new comfort between the two of them will lead to that. Maybe they really are okay.

"Can I have more?" She bites her bottom lip and gives us her sex eyes, and I'm already coming undone, arching toward her as Arlo holds me back.

"You may." Arlo's voice is too amused for him. Too gentle.

I gulp down a groan when she takes me all the way in.

Arlo nips at my shoulder, making me jump. "Be a good girl and work your clit for us."

She raises an eyebrow, but fully gets on her knees and slips her hand between her legs.

"That's so hot, babes."

"Fuck yes, it is." Arlo holds my wrists tighter. "Is my cum dripping out of you? Let me see."

"You came inside of her?" My heart skips a happy beat. That's something Arlo has never done. Not with his one long-time girlfriend, not with a drunken one-night stand. He swore he never would because of the many risks that all boiled down to not wanting to be trapped, and that alone says Jolene is it for him. I turn to meet his eyes, which actually seem to gleam. He's never looked happier.

"Twice." Jolene lets go of me to lean back. The water hits her chest and sends rivulets down her stomach and hips in an image I never want to leave my brain. She opens her pussy to show off.

Arlo groans. "That is spank-bank fodder for life."

"Or we could just do it again whenever you want." Jolene gives him a wicked grin. "I liked it."

"I'm still reeling." He kisses my shoulder. "Now hurry and finish Darius before the water gets cold. I'll order dinner, and then I want to drink bourbon off your nipples."

Jolene surges forward, and I moan to the ceiling as she gets right to work while Arlo holds me tight and directs—the two of them working as my personal team of pleasure-makers.

It feels right. It feels like love between all of us. I allow the stress of the day to wash off me as I'm taken care of by the two people I love most in the world.

When I shout my release, and Jolene takes it all while Arlo praises us both, my heart cracks right open. I turn my head and kiss Arlo.

Jolene crawls up my body, and I take her lips as soon as she's close enough. She cups my cheek, then leans to give attention to Arlo.

In silence, we wash each other, nuzzle and hold each other tightly, unsure of the future but all too happy to live in this moment together. This is going to work. It really is.

Chapter Fifty-Four

Jolene Makes A Decision

JOLENE

I hold Darius's hand as I stand in front of Diggory and Sons. "I'm going to barf."

He squeezes my fingers. "Want me to go in with you?"

"Again no. I put on my big-girl panties today—"

"Which Arlo took off."

My cheeks are hot, and not just my face, but I laugh. "Which Arlo took off. But I also have his handprint on my ass, so I'll be fine."

Arlo told me that since he had to attend a company-wide meeting and he wasn't allowed to rip Jeremy's spine from his body if he came with me, I should *feel* him with me. I feel him all right. With every step and shift, the sore spot lights up.

"Your big-girl handprint."

"I guess that's a thing now." I take a deep breath. "Okay. Wish me luck."

Darius pulls me close, kissing me.

"Lipstick," I murmur.

"Don't care." He pinches my chin and gives me a final peck. "I love you, babes. I'm going to wait right in there for you." The coffeeshop he points at has a cartoon cup with heart-shaped steam coming from it. It's adorable and wasn't the place I went with Jeremy. He took me somewhere a block and a half away, which all makes sense now. "Call if you need me."

"Okay." I give him a tight smile.

He sighs.

I wave him off and smile for real. "I know, I know." The man can read my face as if he's staring into my brain. But I'm going to need to fake it a bit. I know what I'm going to say, but then I walk into the building and look down at that polished glass floor.

How many people mentioned this made them uncomfortable? I've rethought every preconceived notion about this company I thought so much of. I grew up in the pageant world—I should have known better, but had so much hope that I didn't see the danger. The shininess blinded me.

"Nervous in elevators?" The male security guard fidgets with his belt buckle.

I think of Arlo's hand around my throat, of Darius's holding my hand, and step back until the bar bites into my sore backside. I smile, a real one, but at myself in the mirrored walls. "Not anymore." The doors glide open to the eighth floor, and I glance around for the one face I hope never to see again.

The guard leads me to an office and knocks, opening the door when a familiar voice says, "Come in."

Mr. Gant smiles when he sees me and stands, beckoning me in. "Ms. Shah. I was glad you wanted to meet. We have some things to discuss. Please come in."

My heart does a flip, then crashes. He's going to offer me this job, and I'm not allowed to hope for it. I know better now. Fuck, this is going to hurt.

I shake his hand and sit, exhaling a held breath when I feel that ache. "I really enjoyed speaking with you and the others."

"And we enjoyed speaking to you. Actually, I have—"

I hold up a hand. "Let me get this out before nerves destroy me or you offer me something and I forget why I came here."

He tames back his smile and leans forward on his elbows, just like he did in the interview. "I'm listening."

"It's about Jeremy Jung."

His expression changes while I tell him what happened—the way Jeremy asked me to coffee, how I told him I wasn't single, the entire conversation, and then the sneak kiss. I fight not to wipe my lips again as I remember.

Mr. Gant blows out a long breath, puts his hands behind his head and leans back in his chair. "That should never have happened."

"No, it should not have. So, I wanted to talk to you before anything goes any further, because it was very clear that Jeremy gets what he wants at this company, and he has his eyes on me." I've come across people like him before. I may not have stuck around to witness his reaction, but there's typically two responses he would have had—calling me a stuck-up bitch, or he'd think it was adorable that I was playing hard to get. From the way that he didn't hear a thing I said to him, I'd bank on the latter.

Mr. Gant rubs both his hands down his face and clasps his fingers together. "Are you going to press charges against him?"

"Should I?"

"You should. If you need help drafting something, I have someone." He raises his eyebrows in question, and I want to hug him. Okay, so he's not like this place. That's refreshing.

I sigh. "You and I both know that won't go anywhere. But—" I pull two Chicago Police Department envelopes from my bag and hand them over, mentally thanking Darius for that forethought and hoping Jeremy pees himself when he sees the one with his name formally printed on it. "This is a letter documenting what happened—one for him and one for your HR department. The Chicago police have a copy as well. It states that if anyone comes forward with a complaint against him and needs someone to have their back, I will file charges, sit on a stand, and gladly help them in any way I can. And if he contacts me again, he can expect a quick restraining order." I lean forward. "This part is off the record, but if he ever sees me out with my guys—guy—" I'm positive my cheeks go cherry red and I clear my throat. "He better run like the devil is on his tail, because if he gets caught, let's just say 'spineless' will have a brand new meaning for him."

Mr. Gant's lips quirk for a split second, and he nods, tapping the envelopes on his desk. "I will relay this to *all* necessary parties."

I stand and swallow the tight emotion in my throat. "I had so much fun talking to you."

He pushes up out of his chair. "We were so impressed by you, Ms. Shah." *Were*. Well, that's that. I can't fault him. Nepotism is real and makes people sweep problems under the rug, leaving those around them with bound hands because we all have to make a living. I don't like it, but I get it. He can't fire Jeremy, and he can't have someone on staff who refuses to be in the building with him.

Okay, fine, it hurts a whole damn lot.

Mr. Gant shows me to the door and surprises me by walking with me to the elevators. "Where else are you looking?"

I give him the shortlist. And maybe it's out of nervousness, but I also share the interviews I already had, including the train wreck.

His eyebrows raise. "That's an excellent company."

"I'd think better of it if the interview hadn't gone so poorly."

We enter the elevator, and he pokes the lobby button. "I called Mr. Smitt, Mr. Piece of Shit during my internship."

"You interned with him?"

"I did. And he made my life as difficult as possible. But I learned a ton." He keeps walking with me through the lobby.

I appreciate the personal escort because I'm a lot less nervous with a good person walking next to me.

Hand in his pocket, he holds the door open for me. "No matter what happens next, you need to be in this industry as a lead. You get it. Don't you dare waste that talent."

It's easier to believe that now. I imagine Darius and Arlo saying the same thing, because they have.

His added, "I'm sure we'll meet again," as he waves goodbye, is a little harder to imagine at the moment, but I agree, if only to be polite.

When I walk into the coffee shop, Darius is there with a hug and cocoa. I already have a text from Arlo asking how it went. It feels nice to be fussed over, even when the light at the end of the tunnel is so damn dim.

Chapter Fifty-Five

Arlo Finds The Right Fit

ARLO

I'm in the kitchen waiting for the coffeepot to beep when Jolene whispers, "Arlo?" behind me in her sleepy voice.

Grinning, I turn and pull her to me. I missed her last night. She's in Darius' shirt and—I reach down and cup her bare ass—yep. Nothing else. "Morning, angel. Sleep okay?" She was quiet for the rest of the day yesterday, though I understood it. She's grieving the loss of her number one choice, but I caught her sending her resume to three other places before she slunk off for a bath and bed.

"Yeah." She nuzzles my neck, and maybe I'll stay home today and keep her company since Darius had to go to work early.

I grumble when I remember the client meeting I can't miss. There should be a vacation for getting obsessed with someone and needing to stay home to fuck them relentlessly for a few days.

Jolene clamps my shirt in her fists.

I want to stay here forever. Is this what love is like—wanting to be close like this all the time? It's not something I questioned before. I said it to Krisha, but it was just something to say. I loved her in a way, but always felt like I should have loved her more. That's what took me so long to end it with her. I had to figure out if I should give myself to her out of duty, maybe?

When she had told me she'd mapped out my life with her, I'd thought that I'd missed something and had to decide if I wanted to give up what so many craved. I should have been grateful to find someone I get along well enough with. But a year later, when she sent me a picture of her and her new fiancé, I realized I'd been right. She wasn't for me.

But with Jolene against me, sweet and a little fragile at this stage in her life—strong pulse from a strong heart thrumming against my lips—I can't imagine my life without her. I never want to lose this feeling she's created from nothing inside me.

There was always a draw to her. Something akin to a building lightning bolt when our eyes met, but I'd thought maybe it was simmering rage over me being me or annoyance at an attraction neither of us thought would work out. It's this feeling I didn't understand before.

I run my fingers up and down her spine. "Need coffee?"

She grunts.

I shift right, and she shuffles along, still clinging.

There's no stopping the geeky grin on my face. With one hand, I maneuver a cup for her and pour.

"Getting creamer is going to be difficult," I say, kissing her cheek.

Her sigh is long, and she drops her hands from my shirt. "Fine." She wanders to the fridge, bending just enough to give me the slightest glimpse.

"You'll make me late for work if you bend over any further."

I think she's going to dip lower to test me, but she stands back up and spins, sauntering over to me. "I have an idea." She kisses my chin, then trails her way down my neck, sliding her teeth over my collarbone.

I jerk as she bites down. Yeah, fuck work. "Whatever the idea is, I'm in."

She makes a questioning humming sound. "Good. I think you should give me my morning kiss and..." Her whimpers make my ears tingle in the best way as I palm and squeeze her ass. "And then you should go to work." She gives me a peck on the lips and pushes away from me. "And when you get home, I'll be very, very good for you."

Is she starting a game with me or tempting me to make one?

I straighten. "Do you want to edge me, Jolene?"

Her nose crinkles. "If you want to."

I grin. She definitely wants me to take over. *Done*. I snag her waist and drag her against me. "I'm going to need incentive throughout the day." And I know what would get me revved up.

She grips my hard cock through my pants. "Okay. Um. You should know as soon as you leave, I'm going to lie in your bed and play with that wand thingy."

"Fuck if you're going to do that without me watching." Rocking against her hand, I sip from her lips two—three times, loving how they fit so perfectly to mine. I lift her and set her on the counter.

She squeaks when her bare ass touches the cold marble. "Arlo!"

"This is mine." I chuckle and push her legs apart so I can taste her.

It doesn't take long until she's moaning and leaning back to give me more room. When she's good and whimpering, I kiss the hickey I left on her hip. "I want you to do something for me."

She clutches at my hand, and rocks those hips so good. "Anything." She might regret saying that.

I pull her off the counter, turning to face where she had been sitting. There's the slightest line of wetness from where her pussy pressed down. "Clean it up."

"What?"

I put a hand on her back and push her close, my other hand sliding along her damp pussy lips. "Lick up the mess from your needy cunt, and I'll make you come so hard before I leave."

Her brows furrow, and she pouts her pretty lips.

I slowly finger her, pulling out to circle her clit with every fifth stroke. She doesn't want to do what I ask, but there are a lot of things she enjoys once she gets out of her own way. She told me to push her, and what we've been doing lately has been sweet. Tame. Amazing, but not pushing the levels we both enjoy. Plus, her compliance strikes a deep emotion in me that is desperate for this connection with her. It's trust and respect on both our parts. We are each other's safe playground where anything goes. Things like this prove it.

"It's overdue that you don't know how good you taste. Do it, and I will give you what you need. But if you don't want it, I'll stop this and you can join me in the pain that today will bring." I press my erection against her ass.

She moves like she could get my dick in her if she rocks in just the right way.

Adding another finger, I increase the speed.

She glares at me, leans forward, and licks the spot.

I clamp her clit between my soaked fingers and slide up and back. "That's my good girl. Now keep licking. Set your tongue on the spot."

She gasps but does what I ask without hesitation, and I jiggle my fingers. Jolene whimpers, but the sound is different with her mouth open.

"Such a good whore, cleaning up after her soaked pussy. Do you taste good? You may answer."

"No," she says, gasping for breath.

"But you did it anyway to please me."

"Yes." Her hips shift as she gets right on the edge.

"And the dislike is hot, isn't it? You like doing things for me you wouldn't do for anyone else, don't you?"

"Yes, Arlo." Her deliciously sexy smile morphs to her *I'm-close* grimace. "No one else."

My chest swells with pride. "Is my filthy girl going to come for me?" My dick is throbbing, balls tightening. If I rub against her, I may come in my pants.

She falls apart with whimpering gasps.

I play in her slick heat and kiss her neck. Nip her ear. "Best girl, angel. Damn. I'm going to have a hard time walking today."

She giggles something girlish and elated and turns to me, gripping the collar of my shirt.

I give her our morning kiss and hesitantly leave, adjusting myself twice to make it to the door.

Chapter Fifty-Six

Jolene Types It Out

JOLENE

When Arlo gets to work, he texts me in a group chat with Darius.

> I wasn't kidding about needing an incentive, Jolene. Keep me hard all day, like a good girl.

I fan my heated face.

> What did I miss?

> Jolene threatening to edge me, then getting finger-fucked against the kitchen island. GTG. Meeting.

He didn't spill the other naughty thing I did. I haven't stopped grinning since. Why do I love when he makes me uncomfortable? There might be something wrong with me, but it never feels that way when I'm with him.

Darius:

> Ugh, I hate going in early. I also have a meeting but this is fun. Tell me about it.

The first text I send them is,

> It was a good morning. For me.

That should remind Arlo of what we did when he gets out of his meeting. I'd say more, but I want to tell Darius what happened in person so I can see the shocked grin on his face.

Late-morning, Arlo texts.

Arlo:

> Do better, Kentucky.

Darius gives that message a thumbs up.

I squeak in insult. "Better, huh?" In the bathroom, I grab my lipstick, drop my pants, and draw a heart around Arlo's hickey. I snap a picture.

> I wish your cum covered this up.

I send. And then promptly freak the fuck out. What if someone sees that? I can never be president. Not that I would, but now I can't.

Darius:

> I can't walk out of my office without embarrassing myself.

I grin, panic slightly lessened, and text,

> Cover up with a coat, baby.

Darius:

> Then I can be a walking coat rack. Best idea.

He sends an annoyed emoji, then a laughing one.

But Arlo remains silent. Did he leave his phone somewhere? What if he did, and now his coworkers are seeing each message flash onto the screen? I'm about to text him something when dots of typing appear.

A clock somewhere in the apartment ticks as I stare at the screen. I didn't even know we had a ticking clock.

Arlo:

> I had to hide in the goddamn bathroom. My cock is out and I'm stroking. Slide your fingers into that pretty pussy and tell me how wet you are.

I moan at Arlo's words. The visual of him gripping himself makes me oddly jealous that it's not my hand around his cock, but also incredibly turned on. I type back,

> I thought you were edging, sir.

I had to tack on the formality. Maybe out of duty to him or because I know it will please him.

He sends back one word, and I'll never understand how someone can throw a tone into a text message, though it shouldn't surprise me that Arlo has that ability.

Arlo:

> Now.

I lean against the counter and moan as I press two fingers between my legs, sighing at the swell and ache that feels so good to play with. After a few deep strokes, I pull my fingers and snap a picture of them. Guess I won't be a senator either.

> Can I come?

Arlo's response is quick.

Arlo:

Only if Darius says so.

That's new. I grin and play along.

"Darius. May I please come?"

I expect him to say *yes*. To indulge me as he always does.

Darius:

No. Not if I can't hear your whimpers.

I raise my eyebrows, but grin. The ache is tight and needy, and I'm about to tell him I'll call because I know I can convince him, but Arlo steps in.

Arlo:

That's a no, angel. But I want you to fuck yourself with your fingers. Don't you dare touch your clit.

I'm frustrated, but superbly, and I want them both frustrated along with me. So I message, one-handed:

I wish my fingers were one of you.

A moment later...

Fuck, I want more.

And another after that.

I'm close.

Arlo:

Stop!

Darius:

Stop!

I'd send a laughing emoji, but I'm too busy panting.

Arlo:

> I'm going to be useless during this meeting.

Darius:

> I love you. Please write us again soon.

I don't respond because it seems too revealing. I send more messages at midday about my many aches and ask for a countdown of when they'll be home. Then, a photo of my fingers covering my bare nipple. It's a close-up, and I wonder if I was too coy with the image because you can't tell what it is at first.

Arlo:

> Fuck

Darius:

> Yield, babes. I'm dying.

He tacks on three skull emojis.

Arlo:

> Don't you dare fucking stop. I'm going to eat your pussy for an hour when I get home.

A couple of months ago, that would have been punishment. Now I'm soaked.

A beep from the intercom interrupts my rereading of the text chain, and a jolt of distrust rolls through me. Security is calling?

"Yes?" I answer as politely as possible.

"Just the lady I wanted to talk to." Gregory's voice relaxes the tense muscles in my face. Thank goodness it's not Sheena. I've had enough of her interruptions. "There's a package down here for you. I found it tucked under the desk behind a box of paper, so I'm not sure how long it's been here. I'm so sorry about that."

Closing my eyes, I shake my head. "Not your fault." Bet I know who's responsible, though. "I'll be right down."

Gregory doesn't smile much under his burly beard, but he's a *what you see is what you get* kinda guy. I really like that about him. Plus, he doesn't have a sexual history with Arlo—that I know about—so I'm thrilled to deal with him. He apologizes again, and slaps a huge rectangular package onto the top of the desk, scattering two pens and a big envelope.

I help him gather the items and pick up the box, seeing the sender's address and frowning. What would Mom be sending me?

When I get back into the apartment and open it, my heart feels like it needs to hide under a blanket to escape the torrent of inadequacy, rage, and guilt.

And I haven't even opened the Jolene-pink note yet.

Chapter Fifty-Seven

Darius Is Pissed

DARIUS

Jolene goes quiet for the rest of the afternoon and, while I worry a bit, she pushed herself today.

I figure she's lost in numbers and job searching. But after a couple of hours, she needs to come up for stock-market-free air or get out of the tub. I text only her.

> You okay?

She responds ten minutes later.

Joles:

> Yes. But also no. Mom sent me something.

That sounds ominous.

> What is it? Need me to come home?

Joles:

> It's nothing important. You'll see when you get here.

She's contemplating. But she'd let me know if it was something to worry about.

After another hour of pecking at projects, I text Arlo and head home.

We arrive close enough to the same time that Arlo waits for me to jog up.

Sheena is in the lobby. Neither of us speaks to her as we make our way to the elevator.

"I hurt," I say when the doors close. "My balls feel like they weigh ten pounds each and have a cramp."

"I almost came when my dick brushed against the desk." Arlo drops his head back and groans. "I really am going to eat her out for an hour."

We both chuckle, and then I remember her last text. "Her mom sent her something today that she wants me to see, but after that, I'll help. Think we can both do that at the same time?"

Arlo makes an O with his lips. "Yes. Yeah, we're doing that." When the doors open, we rush to get inside the apartment, but both halt when we tumble in.

Jolene lies across the couch in a familiar sparkly pink dress that looks painted onto her. Her hair is sleek, pinned in a half-up style, and she has so much makeup on that it changes the shape of her face. She even has on the tall shoes I thought she'd left in Kentucky.

This is magazine-ad Jolene. Stage Jolene. Sad, fake Jolene.

She takes a swig directly from a wine bottle she has nestled against her hip and turns off the TV. "Howdy."

I step forward. "Your mom sent you your pageant dress from a few years ago?"

Jolene gives a tight smile. "Yep. It barely fits. She'd be so disappointed." She holds up a finger and searches the couch, then hands over a card. "This was in the box."

I move forward to tug the pink note from her manicured fingers.

Arlo drops his bag by the door. Rolling his sleeves up, he kicks off his shoes and sits next to our girl, pulling her up and tucking her under his arm before taking a gulp from the wine bottle. Red today. So, no bubble baths with chilled white. This is fixable. Though the half-full bottle is foreboding.

I open the shimmery note and read phrases like "no one better" and "entrancing" and "I'm so proud of your accomplishments." Those all sound like good things to hear from a parent, but the last line changes the meaning of every word to a twisting knife of cruel expectation.

No matter who Jolene is or what she accomplishes, she'll always be trapped in an image—a snapshot that only shows a small perspective of who she is. This sweet, motherly note has yet again reduced Jolene to a doll instead of a daughter.

I read it again, still in disbelief. "Never forget who you are," I say out loud. My jaw flexes, and I shake my head. *Fuck you, Donna. Fuck you so fucking much.*

Arlo grumbles and hands Jolene back the wine.

She takes a long swig. I hate that I instantly wonder how many magazines the image would sell. Her, ready to walk the stage and take the crown. Instead, she's lounging on the couch, bottle in hand with the tattooed arm of her protective lover, neither of them giving a shit about the time or what others need from them.

I sit on her other side and put a hand on her sparkly thigh. "You okay?"

She pulls her red lips from the bottle and wipes an escaped drop carefully with her manicured thumb. "Mostly, yes. I think I know who I am now. But this"—she signals to herself—"is all I am to her and nearly everyone I've known. This is all I'll ever be." She holds up a finger again even though no one is interrupting. It's a classic tipsy-Jolene trait. "So Arlo. Remember how you said if I wanted to try anything, you'd be there with me?"

"Of course." He leans to kiss her head and pulls a face when her hair crunches under his lips.

She runs her hand up his thigh and rests her head on my shoulder. "I want you to rip this goddamn dress off of me and fuck me. Both of you. Same time. I want you to ruin me or—this part of me."

"Babes, are you sure?" She's found lots of ways to soothe herself through the years. This is not one of those.

"Feels needed. Necessary." She purses her lips. "Or maybe I just want to be fucked really, really well by my men." She huffs and smiles like she's in on some kind of inside joke with herself.

My cock goes harder in my pants. I blame it on the state it's been in most of the day, though the thought of being with her at the same time as Arlo sends quite the rush into my bloodstream.

Arlo takes their entwined hands, extends a finger and runs it up the slit that exposes her thigh, giving the material a little tug, as if to test the fabric. "That sounds like the best sort of evening. You drunk?"

"I'm tipsy, but I read that's sometimes better when it comes to, uh, anal. So..."

"You did some research." He doesn't seem that surprised, and I'm certainly not. I'm sure she's also talked to Hayley about it, and maybe even done some self-play in the shower, especially after Arlo went there and she liked it so much. "And you drank to relax?" His eyes narrow. If she's doing this because she's drunk, he'll shut that down. But he's been exploring that area every time we've all been together lately. I know he's been warming her up for it, and she wants to.

Her bright lips curve up, and she taps his nose. "I'm as relaxed as I can be in this fucking tight dress. But it helps *my body* relax. Get it?"

He nips her finger. "I believe I do."

I cup her cheek and kiss her, tasting lipstick, which is rare since I wasn't allowed to touch her when she looked like this. I stroke her cheek with my thumb and get lost in her fiery, determined gaze. "Here or the bedroom?"

She looks around. "I think here would make things filthier. Am I right, Arlo?"

"You are." He leans in, giving her neck a sweet kiss, then grabs a handful of crunchy hair, tugging until a few pins jut out haphazardly. "Such a filthy fucking whore."

She whimpers. "I love it when you call me that."

"I know. You're also our dirty little slut."

But that word, I know she hates.

She goes rigid.

Arlo waits for her to process, slipping their hands up the inside of her thigh while he gives her neck another sucking kiss.

She sighs. "I am, aren't I?"

"For us, you are. It feels good to not give a fuck, doesn't it?" He kisses her cheek, taking the wine and handing it to me to put on the corner table. "You're our dirty little slut. Say it."

"Yes." She strokes my hard cock over my pants and grins with giddiness. "I'm your dirty little slut."

"Again," Arlo demands.

Demeaning phrases are not my thing, but Jolene's eyes go molten when she looks at Arlo and repeats his words with remarkable confidence. "I'm your dirty fucking slut."

He kisses her hard, pressing her into me, making my cock jump.

He abruptly pushes himself away. Heavy red paints his lips.

I grin, sliding my hand up Jolene's soft arm and gripping a thin strap, then look at Arlo.

When he nods, I jerk.

Jolene gasps as silk rips, flipping a few sequins and crystals through the air. Yeah, that's refreshing.

Arlo kisses the place now free of cloth, then bites. Whimpers fill the air.

I tug down the fabric, exposing her breast for Arlo to suck on. I kiss her neck and repeat a few of her mother's wicked words. "You are entrancing."

Arlo moans in agreement, and tears away her other strap. "Fucking perfect girl. And all ours." He reaches up and swipes his thumb across her parted lips, smearing red across her face. "I want you to turn around and get Darius's cock as deep into your throat as you can. Make me proud."

She turns so fast she nearly tumbles off the couch, but Arlo grips her hips to steady her. So eager to please. I am too. Maybe that's what makes our bond so steady. We're always there for each other, trying to make things perfect.

Arlo gives her sequined ass a light slap, then walks down the hall. And he brings a different dynamic to our bond. He's brought us closer, which I didn't think was possible. I can't imagine us without him though, and I wonder how Jolene feels about that.

I'd ask, but she tugs at my pants with desperation. Time and place, and this isn't it.

I lie back to give her more room.

Arlo returns with a bottle of lube and a condom. He picks up the card, reading it. His jaw flexes, and he shakes his head, flinging the note across the room.

"There's no one better," I tell her as she pulls my cock out and kisses the tip, sending shockwaves through me.

Arlo grips each side of the dress's slit and rips the fabric to above her hip.

She whimpers as if she's about to come.

Arlo's hand comes down hard on her bare ass. "Stop fucking around. Show us what you've accomplished."

Life sparks bright in her eyes, and she takes me down until she gags.

"Yes," Arlo says, rubbing her backside with one hand and unbuckling his belt with the other. "Deeper. Show him how good you are. How perfect."

I groan and drop my head back, then snap it right back up so I don't miss a single second of this moment.

She takes a deep breath and gags again but pushes through so that her tight throat massages my dick.

I can only writhe and moan, riding the line as my abs and my balls tighten. "Fuck, you're making me lose it, babes. I can't hold on."

She pulls back to breathe. "Do it. Come down my throat."

"Yes, angel." Arlo strokes his dick. His movement looks like he's sliding his tip up and down through her folds.

Jolene gasps and shifts her hips. She wraps her lips over my cock and slides down, down, down.

Arlo growls, already looking like he's losing it. "I want to hear you choke on that cock. Give us your tears."

She pushes through a gag and coughs before retreating.

"Good girl. Again. Darius, our little whore is soaked." He pulls back and runs his fist over his glistening cock, thumbing the piercing. "Fuck, I've never been harder."

He jerks her dress farther up and crouches to feast on her pussy and ass.

She whimpers and takes me down again, throat working my length, moans tickling my every nerve to life.

"Babes, I'm gonna..." I can't hold back and erupt hard, yelling and gripping her hair probably too hard in my ecstasy.

She groans and smiles, throat working me down.

I pull her up and kiss her, smearing the remains of her lipstick. "I want to make you come."

"That's needed for what we're going to do to her." Arlo rips the other slit of her dress and drags her backwards into his arms. "Time to get ruined. Take those heels off her, Darius, or someone is going to get impaled."

"Yes, sir." I tug the shoes from her feet, massage a moment, then shuck up her torn skirt, grip the fabric in both fists.

Jolene arches. "Please do it." Her voice is so desperate it makes my dick twitch back to life. "Please."

With two jerks, the fabric rips wider, showing her puffy pussy. "Look at you, babes."

"She's gorgeous when she's all mussed up." Arlo grips her throat with one hand and palms her exposed breast with the other. "Remember that thing we were going to do, Darius?"

I raise an eyebrow. "I most definitely remember."

"What were you going to do?" Jolene asks.

"Give you what we all need." He whispers in her ear, then nips it. "This is who we are, isn't it, angel? Just beings of lust. It's our duty to give ourselves over to our needs and to each other. You know that, don't you?"

She spreads her legs wide for me. "Yes."

He sits up, pushing her aside so he can stand. "Good, because you need to be ruined and I'm restless to taste you."

Chapter Fifty-Eight

Jolene Is

JOLENE

Arlo isn't the only one who's restless.

This dress is too tight and itchy. The rips help ease my mind. I want this outdated, fake version of me to be in shambles, but it's not enough. I jerk at the fabric that remains tight around my ribcage, suffocating me, as usual. That's what it is. I'm fucking suffocating.

Darius jumps into action first, gripping the panels of the skirt, and jerking it even farther apart.

Arlo shucks his collared shirt and wraps the fabric around his fist, pulling me closer, pushing my legs apart and diving in with his lips.

I groan and writhe as Darius twirls his tongue around my nipples, then moves down, spreading my legs wider and joining Arlo. I watch, fascinated, as their tongues touch down, meet, then move back to me. The sensations are such an overload.

And then Arlo moves lower, doing the thing that makes my mind yell "stop!" in the tone of my mother. She would positively die if someone licked her ass, because we're taught that's dirty and wrong, but it's so sensitive and feels so good.

I love that he's going there for me, to push and please me. My dress and my soul are coming unraveled at the very seams.

Arlo smirks up at me, then spits and presses his thumb to that most sensitive area. slowly glides in, keeping his fathomless blue eyes on mine.

I'm done—lost to my body and how good these men are to me. My orgasm is hot rolling waves of pleasure, long and easy.

"You're going to feel so good around my dick, angel." Arlo nips my thigh, making me jump.

They both continue licking, kissing, biting, while gripping my thighs and clutching at my exposed skin.

Arlo surges up, smashing his wet lips against mine. He licks his way into my grinning mouth, kissing me so deep he warms my soul, then rests his forehead against mine. "Are you ready for me?"

The lump in my throat is distracting, but I try to swallow it down. He has no idea how ready for him I am. "Yes."

Darius sucks my clit, ramping me back up for another orgasm.

"Please. I need you." I clutch at them both, gently touching Darius's cheek and also gripping a handful of Arlo's hair until his lips curl in a smiling snarl.

Arlo nips at my hip. "Lie on the floor, Darius."

"Flat?" He moves away from me.

"No," I whine. He's getting good at warming me up, then letting Arlo keep me on the edge for as long as he decides to let me suffer. Which apparently I love, even if I complain about it.

"Straight back, knees up." Arlo holds me back when I go to follow. "Look at me, angel."

I bite my lip and meet his eyes. It's difficult because something shifts between us. I'm overwhelmed by him, just as much as I get sometimes with Darius. He's so big—not physically either, but in his intensity, his energy, loyalty... his love. It's all so big, my heart can't hold in the emotions they stoke in me. They're so different, but the core feelings they give me are the same, not competing, but blending into a mash of love, lust, and need for both body and soul to be touched and held tight.

But now what?

Arlo said he was mine, ours, for as long as I want him. What if that's forever? Can it be that way? My mom would accept it even less than society would. I'm just a little lost pageant queen to her. But to these men, I'm so much more. They see me. I can't help the spill of my soul as I look into Arlo's eyes and know that I'm his. I'm theirs.

"Jolene," he whispers, leaning close to brush his lips so softly over mine. "I love when I can see you thinking about us."

My heart leaps, even when intrusive thoughts rush in. What happens when Mom sees us together? Will she know how much I love this man by the way I look at him? What about others when we're walking around Chicago? Do we hold hands like I do with Darius? No, no, no, this isn't the time for that. I'm moving forward, dammit. Breaking free.

Wrapping my arms around him, I crush myself against him with a whimper, and he opens for me, battling my emotions with his tongue and the tap of teeth. We wordlessly speak to each other, saying what we can't voice out loud. Not yet. I shove his pants the rest of the way off.

He takes me to the floor next to Darius, caging me under him, kissing the hell out of me. His cock lies hard against my hip, and I'd like that to be in me now, filling me, but he's got me pinned. I love the way he does that.

Darius throws his shirt, licks my neck and whispers in my ear. "Can we take this disaster off of you? I want to feel your skin against mine while we fuck you."

"Yes, please." I nod, unseating Arlo's lips.

He growls, then crawls backward and grips the torn fabric pieces, sending a rip into the air and pulling shreds from me. Darius tugs off the stubborn parts that remain until I'm bare and I can finally breathe.

"Straddle me, baby." Darius leans back.

I follow, settling over him, then look back at Arlo. He moves closer, between Darius's knees, and grips my hips while Darius swipes the head of his cock against my soaked slit. He thrusts up into me.

I cry out, arching back.

"Yes," Arlo says with a smirk. "When I saw you fucking Darius for the first time, I thought about what an incredible stripper you would be." He trails his hands up my sides and cups my breasts. "You know your body and how to ride a cock, don't you?"

I nod and roll my hips, making Darius groan.

Arlo pinches my nipples. "I need you to listen to me, angel, and do exactly what I tell you. You must talk to me through this. Can you do that?"

"Yes, sir."

He kisses my neck. "Good girl. Lean forward as far as you can."

I do, pressing tight against Darius's torso. He threads his fingers through my hair and kisses me sweetly. "Hi, babes."

I smile. "Hi."

There's a snap of a bottle and then a chill of dripping liquid against my backside. I tremble.

Darius keeps giving me gentle kisses and stroking my skin in the most mesmerizing way.

Arlo rubs my ass cheeks, then trails down and touches that most sensitive place. "Relax, Kentucky."

I wrinkle my nose. He may as well have told me I was being bad.

Darius chuckles, and shifts his hips so his cock moves slowly in and out of me. "What do you need?"

"You and Arlo." That eases my trembling a little, and I relax. "I don't know what else."

"This." Arlo pushes in with one finger, and my eyes flutter closed at the tightness. He strokes in and out while Darius remains slowly rhythmic.

I shift, needing more movement inside me, especially against my clit.

Darius keeps calmly running his hands over my skin, and it's both calming and making me impatient for more.

Arlo grips under my knee and shifts my leg up as he presses another finger in, making me whimper at the delicious pressure. The heat of his skin presses against my back, and he kisses my shoulder. "It's different with a cock inside you, isn't it?"

"Yes."

"Tell me what you want."

"I want you inside me. I need to be fucked by you both." I'm feral for them. Antsy with nerves and anticipation. "Please, sir."

He peppers kisses over my shoulders and slowly slides in another finger. "Will you tell me if it hurts?"

I give a sharp laugh. "I'll tell you anything right now."

He lifts and slaps my ass hard. "No joking right now. I can hurt you in ways you won't like."

I wince and look back at him.

His face is concerned and serious, and I feel bad for not realizing this was so important to him. It's important to me, too, and I couldn't take this step without them. They make me so brave.

I nod. "I'm sorry. Yes, sir. I swear to tell you if it hurts."

"Okay." He reaches for the foil packet and lube. "Let's fucking ruin you."

I tremble harder. We're going to do this.

Chapter Fifty-Nine

Arlo Owns

ARLO

"**Y**ou okay, Darius?"

With glassy eyes and his jaw set so tight it will be sore tomorrow, my best friend is losing his mind. "I need to fuck," he says through gritted teeth.

As do I. Girl on top is not my favorite, but I want her to ride me like I know she can soon. I've never seen my best friend so damn in love as when she's rolling those hips over him and owning every inch of his cock.

I press my palm against Jolene's back. "Lean again. All the way. And slide your knees up further. I need you open." She does everything I ask without hesitation. The sight of Darius inside her and me lined up to do the same is captivating. This is a first for both of them. And a type of first for me, too. I've never been so impatient to be close to someone, yet so nervous to do so. I could really hurt her. That would wreck me. "Ready?"

Between kisses with Darius, she nods. "Yes, sir."

I guide myself in slowly, squeezing my eyes shut, mouth gaping open at the tight pressure of her muscles.

Jolene gasps and tenses up.

I should have done this first without Darius, but none of us wanted that. "Talk to me, angel. I'll stop."

"Don't stop." She reaches back and palms my ass. "Please. More."

I rock back slowly, then forward again.

We all suck in a breath when I slip through that ring of tightness.

"Oh, my fucking god." Jolene drops her head onto Darius's shoulder and tilts her ass up to sink me in further.

"Fuck," Darius says, and grins. "I can feel your piercing. Damn, that's a lot." He swallows and blows out a long breath.

"Doing okay, angel?"

"Yes. Feels really good. Stings, but I like it."

"You're so tight around me." I move in further against the resistance and squeeze a handful of her cheek. Fuck, she's going to make me come if she utters one moan, I just know it. "Deep breath. Relax this perfect ass again for me."

She listens so well, and I glide in until my hips rest against her soft backside.

Yeah, if humans could overwrite data, I'd have new coding, because I am fucking altered. I'd do anything for them. Anything. It's a new feeling. I've always been that way with Darius, but he's different from everyone who hurt or tried to control me. She's different too. And now she's mine.

I lean over to kiss her neck. "Our perfect girl. How do we feel inside you?"

"Tight." She turns her head to smile and kiss me. "Can you get moving now before I lose my damn mind?"

"Please," Darius adds, arched back with his eyes closed like he is in the most blissful pain of his life.

I bite her shoulder, pull back out, then thrust back in.

Jolene gasps. "How does that feel so good?" She glances back at me like I'm a damned god.

Darius writhes. "Can I move now, please?"

"One more—" I slam against her backside harder, testing and feeling Darius's cock shift with the movement. Fuck, this is the best. Forget any other position. We'll just do this constantly for a while. "And again." Pulling almost all the way out, I chuckle at both Jolene and Darius's tortured groans, then slide back in as deep as I can. "Now you may move."

Darius thrusts up into her, gripping her hips, lips parted with a groan. "Lift up, babes, hands beside my shoulders." He looks like he's in heaven right now, and I can't say anything we've ever done together has touched this experience—just like any experience where Jolene is involved.

Jolene presents herself in the perfect position for us both to have at her. Darius thrusts. Then I do and I'm not going to last. I grit my teeth and grip her hair, arching her long neck. "How's this, angel? Do you like my cock in your ass?"

"So fucking much, sir." Her fingers grip the rug, and she widens her knees. I can tell she wants to move, but we have a rhythm.

"Look at you holding still while we use you. Do you want to fuck us for a moment?"

Panting, she blinks over her shoulder at me. "Yes, please."

"Stay still, Darius." I grit my teeth and hold us all still to regain my control. Everything tingles and wants to break free from inside me.

He grumbles and goes up on his elbows to kiss Jolene's neck. "Fuck us, baby. We feel so good together."

We really do.

Jolene's hips move slowly and unsure at first.

Darius's dick falls from her, and he guides himself back in and lifts his hips to get closer. When she finds a rhythm that doesn't unseat one of us, she really moves, bouncing and spiraling. We grip her hips, fingers linking and squeezing each other.

When I can't take more, I lean forward. "Enough." I hold tight and rail into her. We're all going to have rug burn, but fuck it. If she wants to be wrecked, then Darius and I will be there with her every step of the way. We'll all be banged up tomorrow.

Darius moves as well as he can pinned beneath us, though he doesn't need to.

I slam in hard and fast, moving Jolene along his cock while she whimpers loud and recklessly.

Darius curses and, yeah, I'm there too.

Jolene tightens up, and her hips twitch. I love that I know her body so well that I can pinpoint when she's about to come, and help her into it, or deny her.

I'm not denying her today, though. She can have anything she wants. I press in, all the way, deep as our bodies will allow, and grind.

We all curse as her muscles pulse rapid-fire

I drop my head back and bellow a cry of pure ecstasy to the ceiling as I come violently, utterly losing it.

Darius joins in before his voice tapers off in a laugh. "Holy hell."

This moment. Them. Everything about them is life now.

Darius grips my wrists and pulls me down to cover Jolene. "There's nothing in the world better than that."

She gasps for breath under me.

I peck his lips and tilt her face to me, kiss the tears on her mascara-streaked cheeks and then her forehead. I've never wanted to truly destroy a part of someone before, but she started it. Pieces of her dress decorate our living room, and if she needs more than that, she just needs to ask. "You are a perfect disaster. Did we hurt you?"

She shakes her head. "You prepared me. That was... I don't have the words."

I do. They're right on my tongue, but won't jump. Our situation isn't common, and it's still new. We're under the influence of orgasms right now, and she's just starting out on her path of life and sex. Maybe not long from now she'll have had enough of me, and if I let those words escape right now, I can't take them back. It will be done.

I sigh and kiss her temple. "You'll find them one day. We're doing that again when Darius gets back from his business trip because you were perfect—are perfect."

She blinks back at me, swallows, then lays her head on Darius's chest. "I feel the same about you."

He shouldn't be grinning so hard when I just brought up that he's leaving, but maybe this kind of afterglow is persistent.

I lie over them, inhaling Jolene's faint scent under hair product and makeup. I'm going to wash all of that off of her in a moment, and have dinner with her on my lap.

Soon, we're going to have another talk. A more serious one about the future, because it's our lives now, together, and I don't want anyone feeling out of place in it. Jolene's mother is an issue that needs to be dealt with, because she made Jolene get to a point where she needed our help to rip a part of her away. That won't happen again. I hope we made it better and not worse.

I kiss her and then Darius. They're mine—both of them.

Chapter Sixty

Jolene Spills

JOLENE

"**W**oman, it's so damn good to see your face." Hayley grins wide, leaning in like she's studying me on the video chat.

"Same," I say.

She's beautiful in a cooly ethereal way. Stick-straight, white-blond hair, soft features, and pouty lips that have people asking if they made her mad. All she needs is the smallest amount of color with makeup because everything about her, besides her personality, is pale. She tilts her head, light eyes assessing me. "You look…"

I grin widely. "Happy?" It must be pouring out of me because I've been in a joy bubble since last night.

Her nose crinkles as she nods. "Yeah."

I sigh. "Last night was…" I can't stop smiling but then I crinkle my nose. "Well, it was incredible after my mom sent a pageant dress and told me to remember who I was."

"Oh, fuck." Hayley's eyes widen. "You don't have plans to go back, right?"

I shake my head. "Not a chance. You?"

She shrugs. "I liked it, but it didn't like me. Plus, you can imagine the rumors I'd stoke now." She smiles. "At least I earned those."

Hayley is an unapologetic sexual deviant. I admire how little she cares about what others think of her. At least mostly. No one should hear the things that have been said about her, especially her. Friends stick up for her far more than she does, but we're not always there. I'm really not sure how she's able to turn that part of her off. "I wish I were more like you, Hayley."

She grins. "And I wish I were more like you. It would be nice to have two men wrapped around my finger. Speaking of... did you seal the three-way deal?"

I bite my lips together, close my eyes, and nod.

Hayley gasps. "Fun right? Did you like it?" She leans forward in the screen and grins wide. "Tell me all about it."

I laugh, but share. Not every detail, but the getting ready, choking on hairspray, when the guys got home and literally ripped the dress off of me. Hayley's mouth gapes, and I laugh. Until I think about how careful Arlo was with me. How well he reads my body because he's always watching me to make sure I'm okay. How did I ever think he was callous?

"Mm, mm, mmmm." Hayley looks toward the ceiling, shaking her head. "Did they get you in a Jolene sandwich?"

I cover my mouth as I laugh, then fan my red face. "Okay, yes."

"Love that one. It's the weight or something of the top dude. Feels nice. Like a double hug with orgasms." She takes a sip from her mug.

Remembering I have tea, I take a sip while chuckling. "What's your favorite position? Can I ask that?" I crinkle my nose. She's just so open with information and makes me feel normal about this when it's not normal at all.

"Of course you can, weirdo. Though this feels like a confession." She sighs. "Missionary."

I tilt my head. My free-loving friend has told me to get wild. She's inspired my bravery. In an ice cream world, she's a coffee toffee sundae with sprinkles, pecans, and five cherries in a dipped waffle bowl. I'm a vanilla scoop in a cup. Or I used to be. Now, I have at least a couple of cherries on top. I clear my throat. "Missionary is great. It's sweet."

Hayley props her chin on her palm. "It is. Don't get me wrong, I like freaky sex too, but there's a connection you just can't get when your legs are shoved behind your head, you know?"

"Actually, I know that now." And I feel so proud of that, talking to her. Like I leveled up somehow and enjoyed the practice of getting there.

"Yeah, you do. So you're clearly comfortable in this sexy little trio. Is Arlo a keeper or am I going to need to come over there and kick some obsessed boy butt?" She flexes her arms, showing some impressively defined muscles.

I grin and shake my head. "If anyone is obsessed"—I glance at the open door. It's not like the guys are home. They both had meetings this morning, even though Darius is leaving this evening for his work trip.

"Ooo, my girl is in love. Don't make me jealous, woman."

I glance back at her and nibble my lip. I am in love. Like a lot. Twice. How did I get in so deep, so fast? And why does it feel so right when it can't really happen for real, right? I can't just keep him a secret our entire lives, but then, what about Mom? Dad. Even the neighbors I don't know yet. Darius's work friends. They wouldn't think he was so perfect then. Did I get us into something we actually can't handle? Our future would be—

Hayley's grin melts away. "Someone is freaked about falling for man number two or doesn't like me jealous." I swear she's as observant as Arlo. "Sorry. Did I overstep?"

I sigh. "You didn't. The love thing is, um, a lot. How does that even work? It was just supposed to be like an experiment or something, and I want them both? I don't know what to do here, Hales." Darius and I want to get married. Does Arlo? My eyes pop wide. Am I thinking about marrying Arlo? Holy hell, I am. I can't imagine life without him right now, or maybe ever again. He just fits. How on earth would I tell Mom about that? She will think Chicago is cursed.

Hayley's brows furrow. "It's a little early for *he's a keeper* talk, my friend. Why don't you just enjoy him and see where it goes? That's what I'm doing."

It takes a minute for her words to register. It is early, and I am enjoying him. I'm overthinking again. Who knows what tomorrow may bring, but yeah, last night was big, and maybe tonight will be big, and then Arlo and I have a week alone together. I don't need to think about the future yet and—"Wait. Did you say that's what you're doing?"

"Yeah. Remember my crush? Well, he keeps coming around. We went on a date, like an actual one, not just a meet and fuck. He's... sweet." She seems confused by that.

"Sweet is good."

"Sweet is confusing." She crinkles her nose. "There's something off about him, though, and I can't place it."

Hayley's dating history is more like a *notch on the bedpost* list, so I could see how she'd be reluctant to actually date. And here's where I can help her as much as she helps me. "So tell me all about this date, and when you're doing it again."

Chapter Sixty-One

Arlo Notices

ARLO

I don't need to jog anymore. Running to catch the train home is my daily cardio. However, today, I'm in even more of a rush because the meeting ran late, and Darius heads out at seven to catch his flight to Toronto. That gives us enough time to have dinner and drive him to the airport.

I expect him to be packing and Jolene to be running around in her turbocharged prep mode, but she's sitting on the counter, laughing with Darius. Country music plays through the speakers, and she has a quarter-full glass of amber liquid in her hand. There's a lit candle on the kitchen island that kicks off some kind of berry pie scent.

Her face lights up when she looks at me, and my heart does a liftoff for the skies. But then there's a twitch of her nose and her lips curve down. A flinch?

I set my shit down, wrap my arms around her, and kiss her neck, feeling better with her in my arms. "Everything okay?"

She nods against my neck.

"I'm here too, you know." Darius grins teasingly. Though he's probably not teasing. He's leaving for a week, and it feels really odd.

If he were out of town before Jolene, I'd fill the time with work and women. So it won't be too different, except less work and one woman.

"Yes, you are." I grip his shirt and tug him close so I can wrap an arm around him as well, kiss his cheek, and then shove him away. I look them over—freshly showered, Darius looks smitten, and Jolene is flushed. "You two fucked."

Jolene's mouth falls open. "How'd you know?"

I steal her drink and take a swig. That's good bourbon. "Like I don't know what you look like when you're freshly fucked. And only you can make Darius float around like that." She smiles and tries to take her drink back, but I keep it away. "Give me a kiss first."

Her face is still tense, but she grabs my button-down shirt collars in both hands and pulls me close, planting a bourbon-tasting kiss on my lips that promises me everything. It makes my head spin. But I'm going to have to fall into that with her later because we have to go to dinner.

"Reservation," I whisper against her lips. I inhale deep, smelling soap, but under that, Jolene.

"Oh, yeah. We can't miss that." But she keeps kissing me, and I keep kissing her back. Her mouth is so soft against mine. The sweetest conversation. Almost pleading.

"I can't be late." Darius tugs at me, chuckling. "Help me choose which tie to use for dinner with the business owner tomorrow night."

I pass the glass back over, grinning at her, and walk backwards as Darius drags me down the hall.

Jolene's smile is heart-shattering, and whatever tension was there is now gone. Good. She doesn't need tension in her life. She has me now to deal with it.

Maybe she was worried about Darius leaving. It would be hard to be apart as much as they have finally settled in, then go apart again. I can't imagine it, actually.

Not after her.

Chapter Sixty-Two

Darius Has To Go

DARIUS

I typically enjoy traveling. It's a change from the normal where I get to see new things and talk to new people, but this time, I'm dreading leaving. If Jolene weren't so nervous about money or missing an interview opportunity, I'd take her with me.

Dinner isn't exactly awkward, but it's not home either. Our conversation grows easier as we lean in around the circular bistro table, talking about my work trip and what they'll do while I'm gone. Jolene says, "We'll sulk," just as Arlo says, "We'll fuck," and we all laugh loud enough to make the cranky-looking couple beside us glance over in distaste.

Jolene shifts closer to me, and I wonder if she even knows that she's doing it.

When we're halfway through dessert and cappuccinos, she's back to talking closely with both of us.

"I'm going to miss this." I don't even mean to say it out loud, but I really am.

Both Jolene and Arlo reach for my hands. Then we're back to laughing.

"Me too." Jolene squeezes my fingers, then settles back in her chair. "Feels weird."

"It does." I nod. "I know I'm only gone for a week, but it makes it seem like we're back to being this transient couple who float in and out of each other's lives."

"But you're not." Arlo leans in, eyebrows raised.

"I know. I feel better knowing you'll be together, but still. It's like this part of Jolene and my relationship that we thought was in the past, isn't."

Jolene sighs. "Yeah, it sucks, but it's just a week, and when you come home, I'll be there." She glances at Arlo and gives him a sweet smile. "We'll be there."

We should talk about this. What it all means between us. Talk it out until it doesn't feel like there's a gap between us. They also feel right about the three of us. I know they do.

A shadow falls over the table as someone steps close, and Jolene's eyes go wide. The man is on the shorter side, with sharp features, quirky glasses, and a wide smile aimed at our girl. She smiles back, but it's tight, then her lips part like she wants to say something but needs a cue card.

He smiles. "Jolene. How are things?"

"Good!" she barks. "Good, good, good."

Who is this guy?

Arlo stands, extending a hand. "Arlo Keller."

The man looks kind enough and not at all intimidated as he firmly shakes Arlo's hand. "Lou Gant." He glances at their interlocked hands, then steps back. "I interviewed Jolene."

The kind-enough one at Asshole Works, as Arlo and I have renamed Jolene's first choice of potential employers. "Oh, you work for Diggory & Sons." I stand as well and shake Lou's hand. "Darius Gates."

He sighs. "I do. Jolene and I had quite the meeting before the..." He looks at Jolene and his tight eyes soften. "She has endless potential."

"She really does." Arlo says.

Jolene pops up from her chair. "That's kind. I loved your allocation ideas. This place is fantastic, right? Great food. We'd love to stay longer but Darius, my boyfriend"—she loops her arm with mine, throwing down a line that feels physical between us and Arlo—"has to get to the airport for a business trip to Toronto."

This is full-blown Jolene panic-mode. I shift to hold her hand, squeezing her fingers, and glance at Arlo. He is staring at her with a furrowed-brow expression of confusion. The only time I see this expression on him is when Jolene is involved. Dammit.

Lou's eyebrows raise as he looks at me. "Maple Leafs country. What business?"

"Senior CAD designer at Clausen Innovations."

"Fantastic." Lou turns to Arlo. "And you?"

Arlo's nostrils flare, and there is zero amusement in his expression. "Cybersecurity specializing in corporate hacking prevention. I'm going to go pay the bill. Meet you two outside. Enjoy your evening, Lou."

I watch Arlo go with a tightness in my jaw and shoulders. He's hurt. Obviously he's hurt. The worst part is, I understand Jolene's reluctance to share what we are, especially with a colleague in the business. This is all new, and we need time. I didn't want to leave them for this trip now that this part of our relationship has opened and now I don't want to leave even more, because we need to get through rough patches together and this is going to be a scratchy, itchy, uncomfortable patch.

Lou looks back at Jolene with furrowed brows. His lips purse out like he wants to say something, and I'm curious about what he's thinking. Arlo, Jolene, and I know what's going on here, but what does that look like to the outside? It probably looks like Arlo is impatient and unsocial, because Lou doesn't know him. He thumbs behind him to the crowd of tables and a woman in a blue dress watching us with a curious head tilt. "I need to get back to my wife, but I just wanted to say hello."

"Oh. Okay." Jolene's voice is pitchy and tight.

"Any news on the job front?"

Jolene shakes her head. "But I have another interview this week."

He hums and puts his hands in his pockets. "If you consider it, make sure it's exactly what you want and they're paying you what you're worth."

Her arm lessens the death grip she has on me. "It's hard to know what that is when I'm fresh out of college." She glances toward the door Arlo left and subtly pushes me in that direction.

"Research. You're good at that." Stepping back, Lou turns. "And wait for the right thing. Especially when you have a good support system to keep you afloat." He points to me and then in the direction Arlo went. I like this man and see why Jolene respects him. It truly sucks that things didn't work out for her at his company.

As soon as he's gone, Jolene grabs her purse and bolts for the door.

I navigate the tables as I follow her. "That wasn't handled in the best way, babes."

"I know that," she snaps. "I didn't expect to see anyone I knew. I wasn't prepared." She shoves the door open, looking around frantically and finding Arlo leaning against the building.

He's sullen and stressed, body tight, jaw working. "All set? We should get to the airport." He looks at me when he speaks.

"I'm sorry." Jolene scurries to stand in front of him, reaching up to touch his chest. "I panicked, Arlo. I'm sorry. I don't know how to handle this yet."

He snorts and crosses his arms, unseating her hand. "Maybe start with acting like I exist. We can go from there."

Jolene rubs her forehead. "This is new. I don't have a manual for what we are."

He shoves off the wall, walking toward the car. "Neither do I, but I wouldn't have done that to you. Darius is *your boyfriend?* He is, but fuck, I've never felt more like a dirty little secret until you said that."

I wince. He adores her and, yeah, her introduction was an obvious choice. I'm hers, and he's not. At least in public.

"I know." She jogs after him, and I follow close behind. "That was bad. But he was—"

"Who was he, Jolene?" Arlo turns to her, voice rising. "Someone who interviewed you. He's not your boss or your friend. Most importantly, he's not me or Darius. You tossed me out of your life, pretended I was nothing to you, for an acquaintance."

"I'm sorry," Jolene chokes out. "I didn't mean to."

Passersby pause and snoop.

I grip Arlo's shoulder. "Car."

He growls and swings around to stomp off.

I take Jolene's hand and kiss her head. "It's okay."

"It's not."

"It will be."

She stays quiet, and I hope she can find her words for this, because I'm going to have a hard time getting on a plane knowing my loves are in this state.

I make Arlo give me the keys, and he takes the passenger's seat.

Jolene slips quietly into the back.

The silence in the car is barbed and heavy. I know I shouldn't interfere, but they're mine. I understand them, and I'm leaving them in a few minutes. Halfway to the airport, I clear my throat. "She's not used to this yet."

Arlo huffs. "Switch places with me and say that again."

I nod. "We've been together for seven years, Arlo."

"And Jolene and I have been fucking for a month. I get it."

"You don't, though. Joles and I have leaned on each other through every failure, success, and stressful moment for a long-ass time. You and I have done the same. So much that I know you're going to go home and hit the bag until you fall over. You have habits, and so does Jolene. She's used to leaning on me when she's uncomfortable. It's a habit."

"It still wasn't right," Jolene murmurs from the backseat. "I regret it. I just didn't know what to do."

"Exactly." I nod, smiling at her in the rearview. "You went on autopilot."

Arlo settles deeper into the seat and stares out the window. "Will that change, or will I always be the one on the outside? Am I part of the trifecta, or a visitor to your relationship?"

I stay quiet because he needs to hear Jolene's answer. Me yelling, "Of course you're a cornerstone in our triangle," will only make him feel like I'm being blindly positive.

Jolene leans forward, setting her chin on his seat, next to his shoulder. "I feel so much for you, Arlo. I hope you know that. But I need time to sort out what this means. Relationships like this aren't the norm. Hell, they're not even allowed in our society, so I'm struggling."

"But will you always?"

"No?" Her words tilt up at the end like a question because she isn't sure.

The tension pours off Arlo like a waterfall. "Be fucking honest, Jolene."

"I want you. I..." She leans back. "But I don't know."

And there it is. Another part of our uncertain future. Move forward—Jolene is with me now, solidly moved in and starting her life—then another piece comes in and shakes it up. *Arlo.* He means everything to me, and so does Jolene, but I can't fix this for them, and I really hate that. My chest is tight, and my knee bounces as I pull into the airport departure lane and park. I look at Arlo. "I don't want to get on that plane like this."

The furrow in his brow softens, and he leans to press his forehead against mine. "Safe travels. Call me when you land." He kisses my cheek. "Say goodbye to your girl and I'll drive her home. Pop the trunk. I'll get your bags."

My chest constricts as he steps out of the car.

Jolene looks at me with wet eyes and scoots closer between the front seats. "I didn't mean for that to happen. I'm really sorry."

I smile at her, though it's tight. "We know that. You panicked, and he'll realize that. It's going to be okay. Let him cool off, and everything will be fine." God, I really hope it's going to be okay. I touch her chin and lift her lips to mine. "I'll miss you so much."

She nods and kisses me so sweetly. "I'll miss you too. As many times as we've said goodbye, it feels weird to be apart now."

"It does."

We give our I love yous and both step out of the car.

Arlo hugs me and drops into the driver's seat.

Jolene clings to me and after more kisses and just breathing her in as if I can store her essence inside me until I return, I gather my things.

She gets into the passenger seat, looking small as she keeps her eyes on mine through the window.

My heart is in a vise as I wave, walking backward toward the sliding doors of the airport.

Arlo pulls away from the curb.

My eyes ache. For as many times as we've all been apart, even the thought of being away from them for days is torture.

But maybe it's better this way—me gone so they can figure out how to deal with each other. They'll be okay. I watch the car until it turns, disappearing behind a veil of buildings and cars, wondering if they're talking yet, or if they're both seething, one in rage and the other in regret.

I'm not sure it's going to be okay.

Chapter Sixty-Three

Jolene Is So Sorry

Tension radiates from Arlo like heat billowing off a furious bon-fire.

And I don't know what to do. Pretending everything is fine would be easy—I've trained for it my whole life. But last night, Arlo and Darius ripped apart the last ties to that part of me. At least, I thought they had. It seems I'm not quite past a few things.

Arlo is silent, but his strong jaw twitches, chewing apart his thoughts.

I hate that I caused this, and I also hate that he's holding back from yelling at me. Knowing I fucked up is hard enough, but what's worse is that I don't know how to move forward with this problem. I care about him—that's an understatement—I want to be near him all the time, against his skin with his eyes on mine as we talk about whatever comes to mind. But there's still a disconnect between us. He won't stay with us at night. Maybe that's a normal thing for him, and he will always be that way. There are couples that have separate bedrooms and that's okay for them, but I'm alone tonight and already longing for Darius's comforting presence, or Arlo's big body encompassing me.

If we continue on this path—all three of us—is this how it will always be?

I glance over at his firm jaw and the scowl that is slightly more furrowed than usual. It's amazing how quickly everything has happened—how fast I've adapted to living with Darius and being close to both of them. I want to crawl into Arlo's lap and press my face against his neck. In a different world, one that is more accepting of something like what we have, I'd have proudly introduced him. I'd have tucked myself under his arm and preened about getting to introduce him as mine. But right now, that world feels like a fantasy.

Tonight has made it clear. Something has to change for us. But what? The sex is mind-blowing—everything I never knew I needed. Then there's the comfort of just being around him, laughing with him, and having him protect me and make me feel like I belong in my skin. But it doesn't erase my entire upbringing. I wish it would. It's so easy to play along when we're alone, but around others? One thing is for certain—

"I'm scared." It's the truth, and I hate to admit it, but that feeling isn't going away.

Arlo glances over at me, then back to the road. "Why?"

I snort a laugh. I could tell him it's because I'm in love with two men and the thought of my family finding out could mean disownment. Or that I've never had something that feels this right but is also wrong, but none of that feels genuine enough. It's shallow.

The traffic is heavy as we near the apartment, and everything in this city is loud and unfamiliar. Darius is my rock. He's the one thing that's persisted through the changes of these last few years. My throat tightens, and I wish I were more like him. Stoic and strong. Being able to step out of a problem and look at it from a calmer angle—always knowing things will work out, and mostly being right, or at least carving out a path that works.

I wish I were more like Arlo too, though. He might be somewhat callous, but he's full of passion he wouldn't dare hide. I don't want to lose him or break apart what's starting between us.

He pulls into the parking garage. "When you figure out why you're so damn scared, maybe let me in on it. Unless you would rather call *your boyfriend*." Pulling into our parking space, he turns off the car and pauses. I'm sure it's because he knows me and my ways by now. Even though it hasn't been long, he pays attention.

I swallow. "Do you want the truth?"

He pockets the keys and leans back in the seat. "If you don't know the answer to that, then you haven't a clue who I am."

Gripping the door handle, I look at him—into the blue eyes that are so easy to get lost in, but for how long? *He doesn't settle. He fucks. He doesn't love. He's not my boyfriend.* Yes, he said things changed, then told me he was mine, but does *he* even know what that means? A hot tear slides down my cheek.

His eyes track it. I know he wants to reach out and wipe it away because I know him.

"What if this is just a fling?" I tilt my head as his chest expands with a sharp breath. "What if we're scratching an itch and I ruin my relationship with my family and potential employers, and then you need more women than just me?" And with that out there, I can't just sit. I throw open the door and escape towards the elevator.

A door slams, and fast footsteps echo against concrete and cars.

Arlo grabs me and pins me against a black SUV, crashing his lips against mine, and I'm not sure I've ever felt so strong and so fragile at the same time. His taste is everything. His touch—a gift I never expected. How could I live without this? I might have to.

I kiss him back, wet and hard and with a painful desperation of wanting someone so much, but not understanding how to handle the uncertainty. There's so much uncertainty.

When he pulls away, I ache at the loss.

"Do you feel like this is a fling, Jolene?" His demand tells me there's no way to stall. No time for niceties.

"I don't have a gauge for that, Arlo. I've never encountered anyone like you. Darius has been with me forever, and the short flings I had weren't an option. I only wanted him."

"And now?" He glowers down at me. "And what about now?"

"You know the answer, Arlo. I just don't know how to deal with everything else."

"You get the fuck over it." He covers his face with his hands and breathes deeply before dropping his arms. His shoulders lower. "Fuck."

"Arlo. You know I can't just do that. I'm not brave or unconcerned about what others think. It's a flaw, but I can't just turn it off."

"I know." His eyes are softer as they take in my face. He tucks my hair behind my ear. "Did you love Darius at first? In a month, did you need him like you need me?"

Why would he ask such a thing? Is he trying to compare or relate to what I have with Darius? He can't. It's not the same. "That's not a fair question."

"Why not?"

"Because I was sixteen. I'm not that age anymore."

He leans close, nose against mine, bodies flush. "Then when did you love him?"

I slide my hands up his neck, cupping his face. This feels like dangerous territory, but I can't just ignore or lie about it, so I give in. Give him everything. "When he left. I knew I loved him when he left me for college. I loved him before then, but I didn't realize I wanted him forever until he was gone. If you're trying to compare, or if you're asking anything about my feelings for you, good luck. I feel everything. I'm a fucking mess."

Pushing off the car, he thrusts his hands in his pockets and looks toward the ceiling. I swear his eyes glint with emotion, making mine sting. "Me too."

Chapter Sixty-Four

Arlo Reflects

ARLO

The apartment is painfully quiet when I get home from work. I should be exhausted—I don't think I slept at all last night, even after punching the bag for two hours—but I'm charged and antsy. Because things are up in the air. Unresolved. Being in limbo without answers is not a good place for me to be. And I'm also worried.

Jolene didn't come out of her room all night or this morning. She's responding to Darius's group chat messages, but she's in hiding, and it makes my mind do things I never want it to do. Does she think we're done? Because that's going to be a conflict of interest, even if I don't know how to work this out between us.

It never mattered if someone kept me a secret. It sure as hell does now. I didn't realize how much until she verbally threw a blanket over my head and told me to sneak out the window while she talked to Lou Gant, a man who isn't in her life.

How is she going to act with neighbors, new coworkers, her friends, and especially her mother? So now what? Where the fuck do we go from here?

Darius landed in Toronto and settled into his hotel. Today, he's concerned about us, but his morning meetings went well. He's checking in like his positive hope will fix this broken link between me and Jolene. She's going to need to emerge from her overthinking for us to work on anything.

Though she's not the only one who's needed space. I've thought about yesterday's fight relentlessly. I even caved and called Ian to talk it over. My mom piped in as well. It seems she's changed as much as I have over the last few months. Any bitterness I've held onto in the previous years has slipped away with each word of her calm advice when it comes to Jolene. Mom's right. Ian's right. But patience isn't my forte, and it's getting harder to accept every moment Jolene hides from me.

I put on shorts and a tee, running shoes, lean against the wall next to Darius and Jolene's room, and knock on the door with a knuckle. There's a shuffle from inside, then the knob twists and the door slowly opens. Goddamn, my girl is beautiful. Even sad, with too little sleep and her hair in a messy bun on her head, she's the one I want to look at every day. Forever.

I swallow hard. "Want to go for a jog?"

Her brows furrow, and she nods. Good.

"I'll grab water bottles." I turn and head to the kitchen.

I'm at the door when she walks in looking like sporty sin. We walk into the elevator and through the lobby in silence.

Sheena glares daggers at Jolene and I wait for a comment from her, but none comes. I hope she's moved on.

We start out at a slow pace, but before long, Jolene is speeding up. She must have needed to get out some energy. I've missed her even after just a day of letting things simmer. I want to drag her close, pin her in one of the small alleyways between brownstones, and taste the sweat on her neck. It doesn't feel right though—like it's not my place to do so.

"Okay, enough," she says, gasping for air as we reach mile three. "I can't."

I slow. "Let's walk then."

She puts her hands on her hips as she catches her breath. A few people pass us, looking us over and smiling. At an intersection, she pushes the crosswalk button. "Are you leaving us?"

Fucking finally. Letting her work through things in her own time is a method of torture for me.

I take a swig of water. "Never."

She blows out a breath, though I'm not sure if it's relief or exhaustion. "Are you mad at me?"

"A little, even if none of what happened yesterday is your fault." That lands on her mother. The life she forced Jolene into, teaching her never to be herself. It falls on society. Maybe it falls on me a little for being so damn irresistible to her, and also so pushy for more—for everything.

"It is, though." She blinks up at me, and it's becoming difficult not to drag her to me. Again, too pushy. "I hurt you."

I snort. "Long ago, I fucked up so hard. I don't know how to pull myself out of the mess I made, and then I dragged you into my issues."

She swipes the back of her hand across her sweaty, furrowed brow. "What do you mean?"

We cross the street with a loud group of business people that look our age. They chatter and laugh, and I hope that one day, that can be Jolene, Darius, and me going out for drinks after work. Meeting up with our coworkers and not worrying if we get too touchy with each other. "My family—my father—fucked me up when I was young. And I made that hurt a part of me. I told you we would be nothing but people who fuck and live together when I didn't even believe that myself. I set you up to push me away, asked for it, and then got pissed when you did exactly that."

"Arlo." Her voice is soft. "I shouldn't have said that in front of Lou. It wasn't fair or even true."

I shrug my shoulders. "Sure, you should have. I would have done the same with any other woman but you. I have dismissed lovers like it was my job to do so, and the moment it happens to me, I can't handle it."

"Yeah, but—"

I take her elbow and pull her to a stop, then nearly kiss her, but she wouldn't like that because we're in public. So I dip my head so we're more eye-to-eye. "I was wrong, and I need to give you more time to sort out how you feel about all this. To figure out what you can accept in your life." That was a direct quote from Ian and I'm so glad for his counsel. I don't have a clue what I'd do without him. I'd be way more of an asshole, that's for sure.

"So now what?" She bites her lip.

I go to tug it from the cage of her teeth, but stop short, ball my fingers and let my hand drop. "We keep our private things private, and we'll be roommates in public until you're ready."

"But you—that's going to hurt you like it did yesterday."

Probably. Time will tell if it's worth the pain. "Like you, I don't have a manual for this, but I want you. I'm willing to wait a bit until you figure out what you want." Will she pursue this incredible thing we have or back away? "But I'm not good at pretending, so if I fuck up and embarrass you again, you'll need to forgive me."

"Arlo, no..." She grimaces.

The smallest thread of guilt goes through me, but I clip it away because I need to be myself right now more than ever. I'm not a man who will be hidden away. There's only so long I'll be able to not touch her in public, because that's what *I* need if we're going to be together. If she's mine, she'll lean into me, introduce me as hers, and fucking love that I can't keep my damn hands off her.

But if she's not mine...

I turn and we walk toward our building, keeping too much distance between us. Please don't let it take her long to figure us out, because I know what I want. It's going to kill me if she doesn't feel the same.

Chapter Sixty-Five

Jolene Wakes Up

JOLENE

I jerk awake for the fourth time and glare at the clock. Midnight has come and gone. I stare at the ceiling, which I can't see because it's pitch black. This bed sucks without Darius in it.

And the rest of the apartment isn't so great when Arlo is giving me space. I don't enjoy this non-fighting fight we're in. Arlo is being understanding, but he's also stand-offish. He's not kissing me or touching me all the time. That alone feels like punishment, which I deserve.

We're talking, but without life in the conversation. We're dull—not something I even thought was possible.

"Enough," I mumble and slide out of bed. I open the door and slip through, fist raised to knock on Arlo's door, but it's open. His bed is made and the lights are off. The hallway glows from the living room light that we leave on if we're coming home in the dark. My stomach drops hard. There's no way he's gone out to get laid, because he said he would wait. For a bit. Did he just mean emotionally? No, he said he was devoted to me. That means physically, or I hope it does.

I thread my fingers through my hair and tug until my scalp burns. I want to throw something or kick the wall. My muscles tighten to do just that. I side-eye his punching bag in his cold, empty room. *Fuck*. I'm pushing him away. How much time is he going to give me to figure that out? I walk down the hall. May as well have a damn drink because I'm not getting any sleep tonight. It's so quiet.

The floor is cold because Arlo turned the air conditioning two degrees lower than necessary. Hand on the fridge handle, I eye the bourbon on the counter. That may be too much. When he comes home and I'm drunk, I will definitely say something stupid and accuse him of doing things he said he wouldn't. I'll end up making things even worse between—

"What are you doing up, Kentucky?"

I screech, jerking away from the fridge and bumping into the kitchen island hard. "Ow! Shit."

Arlo is on the couch, shirtless, glasses on, with his laptop open.

Attempting to calm the heart attack I just had, I press my palms to my eyes and blow out a long breath. "You scared the hell out of me."

Arlo sets his stuff aside and crosses the room to drag me against him, lowering my sleep shorts to check the red spot on my hip. "You okay? What the fuck just happened?"

I lean my forehead against his chest and shake my head. "You're here."

He cups my face and tugs at me to look at him. "Why wouldn't I be?" It takes a split second for his expression to morph from confusion to something I hate seeing from him. The disappointment attaches to all of his gorgeous features. "You thought I'd gone out?"

I scrunch my face. "You said you wouldn't." That doesn't stop my damn brain from conjuring up the kind of woman Arlo would seek. But then all I can really see is me with him. Is that just my hopeful mind? "But it wouldn't be your fault if you did. Everything is weird between us."

"That doesn't mean I'd go off to fuck someone, Jolene." He sets his forehead against mine. "I'm just that kind of person, aren't I?"

"No, Arlo. Well, maybe." I wrap my arms around him, clinging to bare muscle. "Sorry."

"Don't be. Why should you trust me?"

I lean back so I can look into his eyes. The glasses are so cute. They soften his scowl. "I do trust you."

"Do you? Because it seems like you think I may have been out fucking some girl."

My jaw tightens. "Don't call them girls."

He raises an eyebrow. "No?"

"No, that's for me. I'm your girl. They're women." Apparently, that's a line for me now.

His grip on me tightens, feeling more like us. "There's my good girl. I like you a little jealous." He brushes his lips over mine, but he doesn't kiss me. It's infuriating how hard my heart is still pounding. "But I promised myself to you, and I don't take that lightly."

I gulp and nod. And here I practically shoved him away from me. "I know."

"You don't. I haven't proved myself to you yet. But I'm going to."

That satiates the tension roaring in my veins and makes me want to prove myself too. I just don't know how. "Are you?"

He stares down at me, face serious. "I don't want anyone else but you." He leans closer, taking my lips with his. His tongue slides against mine, and I'm glad he's holding onto me so tightly, because I full-on swoon against him.

The moment he takes off his glasses, setting them on the counter, and then cups my ass, I know this is more than just a moment of sincere affection between us. His hold on me is desperate.

I cling back like he'll slip away if I let go, but it's not enough. Gripping his waistband, I tug.

Fortunately, he understands I need him right now, and pulls down my shorts as he lowers to the kitchen floor. He shimmies out of his pants just enough to free his jutting cock and leans against the cabinets. "Straddle me right fucking now, angel."

I nearly come at the command and drop into his lap, over his hard cock, and roll my hips, sliding him against me. "Like this?"

"No." He growls, positions himself and slams up into me, making me cry out. "Like that. Fuck me." He holds the neckline of my tee aside and sucks at my neck. "Scream for me." His grip tightens around me to keep me close, but he lifts my chin so I'll look at him. "Be with me, Jolene."

My throat tightens with emotion. "Okay." I roll my hips, riding him as we kiss and breathe in each other's air. My knees hurt against the hard floor, but I don't care. I only need to get him as far into me as possible because he will soothe this ache in me. We stay quiet except for our pleasured moans and heavy breathing, and everything feels right between us. How in the hell would I ever stay away from this man? The thought is painful.

As I grind down onto him, tension rockets forward, almost too soon, but I need it just like I get from him. Hard. Intense. Completely necessary. My stomach and hips tighten. I whimper and moan, arching back to get him deeper.

"Fuck yes. Just like that." He pinches my nipple, making a twisting motion that makes my jaw drop in pleasure. "You're such a good girl."

"For you—" I whimper as flutters begin low in my belly. "Only you." My orgasm is a tight pulse that gets so strong, I'm not sure I'll come out of it. I scream, whimper, and gasp.

Arlo fucks up into me when I can't go on, our flesh slapping so hard, someone's bound to hear us. I fall forward, pressing my face against his shoulder. I can barely get my teeth around the muscle, but it works enough for him to curse loudly and then grunt as he comes.

When the room comes back into focus, we're still lying on the kitchen floor. He's so warm. Turns out I enjoy being draped over him as much as I like his weight on me.

He lifts my face and kisses my lips tenderly. "Angel."

There's no choice but to accept that we are so good together like this. He makes me forget to think, and I need that. And I think I bring some kind of peace he needs too.

I nod, looking over the gorgeous face I love. The blue eyes that go sweet only for me. "Thank you."

"For what?" His voice is raspy.

"For being you."

His grin tilts up further on the right, making him smirk like the sly bad boy he is.

I rest my head on his chest, listening to the powerful thump of his heart.

The way he strokes my back has my eyes drifting shut, but he shifts, sitting up and taking me with him.

He picks me up and carries me to his shower, where we caress and hold each other in the water. And when I'm wrapped in a towel and head to the door, he makes me naked again and pulls me into his bed, where he tucks me under his arm.

I rest my hand on his chest and drift, realizing that being without him is no longer a possibility.

This is him giving me everything.

Can I do the same?

Chapter Sixty-Six

Darius Gets Impatient

DARIUS

A whimper and the sound of slapping skin plus the rocking mattress wake me... again.

I grin and rub my bleary eyes. "We need a bigger bed."

"Good morning," Arlo growls. He has Jolene's face smashed into the mattress as he punish-fucks her. She must have been teasing him again. She's been snuggling him when his alarm goes off so he won't leave the bed or waking him with her slow, teasing mouth. Both make him lose it.

"Fuck, fuck, fuck, fuck, fuuuuccck," Jolene cries as she struggles under him, fisting the sheets, tugging, and popping them off the corner of the mattress as she comes.

Arlo grits his teeth and fucks her harder, pressing her front down so hard, I'm surprised she can breathe.

I'm getting better at watching them go rough. Probably because they really love to go rough.

It's been frequent since I returned from my business trip a month ago. We've settled in further since then... mostly. At home, we're all close and touchy, and there hasn't been the pressurized tension between Jolene and Arlo like there was before.

In public, it's Jolene and me, though she's been gravitating more to Arlo, and if he's had a rough day, her attention is on him. I love what they're building. But they still haven't talked about what's so clear to me.

Arlo slaps Jolene's ass hard and yells as he barrels through his release. When he stops thrusting, my best friend's mood instantly shifts. His hands gentle as he leans over Jolene, turning her face so he can kiss her parted, panting lips. "Good morning."

"Good morning." She bats her eyes. "Was I good for you, sir?"

"No." He nips her bottom lip. "If you wake me with a finger in my ass again, I'm going to tie you to the bed and strap the vibrator to you while I shower."

She grins. "But you love it when I do that."

"But then you pretend you're asleep when I need you. You make me work for it when I need to get up. Bad girl." He slaps her ass again and heads to the bathroom, mumbling about being late.

She giggles and crawls over to wrap her arms around my torso. "Hi, baby."

"Hi." I drag her closer and kiss her head, then roll over on top of her and slip my hard cock into her soaked heat. "Having fun?" Feeling that Arlo just found his pleasure inside her is such a turn-on.

She widens her legs for me and moans as she kisses my neck. "Every day."

The shower turns on, and I lick the seam of her lips until she moans and lifts to kiss me deep. I touch my forehead to hers. "You're so damn wet."

"That's because Arlo just came inside me."

The boldness Jolene has found with Arlo is such a thrill. Besides the *not in public* thing, she seems so much more comfortable being herself with both of us. I kiss a dimple. "Do you love being his little whore?"

She raises her eyebrows at me, then bites her lip and nods. "I really do."

I slowly work in and out of her, forcing myself to focus on the conversation and not on how amazing her pussy feels tightening around my cock. "Do you love *him*?"

Her expression only goes to shock for a moment before she blushes and grins like she can't stop it. "I think I do."

Of course she does. How could she not? I want to take them both and smoosh them together. Tell them to kiss it out and confess how much they love each other. And while it's sort of my place to do so, it's also not. They need to figure it out through processing and patience, if they can. Jolene's still looking for a job. She's still having shitty conversations with her mother. Arlo is catching on that something is wrong with Ian, but the man is playing off that whatever it is doesn't matter, making Arlo antsy. Everything matters when it comes to his family.

And while Jolene and Arlo's relationship feels more solid, it also feels like the structure may crumble if they can't admit their feelings and something in our day-to-day changes.

The shower shuts off, and I loop an arm under her knee, changing our angle. "When are you going to tell him?"

She lowers her voice. "You realize we're making love while talking about Arlo?"

"You and I are good at communicating. You and Arlo need some work."

"Hey!" She shoves at me, but giggles as well. "Soon. When it feels right." She kicks my ass with the heel of the foot I don't have pinned up to her chest.

I press in deep and grind. "Does this feel right, babes? These mornings where your moans and the shaking bed are my alarm clock?"

"Yes, it really does." She kisses me and meets my eyes, making that connection that always seems to stoke more fire for her in my soul. "Don't stop."

"Never, love. I have a lifetime of this for you."

She nods and bites her lip as tingles travel my spine and tighten my balls. I think we both sense Arlo and look over to find him watching us from the doorway, arms crossed and smiling.

He looks happy. Content as I've ever seen him. But I know it's hard for him because he's told me it is. He's shown more patience over the months than I thought he possessed, though the incredible sex, morning kisses, cuddles after rough days, and laughter at dinner certainly helps.

"Coming," Jolene whispers, gripping my ass. "Darius."

I grind down hard into her pussy, and when she cries out, her inner muscles knead me into a forceful orgasm. I settle my weight on her and sigh, kissing her neck. "I love you, baby."

She gently rakes her nails over my neck. "I love you."

"That was a good one." Arlo presses his hand to the mattress and kisses Jolene, then me. "I'll make coffee. Leave in ten?"

I hum an agreement and kiss my love, basking in the heat of her body. I can take a two-minute shower, I think.

But no matter how much I bask in these calm, beautifully normal moments, we can't stay like this forever, even if it seems perfect right now.

Jolene is going to have to confront things about herself that aren't comfortable.

And Arlo isn't a man who can live unsettled.

Chapter Sixty-Seven

Jolene's Luck

JOLENE

I'm cleaning out the fridge when I get a call from an unknown Chicago area code number. Maybe it's another interview that will turn into yet another offer for an unpaid internship. Yippee.

I answer anyway, because I'm still waiting for that dream job. "This is Jolene Shah." How would our names work if we all stayed together? The Shah-Gates-Keller family? The Shateslers? The—

"Hello, Ms. Shah, this is Martha from Thrummends Finance. You interviewed with us a couple of months ago."

I raise my eyebrows high. "I remember. How are you?"

"Doing great. Thanks for asking. I'm calling because we'd love for you to come back in for another interview. Would you have time this afternoon?"

I'd fall out of my chair if I were sitting. I have a lot of time, but not a lot of time for assholes. "Would the interview be with Mr. Smitt?" I grin, remembering Lou's nickname for the rude man. If I never see that grump again, I'll live a happier life.

"Actually, he retired." The grin in her voice is clear. "We have several critical positions open, and your name came up."

My jaw drops. I liked nearly everything about Thrummends except for the CFO. This could be it. *Finally.* "In that case, yes. I have time."

***

I pause at the black doors of the Thrummends building, one block inside Chicago's financial district, and pull out my phone. I smile at Darius's good-luck-meme-blast and dial Arlo.

He answers on the second ring. "You on time, angel?"

"Yeah. This is a good thing, right?" I'm so nervous about messing this up again.

"Your name came up in the financial circle. That's good. You're going to do great. Get in there. Be you and they will love you."

I bite my lip. I want to tell him I love *him*. It's right on my tongue, but I should be with him for that, and he hasn't said it either. "Thank you. I'll see you when I get home."

"We'll celebrate, no matter how it goes today." It's incredible how much he can settle me with his words. Just like that, everything is going to be fine. No matter what. Then he says, "Is your ass still red from this morning?" and I get a much different set of feelings. Hot and bothered, but also protected and never alone.

"No. It faded by lunchtime. When I think about it, though, I can almost feel it."

"Good. Tonight."

"Tonight." I hang up and step inside.

Martha's blond head pops up from behind the sleek steel reception desk with backlit letters of the company name. She stands. "Ms. Shah. So nice to see you again."

When I met her for the first time, she was in a black dress suit with her hair in a tight bun. Today, her hair is down in wild spirals, and she's in a bright green flouncy blouse and slim gray capris that show off her ample curves perfectly. She looks so much more comfortable—happier—than before.

She directs me down the hall. "Come on. They're all in here."

It's the same conference room I was in before, but instead of blank gray walls, there's an enormous canvas that's covered with a teal, gray, and gold marbled effect. Only one other thing is distinctly different.

"What are you doing here?" I blurt before I can remember to act professionally.

"There she is." Lou Gant stands at the head of the conference table and comes over to hug me. "Well, Mr. Piece of Shit finally retired—"

"Thankfully," says the older man in the room. I remember him, but today he wears a big smile instead of a constipated frown.

"Yep. And so I was called in to help steer the ship." Lou points to him. "You've met Olsen, right?"

"I have." We shake and go through the business how-are-yous.

Lou signals to the chair next to him. "Has a decent company scooped you up yet?"

Do not get overly hopeful, Jolene. He's not going to just hand you a job even if Martha said "critical positions." However, my freaking name came up. It's really hard not to fist pump right now.

I shake my head as I sit. "Nope. I've heeded your advice and have declined six unpaid internships."

Olsen snorts and shakes his head. He taps a black folder under his palm.

Lou stands. "Glad to hear it. Olsen is going to tell you a bit about our new structure system, and I'll be right back."

A little odd for an interview, but okay. I turn toward Olsen, who enthusiastically opens his folder.

By the time Lou reenters the room, my head is spinning, and I've filled two notebook pages with company notes along with benefits, insurance, and vacation info that are impressive compared to any of the other places I've interviewed with.

"Questions?" Lou holds an envelope out to me.

"Uh…" It has my name and the date printed on it. "Should I open this?"

"Later. Go home and talk it over with your—" he tilts his head. "—people."

My cheeks heat, but I power through. "And what am I discussing?" Let's just make sure things are clear here and I'm not letting hope and desperation impede logic. This hasn't been an interview.

Lou leans back, fingers linked against his stomach. "How you're coming to work here as soon as possible. How long do you need before you start?"

I laugh. Like a loud, echoing bark of a laugh. "That's it? Do you need me to crunch numbers or something?" He can't be serious. It can't be this easy, not that it's been easy.

He waves me off. "We already did that."

Olsen holds up two fingers. "Twice. We thought your insight was outstanding."

"Mr. Smitt didn't."

"Nothing was good enough for him," Olsen says.

Lou nods in agreement.

I don't know why I feel the need to argue, but I can't stop myself. "But I didn't exactly handle myself when things went south."

"You didn't burst out crying like the man after you." Olsen scrunches his face. "I hope he's okay after that."

"Smitt left a pile of burned interviewees in his wake." Lou claps, making me jump. "But you're here, and business is settled for now. Want coffee? I want coffee. Let's go."

In a haze as I process what the hell just happened, I shake Olsen's hand, stuff my envelope in my purse, and follow Lou out the door.

He peeks into three offices on the way out to introduce me and ask people if they want anything while he's out. When we step out of the building and wait at the crosswalk, he nudges me with his elbow. "You're not going to say 'no,' are you? Because I'd really like to have you on my team. I know what happened with Jeremy was rough, but I promise I do *not* condone nor—"

I wave him off. "I was in beauty pageants. That gave me too much knowledge regarding how nepotism is handled—or *not* handled—in the workplace. Is that why you left Diggory and Sons?" I grimace, eyeing the last of the passing cars as the walk light flashes. "Sorry. I know that's prying. Don't answer. I'm familiar with privacy policies and non-compete agreements." All financial places make their employees sign them, so there's no way to switch companies and take clients and secrets to the competition. I don't know how he avoided one.

"I can't believe you're only twenty-two. We are going to have the best team in the city, Jolene." He grins widely. "I didn't have an NCA because my wife's girlfriend is one of the best lawyers in the city and was present during my negotiations."

I stumble-step and open my mouth to say... I don't know what. His *wife's girlfriend*. He's like me or us or what?

Lou flicks his eyebrows at me, then points at a cafe table two men are stepping away from. "Hurry. This place is busy."

We sit while a server grabs the dirty dishes and takes our order. When she's gone, Lou stays quiet. I feel like I've known him far longer than the few interactions we've had.

I swallow hard. "I'm glad she could be there for you like that."

"She is an amazing woman. As is my wife."

He tells me how they met. How he knew his wife would be his the moment he saw her, but she'd been in the worst place since a disastrous breakup, and then how a decade later that ex reached out to apologize. He encouraged their reconnection, if anything, so his wife would have closure. Grinning, he tells me they didn't expect that a reconnection would turn into what it did.

I have questions—of course I do. I ask whether they live together and if they have kids.

He's so open to sharing that it makes my soul swell.

I take the first sip of my new favorite latte. "How do you deal with…" I glance around at the people at the surrounding tables and the passersby. "Um, everyone?"

He leans forward conspiratorially. "We hold on to those who accept us and let go of those who don't."

If only. "That sounds very simple in theory."

"And it takes a lot of painful practice." His nose scrunches. "I lost some people in my life, and that hurt. But if someone can't see how happy we are, and worse, wants to stop us from being happy, then they don't care for me enough to be part of my life."

My throat is tight. "I'm sorry some people didn't accept you." Am I going to cry? I swallow it down. Nope. Not today, and not in front of this awesome person who might be my new boss.

Lou's eyes go soft behind his glasses, and he tilts his head. "I have a confession."

What else could this man tell me he hasn't already? "Oh?"

"When I saw you at the restaurant, I could have left you be. Wandered off home, and we would still be here today talking business without this additional topic. But I saw the three of you, and I knew.

My wife knew. And I guess I was excited for you, like I'm excited for us, and wanted to share that. I'm sorry if I caused strife." He flinches. "I didn't read you all totally wrong, did I?"

My stomach drops, and I reel through the memories of that night to pinpoint what he saw, and realize he saw *us* happily together in a relationship. He probably noticed the way we all act like the other two hung the moon and spit out the stars. Denying that I'm deeply in love with two men would be such a lie. I sigh, and I feel lighter. "Uh, you didn't read that wrong. But I caused the strife. Not you."

He shrugs a shoulder. "I assume it was new?" His smile is warm and not judgy, which I truly appreciate.

I nod. "It was our first outing since, um, connecting."

"That makes sense. Before I invaded, the three of you just exuded togetherness."

Did we? I lean back and huff a laugh. "And then we got into a huge fight."

"Yeah, I picked up on that. Everything okay now?"

"Kinda." My breath evens out. This feels oddly good to talk about. "We're not public. I don't know how to do that, or really how to navigate whatever it is we are."

"Oof. It's a tough road." Lou drains the rest of his cup. "But so is life. There are so many things that are out of our control, especially other people. You can't decide what someone is going to think about what you do."

Deep down, I know that. I do. I've been judged my whole life, but I don't want to be judged in this, dragging my men with me as people mentally score us so low with only a glance. They don't get it, and they never will.

"You just have to do what makes you happy. They're good to you?"

I lose the battle with the emotions in my throat. "Yes," I rasp. "I'm so happy with them."

"Good. Then go call a family meeting and discuss what life would look like if you worked for me and made our company into the financial empire it can be."

We part with a hug, and he makes me promise to call him about the job soon.

From there, I walk to Millennium Park and text Darius and Arlo to tell them it went well and I'll fill them in at home. I want to tell them both at the same time and see their faces. I need both of their responses.

I find a bench and look around at the couples, joggers, business-people and wonder what their relationships are like. There are families of all kinds, but none that seem to be more than the regular. None are like I am. We are.

Blowing out a breath, I lean back and let the late-summer sun warm me.

I didn't realize how lonely I was with my thoughts. Sure, I share with Hayley, Darius, and Arlo—mostly. But I haven't shared myself with friends or my mother since I made this major change in my life. I'm not ready, but I'd like to be.

Chapter Sixty-Eight

Arlo's Dilemma

ARLO

I stare at the numbers on the employment proposal that Lou gave Jolene.

So does Darius.

Jolene uncorks the bourbon and takes a swig from the bottle, then hisses at the sting as she leans back against the counter. "So. Um. I..." She laughs and takes another swig.

"That pretty much sums it up," Darius says, shaking his head. He blows out a breath and tugs her against him. "This is amazing, babes."

"So much," I add. I signal for her to bring that over to the kitchen island, because this is a celebration. The kind where we should be on a yacht headed to the Caribbean. Our girl just carved out her place in Chicago. There's no way for anyone to deny she belongs here now.

"And Lou knows about us?" Darius keeps staring at that big fucking number. "Like... knows-knows?"

Jolene's head bobs, and she hands the bourbon to me.

I tip it up and let the fire in my throat reset my brain. The aftertaste is caramel and wood, and will always remind me of my Kentucky girl.

"Okay." I huff a laugh. "Lou is cool, and I don't even have a thought about what to negotiate with this package. Maybe... days off? Why didn't you say yes?"

"Because I didn't open it until now. Do I call him? What should I do?"

"Do you think you'd like the job?" Darius asks.

"Yes." Jolene leans against my arm and sighs. "I know I'd love it. It's exactly what I want to do."

Dragging her between me and the island, I rest my chin on her shoulder as I browse the benefits. "Then you ask for anything additional you want and accept." I kiss her neck. "I'm so fucking proud of you. Look at this big-ass signing bonus. That's there because you are exactly where you need to be and did just what you needed to do."

The way she beams at me should be illegal because I think I'd do anything to get it again in the future.

I tap her nose. "You're taking us out to dinner."

Darius reaches across the island and strokes her cheek. "In France." He snorts. "This is wild."

I laugh. "Right?" I turn Jolene toward me and kiss her hard before pulling back and giving her a peck on her forehead. "How do you want to celebrate?"

She grins, biting her lip like she really can't believe this is happening. But it is, and there's paperwork to solidify it. I knew it.

Darius definitely knew it. He's grinning too, thumbing through the contract.

Jolene presses her hands to her cheeks. "Maybe we can—"

My phone rings on the kitchen island. It's Mom, who never calls me unless she's demanding I call and catch up with my sister.

"Hold that thought." I roll my eyes and give one more kiss to Jolene's neck before stepping away. "I have to take this." Stepping toward the living room, I answer. "Hey, Mom."

"Arlo." The way she says my name is pain and tears and utter anguish.

Panic shocks my spine. "What's wrong?"

She takes a jagged breath. "It's Ian. He collapsed at fourteen-hundred hours after leg and chest pain. They think it's a pulmonary embolism and are doing more testing, but his stats are terrible and—" her sob makes my skin tight. "—they're not sure he's going to make it through the night, much less surgery. Your sister is on the way with the family, and so are Ian's brother and nephew. Can you come?"

Old man stuff. The weight loss. Those damned bags under his eyes that weren't going away. This can't be happening.

Jolene entwines her fingers with mine, and my world stops spinning.

I hang on tight. Squeeze. With a gulp, I nod. "I'm on the way. Are you able to text me your location?"

"Yes. Thank you."

As soon as I hang up, my eyes sting. I'm shaky and everything's too tight. Dragging Jolene against my chest and breathing her in helps. I can't lose him. Even the thought of it is too much.

Darius places a hand on my back. "Can you talk about it?"

With a few cracked words and a sniffle, I tell them what I know, then tip Jolene's face up to kiss her.

She squeezes me tight, and I'd love for her to be with me today, but she can't be. I step back and slip my shoes back on. "I have to go."

Jolene nods. "I'll get dressed."

Darius takes a step to follow her. "I'll drive."

I grip her elbow and pull her close as I shake my head. How do I tell her this? "My family will be there. All of them."

Her brows scrunch. "Okay."

I press my forehead to hers. "This is going to be rough for me, angel. If Ian—" I swallow again to keep my voice as steady as possible. "I'm going to be a wreck. And I'm going to need you close."

She cups my face with both hands and sniffles. "I'm here."

"I know. But I can't pretend we're not together today. Do you get it?"

"But I want to be there for you."

"And I need you, but not with my sister there. I don't know how she'll treat you, but if it's like she treats me, I can't worry about you when I'm worried about—"

"Hey." Darius runs his thumbs over the tight muscles in my neck. "It's okay. I'm going to order a ride for you, and the moment you find out anything, you let us know. We'll do anything to help. You know that."

I catch his gaze and nod in thanks for his understanding. "I'll keep you posted."

Jolene crosses her arms, but it's more like a self-hug. Her distraught expression adds to my distress.

"I'm sorry. I just can't. Stay here with Darius, and I'll call in a bit when I find out what's going on." I hug Darius and then turn to my girl, take her face and kiss her. I wish I could make everything better for her, but I can't, and I have to fucking go, dammit.

I can't even look back at them as I haul myself out the door for fear I'll cave, pick her up and make her come with me when she's not ready.

Chapter Sixty-Nine

Jolene Makes A Choice

JOLENE

Arlo doesn't want me there. I shake my head at myself. No—he doesn't want me there when we're not fully together. I feel like such an ass for keeping him at arm's length for so long, because there is nothing worse than the feeling that I need to run down the hall, catch up, and go with him.

Poor Ian. And Yolanda. I want to see them, and be there for her and, obviously, for Arlo.

I want to meet this sister of his and figure out why she'd keep their monster of a father closer to her than her brother and see what the family she's built is like. And if Ian… I can't even think about it, and it's not like he's my family, even if it feels like he is. He has to make it through this. I've grown to love that man.

The letter on the kitchen island is my future, proof I'm an adult who can fend for herself in this world. But I don't feel like an adult because I'm locked in my childhood with my narrow perspective of what things should be like according to… who? My mother and her pageant friends? What is wrong with me? Arlo needs us, and we're here, not with him. Not supporting him when he needs it most.

Darius stares at the door, hands on his hips. His eyes are watery, and he doesn't need to say a thing because I get it.

I ball my fists. "We should be with him. We're his and he's ours and we're supposed to take care of each other."

Darius's head bobs. "I know."

"Fuck," I yell. "I should be holding his hand, being his rock, and making sure he has everything he needs because I love him. He's what I want in my life. *Him.* Him and you."

Darius stretches his arms as if he doesn't know what to do with his hands, either. "Good. Me too. What are we going to do, babes?"

I grab my phone from my purse, then walk back to the bedroom. Darius follows and grabs a bag, throwing a blanket in it and some books.

Mom answers after two rings. "And here I thought you had disappeared off the planet."

That happens when I can't share what's going on in my life without catching hell for it. "I know, Mom. Sorry, I've been quiet. I've been going through some things."

"Aw, sweetheart. Problems with Darius?"

I glare at the phone. "No. Not at all. He's wonderful, as always."

Darius raises an eyebrow at me, and mouths "speaker."

I push the button, and he goes back to packing, grabbing a phone charger and stuffing it in the bag.

"Do you need to come home?" Mom sounds so hopeful. "I'll get a ticket right now."

Darius and I roll our eyes in sync.

"No," I say. "But I need to tell you something. I'm not sure you're going to like it."

She's quiet for a moment. "Well, try me. What's going on?"

I swallow hard. This is not something I ever expected to tell my mother, but here we are, and I can't deny this anymore. "I'm with Arlo. He's my boyfriend."

"What?" The expression that her tone conjures in my mind is a near snarl. "Where's Darius?"

"I'm here too, Donna." Darius stares at the phone, waiting for a response, but there's none.

My jaw clenches at his worried expression. I stare down at the link to my mother, wishing I had done this on video or in person, not that she'd have let me leave Kentucky if I'd have gone there to talk to her about this. "We're still together. They're both my boyfriends."

She makes an odd sound, somewhere between a scoff and a laugh. "What? Jolene, that doesn't make any sense."

"I know it's unexpected—I didn't expect it either—but I love them both, and we're trying a relationship with the three of us." My insides ball like they're trying to hide from this conversation. "And it's going really well."

I want to wake up with Arlo every morning and play—pushing each other in ways that expand who we are. And I love Darius's sweet quietness and how he reads both Arlo and me like it's his job. We are a team, and I need to fight for that, even against my mother.

"You're kidding with me. This is ridiculous. Jolene, you can't—are you *with* them? Like you're not in bed with Arlo, right?"

I'm in bed with Arlo as often as my body allows, but I'm not making this conversation more difficult than it already is. "I know this is hard to understand, and one day, when there's time, I'll sit in front of you and we'll really talk it out so you can understand how I feel. The three of us will come to Lexington and—"

"Jolene, this isn't funny." Her voice goes pitchy. "Don't joke around."

I wince. "I'm not joking. Again, I know this is not what you ex-pected—"

"It's not right. If this is what happens in a city like Chicago, you need to come back home."

Darius sits next to me, pressing his warm arm to mine.

My heart hurts, but I swallow the emotion down. "I think this happens when people fall in love. And maybe you don't consider it normal, but that doesn't make it wrong. But besides that, I got a job offer today, and it's more than I ever expected in a position I am going to love so much."

I wait for a reaction to the subject that she should approve of, but the line is silent. I sigh. "My home is Chicago, Mom." I look up into Darius's wet eyes and tug at his strength and the way he loves me. "Here with Darius and Arlo. This is where I'm starting my life, and I'm so happy."

He pulls my hand up to his lips, kisses my knuckles, then whispers, "I love you," against my skin.

"Jolene," Mom says in a harsh tone. "Don't you dare ruin your life like this. You come home, by yourself or not at all."

My face scrunches with emotion, and I sniffle. "What do you mean?"

"That man isn't welcome here. Do you hear me? And neither is Darius if he's going to let you do something that-that... disgusting. You need to come home and figure yourself out."

"Donna?" Darius's voice is steady. "I know this isn't a simple thing for you to understand, but there's nothing disgusting about how much we care for each other."

"And what does your family say about this?" It's an obvious threat. An, *I'm going to talk about this with them if you don't back down.*

Darius sighs. "They won't be surprised at all. They love Arlo and Jolene. It makes sense."

Nothing fazes his family, so he's not wrong. I just hadn't thought about anything other than my mother's reaction because she's always fazed by my decisions. Though this one is the wildest I've ever made. It feels so right, though. Even now.

"I'm not speaking about this with you," she says back too harshly.

"Mom." I wipe a tear that spills over and steady myself. "I am feeling more like myself than I ever have. I really hope you can eventually understand that I love them. And if Arlo and Darius aren't welcome around you, then I'm not either."

The line clicks off. My mother hung up on me—cut me off. Okay, then. It is what it is and, like Lou said, I can't control her, only me. And I need to be there for Arlo.

"I love you so much." Darius pulls me against him. "You okay?"

I wipe my tears with my palms. It's not like we didn't expect her reaction, and there's relief with it being done, even though my heart feels squeezed and shaky. "No. But there's no time for that."

"It will be okay. It will." He pulls me up from the bed, clearly as eager to get to Arlo as I am. "Let's go."

Arlo Breathes Easier

ARLO

It's forty-five minutes before I'm allowed to see Ian, even though my mother is there with him. I've paced the waiting room, bugged the nurses, sucked down a cup of the worst coffee, until, finally, a doctor comes in and calls my name.

When I step into the hospital room, I can barely focus on Ian's pale face. All the tubes and the five machines surrounding him, beeping and flapping as they deliver meds and oxygen, drain fluids, and work as a unit to keep him alive, are a shock. He really may leave us.

Mom pops up from the seat beside the bed. The moment she hugs me, she breaks into sobs.

I can't hold in my own tears.

My mother doesn't cry. She's a stoic hard-ass who keeps her emotions inside a locked armory box in some hidden dungeon of her soul. Then again, Ian did a hell of a job unlocking a lot of things in her and me.

I kiss her head and clear my throat. "Give me all the details." Maybe we can do something.

"Well, he's been going through a few things." She hiccups and wipes at eyes so bloodshot, the blue looks neon. The floor pulls her attention, and I know something's not right beyond what happened today.

"His old-man stuff." I squeeze the bridge of my nose to ease the pressure in my eyes.

"Sorry. There wasn't anything for anyone to do, and it didn't seem like it was much of a big deal. But…" She looks toward Ian and sighs.

The Keller family way—either make fun of it, or pretend it doesn't exist. My jaw is so tight I have to open my mouth to flex it. "Big deal or not, I would have liked to have known. I'm sure both of you could have used some support."

Mom's face scrunches, and she nods.

I tug her into a hug.

She clings to me, breathing in tiny jagged breaths, until her phone buzzes. "That's your sister. I'm going to wait for her at the elevator. You can…" She looks at Ian's still body and nods before stepping out.

I walk over to Ian's side and take his chilled hand. "Don't you die on us, asshole." I kiss his forehead.

His lids twitch, then flutter open. His eyes roll as he tries to focus on me. "Arlo," he slurs, voice raspy. He squeezes my fingers. "You caught me on a bad day—" he pulls in a sharp breath, making the pegs of the oxygen tubes press deeper into his nostrils, and a machine beeps. "I didn't brush my hair."

I smile, jaw and throat painfully tight. "Well, I'll be handsome enough for the both of us."

"As always." He sounds drunk. They probably have him on some potent drugs for the pain. He puts his hand over mine. "Let's save the bullshit for later and pretend we're at the bar. Can we do that?"

He knows how much I hate that, but if it's what he needs… I swallow hard and nod.

"How's your girl?" he says, grinning.

If we're pretending everything is fine, I shouldn't tell him she's not mine yet and I'm not sure she ever will be. There are too many hang-ups and societal rules for her to be mine, but the man is dying. I'll tell him anything to keep him hopeful and here.

And that means not discussing the emotional bullshit—how he's been the best father to me and an incredible friend. How I wouldn't be who I am, doing what I do, without his support, and I will take his lessons with me to the grave. He's made a mark on every person's soul he ever met, but he knows that already. We show him how much he means to us when we conquer our world fueled by his advice. And because I would drop everything to be here and so would everyone who knew him. But if I say that, it's over. He'll know we think he's done and may stop fighting.

So I tell him about Jolene's job offer.

"She's going to be just fine." Ian grins, blinking slowly. "And she has you two. When are you going to make that official?"

If we were actually in a bar instead of the hospital where his eyes are half-closed, he'd realize how big of an effort it's taking me to appear so nonchalant. "When she's ready," I lie. "I'll take her and Darius to a Caribbean island and have a talk about weddings, receptions, and where we're going to raise a family."

"Closer to our house, obviously."

I nod. "Obviously." And while I may have fabricated this future out of quick necessity, the vision also slams into me with painful force.

The three of us in our morning routine at our house. Making break-fast. Ian and my mother walking into the chaos of kids and dogs because they're always welcome. Darius lifting our littlest daughter into his arms because she makes him carry her around like the princess she is while the others bicker over which pancake toppings are best. Me, taking a moment to stare down my girl. Jolene looking hot as fuck in a suit because she's signing another huge deal, and my glance telling her I'm going to enjoy taking that off her later.

Fuck me, I want that more than I could have ever in my life imagined.

He grins. "Grandkids like you? The world is in for it."

"It is. In a couple of years, though. We're not ready for that." *Stick around, old man, and let's see.*

"A couple of years sounds perfect." Jolene's voice makes me spin. She's here.

Darius stands behind her, leaning against the doorframe with a huge grin on his face.

She tilts her head. "That gives me time to settle into my new—"

She doesn't get the last word out because I dive forward, cup her face, and crash my lips down on hers. She's here, wrapping her arms around me to bring me closer, and kissing me back, not seeming to care if others see.

I pull back but keep her close, because I have to. It's required. "You're here." Fuck, I needed her here.

"I never want to be away from you when you need me." She stares up into my eyes, connecting us like some weird soul-bound attachment. It makes no sense, but I want this feeling forever.

"So, you're mine, angel?" I glance at Darius. "Ours?"

"Yes." Her chest rises and falls, and she strokes her knuckles down my cheek. "I love being yours, Arlo."

There's a pause in the room, because I want more from her and want to give her more. I want to name our feelings, but we're in a hospital and it's not time.

She swallows and leans to give my lips a peck. "I'm tired of denying the truth."

"Good." I cup Darius's neck and pull him close until his forehead meets mine. He called it. I thought that getting along with Jolene would be difficult, and that it would be impossible to love her like he said I would. I was so wrong.

He pushes off the doorframe and pulls me into a one-armed hug since his other is busy holding a big carryout bag.

I sink against him, pulling Jolene with me. I needed them so damn much. It's like a weight just dissipated from inside my chest. These are my people. I glance over my shoulder.

Ian's grin is knowing, though tired. "Come, tell me about your day before I get another hit of the good stuff from this machine and fall asleep."

Jolene breaks from me and approaches the bed, taking his hand. "Well, I got an amazing job offer."

"Well deserved. Congratulations."

She beams. "Thank you. But then Arlo told me one of my favorite people was in the hospital."

"Bah," Ian says. "You're pulling my leg."

"Nope. Here you are. In a hospital bed."

His raspy laugh is slow and tired. "What else?"

"Uh, well, I told my mother that I was in a relationship with Arlo."

I step against her back, slipping my arm around her waist and tilting her face to mine. "You okay?"

She looks like she's a moment away from bursting into tears before she swallows it down. I know her expressions now. That conversation did not go well.

"Fuck, I'm sorry." I rest my forehead against her hair. *Fucking Donna.*

"I can't control what others think about me." Jolene's words are too steady. It's like she rehearsed the phrase.

One machine makes a whirring noise.

Ian shakes his head and closes his eyes. "She'll come around when she sees how good you all are for each other. You have a good heart, Jolene. Darius, you too." His lips curve up in a sleepy smile. "I guess Arlo is pretty decent as well."

Jolene looks up at me with teary eyes. "He's amazing, and I'm very lucky."

"Not luckier than I am." I tighten my hold around her waist and kiss her shoulder before patting Ian's chest. "Rest."

Jolene nods, pulling his thin blanket higher. "Yes. Do that, and we'll all be here when you wake."

We're going to be here. Through his surgery. Recovery. Together, because we're a family.

I turn back to see Darius hugging my mother. My sister stands behind them with her husband and my niece.

Jolene slips her hand in mine, and waves like this won't be horribly uncomfortable for all of us. "Hi there. You must be Samantha." As she drags me forward, she squares her shoulders, and her smile lights up the room, but it doesn't fit the woman I've grown to love.

This is what Darius was talking about. This must be stage Jolene, and I have to say... it's a little hot that she can switch it on and off like that. She hugs my mother, offers a hand to my sister, then brother-in-law. She smiles at my niece, introducing herself to her as well, even if the toddler hides against her father's chest.

She's so good at this. Jolene has mastered being confident in socially awkward situations, even on a day when I know she's struggling.

That part of her past that she rejects—her training, poise, her pageant queen mask—is still a part of her makeup. I wonder if she realizes how incredible it's made her at handling situations like this?

It's easier to talk to my sister, with Jolene paving the way. She makes everything calmer just by being in the room.

I hope she understands how appreciative I am that she's here with me, touching me like she's truly mine? She should. She will.

Chapter Seventy-One

Darius Is Complete

DARIUS

Mid-morning light beams between buildings as we drive home from the hospital. Jolene falls asleep in the first five minutes, tucked under Arlo's arm in the back seat. His eyes are closed, head dropped back as he quietly sings along with the radio. There's a calm relief, despite the exhaustion through the night and early morning hours.

This could have gone differently if we hadn't been there for Arlo. I couldn't be more thankful that Ian made it through surgery. He's not in the clear, and the road ahead is going to be hard. He's going to need a lot of help he's probably going to reject, but as Yolanda said through happy tears, "He'll just have to get over it."

Arlo's sister is a snarky beast, but was no match for Jolene's southern bless-your-heart mentality, and they somehow became kinda-friends through the night.

Things got even easier when Arlo's niece attached to her uncle and fell asleep on his chest until Sam's husband took their daughter to settle in at Ian and Yolanda's house. It's the first time I could see Arlo so clearly as a father, and I like the idea of it, maybe a little more than I should at this point in our lives. One step at a time.

After Ian went in for surgery at the crack of dawn, Arlo and Sam went for a long walk around the hospital ward while Jolene and I talked with Yolanda and Ian's family. When the siblings returned, they seemed less tense around each other.

Throughout the night, the three of us held hands and checked on each other with words and touches. I'm positive it was clear we were together, but no one stared too long or asked what was going on between us. I'm sure we'll have to field questions soon, but we'll be able to answer them honestly, because of something I knew long ago.

We're perfect for each other. All three of us.

Pulling into our spot, I turn the car off, look behind me and grin at my loves.

A week ago, I caught up with a friend from college. When I told him about Arlo and Jolene, he asked how that worked—how I could watch them together and not feel possessive or jealous over what they share.

I didn't really have an answer except, it's how I am.

But seeing their connection today, and how they're now snuggled up completely at peace with each other, makes me overwhelmed with love for them. Maybe it works because I'm in the front row, watching the people I love the most fall in love. And they love me too. They get lost in each other, but they always look to me for approval, wanting guidance, or to share this joy we feel so strongly. I don't feel outside of them. I feel right with them on their journey, and I'm so blessed to experience their happiness—our happiness—even in rough times.

Arlo peeks open one eye and yawns. "We're home?"

"Yeah. Let's go to bed."

He checks his phone in case of updates from Yolanda and then tugs a grumpy Jolene out of the back seat and into his arms.

She grumbles until he puts her down, and she drowsily follows us to the elevator where she leans against him and holds my hand. We're in a silent, sleepy bubble as we walk down the hall and step inside the apartment.

Arlo grabs a glass of water, while Jolene kicks off her shoes, stumble-stepping with exhaustion.

She wraps her arms around my neck. "Yeah, okay, now carry me."

I chuckle and lift her by her backside, walking down the hall with her legs wrapped around my hips.

Arlo follows, then ducks into his room and into the bathroom.

Jolene and I do our evening routine even though it's nearly eleven in the morning. I swear she has her eyes fully shut as she tumbles into bed, sighing as I cover us up with the duvet.

Arlo comes in a moment later, closes the curtains, and slips in beside Jolene. "Thank you for being there for me today," he whispers, eyes closed.

Jolene turns toward him and snuggles against his chest.

I loop my arm over both of them. "It's what we do."

Chapter Seventy-Two

Jolene Makes A Mistake

JOLENE

I pause outside the front doors of our apartment building after dropping off paperwork to my new employer. I'm employed. Officially under contract after two days and one round of negotiations. I now work from home on Fridays and will be up for a scheduled salary review after six months. It's an amazing day.

I nod with my phone to my ear as if Lou could see me. "It's all signed, and Martha put it on your desk."

Lou whoops. "Monday then?"

"Monday. I can't wait. And Lou? Thank you. Not just for the job opportunity, but for everything else, too."

"I'm so happy for you, Jolene. Hey, do you and your guys like barbecue? We'll barbecue. Our house. It's a done deal. Maybe next Friday. Say yes."

I laugh. "Yes."

He's been so helpful just by being himself—supportive, accepting, kind.

More than I can say for my mother, who had my father call me to ask if I'd been joking about Arlo. When I told him I wasn't, he told me I'd disappointed him and I should call and apologize to my mother once I figured myself out.

Darius nearly had to tackle Arlo to keep him from taking the phone from me until I told Dad I was disappointed that my family only loves me if I follow exactly what they think I should do with *my* damn life. My men stared on, wide-eyed, as Dad cleared his throat and told me we'd talk about it later. That was father-speak for, "This is too uncomfortable to discuss because I know I'm wrong." My new, amazing job wasn't even brought up.

But Darius and Arlo were there to lift me right back up, because that's what they do for me. That's what we all do for each other.

I grin and step into the building. As if I needed to be brought down from my great mood, Sheena is at the front desk. My grin disappears, but I hold my head high and walk past, my heels clacking on the tile of the silent, cold lobby.

The elevators feel like they're a mile away when Sheena clearly says, "Slut."

I stumble to a stop and turn to her and her cocky grin.

She raises an eyebrow as if she's not on duty at her job nor has a speck of kindness in her. Like she's not also a woman.

"What did you say?" I know what she said.

She clears her throat and lifts her chin. "I called you a fucking slut."

That should hurt. It should hurt a lot. I should fight rage tears at the audacity that someone who works in this building would say that to me—that anyone would say that to me, much less while I'm minding my own business, but my throat isn't even tight. Walking away is the best thing to do, because Arlo was right. I don't need her to like me. However, it's time for her to leave us alone. It's not okay for me to walk into the place I belong and have her try to make me uncomfortable.

"Why would you say that?"

"Because that's what you are. I know your type." Sheena's smugness draws a little tighter as I paste on my pageant smile and step up to the front desk.

"You don't have a clue who I am." Setting my elbows on the counter, I hold her stare. "And I don't care if you ever do, but it's time for you to leave us alone. Arlo doesn't want you, Sheena. You need to move on."

That wipes the grin off her face. I turn to leave, but there's a click, and her nails tap under the counter. "Do you think Arlo's your boyfriend or something?"

I furrow my brows because it feels like a silly question. "Yes."

She tilts her head. "Does he fuck you hard, *Ms. Shah?*"

"Yes." It's none of her business, but the word pops out, anyway. I bite my lip. "And he's so sweet to me." She doesn't know who he really is, either. She was just a fling and never got how much goodness he has in him. Bad for her but lucky for me.

Her grin returns with a gleam of maliciousness in her eyes, reminding me of some of the too-serious competitors. The ones who will spread a completely false, yet harmful rumor without batting an eyelash.

"*Sweet?*" She shakes her head. "Now I know you're lying." There's another click and her tapping nails. She's fidgety. "He had me wrapped up too, divvying out his attention like moldy bread crumbs. That's a mistake, little girl."

"Don't call me *girl*. Only he gets to call me that."

She laughs. "Liar. If he calls you anything, it's probably *princess tight ass* or *dumb bitch*."

There's no point to this. "Good luck, Sheena. I hope you find what you're looking for."

"I did. And you still don't get it. It's our game. He's leading you on. You really think he's going to settle with someone like you? That's not him. I know him."

"You really don't, and never will. And now you're bordering on harassment that needs to end."

More taps. "You sound like a jealous girl in love. Too bad it's with Arlo. He doesn't do that."

He does, though. I can feel it in the way he looks at me and touches me. The way he seeks me out for morning kisses and when he gets home, he hugs me like he's waited all day to have me in his arms. "You have no idea how hard that man can love. And, yeah, I love him back so much." I've felt it for months, but declaring it feels like a weight lifted. Of course, I love him.

"You love Arlo? The man who tells all of us not to love him back?"

He did that, didn't he? "It's impossible not to. Please stop trying to win him back. Move on. He's not interested." I don't say, "Back off, bitch, because he's mine," but that's how I'm feeling, and I'm sure it's implied by my tone.

Sheena smiles. There's that odd click again, and she rests her elbows on the desk and cups her face. "You're an idiot. I hope Arlo enjoyed that little show because even if you were this week's fuck to him, you're done now."

"What?"

There's a buzz, and she giggles like a kid, then taps the machine under the counter. "Yes, sir?"

Arlo's voice comes through the speaker. "Get up here, Kentucky."

Sheena takes her finger off the intercom, snaps, and signals to the elevator.

My stomach drops, and I'm positive my face blanches. "He heard all that?"

"He did." Sheena cackles. "You can tell Mr. Keller I'll be ready for him. In fact, I'll just swing by on my break. I bet he'll fuck me in front of you while you're boxing up your shit."

That won't happen, but I can't think of an argument right now because I'm in trouble. He told me to ignore her, and we still haven't said the words to each other that I feel so strongly about or discussed our future. I walk to the elevator, stomach roiling, while Sheena cackles, throwing more barbs in my direction.

Chapter Seventy-Three

Arlo Loves

ARLO

I turn to Darius and lean back against the wall. "She loves me."

He chuckles. "Yeah, obviously." Of course, my best friend would know. I do too, and I simultaneously want to redden Jolene's ass and wrap her in my arms so I can kiss her a thousand times.

Those words are for *me*, not Sheena.

I push away from the wall and pace the living room. My muscles feel like they're going to pop off my body. I need her in my arms right fucking now. She loves me. *Me*. Someone who pushed her away, warned her against this and yet, I'm happier than I can ever remember feeling.

Do I meet her at the elevator? No, I'll just tackle her in the hallway and probably get complaints because I don't care who sees how much I love her. I'd show her right there in front of all the neighbors.

"How are you holding up?" Darius asks, head tilted as he studies me.

A laugh rolls out of me. "I'm coming out of my skin in the best way. You knew about this." It's not a question.

"Pssh." Darius grins with complete joy. "Again, so obvious." He watches me tread a line on the living room carpet. "She's loved you for a while. Just didn't know when to say it. She told me, though. And Donna."

"Did she really?" My chest squeezes. I know how that conversation went.

"Yeah." He leans forward, propping his elbows on the kitchen island. "She said some sweet things about you. I mean, they went unheard, and now Donna is giving her the silent treatment, but still."

Everything about Jolene is sweet, but it's wasted on her goddamn unsupportive mother. I knew she was struggling with guilt, that she was keeping secrets from an important person in her life—someone who's not speaking to her right now. I didn't expect that she'd tell Donna that she loved me.

Fuck me. I will spend everyday making her know how perfect she is to me. How thankful I am that she would face her biggest fears to be with me.

Darius keeps his eyes on me, expression calm and content. We're not lovers, but we love. What I feel for him isn't all that different from what I feel for Jolene. They're both mine, and I'm definitely theirs, but I need a final check-in with him before I tell her what she means to me.

I run my hands through my hair, then sit on the arm of the couch and start rolling my sleeves. "This is what you want, Darius?" I keep my eyes on him. "Her being with me, too? You're okay with having us both for good?"

"Hell. Yes." He nods, standing up straight. "You two are everything to me."

The door clicks open, and our girl steps inside, a little pale except for her pink cheeks. She swallows and puts on that smile that's a bit too toothy and makes her eyes go too wide. "Hi. How was work?"

Darius snorts a laugh and presses his fingertips to his lips.

I raise an eyebrow. Is she seriously trying to pretend I didn't hear her just tell someone she loves me? "Come here."

She drops the smile quickly. "I'm sorry, Arlo, I—"

"Don't you dare say you're sorry. Come here." I beckon her with a finger.

She steps out of her heels and sinks to her knees. Her tight skirt forces her thighs to stay pressed together as she crawls her way to me. Fuck, she's such a good girl. So damn perfect. Each inch closer makes my heart beat fast in my chest and also in my cock. When she's in front of me, she puts her palms on my knees and looks to Darius like he may rescue her.

"Nope." Gripping her chin, I drag her gaze back to me. "This is between us."

"You're mad?"

I'm so fucking elated I feel like I might burst. "Far from it. Say it to me. Not to Darius, not to fucking Sheena, or your mother. Tell *me* what you feel for me."

The slight fear in her eyes softens, and she leans into my touch. "I love you, Arlo."

Gripping the back of her neck, I pull her up into my arms until we're eye to eye. "I love you so damn much, angel. I never imagined I could feel like this about a woman. Do you understand me?"

Her eyes go all watery like they do when she's overwhelmed. "I understand."

I crush a kiss to her lips and lick until she opens for me with a moan. We are relentless with our mouths, teeth tapping, breathing in stolen gasps. I drag her against me, and she straddles me to get closer, but we end up sliding off the couch arm and onto the plushy cushions.

Jolene giggles, keeping her arms tight around me, mesmerizing me with her dimples and curves against me.

Darius sits beside us and gives Jolene a brief kiss.

I reach to take his hand. "I love you too, you know."

"Oh, I know. You show me all the time, and I love that about you. I'm so happy for the two of you, and for us. We're going—"

The knock on the door makes Jolene grumble. "That's probably Sheena. She told me you'd—nevermind." She crinkles her nose.

I rub at the cute wrinkle. "Nuh uh. What did she say?"

Jolene gives a long, exhausted sigh. "That you'd fuck her while I packed up my things."

I huff a laugh. "You tried to pack once. Remember how that went?"

"I don't think I'll ever forget that." She glances toward the door. "Just ignore her. She's hurt or stubborn, or just kinda mean. I don't know."

All of those things and more. I should have known better, though, and I need to correct that for good. "Let's find out. Darius, would you mind?" I lift my chin toward the door.

He raises an eyebrow but stands and crosses the room.

I push myself up from Jolene and sit back on the chair arm.

Darius opens the door, revealing that Jolene's guess was correct.

Sheena strolls in, uninvited and highly unwelcome. "I tried to warn her, Mr. Keller."

Darius keeps the door open, but glares at the back of Sheena's head.

"Warn her about what?" I ask.

"Acting like you two are involved to make me jealous."

That is a new level of delusion, and now I'm concerned this building won't be safe for us while she's in it.

I glance at Jolene, and she's already looking at me, trusting me to lead her wherever I think is best. The difference between what I thought I liked and what I found I needed from a woman is so vastly different it's laughable. "Stand up, Jolene."

She does without pause.

I do as well, stepping behind her and caging her throat. "Were you acting, angel?"

She lifts her chin, giving me more space to grip and do whatever I please. "No."

"I was for a little while." I tilt her head and kiss her neck. "Acting like I wasn't obsessed with you from the second I saw you."

"Sir?" Sheena's voice is a tiny chirp.

I narrow my eyes at her. "I'm not your sir. And this isn't about you. Never has been." I step in front of Jolene and kneel.

Her gasp would be inaudible to anyone who wasn't paying attention to her every breath, like I do.

I hug her thighs and look up at her. "You're the only woman in my life, forever."

She smiles, and her bourbon eyes threaten to spill over in the sweetest way. "I'd say you're my only man, but…"

Darius slides up behind her, wrapping his arms around her waist and nipping her ear. "You're mine too."

I glance back at the closed door. "She leave?"

"The moment you kneeled. Hi, babes."

"Hi, baby." Jolene turns to kiss him, and my own eyes ache. I love how they are together.

How we are.

Just fucking perfect.

Chapter Seventy-Four

Jolene Accepts

JOLENE

"Shhh," Arlo says.

I'd threaten him and tell him to behave, but that's a pointless endeavor. Arlo does what he wants when he wants. And at the moment, he wants to torture me by fingering me under the slight edge of a towel. We're under an umbrella, and this island resort is relatively secluded, but there are still people out here enjoying this gorgeous Caribbean day on the beach.

"I think we should move." He grazes my clit.

I bite my lips together, but there's no stopping the whimper that comes from my throat. My face heats far more than the touch of sun I've gotten on my face these last couple of days. "What?" I try to turn from him.

He stays with me, fingers sliding in deeper. "I think we should move. Maybe into a neighborhood like Westloop or Old Town?"

Darius flips the page of his book. "I love the houses in Wicker Park."

"Why? Why are we talking about this *now*?" I'm getting closer, and if he makes me scream on the beach... no, he knows better. Right?

Arlo leans to bite my shoulder. "You and Darius have full conversations while you fuck."

I huff a laugh, but it melts into a moan. "Yeah, but this is making me think about taxes. You want me crunching numbers while your fingers—"

He licks my bottom lip, and grins in that gorgeous boyish way he does when he's fully unguarded. This damn beautiful man can do anything he wants to me when he looks this happy. "What if I told you I want a house with an enormous California king bed that will give us all kinds of room to do things like this?"

I give in, and rest back on the soft towel over warm sand, spreading my legs just a bit. "Slightly better."

"Good girl," Arlo whispers, stirring his finger inside me.

Darius leans from his book and kisses my whimper. "We could funnel your entire salary into funds and have a down payment pretty quickly."

We could. And while it's a big step, it has my brain making a spreadsheet of fund options I'm going to have to replicate when Arlo lets me open my laptop again.

He tsks and pinches my clit, chuckling when I yip. "So distracted. It's for the best, anyway." He pulls his fingers back and sucks them just as a figure approaches the edge of our umbrella.

"And how's our favorite trio this afternoon?" Walt the bartender says.

Would it be weird to say horny? The entire staff of El Escape Azul has embraced that we're a threesome like that's a normal thing on Simona Island, even if I'm still navigating these odd feelings about our relationship.

"Enjoying the weather," Darius says, turning over and sitting up to speak to the man with the wild bleached pompadour.

"And the company," Arlo adds, kissing my shoulder. "You want a drink, angel?"

Walt waits with a wide smile.

I purse my lips. "You know what I'm going to say."

"One of my most fabulous rum punches for the queen." The bartender writes in the air like he's taking an order.

"Add coconut water, please." Arlo tugs my bikini strap down, probably checking to make sure I'm not getting too much sun.

"Noted." Another air message from Walt. "And for the gentlemen?"

They order their drinks as well, and we all lie back when Walt wanders back towards the hotel.

"I really love it here," I whisper, eyes closed and breathing in the warm, salty breeze.

Darius takes my hand and pulls it to his lips, kissing my palm. "I can't think of a better way to enjoy your bonus. Thanks for sharing with us."

I nod. "We should share an orgasm because Arlo got me all worked up."

Arlo sits up and starts gathering our bag. "Let's go."

Darius laughs. "Walt is bringing us drinks, and I think there's a sandcastle contest in a few."

"Oh, yeah," I say. "Helena mentioned that."

It took me days to build up the nerve to call local travel agents and explain that I needed a vacation where a polyamorous throuple would be welcome but also secluded. Helena was the kindest, had the best deals, and didn't even pause as she told me she had a *throuple* of places in mind. I about fell out of my chair laughing. Then I signed on with her and made another connection in the city.

"While that sounds fun"—I sit up as Arlo tugs at the towel under us—"it's not going to make me come."

Arlo freezes, then leans in to kiss me. "Fuck, I love you so much."

I grin. He might have been the last person I thought would be so giving with those words, but he says it and shows it often. Every day.

He takes Darius's book from him. "Orgasms await. Move your ass. We'll catch Walt on the way in."

Darius groans, but he's grinning, too. He takes my hand and pulls me up.

The other people we pass are clearly in love as they lean against each other, play in the waves, and rock in the hammocks hanging between palm trees. I see what Lou was talking about. It's exciting to see people in love. I want to share what we have together, because it feels so perfect for who I am.

I'm happy for them, and I'm so happy for myself.

There's not a moment of doubt that Darius and Arlo are the men for me. That they love me exactly as I am, the good and bad. Obsession-worthy and annoying. They look at me with love, not judgment, in everything I do, and this beautiful island adventure we're on is just the start of so many more.

Chapter Seventy-Five

Epilogue: Hayley Arrives

HAYLEY

Cars line the streets of a pretty neighborhood in Chicago. It's beautiful and lush, perfect homes with nice cars, bikes on lawns, and dogs yelling about all the things dogs yell about. It reminds me of Lexington, creating a sour itch in my stomach.

I wish I had better feelings toward my hometown, especially right now when I want to love this place where my best friend now lives. But my anxiety is loud.

Maybe it's just that my brother is acting weird again, though that's not unusual. He's asking if I'm planning on coming to the house soon, tacking on a nice dig of, "since you're such a mess and can't decently plan anything."

I'm actually a great planner, thank you very much. I'm also a mess. A mess who isn't interested in heading back to the land of bad juju.

Going back to the place I grew up isn't exactly a joyride for me. It's a choice when I have zero dollars left—which has happened more times than I'd prefer. It boils down to staying in the decrepit house of shitty memories I grew up in until I get enough cash to get to a place that looks fun to live, or move under a bridge and become a toll troll... tempting, but I don't like being cold. But things are better now. I have a job in freaking New York. One I love. And I'm dating a guy who's actually nice, even if there are a few red flags. There are always red flags. No one is perfect.

I scrunch my nose. Maybe I should swing by Lexington to check the house, though. I hope Kenneth isn't trying to sell it out from under me again. It's not rentable, so that's not an option.

Kenneth probably has one of his friends staying there and wants to make sure I'm not around to have sex with them. As if I would lower my standards for his legion of dumbassary. I mean, Zephryn is a fuckboy and would be a fun night or two if Kenneth didn't find out. And I'd give Micah Milford whatever he wanted if he weren't already claimed. Married his high school sweetheart, went soccer pro and is now retired from the league? He's probably floating around on a yacht, never to be seen by my eyes again.

The driver stops in front of a stately craftsman. "Is this the place?"

"Uh, probably." I scroll through my phone to tip while she grabs my bag from the trunk.

Intrusive thoughts, begone. Today is about catching up with Jolene and her men. *Her men.* I love it.

Of all my pageant friends, she's the last I'd picture doing something like I would totally do if I weren't with one man for the unforeseeable future. Jolene Shah is a damn delight, and always had this fabulous rebellious streak when it came to pageants. It called to me the second I met her. Though she only flexed it enough to make her bold while she played the part they wanted her to play. It superpowered her in the pageant world.

Me, not so much. Some ladies have the looks, money, and reputation to go all the way. I didn't have any of those things. Just the heart. I liked the stage and the competition. I even enjoyed grinning with utter joy to make the judges uncomfortable after they'd given me low scores because of my shape or because they didn't like my alcoholic father or jackass brother, who was always in trouble. It's hilarious that he's a lawyer now.

Or maybe they didn't like me and the rumors everyone loved to spread about the girl from the wrong side of the tracks. I swear you'd think a small town would be nicer to a kid whose mom abandoned her, but no. No grace for someone like me. Not until I met Jolene, and a few of the pageant women who pretended I wasn't dirt poor and unwanted.

Before I can ring the doorbell, the door flies open and a fury of dark hair and a silky blue fabric tackles me, sending me back a few steps. "Oh my God, I missed you so much! Your hair! You look so pretty. How's life?" Jolene is just the best. I needed this.

We hug, swaying until I get dizzy and let go.

"I missed the hell out of you, woman." I flick my now shoulder-length strands. "Yeah, last month I did a mud 5K and got stuck on an obstacle. It took three attendants to detach my hair from a log while I lay tits-down in a freezing mud puddle. It was like a really uncomfortable spa treatment. My time sucked, so I chopped it off the next day. And life is... good."

I scrunch my nose at the odd foreboding sense that something is off. Things are typically off with me so my inner sense could be that someone might be rude to me here and I'll need to control my temper, or that I return to New York to find my weirdo roommates have removed my barricaded bedroom door, found I own practically nothing, and rented out my room. I hate it when that happens.

"That was a hesitation," Jolene says.

I wave off her questions. "Later. Right now, I want to hug Darius and meet the other corner of your triangle. Oh, and—" I snatch her hand and gasp at the two rings that sit together. The ring with the single amber stone is so sparkly, and the other ring holds two pretty diamonds that cradle the amber one. "Damn, that's a gorgeous set. Six months?"

"Yes. Though Arlo pushed for three. He's impatient." Her grin is contagious, and I'm so glad I'm here. I needed this reminder that people can make it.

I might have reservations about Alonso, but I think it's just that my past has jaded me. He's nice to me. I've even told him about my past, and he didn't crinkle his nose and dump me on the spot, which is more than most men who seem to want a woman who is unabashedly sexual, but only for them... like ever. I guess they don't like that we learned through the years how to be confident in the way we are.

We step into the house. Army decor and photos line the walls and shelves. I raise my eyebrows. "This is something."

Jolene laughs and takes my hand to lead me down the hall. "Arlo comes from a big line of military people, but he went a different route."

"Well, he's certainly stacked like a marine." She sent me a picture of the three of them in front of that shiny bean statue, and he is very nice to look at. But the best part was that he was staring at her like she was the North Star instead of at the camera, which has endeared him to me forever. She deserves to be loved with every ounce of that man's being.

"He is something else." The way she says it makes me grin. *Lucky girl.*

We pass into the kitchen, where two dozen bottles of wine, liquor, and fancy flavored sparkling water line up. I trail a finger down a bottle of one called Raspberry Rumble. "Fancy meeting you here, sexy."

"Let's get settled with a drink, then we can join the party." Jolene rummages around the island, settling on bourbon for her and that raspberry tease for me. She snaps and pulls a bottle of electrolyte water from the fridge. "And Ian needs a drink."

I settle my elbows on the counter of the bright kitchen as she pours. "Aw, the soon-to-be-stepdad-in-law. You got the top prize, *angel*."

Jolene laughs and throws a lime slice at me, which I snatch and bite. The sharp sourness makes me pull a face. I'm happy for her. Both Jolene and I struck out with fathers—both too busy working or drinking to do something like raise a daughter. I got the bonus of a brother who likes to make my life hell. *Ha. I win.*

"How's he doing after the last surgery?" I ask.

"Much better. Says he feels five years younger."

She glances through the glass French doors where thirty or so people mill around a balloon arch and sit at tables with white tablecloths. The revelry is obvious. Everyone is smiling and laughing, holding red cups. Three little kids do a terrible job at playing cornhole, but look cute as hell trying to throw beanbags. But it doesn't look like any of Jolene's family is here. "Did your mom come?"

Her grin fades. "No. But that's her choice." She glances out the window at the crowd. "The people who need to be here are, and I can't ask for more than that."

I nod, walking around the island to hug her as she pours my water. Maybe I need to head back to Kentucky just to leave a flaming bag of dog poo on Mrs. Shah's doorstep. A sack of crap for a—

My phone buzzes in my pocket, but it's an unknown number. No one calls me, so I ignore it. "So what are you—"

Buzzes start again. Three times.

"Sorry, let me see what the hell is going on here."

And it's a text message.

> To Hayley McAdams, he's married. Don't bother returning to New York. There's nothing here for you. Check your email.

I roll my eyes as I tap over the keys to open my inbox. This better not be an elaborate scheme to download spyware onto my phone. Been there and done that. Twice.

But when I open the message from a Mrs. Annabelle Getty, I kinda wish it were some malware, and not this malicious information. There's a pasted-in photo of a wedding announcement three years ago between my boyfriend and his pretty wife I knew nothing about. *Alonso W. Getty*. And here I thought his name was Alonso Winston.

There's also a forwarded email addressed to my company's human resources department with a pile of links to my old camgirl site and the gentleman's club I worked for.

Just lovely.

From the article, it looks like Mrs. Getty is Alonso's mother. Is he in as much trouble as I am? Doubtful. Why do moms hate me so damn much? Probably because I can't see their red flag sons when they fold themselves up so nicely and slide right into my pocket.

I glance at the adorable cuckoo clock hanging by the sliding doors. Time of death on Hayley's career and love life. Four thirty-six.

"Everything okay?" Jolene asks as she slides the sparkling water over to me.

I blink my squinted eyes, drop my tongue from the roof of my mouth, and sigh. "Things could be better, but sure. Yep." I pop that P a bit too hard, and reach for the vodka, because when shit hits the fan, there's a checklist for getting through it, and water, no matter how fancy and delicious, isn't on the guest list.

"So how's your New York guy?" Jolene asks, though with caution as if she knows what she can't.

I smile and pour. "He's not mine." As usual.

She cringes. "Did you break up?"

"Oh, yeah." I just wish he hadn't changed my entire path as well as being a cheating dickhead. I liked that job. Liked him too. But that's how life goes, doesn't it? Find what you want, have it snatched away, then rebuild again and all the agains. I clear my throat. "But that's a story for another day because the cards of life lined up for you like they should, and we're celebrating that." Jolene is a good person who makes excellent decisions. She knows how to behave appropriately when it matters most, and that's one of the many reasons she's living her best damn life. Speaking of—I raise an eyebrow and lean on the marble counter. "So. Are you going to do the interview?"

Nothing like being offered a large sum for a polyamorous photoshoot with your fiances. My best friend really is living the dream.

She scrunches her nose. "I'm not sure yet. It's um, a lot."

"A lot of money and a lot of fun. You should."

"Yeah, it's just... moms, you know." Her eyes widen. "I didn't mean it like that. Sorry."

I wave her off. "All good. You know I know we both need therapy for our mommy issues. I just need a little extra for the dad and brother too. But seriously, you're in love, and the pageant world is full of curious beasts. That won't go away. May as well profit off of it."

She sighs and glances out the window.

The sexy tattooed monster that is her fiancé lifts his head like he feels her gaze.

Even my stomach does a little twirl at the prey drive that man has. "Your taste is exquisite, my friend."

"Yeah," she says like a sigh.

He strolls toward the house, and Darius sidles up next to him.

"Looks like we've been discovered." I lift my glass. "Cheers to you and this amazing mess you've gotten yourself into. May we all be so lucky."

***

Thank you for reading How We Are! I hope it resonated and leaves you with some hope or joy or just a good feeling of entertainment. And I hope you are ready for book two, because it is on the way! Keep reading for more information on that.

If you have a quick second, it would mean the world to me if you'd rate and review so amazing readers like you can find it!

All the love!

Until next time,

Poppy

Chapter Seventy-Six

Next up...

How We Began

When your first adult relationship and your budding career implode on the same day, apparently you crawl back home with your tail between your legs.

Lucky me.

I'm a ball of disappointment that'll give my horrible older brother endless *told-you-so* ammunition.

But when my lifelong crush Micah and my brother's playboy best friend Zephryn pick my drunk, broken self up from the airport, I realize coming home might be even more complicated than I thought.

Micah's all brooding intensity and gentle hands, even though the former soccer star's dreams died with his divorce.

And Zephryn is made of reckless charm. He's the party boy who's never met a rule he couldn't break or a fight he wouldn't start for someone he cares about.

They're opposites, and somehow exactly what I need—together.

But my brother's voice won't stop reminding me I ruin everything I touch.

Maybe he's right. Maybe I'll destroy the best thing that's ever happened to me. The two best things.

Get ready for this scorching, emotional MMF romance with a protective playboy, a broken dom, and the hot mess who might be their perfect match.

Now check out a sneak peek of Holiday Hotel and visit Simona Island, our favorite trio's vacation spot!

Holiday Hotel – A Tropical Christmas RomCom (3/5 spice level)

CHAPTER ONE—PACK YOUR BAGS, MRS. CLAUS

W hoever invented corset boning is definitely on the naughty list.

This red velvet monstrosity makes breathing problematic, and there's marabou stuck in my lip gloss. But it will all be worth it when James walks down the hall and finds me stretched out on the living room rug.

It's been one month, three weeks, and five days since he's touched me or kissed me or even tried to catch a glimpse of me in the shower. I can't remember the last time we laughed ourselves into a vigorous ab workout or the last time I earned one of his you're-a-goof-but-you're-my-goof grins.

That changes now.

Blowing aside the poofy ball that keeps bombarding my cheek from my Santa hat, I shift in my corset to see which angle is best. On my stomach in a pin-up pose with my ankles in the air and crossed, I think. Good cleavage angle with that one.

The clock I put on the wall yesterday says seven fifty-three, and James will be heading for the front door at eight to run. In this sexy Mrs. Claus getup, with a playful pose with my candy cane rod, I'm going to get us out of this stagnant stage in our relationship. He will love it. I wince and reconsider my hopes. He will pay attention and hopefully remember that he likes my company for more than movies on the couch.

The tight ball in my stomach could be from the steel boning tucked in crimson velvet, but my sweaty palms tell me it's beyond that. I need more fun times and I'm going for it. Besides, Christmas is the ultimate time for antics. It's also a time for decorations, but I'm missing those. With our recent move, that would be too much stress, according to James. That's valid, as I take holiday decor to a ridiculous degree, but I still have antics—my wheelhouse—and it's been a while since I allowed myself to fly free.

We need a push. We've been working nonstop—him at his new location and me on a particularly demanding client—all while un-boxing. And we were drifting before the move, existing side by side yet alone. Maybe while making the best of this untypical holiday, I'll start a new tradition. The Mrs. Claus surprise—pre-coffee Cozette laid out on a fuzzy white rug to set the alluring scene, ready for a fun-filled day of sexiness.

Footsteps. He's awake and moving from the bedroom. My heart smashes against the corset's marabou trim. I'm shocked he didn't notice how excited I've been over the last few days. Was this the best idea? I shake that thought away. I think I'm sexy, and so will he. It will be fine. One deep breath and I prop the end of the thick candy cane stick in my mouth, mindful of my bright red lipstick, and throw my shoulders back, displaying my heaving bosom, which I don't need to fake because I'm panic-panting.

"Cozette?" James asks from the hallway. "Why do you have Christmas music playing so loud?" He steps into the living room and keeps going toward the door, eyes on his phone, probably routing his morning run.

"Ahem," I mumble around peppermint.

When he drags his eyes up, they pop in surprise for a split second, then sink into an expression he aims at me when I've done something out-of-bounds—a blank hazel-eyed stare, plus the slightest nose scrunch.

But no heat.

No interest.

No sexy.

"What are you wearing?" he asks.

My eyes widen. Heat burns my cheeks at this asinine idea. I'm onstage and the one person in the audience, the man who is supposed to love and support me, just discarded his complimentary tickets to this performance.

"You know what? Fa la la you and your little dog too!" I leap up and bite back a hundred angry, hurt words that would only give him more ammunition to judge me. Sorry for trying to have a sexy Saturday before the holidays.

"I-I don't have a dog." He tugs at his winter running shirt and eyes the door to freedom.

I chirp a crazed note of sarcasm. "Well, get one to keep you company, because I'm gone."

Hey, now that follow-up turned out better than expected. One micro-win for me. With a pivot on my shiny red stilettos, I catwalk down the hall. My fast strides send a chill over my bare backside, as the sexy Mrs. Claus skirt I'm wearing isn't exactly full coverage. At least the Santa hat is keeping my head warm.

James used to have fun, used to smile at my shenanigans. He's never been the kind to tackle me, though I'd appreciate that treatment when my lady parts are busting out of a scrap of red velvet and I'm sucking on a candy cane as if it's the best lover I've ever had. Hell, it's the best lover I've had in months.

I'm getting nothin' for Christmas except a Cozette-is-weird face and a *What are you wearing*?

I tug my teal suitcase from the closet shelf and pitch in my clothes from the oak dresser. Everything in our bedroom is beige or wood except for two bright, patterned throw pillows I bought while James was at work. He shoves them in the closet each night, and I toss them on the bed each morning.

"What are you doing?" he asks from the doorway.

"I told you, I'm out, done, finito. It's the motherfrolicking end scene, James."

"Cozette." His tone as he groans my name is an exasperated complaint about my overwhelming nature. Or that's what it sounds like to me. "You need to tone it down. You're upset."

My cheeks heat again. Yes, I am *upset*. I've let this man "tone me down." My style, my language. I've altered everything about me because feelings and bright things make James squirmy.

"How could I let this happen?" I whisper to myself.

"What?"

I move to the closet, jerking everything that's not black or gray off hangers and cramming it all in the suitcase. "We've been together for two years, and I've pushed myself aside to be what you want because I love you."

I'm not feeling the love at the moment, and my heart is racing for freedom instead of embracing my this-relationship-is-over panic. That can't be good.

"Cozette," James grumbles, rubbing his forehead. I wait for him to continue into a reprimand as he always does. Three...two... "That's not—"

There it is.

"No." I slam my suitcase shut, but it won't close all the way. I jab the cascades of unruly fabric inside with my finger. "It is the truth. Somewhere along the line, I forgot about me in this relationship. Today I let myself out, and you don't want me. You want tame and easy and boring. I'm not that person, James. I'm sexy Mrs. Claus, and you're not my Santa."

"This is about sex?" He displays his palms at me, lanky fingers splayed. They haven't been in my vicinity for too long. So long, I'm not sure I want them on me anymore. "I guess it has been a couple of weeks," he says. "Sorry. I'll try to—"

"Hold it right there, Jack Frost." I jerk my bag off the bed, tuck an accent pillow under my arm, and brush by him to head toward the bathroom. "That's the problem. You shouldn't have to try. When it's been over a month, and you walk in the living room to me fellatioing a candy cane while wearing this getup, the obvious path is to replace the peppermint stick with your dick. Your mind didn't even go there."

If our sex life had been a passionate romp long ago, I'd worry about stress from his job or the move, but that's not it. We don't match. Never have, and I'm not sure why I thought a relocation would somehow make things better between us.

"It's fellating. And it's not always about sex, Cozette."

I shove toiletries and makeup into a shoulder bag. "No, it's not. It's about talking, laughing, going out, and making up words like 'fellatioing' because it's more fun to say. We act like we're settled down with kids, but we don't even have pets tethering us to this tiny prison. Is it too difficult to leave the house on a Friday night? Maybe go to a brunch and meet other people our age? You don't want me to explore without you, but you won't leave the apartment. There's a massive city out there, and I've gotten only as far as the coffee shop."

"We've gone farther than that." James tugs at the waistband of his running shorts. "I'd rather stay in. I enjoy our quiet time." His monotone voice grates on the one nerve I have left.

"It's all quiet time!" Except for now, because I'm yelling. "Not to mention, you haven't even attempted to stop me from packing. We're done."

I zip the bag closed, exit the bathroom, and drag the suitcase, my laptop bag, purse, and throw pillow down the hallway, bumping into the wall twice. The stilettos aren't helping my graceful exit.

"What do you want me to do, unpack your stuff?"

"I want you to care," I toss over my shoulder.

At the front door, I eye my corset and gratuitous cleavage. "Ugh." I drop everything to the floor and shuck my shoes.

James steps aside as I pass him on my way back to the bedroom. How can he not get this? Did the hundred times I've asked to go out not give him a clue to my state of mind? I should have gone alone, met some friends or taken on some smaller local projects, but he'd pout if I went exploring without him, and when he went in search of running routes, I had no hope of keeping up with his speedy strides.

I pause in the bedroom and take a cleansing breath. "I want you to show an ounce of emotion that the woman you claim to love is leaving you."

The black sweatpants I left in the drawer are good enough for now. While I think it'd be poetic to walk away dressed as a holiday temptress, it's December in New York. I've had frostbite-free legs for twenty-five years, and I'd like to continue that streak.

"Hey, don't go. We can work this out. The Christmas party is tomorrow."

I stop dead in my tracks. "Oh, is my presence requested at your holiday party? Your boss will not like this breakup one bit, and you know why? Because I'm the only one who talks. I'm entertaining." Regathering my pile of stuff, I head to the door. "At least someone appreciates that."

Stomping my bare feet into my boots, I shove my stilettos into my winter coat pockets, loop my laptop bag and purse over my head, and walk out the door. "I'll pick up the rest of my stuff later."

"Cozette," he says from our apartment door.

The elevator dings. He's not even going to follow? Fully dressed, with no obligations but his self-imposed running time, he stands in the hallway, one foot from the safety of home, watching me walk away.

The stupid part of me that thought he'd simply try when our relationship boiled down to this inevitable moment withers away as the elevator doors shut. Sure, he takes longer to vocalize. Unlike me, he thinks everything through before he speaks, but still. He won't even attempt to convince me to stay?

Leaning against the wall, I wipe away a dumb, hot tear.

Two years of sweet moments had dissolved into bitter boringness. It's over.

James further dashes my teeny hope of a passionate reunion when I get to the empty lobby. He and I have watched enough romance movies to know that when one person leaves, the other sprints the stairs, or races through the airport, or borrows a flippin' bicycle to cut off their true love's escape.

They do anything to win them back.

But James doesn't burst through the stairwell door, chest heaving and stammering about what a fool he's been. I'm absolutely certain he's already gone back into our apartment.

Oh, he'll consider coming after me, pace the hallway while biting his thumbnail, antsy because he's missing his typical running time. Then, he'll call his twin and they'll chat about how irrational and reckless I am. How my exit is one of my tantrums and I'll return home forthwith. Except they'd never use "forthwith." Too uncommon.

My luggage wheels rattle across beige tile as I roll my suitcase to the door. Outside the glass doors, people pass, bundled up in scarves and hats. The city is a wall of gray stone that blocks out the sky.

I have nowhere to go. We moved three months ago for James's programming career. Since then, I've been working my virtual event planner job from the couch or coffee shop. The closest friends I have are the three baristas on rotation, and only one of them remembers my name. But I do exemplary work when caffeinated and free from beige everything, so that will be my think-this-through spot.

The ding of the elevator makes me jerk to attention. Maybe? Possibly? Could it be?

The doors slide open and a couple hobbles out, bundled up in near-matching gray wool coats. Snowflake-white hair peeks out from under her beret and from his fedora. He leans on a cane, and she leans on him like they're posing for a greeting card geared toward couple goals.

How many times have they broken apart and patched themselves back together? He mumbles something laced with the rasp of decades, and her lips quirk, revealing aged beauty carved from a million laughs.

Past them, the elevator clanks shut. The glowing yellow floor number stays halted on L.

James will expect me to come back. It's my M.O. Freak out, cool down, slink home. I'm reliable like that.

Not today.

I swing open the door and slam into an arctic wall of cold. A squeak crosses my lips, promptly freezes, plummets, and shatters on the concrete. Why did I ever agree to move to this popsicle hell?

The hundreds of holiday-decorated windows a few blocks away help thaw me out a little. And it's rumored that I can find any obscure material item in city stores. Oh, the pizza and bagels are so delicious that nowhere else in the world could hope to replicate the taste and texture, but whatever—it's cold.

As I shiver my way to the coffee shop, cars travel the potholed grid like Pac-Man chasing dots while ghosts follow, weaving between each other and popping out of adjoining streets. All I can smell is frozen concrete and exhaust. The dancing neon mug in the window just beyond a wall of steam billowing from a sidewalk grate is a beacon in this gray, frantic world. I take the seat closest to the back to keep away from the frigid whoosh each time someone enters, but it's still freezing. The woman next to me scowls at my haul of bags, and I refrain from flipping her off as I place my throw pillow on the seat to mark it as mine. At the counter, I'm greeted by one of the baristas who doesn't know my name.

Marco is an aspiring actor from Venezuela. He lives in a flat with four other theater friends—one of whom steals all his rice pudding and he is not pleased. He spells my name C-O-S-E-T.

The cup of chocolate ganache peppermint espresso with cream and whip warms my hands. After one sweet sip that heats a path to my soul, I declare it the ultimate beverage for a 9:00 a.m. breakup. I fish my phone out of my overstuffed purse. No calls. Fine, then. It looks like I'm headed home for Christmas after all.

I'd told my parents we were staying in New York because of James's new job and the holiday party, but that's not an issue anymore. North Carolina, here I come.

Dad answers on the second ring. "I was about to call you. Hello, daughter of mine from the great big city of New York!" He sings "New York" so loud I have to pull the phone away from my ear and the scowling woman levels up her bitch-face.

When his long note tapers to silence, I tuck the phone back against my ear. "Hello, father of mine, who now gets to spend the holidays with his loving daughter."

"What? Did James get off work for Christmas Eve?"

"No, but we broke up, and now I get to come home for Christmas." I take a deep breath to calm the tightness in my throat. "Yay."

The woman stops scowling and stares into her coffee cup.

"Oh, Cozette. Sorry, sweet pea. Can you work it out? You two have been together a while, and you just moved. It's probably stress."

It's boredom, actually. A nonstop need to bolt to the door and be loud, reckless, and alive has been biting at my toes for a while, and that doesn't match James's need for the safety of dead quiet.

"Coming here with him wasn't smart," I say. "I thought since New York has so much to do, we'd explore and reconnect, but nothing has changed." Except me, as I've tried to make myself what James needs. "I can get a ticket and fly out this afternoon."

"I'm sorry it didn't work out. Maybe you need time apart. And about Christmas...we're in Quebec, remember?"

What are my parents doing in Canada? It's colder there than in New York.

"Nope, I don't recall Quebec."

"Mom didn't mention it? Huh." There's shuffling and mumbling. "Oh. Mom says she didn't want to bug you with details during your busy season. We figured since you and James couldn't make Christmas, we'd head up north. She's always wanted to see the nativity tour, so we're staying in Old Quebec, and they've decorated everything—I mean everything. We've walked into a Dickens Christmas village."

"That sounds nice. Chilly, but nice." I don't want to go to Canada. It doesn't have my carousel or smell like cinnamon pinecones.

"It is. I'd tell you to come here, but we could only book because someone canceled two minutes before we called. Hang on, and I'll go see if there's another room available."

"I don't want to interrupt. Can I go to the house?"

Dad hisses through his teeth. Ooh, that's going to be a no.

"Oh, well, you know that Airbnb thing?" he asks, and I visualize him scrunching his face and biting his lips until his mouth disappears into his dark, gray-speckled beard. "A family rented the house for the week."

"You let someone rent the house?" I take a long gulp from my cup, washing down the last vestiges of hope for a normal holiday.

"Yeah. They're pleasant folks. Just a family wanting to visit the lake during the winter vacation."

"What if they steal everything?" Someone is sleeping in my bed right now or staring at the old photos on my pin-board. I don't live there anymore, but it's the house I grew up in, and my parents didn't change my space.

"We locked up the important stuff."

"What if they have six dogs that eat all the furniture? Oh! Or they make a porno on the couch?"

"Cozette," he chides. "Like that couch hasn't seen its fair share of—"

"Dad!"

He laughs in rolling melodic waves. "Sweet pea, it's fine. I'll check on an additional room and call you right back."

We hang up and I pull out my laptop, opening emails. There's one request for location research on the East Coast. Easy peasy. Another requests a forty-person full workshop design in Portland. Fun.

Too bad I didn't have any clients over Christmas; otherwise, I could pop into one of the events I plan. Some of my clients beg me to show up in person to the conferences I set up while sitting on the couch in my yoga pants. Not having to wear a suit and heels is a massive bonus after years of doing so.

I accept the two and get to work creating new client spreadsheets. I may not know where I'll sleep tonight, but these electronic folders are perfect: ordered, to the point, and exactly like the others—on the path to success with little fuss.

I've planned gatherings my entire life, starting with my fourth birthday party. When Dad told me that taking my ten best preschool buds to Disney World's princess castle wasn't within the budget, I sat on his lap and instructed him to look for something similar. We found a princess and unicorn duo that would come to the house for pony rides and pictures. The decorations and details were easy once the entertainment fell into place.

After that, it was friends' parties and school functions, then city festivals. By the time I graduated high school, I'd built a résumé that some people twice my age with full college degrees didn't have yet. A huge, international conference company hired me two weeks out of high school, and each year I received a higher title and more demands of my time.

I just get it, and I love it—the budgets, the people, coordinating a hundred things at once and having parts go wrong. There's a thrill in having to turn on a dime and work a secret miracle to keep things appearing like they're not falling to pieces. Everything about it is what I want in a career, except for the hours. There was no life outside of conferences. I faced hundred-hour workweeks and so many flights, I'll have frequent flyer miles for a decade.

I made so much money in exchange for my early twenties.

My phone beeps.

It's James.

James:

> Hey, where did you go? Come back home so we can talk.

Nope.

The phone chimes again, and this time it's Dad calling.

"Hi," I answer and brace myself for a very wintery holiday.

"Bad news, there's nothing available. The nearest vacancy is miles away, and the innkeeper said she wouldn't put anyone she loved there."

I'm sad but relieved. Alone for the holidays, but not destined for the arctic. "That's okay. I'll think of something."

"Need us to come back? We could go to a B&B."

I love my parents so much. "No. You two kids have fun. I'll let you know what I'm doing in a few."

That puts me on the clock. If I don't have a solid location in the next hour, the dad timer will detonate, and my parents will be on a plane and not living out their Dickens fantasy Christmas.

We hang up, and I jump feetfirst into an internet search. The potential Christmas getaways are endless. Disney? Booked. Christmas spa excursion at Hershey? Booked. A wine country Christmas in Cali? Not this holiday.

Tropical locations keep popping up in my search. Hanging out with Santa by a palm tree while I drink yuletide cheer out of a coconut? Yes, please.

The options are daunting. Hundreds of self-proclaimed paradises vying for my attention with deals that may or may not be a dream come true, and in locations I've never heard of.

Helena. I need Helena.

I scroll through my emails to find the best travel agent ever's contact info. She's assisted with many of my out-of-country event bookings and cuts the best deals.

However, booking three days before Christmas? Maybe she can work a miracle.

"Cozette," she says, in a tone that wraps me in a winter hug. "Happy holiday season."

"You, too. I have a request, and it needs to be speedy quick."

I explain my predicament in less than a minute without taking a breath.

"Oh my. Give me your budget, what you're looking for, and I'll see what I can do. You have to leave today?"

I'd get a hotel room, but that's not plan A. As pissed as I am, if James starts his super sad lament highlighting the good times we've had and poses a convincing argument about how we'll work it out, I'll cave. It's best if I surrender thousands of miles away so I have time to come to my senses and realize this has gone on too long.

"I'd prefer it, yes."

"Woman, that's a tough order. Most flights for the tropics leave JFK in the morning, but...maybe today we'll get lucky." Her sweet voice whips to schoolteacher-fierce. "Give me your needs."

She's in business mode, and I love that about her. Someone is on my team.

"Five grand, max," I say. "But I'd prefer under three, a week stay, tropical weather, alcohol, all-inclusive because bikinis don't have pockets, Christmassy, and fun. Oh, but not a family resort. That's entertainment I'm not ready for. Peaceful ocean sounds, sans screaming."

Clicking and scribbling sound through the line. "Mmkay, I have four places in mind and your credit card on file. Do you trust me?"

"I do," I say with a nod.

"Gonna burn up this card. I'll call you with details."

She hangs up without another word, and I smile into my now-chilled beverage. Still chocolaty.

The scowling woman stands and taps her fingers on my table. "Good for you, hon."

"Thank you." It is good for me. I'm bailing out of this coldbox and away from Mr. Boringpants. I'll sing drunken carols with surfer Saint Nick and stick my toes in the sand on Christmas morning instead of snow.

I roll up my puffy sleeves and get cracking on venue research to keep busy. The temptation to browse the net for the tropical places Helena could send me is strong, but then I'll fall in love with an unavailable resort, and anywhere else she finds won't hold a candle to my long-lost paradise.

A half hour later I'm tapping my empty cup, boots propped on my luggage. The phone rings, nearly sending me into the air. I fumble it, then answer.

"Get thee to JFK," Helena announces. "Your flight leaves in one hour and twenty-three minutes for Simona Island."

***

Jump into Christmas antics in Holiday Hotel... https://books2read
.com/Simona1UBL

Also by Poppy Minnix

Faetales Romantasy Novella series, 4/5 spice

The Springfest Sprint: Book 1

Stealing the Bogeyman's Bride: Book 2

Rescuing the Unseelie King: Book 3

Duet of the Gods Mythological Romance series, 2/5 spice

My Song's Curse: Book 1

Song's Gift: Book 2

Simona Island RomCom Series, 3/5 spice

Holiday Hotel: Book 1

Caribbean Competitors: Book 2

Choosing Us Menage Series, 5/5 spice meter)

When We Tried: Book 0.5

How We Are: Book 1

Standalones:

Dasher (The Claus Club: Paranormal Romance, 4.5/5 spice)

<u>Coming Soon...</u>

How We Began (Choosing Us #2)

A Grim Proposal (Faetales #4)

Acknowledgements

Where to even start with thank yous?! How about with Mary Cain, who is and always will be my favorite editor and book bestie. Go read her books, because she's an incredible author and you'll love her work just like I do. This book wouldn't be as pretty as it is without her help and the fantastic comments from amazing beta reader Ellen Tennant! Also, thanks to Lara Elmore for loving this trio as much as I do back when it was just a bunch of episodes on Vella instead of the epic it became. Getting to know her and her fabulous work has been a complete joy! My morning Inkerscon mastermind sprint group was incredible at getting me going on these edits and keeping me inspired. Y'all are the absolute best, and so are Alessandra Torre and Terezia Barna for the brilliant advice, answered questions, and providing the most inspirational place around for learning and networking.

So much goes into creating a book, and I couldn't have done this alone. Thank all the amazing people for the inspiration, non-judgmental support, and advice I've received along this path.